Biblioasis International Translation Series
General Editor: Stephen Henighan

1. *I Wrote Stone: The Selected Poetry of Ryszard Kapuściński* (Poland)
Translated by Diana Kuprel and Marek Kusiba

2. *Good Morning Comrades*
by Ondjaki (Angola)
Translated by Stephen Henighan

3. *Kahn & Engelmann*
by Hans Eichner (Austria-Canada)
Translated by Jean M. Snook

4. *Dance with Snakes*
by Horacio Castellanos Moya (El Salvador)
Translated by Lee Paula Springer

5. *Black Alley*
by Mauricio Segura (Quebec)
Translated by Dawn M. Cornelio

6. *The Accident*
by Mihail Sebastian (Romania)
Translated by Stephen Henighan

7. *Love Poems*
by Jaime Sabines (Mexico)
Translated by Colin Carberry

8. *The End of the Story*
by Liliana Heker (Argentina)
Translated by Andrea G. Labinger

9. *The Tuner of Silences*
by Mia Couto (Mozambique)
Translated by David Brookshaw

10. *For as Far as the Eye Can See*
by Robert Melançon (Quebec)
Translated by Judith Cowan

11. *Eucalyptus*
by Mauricio Segura (Quebec)
Translated by Donald Winkler

12. *Granma Nineteen and the Soviet's Secret*
by Ondjaki (Angola)
Translated by Stephen Henighan

13. *Montreal Before Spring*
by Robert Melançon (Quebec)
Translated by Donald McGrath

14. *Pensativities: Essays and Provocations*
by Mia Couto (Mozambique)
Translated by David Brookshaw

15. *Arvida*
by Samuel Archibald (Quebec)
Translated by Donald Winkler

16. *The Orange Grove*
by Larry Tremblay (Quebec)
Translated by Sheila Fischman

17. *The Party Wall*
by Catherine Leroux (Quebec)
Translated by Lazer Lederhendler

18. *Black Bread*
by Emili Teixidor (Catalonia)
Translated by Peter Bush

19. *Boundary*
by Andrée A. Michaud (Quebec)
Translated by Donald Winkler

20. *Red, Yellow, Green*
by Alejandro Saravia (Bolivia-Canada)
Translated by María José Giménez

21. *Bookshops: A Reader's History*
by Jorge Carrión (Spain)
Translated by Peter Bush

22. *Transparent City*
by Ondjaki (Angola)
Translated by Stephen Henighan

TRANSPARENT CITY

TRANSPARENT CITY

Ondjaki

Translated from the Portuguese
by Stephen Henighan

BIBLIOASIS
WINDSOR, ON

FIRST EDITION

Library and Archives Canada Cataloguing in Publication

Ondjaki, 1977-
[Os Transparentes. English]
    Transparent city / Ondjaki ; translated by Stephen Henighan.

(Biblioasis international translation series ; no. 22)
Translation of: Os transparentes.
Issued in print and electronic formats.
ISBN 978-1-77196-143-1 (softcover).--ISBN 978-1-77196-144-8 (ebook)

    I. Henighan, Stephen, 1960-, translator II. Title. III. Title:
Os Transparentes. English. IV. Series: Biblioasis international
translation series ; no. 22

PQ9929.O53T7313 2018   869.3'5   C2018-900214-X
                                              C2018-900215-8

Edited by Daniel Wells and Eric M.B. Becker
Copy-edited by Emily Donaldson
Typeset by Ellie Hastings
Cover Designed by Zoe Norvell

REPÚBLICA
PORTUGUESA
CULTURA
DIREÇÃO-GERAL DO LIVRO, DOS ARQUIVOS E
DAS BIBLIOTECAS

Funded by the Direção-geral do Livro, dos Arquivos e das Bibliotecas
PRINTED AND BOUND IN CANADA

for Renata
and
for Michel L.

the time of remembering is finished
tomorrow i'll weep
the things i should have wept today

[from Odonato's crumpled ticket]

"you still haven't told me what colour the fire is..."

Blind Man spoke towards the kid's hand, which was gripping his arm, the two of them terrified of standing still in case the tongues of flame bursting out of the floor in search of the Luanda sky engulfed them

"if i knew how to explain the colour of the fire, elder, i'd be one of them poets that goes around babbling poems"

in a hypnotized voice, Seashell Seller moved where the heat pushed him and led Blind Man down more or less safe paths where the water gushing out of the burst pipes opened passageways for anybody who dared to move in the wind-lashed jungle of the blaze

"please, you with your good vision, go see, i feel it on my skin, but i still want to imagine the fire's colour"

Blind Man seemed to be begging, in a voice used to giving more orders than caresses, Seashell Seller felt it showed disrespect not to reply to such a specific request that asked, in a tender voice, for information that simply was about colour,

though also difficult and perhaps impossible to ascertain

the kid pulled up hot tears from inside himself that took him back to childhood because it was there, in that realm of unpremeditated thoughts, that a flowery reply might come to life, bright and faithful to what he was seeing

"don't let me die without knowing the colour of that warm light"

the blaze cried out and even those blind to the sight must have felt a yellow sensation that invoked memories of grilled fish with black beans cooked in palm oil, a hot sun over a beach at noon, or the day when battery acid stole away the thrill of seeing the world

"elder, i'm waiting for a child's voice to give you a reply"

seen close up, or far away, the night was braided blackness and enclosure, the hide of a nocturnal beast oozing sludge from its body, there was a timid gleam of stars in the sky, the languor of certain whitecaps and the seashells on the sand popping open in an excess of heat, human bodies undergoing involuntary cremation and the city, sleepwalking, wept without the consolation of moonlight

Blind Man's lips trembled into a sad smile

"don't wait, lad, our lives are almost broiled"

the clouds far away, the sun absent, mothers yelling for their children and the blind sons didn't see this city's mindless light sweating beneath a bloodthirsty cape, getting ready to receive a deep dark night in its skin—as only fire can teach

the tongues and flames of hell stretched out in the visceral sauntering of a tired animal, rotund and resolute, fleeing from the hunter with a renewed will to go farther, to burn more, to bring on more heat and, exhausted, to try to burn bodies that were losing their human beat, their inhaled harmony, hands that stroked hair and happy pates in a city where, for centuries, love had uncovered, amid the clouds of cruelty

one or another heart to inhabit

"elder, what was the question again?"

the city, bloodied from its roots to the tops of its buildings, was obliged to keel over towards death, and the arrows that announced its passing weren't lifeless arrows but rather flaming darts which its body, howling, received as a sign of its foreseen destiny

and the elder repeated his desperate line

"just tell me the colour of that fire..."

Odonato listened to the voice of the fire

he saw it grow in the trees and the houses, he remembered childhood games, the fire was made with lines of gunpowder stolen from his stepfather's store, labyrinthine designs in slender quantities, on the ground, then a match setting off the dangerous game until, one day, out of curiosity and determination, he decided to try putting a tiny powder trail in the palm of his left hand, without hesitating, he lit his flesh and the pain—this was the mark that he was running his finger over now while a huge fire consumed the city in a gigantic dance of yellows that echoed to the sky

the fire roared

Odonato was no longer strong enough to sketch a minimal expression of horror, or a vulgar smile, with his lips, the heat was burrowing into his soul, his eyes were burning up inside

in the end crying wasn't about tears, it was preceded by the metamorphosis of internal actions, the soul had walls—porous textures that could be modified by voices and memories

"Xilisbaba..." he looked at his hands and didn't see them, "where are you, my love?"

on the first floor of the building, Xilisbaba had soaked her body in water to protect herself from the fire, she was breathing with difficulty and coughing slowly as though she didn't want to make a sound

in her hand she clutched a small piece of sisal, in imitation of the piece that her husband had tied to his left ankle, Xilisbaba's movements and her sweat unravelled the threads of the bracelet into sodden fibres that then covered her feet, the others looked in her direction, guided by the sounds they heard and by the image of her floating hair

outside human voices were shouting

the women's hands reached for each other, a delicate, muted gesture, more to share misgivings than body heat

Strong Maria felt the need to summon other strengths to soothe her friend's tears

the tears ran in even streams down Xilisbaba's face, Strong Maria tried to look at her face, made out her features—salty slopes—detected her sadness from her easy air, tried to take her pulse, but the pumping of Xilisbaba's heart, thinking about her husband isolated at the top of the building, was only a stealthy murmuring of her veins

"Maria... i want to see my husband one more time... to talk to him about the things people keep quiet about for their whole lives"

Strong Maria's hand gripped her in a comforting clasp and Xilisbaba let herself go and slid—her clothes, her shoes, her hair and her soul—down the wall to the floor

"just calm down, sis, fire's like wind, it shouts a lot but it has a tiny little voice."

the Building had seven floors and breathed like a living body

you had to know its secrets, the profitable or pleasurable characteristics of its warm breezes, the workings of its old pipes, the stairs and doors that didn't lead anywhere, various crooks had felt in their skins the consequences of that accursed labyrinth whose creaks betrayed people's movements, and even its residents tried to respect each corner, wall and staircase

on the first floor the burst pipes and an awful darkness discouraged the distracted and intruders

water flowed in a steady stream and served multiple ends, the whole building's water came from this floor, the business of selling it by the pail, the washing of clothes and cars,

Granma Kunjikise was one of the few to cross the flooded territory without wetting her feet or having a tendency to slip

"*that's a river,*" she used to say, always in Umbundu, "*all that's missing are the fish and alligators*"

the old woman arrived in Luanda days after the death of Xilisbaba's real mother and, unable to endure her hunger, barged into the funeral service confessing her urgent need amid tears, apologized for her attitude and, establishing her firm use of a muttered Umbundu, looked deep into Xilisbaba's eyes and said "*i can pray for the death of the one who died, my voice reaches the other side...*"

Xilisbaba, who already knew how to read the truth in life, greeted the old woman with a goblet of red wine, gave up her place, asked them to bring a plate of food with the best fish stew from the funeral dinner and took care to warn them not to serve it with cassava flour because the lady was like her, she needed cornmeal to withstand the craziness and the rhythms of Luanda

"*your mother is laughing,*" the old woman said

"you're my mother now," Xilisbaba replied

during the funeral, and after the debts incurred in order that the lady might have the food and drink she deserved in her honour, Odonato became even thinner than the usual limits of penury allowed

Xilisbaba noted that her husband was growing more silent, he spoke with the children, he talked over trivial matters with the neighbours, he tried to find work and repair the radio's batteries, which gave off no energy in spite of being set out in the sun

but all of his gestures, his morning walk, scratching his head while reading the newspaper he'd found in the street, dressing or stretching, all of these gestures had ceased to make a sound

the woman understood that, in a certain way, it was her husband who was really in mourning,

in her eyes he was far away, Xilisbaba saw him still young and dreamy, daring with his hands and mouth, in the time when he used to surprise her on the flooded first floor, she coming upstairs with her fruit, he squeezing the fruit against the body of his wife who laughed in the surprise discovered late in the afternoon

Odonato barely moved his fingers, the fingers of his right hand caressed the ring on his left hand, Xilisbaba saw Odonato slip the ring off his finger and put it in his pocket, the finger's diameter no longer wide enough to secure the wedding ring

13

he breathed deeply

oxygen molecules flooded his heart, then his veins and his head, renewed energy travelled to his body's extremities but the phenomenon had already broken loose

what's hidden is like a poem—it can come out at any time.

his feet were accustomed to covering many kilometres a day, they were old feet on a young body

Seashell Seller enjoyed treading the sand of Luanda Island's beach and the shimmering earth of his nightly nightmares, he had a house in the neighbouring province of Bengo but he had fallen in love with Luanda early on because of its salty sea

he called the sea the "salty sea"

and he stared at it each day with the same love, as though it were only yesterday that he had gotten to know it with his skin and his tongue

he waded in slowly—as if he were touching a woman—tasting the salt, and relived the ever-present terror of diving down for as long as his lungs allowed and his gaze withstood it, he got to know the rocks and the dories, the fisherman and the hawker women, he carried the hot smell of dried fish ground into his hands and, above all, he got to know the seashells

the seashells

he had grown up in Bengo, between river and river, between tilapia and tilapia, but one day he discovered the salty sea with dories, oars for rowing, and seashells

"elder, you could still make me one of those oars"

"you don't have a dory and you don't go out on the sea"

"...i want an oar to row right here on land: to row through life!"

on the beach of Luanda Island he was seen as an industrious and honest youth

he helped to carry fish, always with a congenial, innocently seductive smile, he made sales and deliveries, he sent salt and money to his relatives in Bengo

Seashell Seller's feet, over the course of the years, crystalized like the bottoms of the dories' hulls on Luanda Island, shards and nails were no more than an itch to him, but in spite of this he wore leather flip-flops given to him by his cousin

the threaded beads around his neck

the seashell bag on his back, his half-closed eyes, which revealed no secrets

he had heard people talking about Strong Maria, dedicated to so many financial activities, and he thought that maybe he could interest her in his seashells

he had them in all colours and shapes, for practical purposes or simple adornment, in so many formats and prices that it was impossible to run into this young man without succumbing to the temptation of keeping a seashell for immediate or future use: to women he spoke softly, to give space to each one's needs and imagination, to bus conductors he offered seashell pendants that they could offer to their lovers to hang in their hair, to men he made practical suggestions about how to use them at the office or in their cars, to ambassadors' wives he presented the seashells as exotic objects that no one would ever think of giving as Christmas presents, to makers of lamps he spoke of the advantages of enormous hollow seashells and of the effect of the light on that marine material, to priests he pointed out the difference they could make to an altar, to old women he recommended them as keepsakes, to young women as original trinkets, to children as toys to make other children jealous, to nuns he sold seashells stuck together in the form of a crucifix, to restaurant owners he sold them as appetizer plates, to seamstresses he emphasized the material's creative potential and its tinkling sounds, to hairdressers he made clear that beads had already gone out of fashion and, to thieves, Seashell Seller hastily excused himself for the fact that he was carrying nothing more than a bag full of worthless junk.

it was at a red light that Seashell Seller met Blind Man, lowered his bag from his shoulders to the ground, and Blind Man enjoyed the noise of the shells

"you got good hearing?"

"i don't get it"

"you hear really well?"

"i only have average hearing, you talkin' about the noise in the bag? they're seashells"

"i know they're seashells, my name may be Blind Man but i know how things sound, it's not that…"

"so what is it?"

"it's that i can hear the noise of the salt inside the seashells"

Seashell Seller didn't know what to say, Blind Man didn't say a thing

the light stayed green but neither of them moved.

Xilisbaba got out of the *candongueiro* with bags of vegetables, accompanied by her daughter Amarelinha, Seashell Seller's lips pinched, he didn't understand Amarelinha's expression as she sweated and balanced other bags

"what was it then?" asked Blind Man.

"i don't know," Seashell Seller hoisted his bag again

the noise of the seashells, or of the salt, caught Amarelinha's attention

her body passed close to them, but only Blind Man thought about how many aromas that body carried: ripe mangoes, nocturnal tears, black tea, papaya-root tea, dirty money, Omo detergent, old sisal, newspaper, carpet dust, grilled fish with black beans, and palm oil

mother and daughter were walking rapidly towards the building, they went inside skirting the puddles near the empty shell of the elevator, Amarelinha hoisted up her dress a notch and followed her mother, who knew the stairs better than she

on the fourth floor, already panting, they met their neighbour Edú

"how are you, Edú, are you better?"

"i'm not gettin' any better, i haven't got worse either, i'm still alive, Dona Xilisbaba"

"that's good"

"i'd like to help but i don't have the strength," he opened his enormous hands in an apologetic gesture

"don't worry, it's only two more floors"

"is that water down there under control?"

"yes, like it always is"

Edú lived permanently on the fourth floor, and the farthest he had travelled was from inside his apartment to the corridor, which was open at its ends to the elements, to smoke or breathe in the polluted Luanda air, he walked with difficulty and was being seen by international specialists fascinated by his case

he had a gigantic hernia next to his left testicle, something that was called a *mbumbi*, whose size fluctuated according to climatic conditions but also obeyed psychosomatic factors, this was why he was visited by a varied gamut of scholars, from the hard sciences to the social sciences, as well as metaphysicians, traditional healers, and even some people who were just inquisitive, so people said, he had not accepted the invitations of Angolans, Swedes, or Cubans to operate because no one had yet offered him a sum big enough to pay down his fear

"aside from that, i'm used to being this way: to each his own..."

Amarelinha looked at the floor, waiting for her mother to catch her breath so they could continue

"your daughter just gets prettier every day," Edú commented "one of these days she's going to bring home her boyfriend"

Amarelinha felt trapped, smiled out of courtesy, they climbed the rest of the stairs in silence

on the fifth floor lived Comrade Mute, serviceable and silent, an excellent barbecue cook due to his secret method of preparing the charcoal, especially in cases where there was little charcoal from his apartment came the sound of muxima music sung by Waldemar Bastos and Xilisbaba remembered her husband again

Comrade Mute was sitting at the door peeling potatoes and onions from two enormous bags and Amarelinha was startled again by the patience with which this man completed his chore

everyone knew that when it came to peeling Comrade Mute was a tireless perfectionist

"hello," he murmured

"hello," Xilisbaba answered

the neighbours were in the habit of borrowing his sharpened military knife, the hawker women from the ground floor, who sold hot snacks and blood-sausage sandwiches to passersby in a hurry also called upon his domestic services to prepare their French fries in oil

they had reached the sixth floor

Amarelinha dropped the bags at the door of their apartment and knocked twice, gently

Granma Kunjikise came to open it

an old metal watering can awaited Amarelinha on the gangway and the row of colourful flowerpots were carefully watered, Amarelinha had precise, delicate gestures, as if she were Granma Kunjikise's blood granddaughter, and the same hands, which in the afternoons were busy threading beads to devise necklaces, rings, and wristbands as girls devised reasons to buy them

"we're going to do good business, my little darling," Strong Maria, the resident of the second floor, used to tell her, "you provide the workforce and i'll make the direct sales to clients"

beneath her husband's alert gaze, Xilisbaba arranged the things in the kitchen cupboards, Odonato watched people by paying attention to what their hands were doing, he liked to watch Granma Kunjikise cooking slowly, he was pretending to read the newspaper but was admiring the rapidity and precision of his daughter's bead-threading movements, he himself had been gifted in wood working but his full-time job as a civil servant had eroded that part of his sensibility

"stamping documents...that's what dulled my sensitive hands"

Odonato was watching the hands and the food: all of it provided by or found among the leftovers from the supermarket where some acquaintance worked

"now we only eat what other people don't want," he commented

"it's a sin to throw out good food"

"it's a sin not to have food for everybody," concluded Odonato, leaving the kitchen and heading for the balcony

he looked out over the city, the chaotic bustle of cars, people in a hurry, hawkers, Chinese motorbikes, big jeeps, a mailman, a car that passed by with the alarm on, and a Blind Man shaking hands with a young guy carrying a bag

"worried about something?" Xilisbaba approached him

"there's no news from Ciente, nobody knows where he is"

Ciente-the-Grand, Odonato's elder child, spent his adolescence drifting from bar to bar, he had been a partner in a famous discotheque but ended up as a doorman who was always late for work, he stole needles in a pharmacy, becoming a habitual heroin user, and, later on in his young life, after being accepted into a Luanda Rastafarian group, stuck around for the weed and the petty thievery

aimless by vocation, he woke up early in order to have more time in which to do nothing, and nourished an obsession of eventually owning an American Jeep Grand Cherokee, his friends called him "Ciente-of-the-Grand-Cherokee," and this was rapidly abbreviated to Ciente-the-Grand

"is there anything we can do?"

"just hope that he doesn't do anything else stupid."

the Mailman sweated and used a sodden handkerchief to wipe away his sweat, months had passed since he had requested that his boss, a fat mulatto from Benguela, give him a moped for his arduous delivery work "a moped? don't make me laugh, you'd be lucky if we gave you a child's scooter, if you don't want the job somebody else will, a moped... look at this guy!"

the Mailman thought he might have more luck if he put it in writing

he wrote seventy letters by hand, on blue paper of twenty-five lines, all duly stamped, and delivered them among the upmarket clients of Alvalade, Maianga, and Makulusu, not forgetting to include Members of the National Assembly, influential businessmen and even the Minister of Transportation

he explained the combination of factors, the kilometrage required by his occupation, the geographical discontinuities and, invoking an improvised international standard for mailmen, he requested, at the very least, an eighteen-speed bicycle with guaranteed maintenance by the competent authorities but

he never got a reply

"your work is to deliver letters, not to write them," the boss laughed

the Mailman decided to take a break, he opened his leather bag and chose a letter at random, opened it carefully and checked he had a little of the white flour paste that he used to reseal the letters he read

it was written in a pretty yet uncertain hand and, in the margins, there were drawings of birds and clouds, other signs recalled geographical coordinates identical to those he had studied, during the time of the Portuguese, in his native city

"you want a hot snack on a toothpick, Comrade Mailman?" asked Strong Maria, while she made the embers dance

"i'd have it if it was on credit, i'm short on dough"

"i only give credit with a cash advance," she laughed

"then you're a swindler! that's anti-credit, can you even do that?"

"is there anything you can't do here in Luanda?"

the Mailman swallowed the saliva from his combined hunger and thirst, Strong Maria felt sorry for him, but sorrow didn't give her an income and the city was too costly to cosset him "you reading other people's mail, Comrade Mailman?"

"it's just a distraction to distract me, i'm like a child: i forget everything right away"

Strong Maria stirred the embers with her fingers, blew on the charcoal with a firm breath and, between threads of smoke, regarded the Mailman

"if only i could learn how to forget..."

the Mailman grimaced, trying to expel a little of the heat, he asked for a glass of water, reread sections of the letter and confirmed that it had been posted from the city of Sumbe

"good news?"

"i don't know, who lives up there on the fifth floor?"

"Comrade Mute"

"is he gonna give me a good tip if i go up the stairs?"

"i can't say..."

the Mailman stopped on the first floor to let his eyes adjust to the darkness

water ran down invisible corridors, it wet his feet over the tops of his worn-out sandals

at first he felt vertigo, an upside-down vertigo, it wasn't his head that swirled, it was his feet that seemed to want to rehearse tiny dance steps

«maybe it's hunger» he thought

hunger which drove people to the most bizarre sensations and the most improbable actions, hunger which invented new motor skills and psychological illusions, hunger which broke new ground or prompted misfortunes, but no,

he figured out it was the site, because there was an odour there that wouldn't let him feel it, and a wind that didn't want to blow, the water, which was detectable though it could not be seen, obeyed an unnatural ebbing, maybe a circular force

"the things you think in the middle of the day... or in the midst of hunger..."

his eyes adjusted to the darkness and made it seem as though he were isolated from the outside world he listened to the street sounds which reached him as though filtered, barely conveying the essence of conversation or thought

"to make it worse, somebody's still probably gonna accuse me of smoking weed during business hours"

the light's colour couldn't be explained, it invented yellow tones on the dirty white of the wall, dipped into the water to reinvent itself in greys that didn't know how to be dark; the water reflected tiny blue beams, reddened, concentrated waterfalls, back into the Mailman's eyes

his thoughts were better ventilated, his hunger softened

"if it's gonna be like that, it's better to hang out here for a while"

when he went to lean back on the door of what had previously been an elevator, he sensed an internal heat coming to life in his testicles, he hadn't felt the sensation so sharply in a long time, he glanced at the entrance, then at the stairs, nobody was around

he passed his hand lightly over his trousers, felt his penis in near unrest in his torn briefs, closed his eyes, absorbed one more time that absurd shamelessness

his testicles remembered

he felt disconcerted, covered the front part of his body, breathed deeply; damp thoughts invaded his mind, sweated inside him as though a childhood fear were gripping him, amused

only later did he go upstairs

wondering at the silence

he didn't see anyone on the landings, and was surprised by the absence of children

he heard, when he reached the third floor, a voice that sang a lifeless melody from an old 45 turntable

it was jazz

he arranged his heavy bag, shifting it on his shoulder, and felt a pleasant relief

his skin's usual outlines returned to the spot where the bag had been pressing down, he made circular movements with his fingers, he revelled in the feeling of his skin returning to its place, he caressed his other shoulder as well, which felt misshapen

the postal bag's long strap was made of a material that imitated a sturdy rope but which had never in all these years fretted at him, his shoulders alone knew the secrets of that texture, a kind of provisional scar, customarily dealt with by changing shoulders and giving himself circular caresses

"at least a bicycle, it doesn't have to be motorized"

he approached slowly, straightening the antiquated, dusty card that identified him as a National Postal Service worker, took the letter again and, with a quick glance, confirmed he had closed it again, then he pretended to reread the address

fifth floor, Maianga Building, to the bearer, ps: it's the building with the huge pothole in the ground floor, you can't miss it

Comrade Mute peeled potatoes without smiling, he occasionally fondled his lavish moustache, left his flip-flops nearby, but it was normal for him to move around barefoot, even in the presence of neighbours

the Mailman coughed

somewhere in Luanda, far from here, a parrot whistled the same melody coming from the turntable, the Mailman looked at Comrade Mute with the sharpened knife in his left hand, the potato dripping a turbid liquid

"excuse my bare feet," Comrade Mute said at last

"make yourself comfortable, i'm a simple mailman, i'm here to bring a letter to the fifth floor"

"it must be a mistake, nobody ever wrote me a letter"

"no mistake is possible, do you want to see it?"

"my sight is terrible," Comrade Mute dried the knife on the left leg of his trousers

"just take the letter, my friend! my boss gives me hell if i bring him returned letters"

"okay, leave it on the table"

"what table?"

"the one inside"

Comrade Mute continued peeling potatoes at a feminine rhythm, his gaze so far away that the Mailman no longer doubted the man seated there, with the knife in his hand and a pile of potatoes still to be peeled, didn't see very well

and now he didn't see him

should he stay propped up in the door, should he break into a run or a shout, should he enter the apartment or not

"with your permission," stuttered the Mailman, entering the apartment

half the noise came from the music, the other half, enchantingly cadenced, was the uproar made by the turntable's old needle

the Mailman dropped his bag in the entrance and advanced to the edge of the little table

two scarlet threads crossed the room like a double-sided clothes rack, making it possible for the speakers to sit on the little windows that gave onto the hall

the sound of a trumpet massaged his shoulder, whistled softly in his sweaty ears, induced him to sit down and seek out another glass of water, he glanced towards the door, glimpsed the resolute, rapt and abrupt gestures of Comrade Mute, saw his knee was moving from side to side with a measured rhythm which was not that of the music

"can i grab that glass of water?"

Comrade Mute's silence said yes, the record came to the end of side A, the needle persisted in searching for more jazz notes

"put on side B, that trumpeter's only real good on his B-sides," Comrade Mute said

the Mailman drank the water and wanted more, but kept his want to himself, on the living-room walls strange figures reclined in photographs and posters written in foreign letters, some were photos of singers, others had close-ups of hands on pianos, saxophones, or thick microphones, he recognized one of the figures on the wall as a face he knew from somewhere, he went closer, wiped away the sweat that was running over his eyebrows and read the name, it was the same as on the record whose B-side was now playing

he heard voices from outside, set down the glass, approached his bulging mailbag, an old woman with white hair approached Comrade Mute, they spoke

"*on thursday i'll bring you the root, there weren't any today, are you better?*"

"if i'm better? i don't even know, i'm not worse either, that's what matters to me, but i've got aches in my body, inside my bones..."

the old woman bid farewell with a feeble gesture, climbed the stairs, the Mailman took advantage of her departure and left the apartment

"i found a glass of water"

"you did right, my apologies for not even bothering to get up, i'm not feeling very strong"

Comrade Mute turned from the pail, picked up a former barbecue fan, huge and worn-out, he fanned himself three times, the man had a sort of secret pact with sleeping sickness, a sort of fever and discomfort which, in the absence of treatment, clung to him for years, its symptoms disappearing then returning again

"stubborn old sleeping sickness" Comrade Mute gave a slow smile "already diagnosed by doctors... it's a chronic thing"

the Mailman scratched his head while he thought of something to say, he hoisted his mailbag, wiped his hands on the sides of his trousers

"well, anything you need, just let me know"

"thanks, the soft drink can wait till next time, i'm flat broke"

"sure, boss" the Mailman said by way of goodbye

on the stairs, Granma Kunjikise looked the Mailman in the eyes, he looked away

he felt good, he didn't have much to hide and he had never caused distrust in old people, especially those whose heads were already white

Granma Kunjikise smiled, let out an almost inaudible murmur and resumed her walk towards the sixth floor

where she met Odonato, who was staring into the distance

Granma Kunjikise saw him from the back in the thinning sunlight and shuddered as she hadn't shuddered in a long time, she closed her eyes, made an effort, wanted to shed two or three tears, to purge herself of that vision

but the truth is clear and acquainted with the secret pathways that lead to its destination

"*Nato...*," Granma Kunjikise called, very softly

Odonato turned around slowly, leaving the old woman neither space nor shadow for doubts

the sun, divided into slices of intensity, hot and perpendicular at that hour, the sun, its sheaves of light crossing sidereal distance and immensity, travelled along the man's body without obeying the logical limits of his anatomy

there was light that enveloped him and light that no longer touched him

"*Nato... your body...*" the old woman laid her hands on her chest, as she'd done since she was a girl, whenever she wished to calm down

dwindling rays of sunlight, of the most extreme slenderness, sad fine yellow-coloured threads crossed the peripheral zones of Odonato's meagre body, on the flanges of his waist, on his knees, also on the backs of his hands and shoulders, the remote light passed through him as though a human body, real and full of blood, might resemble an itinerant sieve

"take it easy, Mother," Odonato came nearer

"*it's not that,*" Granma Kunjikise said, "*i'm thinking about your family, about the people from your house... my poor daughter!*"

Odonato went to fetch the water passion-fruit smoothie that the old woman adored

"we don't have any more sugar, but drink it"

the stereo from the fifth floor was audible there, the old

woman stamped her foot and smiled at Odonato, arranged the garments that covered her shoulders and part of her neck

her hands dry, her skin drooping, her gestures decisive

"did you see it, too, Mother?"

Granma Kunjikise looked him in the eyes, which was how she spoke to those who didn't understand her Umbundu, she told him many things, things she had divined or learned long ago, but understood only now, in that heated instant

"*i saw the future,*" the old woman murmured.

the sound of the siren reached the sixth floor

inside the vehicle, the Minister told his driver to stop, to go take a long walk, he would call when he wanted to be picked up

but the Minister didn't want to be picked up

"are you sure this is the building?" he asked before getting out

"this is the one, don't you see that pothole there, Comrade Minister?"

"yes"

"then this is the building in Maianga with the pothole on the ground floor, that pothole is really old, boss, i could spin you a yarn..."

"not now," the Minister interrupted, getting out of the vehicle

his bodyguard was getting out but the Minister ordered him back inside

"but, boss..."

"that's an order, get out of my sight"

the bodyguard hurried back into vehicle without looking back, the hawkers observed the Minister's clothes with suspicion

the driver disconnected the siren, the traffic was impossible, the vehicles almost weren't moving at all, once or twice around the block could take more than forty-five minutes, a police officer recognized it as a government vehicle from the licence plate and gestured to the driver to ask if he wanted to get through the driver gave him a negative look, the policeman appeared confused

the Minister reached the building, wiping the sweat off his forehead, keeping his yellow handkerchief in his left pocket, he stepped into the darkness, went up the first steps and listened to the dripping water, he let his eyes become comfortable with the darkness and his hands absorb the coolness

"are you there?"

a kind of silence replied to the Minister's serious voice, he proceeded, soaking his shoes

"they say Jesus walked on the water! like fuck he did!" he said, rankled

on hearing noises on the staircase, he tried to hide alongside a gigantic column, a whistle, surprisingly in tune, preceded the person coming down the stairs

he was frightened by his own breathing, he knew he was hidden in an awkward place, he was a Minister wearing an expensive suit, a delicate silk tie and shoes bought in Paris

he resolved to act, emerging from his hiding place, he observed, in the ashy half-light, the approaching figure and decided to speak in an authoritative tone

"who goes there, identify yourself immediately"

he heard the sound of another body ceasing to move, and waited

that other body deposited something on the floor

"i'm on my way out, i'm the Mailman without a bicycle or a motorcycle, i only have letters"

"what letters?" inquired the Minister

"the letters i wrote"

"you write letters or you deliver them?"

the Mailman came closer, descending the remaining stairs, he felt the nauseating aroma of the Minister's expensive cologne, he imagined what his clothes must be like but didn't work out who he was

"please excuse a simple comrade, but may i ask the gentleman's name?"

"you don't know who i am?" he started to move in the direction of the exit

"i can't say that i do"

"then it's better not to know"

the Minister returned to the daylight, hurrying, he slipped on a pan that Strong Maria had left in a spot that wasn't usually taken by those leaving the building, the children who were playing on the sidewalk made fun of him, imitating his straitened effort to straighten his clothes and dark glasses

the Minister searched for his absent vehicle

the traffic remained dense and he had forgotten his phone in the ministerial vehicle, he began to feel the sweat coming to life on his neck and in his armpits

"could you lend me your cellphone?" he asked Strong Maria

"good morning, comrade"

"yes, good morning, but will you lend it to me or not?"

Strong Maria, in a smile-drenched movement, withdrew her cellphone, which was also sweaty, from inside her bra

the Minister hesitated, leaving the lady's hand dangling in the air, the Mailman appeared with his eyes closed, getting used to the city's intense brightness, the Minister pulled his handkerchief from his pocket, wiped the cellphone and made his call

"i'm just imagining him," the Mailman said, deep in thought

"just a minute, one thing at a time"

the line of seated women ceased all activity to watch the man in a suit and tie grasp the snack-seller's phone with his yellow handkerchief

"the phone doesn't have any credit, madam!"

"you asked for the phone, sir, you want credit too? i can ask the kids to go buy it"

"that's it," the Mailman interrupted, "the gentleman is a comrade minister! i don't know if you got my letter..."

"what letter?"

"...speaking about the lack of means of transportation in the central services of the Post Office" "hey, man," the Minister was sweating and starting to look worried, "don't you have a cellphone?"

"i have one, but it's identical to this lady's"

"how's that?"

"just like it—without credit"

"oh, fuck!"

the children had encircled the Mailman and the Minister

"can you give me back my phone, Comrade Minister?" Strong Maria spoke deliberately

"of course, it's useless"

"but to get back to the subject, Senhor Minister, please take note of my petition for a two-wheeled vehicle"

"i've got better things to do, man, talk to your superiors"

"but, sir, being superior in the Ministry, and also superior to my boss, aren't you my superior, too?"

"have you ever seen an Angolan mailman going around on a motorized vehicle during the working day?"

"there's a first time for everything, Senhor Minister, i'm sure that you, sir, remember my letter, written on paper of twenty-five lines, with a seal, white glue and old-fashioned handwriting"

the Minister looked around in search of his vehicle, he was sweating a lot, the Mailman examined his bag, convinced that he would find a copy of one of the letters he'd sent

"boys, did you see a blue car, from the Ministry? it's probably parked right around here, do you want to take a look around the corner?"

the boys smiled, eyeing each other

"we can't leave here, comrade, our mothers don't like it"

"these ladies are your mothers?"

the women wagged their fingers

"that's why we can't leave, Comrade Minister," one with arms crossed said in a mocking tone, "these ladies tell on us to our mothers every night"

the car arrived, honking to clear the way between the civilian cars that did not belong to ministries

"Comrade Minister," the Mailman touched the arm of the Minister, who shook him off and resumed walking, "i just wanted to give you the letter, it might be here"

the Mailman followed the Minister towards the car, talking and rummaging in his bag, the bodyguard hurried up and, even though he had already opened the door for the Minister, took down the Mailman with a movement so fast that the children were unable to repeat it later in their re-enactments

"lay still until the car's out of sight, understand?" said the bodyguard while he dealt the now subdued Mailman a vicious slug in the face

the vehicle moved forward and stopped a few metres up ahead

the Mailman, already back on his feet, cleaning off his trousers, sat down again quickly, the driver called over one of the children, he approached the car window and the Minister himself handed the boy an envelope

"give this to the lady who keeps her phone between her boobs"

the little boy returned and helped the Mailman pick up the letters and other waterlogged papers spread over a muddy pool, and grabbed a blue sheet of twenty-five lines

"pretty handwriting you've got," Strong Maria said

"i studied in the time before," the Mailman smiled with his swollen lips "i got beaten up a lot at school for forming the letters so well"

Strong Maria opened the envelope delivered by the little boy, inside was a telephone card worth ten dollars

she scratched the card, then grabbed the letter with the blurry blue ink and the drenched seals

"you want a soft drink, Comrade Mailman?"

the Mailman glanced up the street in the direction the Minister's car had disappeared

"no, thanks, i've got a lot to do"

"can i keep this letter?"

"sure you can, i've got lots of them, see you tomorrow, everybody" hoisting the mail bag onto his shoulder, the Mailman set off in the opposite direction from the ministerial vehicle.

Nga Nelucha got out of the *candongueiro* on Maianga Square and didn't look at the Mailman who, for his part, was waiting to cross in the midst of the crowd, which was hoping for a break in the traffic so they could get on with their lives

life is made in the city, on the asphalt, in the midday heat

with dusty feet, a sweaty forehead, her hands weighed down with plastic bags of fruit and vegetables, Nga Nelucha stopped at the entrance to the building and asked Strong Maria for a really cold soft drink

"this is what you call hot weather," she said as Strong Maria passed her a locally manufactured Coca-Cola which, according to general belief, was better than the international variety

"back in the time before, people even carried parasols in the street to give themselves a little shade, now you only see umbrellas when it rains"

"it's true, i remember that too"

"you don't remember a thing, don't make stuff up, you're a kid, don't shoot your mouth off"

Nga Nelucha laughed, she had an appealing smile with pretty teeth and plump lips that set her life in motion with every chuckle, her eyes, which in the morning were limned with a bright mascara, were now surrounded by slippery pink stains over her dark skin

"godmother, weren't you there when the trouble happened?" asked the boy they called Little Daddy, his body ebullient and dripping with fresh water

"what trouble you talkin' about?"

"a Minister came and punched out the Mailman"

"you kids are making stuff up..." Strong Maria arranged the ice inside her enormous plastic coolers, "did you see the Minister punch somebody out?"

"Minister? Mailman?" Nga Nelucha looked confused

"yes, godmother," Little Daddy agreed, "it was the Minister's guard, but the Minister didn't complain or stop him"

"that really nice Mailman? poor him"

"yeah, him," Strong Maria confirmed, "and all because of the moped he wants to deliver his letters"

"did they really beat him up?"

"it was just a shove that kicked up a bit of dust"

"that's because it wasn't you who experienced it, godmother," Little Daddy laughed, he washed out his big pails, "a security guard's punch hurts like hell, you can't even imagine it from far away, but those hands have all the weight it takes to give a good slug, godmother, it hurts like a sonofabitch"

"you come a long way, Nelucha?" Strong Maria tried to change the subject since other people were approaching to listen to the conversation

"not far, from the Prenda Market, i went to buy a few vegetables and fruit, too, Xilisbaba's going to need it"

"we gonna have a party, godmother?" Little Daddy asked, getting ready to go upstairs again

"who's 'we'? did somebody invite you?"

"i figure i'm already part of the family, godmother," Little Daddy laughed, grabbing Nga Nelucha's bags to take them upstairs

cunning Little Daddy had appeared in the building years ago, with his biddable manners and clever courtesies, but had soon revealed himself to be a child with attentive eyes and agile hands, an oblong body like a tilting palm tree smiling at any squall that came his way

"if he didn't spend so much time washing cars, he could've been one hell of a basketball player"

when they reached the fourth floor, Nga Nelucha was sweating with fatigue, Little Daddy, on the other hand, was still cool, damp from his recent run through the burst pipes on the first floor

"nothing like a bath... everything okay, Senhor Eduardo?" he greeted

Edú was returning slowly from the fifth floor, in his hand he held the thermometer he'd borrowed from Comrade Mute, he dragged his feet, moving as though in slow motion like a cartoon that's too slow to entertain the children

"another fever, Edú?"

"not yet"

"so why'd you go get the thermometer?"

"So that Mute has to come here to get it back, otherwise he'll be up there all alone, and me, too, this way we've got an excuse to talk to each other"

at home, Nga Nelucha, heading for the kitchen, asked Little Daddy to leave everything on the floor, parsley leaves, Gimboa, slightly withered mucua pulp, old avocados and lettuce decorated the bench next to the stove

"godmother, can i drink a little ice water?"

"take yourself a soft drink, i'm grateful for the help"

"thanks, godmother"

Little Daddy served himself the soft drink and left, greeting Edú again and asking him if he needed help to walk

"you think i'm old or something?"

Little Daddy let a sad expression trickle into his crooked smile

having arrived in Luanda from the south, he'd spent years in a fruitless search for his mother's whereabouts, respected in the building for his gifts of honesty and punctuality, both uncommon in people from Luanda, Little Daddy was an assiduous watcher of the television program *Meeting Point*, created precisely so that displaced Angolans could learn the location of people from whom they had been separated by the war

Little Daddy left in sadness, consoling himself with the taste of cold Coca-Cola, and joked

"Boss Edú, that Coca-Cola 'made in Angola' has a lot more punch!"

Edú hawed at length, closed the door and made his way to the kitchen "kids these days, when they tell you they wanna help, they're just taking the piss out of the elders, just because my privates are swelled up does that mean i can't walk?"

"leave it, honey," Nga Nelucha was in a good mood as she stirred the food, "he just wanted to help, Little Daddy always serves others"

against the sound of National Radio, which was playing a medley of Carlos Burity's music

and in spite of his problems with his leg, Edú showed that he was still a potent stepper in the Luanda style, the couple smiled and danced, Edú led the passes of a hip-swaying kizomba in slow undulations without treading on the recently arrived fruit or brushing the plastic bags, beneath the attentive, concerned gaze of Nga Nelucha, whose mouth was soon saturated with a smile of disbelief at the elder's moves

"you think my mbumbi's king? now i'm living adaptively! with this mbumbi, i'm inventing new steps, don't you see i'm already swivelling my knee like a soccer star? onwards and upwards..."

Nga Nelucha laughed, she let one of Edú's hands seize her waist, the other slid down to the vast contours of her ass, a hot sweat invaded the kitchen and the soft music went on, making the couple close their eyes without losing track of the contours of their apartment

"don't you remember that fateful episode? ay, oh..."

back when there was a curfew, parties were full of people who wanted to drink, eat, and dance and it was literally prohibited, because of the curfew, to leave the party

anybody who stayed past midnight could return home only after five-thirty in the morning, the time when, foreseeing the sunrise, sweetly exhausted bodies ask for a place to sit down, a last cold beer, and a plate of muzonguê.

it was normal, in that time, after the soup, for a party that was winding down to heat up again, continuing for some people until ten o'clock in the morning and, for the most insistent partygoers, it would be transformed into the so-called

35

"continuation," where the men would go off to buy fish or meat, potatoes, cassava meal, manioc, but, above all, liquid sustenance, bottles, cans, or barrels of beer, so that, around two in the afternoon, the pace would pick up again beneath the aroma of the women's seasonings, in an afternoon that would stretch out into a new night

"ay, our mandatory curfews..." Edú smiled with closed eyes remembering the final night when he had made her his

"excuse me, young lady, what's your name?" he had approached Nelucha, crumpled white linen suit, open-necked shirt and a golden crucifix gleaming against the dark dampness of his skin

"Nelucha," she smiled, timid

"do you dance, Nelucha?" he offered her his hand and his smile in a way that made the request more than irresistible

hence, in the way in which the lady allowed the gent's body to draw close, began the interplay of corporeal energies, the closeness of his mouth to her neck, the settling of one's hands on the other's body, the complicity of the smile, and the steps that evolved with ever more intimate contact, legs that brushed against each other to see if it was possible, waists that revealed intentions

and Nelucha, without revealing herself, had already consented even before the culminating hint

"but is it Nelucha with *x* or with *ch*?"

"why, boy?" Nelucha drew back from his neck and asked in a serious voice

"tell me, girl"

"it's with *ch*"

"so we're going to scratch out your name, now pay attention"

Edú's challenge wasn't to write the name on the floor, an act of which he judged himself capable, even with the challenge of it being with a *ch*, the issue was that the music might not give him time to accomplish the deed with the graceful nonchalance to which he aspired

Nelucha, looking back and forth between the floor and Edú's calm face, was visibly impressed, the man had mastered *kizomba* technique to the point of not touching the other couples who danced nearby, having avoided even the icing from the cake that was spilled over the dance floor and the children who ran past

"if it's all right with you, we'll write the *ch* during the next song," Edú concluded when the song ended

"i don't know what to say," Nga Nelucha smiled, speaking the same sentence now in the kitchen that she had said years before

"then don't say anything," Edú joked, opening his eyes

Nga Nelucha gazed at the kitchen floor, the broom was intact, and even the fruit that had rolled out of the bags hadn't suffered any damage

"you're still a really good dancer"

"we do what we can, the *mbumbi* gives a certain rhythm to the curves," Edú laughed

Nga Nelucha picked up her things, set out the bags along the bench, put away the dishes, turned on the tap to wash the vegetables

"we have to talk, Edú"

"again?" Edú feared that the subject in question was too serious for that hour of the day

"i was thinking again about this business of the *mbumbi*, it's a serious issue, Edú"

"and i'm the one who drags it around with me everywhere, you think i don't know that?"

"but then why don't you just make up your mind once and for all? you could take up one of those doctors on their offers, they're important people, with knowledge, they can solve the problem easily"

"ah, solve it, hmm? and if it goes wrong?" Edú got irritated when people came to talk to him about the surgery that would eventually free him of the gigantic lump, "don't you know that *mbumbi* is related to the testicular area? how can i be sure what'll happen down there in the privates..."

"you don't know, and neither do i, neither of us is a doctor, but you get visits from doctors from so many countries, one of them could explain it better to you, you don't even let them talk"

"talk, talk... and i already told you that a traditional healer friend of mine is the one who's looking after this business, until he makes his decision nobody's messing around down here, do they think this shit here belongs to the masses, or what?"

"Edú, calm down, honey, the other day i was speaking with my sister, and she said a few things about this that made a lot of sense"

"said what, exactly?"

"you already said you want to wait, that's all right by me, you have to hear everybody's opinions, the healers' but also the doctors', so many people come here, journalists, American television... have you thought about that?"

"about what?"

"these days people go on tour, there's all kinds of galas, sporting events, exhibits, expo-this and -that, all the artists go on publicity tours"

"publicity tours?"

"yes, you could go on a publicity tour, instead of the doctors coming here, we could be the ones who go to them... visiting clinics, newspapers, television stations, and like that we could go get to know other countries"

"i don't know, Nelucha... all that travelling... dancing is one thing, but staircases, airplanes, i don't know, and they're gonna make us pay the bills..."

"they won't make us pay a thing, that's what my sister says, they pay the expenses and if they want to operate on you, you just say you'd like to see another doctor and then we go on to some other country, my sister's an experienced event organizer, she can be our agent"

"agent? this sounds like a promotional tour for the Kassav'," Edú chided, though the idea didn't displease him

"she can come over here one day and explain the plan to us, just think about it, first the usual circuit, Portugal, South

Africa, Namibia, then Europe, with the Frances and the Italian Spains. and if all goes well, America, New York and Miami"

"then who knows, Japan and China, now that the Chinese are coming here they should know about a *mbumbi* of this size..." Edú sat down on the tiny stool which, because it was strong, was reserved for his use, "tell your sister to come on over, it sounds like we're in business"

on the sixth floor, Xilisbaba entered her apartment and felt a coolness that displeased her

the intense silence was barely ruffled by the jazz notes coming from the fifth floor, the half-closed windows, the drip of the kitchen tap in its sure rhythm, and a beautiful light cast by the holes in the old living-room curtain

"Odonato? Mama?"

she put down her meagre bags in the kitchen, Amarelinha had already sat down in the living room to check out the threads and beads she had brought for new bracelets, Granma Kunjikise emerged from her room, dressed in her striking traditional robes

"white robes, Granma?" Amarelinha smiled, "is it party day?"

"*a day of misfortune, that's what it is*"

she continued walking with her silent steps, came into the kitchen and kissed her granddaughter on the forehead

"good day, mama," Xilisbaba greeted her

"*good day, my daughter*"

"did Odonato go out? did he go out to look for work?"

"*i figure he went looking for something else, he's up top*"

up top, in the parlance of the building, was on the rooftop terrace, a wide, cluttered space, frequented by whoever wanted to go there, an open-air courtyard for abandoned chairs and water tanks, both empty now that water was no longer lacking in the building, which is to say that it was often lacking in the taps but never in the burst sewer pipes on the first floor

there innumerable antennas lay quiet or danced in the wind, those from the old days, decrepit, crooked or even

39

wavering, and the most recent ones, large and small, parabolic, of the kind that seized news and voices from other, more international places, they were also a source of some income since the neighbourhood took advantage of the building's height to serve some of the surrounding houses

Odonato was on the edge of the terrace, regarding the city, its ancient dust, its trees, the Mutu-Ya-Kevela School, formerly known as Salvador Correia High

"i don't like you to be here on the edge"

"there's lots of stuff i don't like, either," Odonato wasn't in a good mood

"you feel like cooking? i brought vegetables, fruit, and fish for grilling"

"Baba," Odonato took a deep breath, as though he were breathing in all the dust in Luanda, "i've decided i'm not going to eat"

"you're not hungry? you don't want to eat lunch?"

"you don't understand. i'm not going to eat any more, i'm sick of leftovers and other people's slops, i'm going on a public fast"

"oh, honey," Xilisbaba didn't know what to say

she approached her husband without looking at him

seen from here, the city was simpler, the painful weight of its problems, its dramas, didn't get under his skin and into his eyes in the same way

"what's beautiful in this city, Odonato... are the people, the parties, the rhythm, even the burials"

"we've spent many years, Xilisbaba, looking for beauty to put up with ugliness, and i'm not talking about the buildings, the holes drilled in the street, the burst sewage pipes, now is the time to face what's wrong"

"where i come from, the elders used to say it's good to take the long view, to cross the river with the far bank already in mind"

"where i come from, the elders used to say that to cross the river it's good to know the alligator's schedule" the sun sent metallic gleams dancing from antenna to antenna, the wind had ceased, car horns and sirens crossed the city in the direction of the sea's vastness, the swallows were resting in the shade, feeding their young

Xilisbaba touched her husband's cold hand, lifted it to her lips to give it a soft kiss, her old gesture of soothing tenderness, her breathing changed, her gaze took on the fear of those faced with something they don't understand

"don't be afraid, please," Odonato, too, had tenderness in his voice

"Odonato..."

"i know"

the light vibrated differently in his hand

a translucency toyed with reflections in his veins, Xilisbaba watched attentively so that the minutes would give her certainty

looking at him carefully, Xilisbaba saw, without seeing, the blood running through her husband's veins, his beautiful, exhausted hand, the callouses on his most worn fingers, and that kind of vision that was an uncertain foreseeing, as though he understood the course of his blood and outlined with his sight the bony movements of his fingers

"i know, Baba; i'm becoming transparent!"

Ciente-the-Grand, Odonato's eldest child, had been sleeping at his friend The Real Zé's house for several days, where they started the day with a long joint shared between smiles and coffee

the annex that The Real Zé rented on the other side of Maianga Square wasn't far from the building, close to the Presidential Palace

it was in another, lower building, inhabited above all by Luanda's Rasta community, to which The Real Zé had belonged in the time before he'd become a professional crook

"my friend," The Real Zé began, "living here right under the boss's boot is awesome, you're never without water or light—and as for a generator, we don't even need it! and when the light goes out, the whole city in darkness, and us—no problem!—we're sittin' pretty, when the Man came here to live in the palace, we cheered him"

"yeah, i heard..." Ciente-the-Grand opened his eyes with difficulty

"only snag is, i'm stuck with this jinx, don't even know if it's from birth or what, jinx goes right along with me, business don't go my way, i swipe, i'm caught, i try to swipe, guys beat the shit out of me, i swipe, i can't unload the goods, pain in the ass!"

"yeah, i get it"

"you don't get shit, because you don' even know how to smoke, you just stay stoned, but you don' even get it, now i'm gonna cut you in on a deal i got here... pure business, but you're gonna command the operation"

"okay"

"deal's in a store... i got a bunch of lowlifes there who wash cars, they already gave me the inside dope, the store owner's gonna spend the weekend in Benguela, two dumb-ass guards, the gang can go in and take it cool"

"swiping food?"

"what food, don't you be a dumb-ass, too... the store's just a front, the guy inside changes dollars, and now the Euro's lookin' sweet, you get the picture?"

"yeah, i get it"

"you don't get shit, but it's okay, i'll give you directions, and you go twelve hours without smoking up so you're in shape for Operation Cardoso"

"ah, but are the twelve hours up yet?

"whoah, you're thick, we'll talk later, but you're gonna have to get a piece"

"yeah, i ain't got a thing, i'll talk with my cousins"

Ciente-the-Grand hadn't shown up at home for months

earlier, in a somewhat more stable period, punctuated here and there by petty thievery, cellphones, tires, jeep grilles, robberies on the beach, it was customary for him to appear at his father's home on Sundays to sit down to a good meal, after a while the situation got worse and members of the Rasta community, who knew of the father's existence, warned Odonato of Ciente's degeneration

he had been expelled from the community for failing to follow its rules and for having expropriated funds intended for the annual commemorations, nobody touched him, he was just expelled with loud threats, above all out of respect for Odonato

"you know we respect you, mister, but he can't show up here no more"

Odonato collected some money and handed it over to the Rastas to clear his son's name, Ciente disappeared for months, relatives in Benguela had seen him in the south, later he was glimpsed smuggling in Cunene, close to the border

he was able to hold onto some money from his business, including his ill-advised participation in some excursions to the mouth of the Cunene River in search of diamonds, but he never got beyond the various camps where idle chatter took place, there was bathing in the river and generous amounts of weed were consumed,

when Ciente returned to Luanda, just as confused as when he'd left, he met The Real Zé, famous bandit, swaggerer and good dancer, a ruffian known for his fame for having, as an innate characteristic, incredible luck, which he called "the jinx"

"actually, you guys call it luck because it's not you who have to take the rap..."

the truth is that it was common to get caught and normally he didn't escape his nocturnal adventures unscathed

what the populace called luck was the number of times The Real Zé had been involved in physical confrontations with the populace or the police, and from which, after recuperating, he returned to his normal state, smiling and planning his next coup, as though he'd been hit by total amnesia regarding the pain his previous actions had brought upon him he'd been shot seven times without ever having fallen into a coma, the seventh time a stray bullet had struck him unawares as he was returning from a discotheque on a motor bike at six in the morning

stopped at a traffic light, he felt a strange stickiness around his belly and saw a huge bloodstain on his trousers, he continued home, he asked his sister to come and visit him at the Military Hospital in two hours with clean clothes

"Military Hospital? are you crazy, or what?" the sister tried to object

"hey, you shut your mouth, here i am shot up at six in the morning and you want to fucking argue? i'm tellin' ya, come and find me in the Military Hospital, give them my name, if they ask who i am, tell them the colonel's bodyguard, that's all"

he arrived, weak, at the front door of the Military Hospital, got off his motorcycle, parked it close to the security hut where two guards opened the gate

"please, comrade, just call a doctor, tell him i was shot in the stomach"

"but are you a soldier? out of uniform?"

"comrade, my boss went home, we were coming out of the discotheque, there was a shot, i tried to protect him and they shot me"

the soldiers, confused, confirmed the bullet hole and the blood on the stomach of the supposed bodyguard

"but who's your boss?"

"comrades," The Real Zé began to close his eyes, "i'm gonna pass out now, if anybody asks, i'm Colonel Hoffman's bodyguard"

the surgery went well, the Cuban doctor who operated on him was fascinated not so much by the soldier's having walked into the hospital on his own two feet, that's to say, on his own two wheels, as by the difficult route the bullet had taken through his body, avoiding by millimetres any organ that compromised his vital functions "you, *compañero*, are an *hombre* with *suerte*," the doctor smiled as he saw The Real Zé wake up, "this one's not going to be the end of you"

"thank you, doctor, do you know if my sister's arrived yet? i don't like these hospital clothes"

"your sister, *sí*, and a very big *hombre*, said he was a colonel by the name of Hoffman"

The Real Zé trembled

his intestines were invaded by torrential stomachache that sent his hands to his belly

"are you *bien*?" the doctor asked

"it's just that i'm not ready for visits," The Real Zé was sweating

"don't sweat it, *hombre*, your sister, your boss, it doesn't matter if they come in" the doctor admonished

the sister approached with a worried look as though, even looking straight ahead, she were making signals that aimed behind her, slowly, behind the sister, a big, tall, white-bearded man, entered as well and stood next to the door

the sister set down the clothes and asked in a whisper

"and now?"

"just keep calm..." The Real Zé recovered the rhythm of his breathing, "everything's okay, just get ready to make a strategic retreat, did you warn Ciente?"

"yes, he's on his way"

the sister withdrew without looking at Colonel Hoffman, the door closed on a hard, hospital-like silence, the serum bag dripped drops in a halting rhythm that could almost be discerned by the two men present

"do you know who i am?" the colonel's serious voice resounded

"my friend, you must be..."

"friend from where?" Hoffman interrupted, "did we go to daycare together or what? i grew up in Moxico, who are you?"

"my name's José, better known as The Real Zé"

"better known? better known where?"

"here in the city of Luanda"

"you guys from Luanda are obsessed with making a splash... right?" Hoffman said in a threatening tone

"you're right, colonel"

"you send them to call me this early in the morning? do you know who you're talking to?"

"i didn't send them to call you, colonel"

"but they called me from reception to tell me my body-guard was here, do you think i go around with bodyguards? have you taken a good look at the size of my body?"

the silence alone took over the room

"when your friend arrives, you're going to leave these facilities without making a peep, you get it?"

"yes, colonel"

"you never met me, i wasn't here"

"yes, colonel"

the big-shot Colonel Hoffman withdrew, murmuring a threatening, barely audible, "hmm!"

The Real Zé got dressed and prepared to leave the hospital, in spite of his pain, when his sister came in, The Real Zé was ready

"you can leave already?"

"it's not that i can or can't, it's that i have to leave"

Ciente-the-Grand had borrowed a hearse and entered the Military Hospital on the pretext of removing a dead body in an advanced state of decomposition, The Real Zé left the grounds lying down, covered in a blanket, and the guards refused to search the car before it left

moments earlier, the sister, sitting in the front seat, was forced to shed a few tears

"either you cry now or you cry at home when i give you a couple of slaps"

once a few days had passed, they laughed at the story, Ciente was given the mission to recover the motorcycle from the guards at the Military Hospital

The Real Zé was utterly convinced that the mission would be unsuccessful and was surprised by Ciente-the-Grand's loud arrival on the motorcycle, which looked sparkling clean, as though it had just left the factory

"how did you get it?"

"i said i was Colonel Hoffman's other bodyguard, and they even washed the motorcycle"

The Real Zé gave Ciente-the-Grand two hard slugs in the face

"you makin' fun o' me, or what? didn't i tell you what went down there?"

"but..."

"shut your goddamn mouth, nobody can ever use that name again, the man's dangerous, you guys didn't see his face, that's the end of tales about the colonel from Moxico!"

in spite of his anger, that was the day their friendship began

but

they never again mentioned the name of the mysterious Colonel Hoffman.

Blind Man yearned for colours, all colours

this business of once having seen the world around him as a foggy memory—mist from a recently forgotten dream—he felt within him a tenacious yearning for colours, he knew how to imagine them, the warmth of a reddish yellow, the peace of sky-blue, the fresh pink of the inside of a papaya and even the implacable simplicity of white

"Nganda Zambi could still lend me a light, just once in a while, even if i always had to pretend i was still blind"

"are you talking to yourself, Comrade Blind Man?" Strong Maria said with sympathy in her voice

"i was having a thought, did you hear me, ma'am?"

"i didn't understand a thing"

"it wasn't for understanding, i was remembering colours"

"then you've seen colours"

"you know, colours aren't just for seeing, there are colours i know in my skin, in my hands, life has lots of different spots... comrade?"

"Strong Maria"

"i like your name"

Seashell Seller gave Strong Maria a nod, took Blind Man by the arm and off they went, there was lots to do, the bag was full of beautiful shells with the smell of salt in the depths of their folds

"they smell of the colour of the sea, those shells of yours," Blind Man said

they wandered down the city's potholed sidewalks and, except for a few warnings from the Seashell Seller, Blind Man seemed to see, if one can put it that way, each trap that lay in wait for him

"are you silent from sadness or from thinking about matters of the heart?"

"excuse me, elder, i'm just thinking along the way, at home they told me about a woman with money who was going to buy lots of shells from me, i'm still remembering"

"i know you're remembering, you just spoke to that girl with the colourful name"

"how do you know that?"

"because people have smells, i'm familiar with that girl's skin, what's her name?"

"Amarelinha…"

they continued in silence, Seashell Seller did not seem to be prepared to speak and Blind Man did not seem to be prepared to force him to speak, they passed Noah's Barque, they greeted people from a distance

"good morning, Noah, how's your ark?" Blind Man loved this joke

"everything's great, watch where you step," Noah replied with equal provocation

after crossing a few intersections, they reached a peaceful square with immense houses, Big-Man houses with guards at the gates, some with two or three soldiers, others with those guards from private security firms

they tried to find out about the house of a lady who answered to the name of Pomposa "hey, watch out for the guards," Blind Man said

they knocked again and a strange voice, in a strange language, said something in a tone that ordered them to wait

in the front-door peephole, a short Chinese man appeared with very whitish skin and a curious gaze like a pair of parakeets

"comrade, we're looking for Senhora Pomposa's house"

"Senhora Famosa?" the Chinese man said

"no, i think it's Pomposa, the wife of a Senhor Minister"

"she car brue Vorvo?"

"i don't know, comrade"

"yes, that's the one," Blind Man shouted, "i'm blind and even i know the Minister's car is a Vorvo"

"house have guards, you sell fish?"

"no, i sell seashells"

"sell what?"

"seashell"

"say shall?"

"let's just say we get out of here," Blind Man laughed, "this Bruce Lee guy is mixing Kimbundu with Chinese!"

"seashell, comrade, to decorate the house," the seller showed him a small, pretty pink seashell, which he was holding in his hand

"Chinese always little money, no buy"

"keep it, it's on special"

"me like special, you no have fish?"

"no"

the Chinese man accepted the seashell and closed the peephole, Seashell Seller, then Blind Man, made their way at a leisurely pace to the enormous house, which was surrounded by guards, and had the Volvo parked inside the gate

"hey, get lost, there's no point in asking for anything here"

"apologies, comrade, i came here to make an offer"

"offer what?"

"they say the lady of this house is looking for my seashells"

"seashells from the sea? are you sure?"

"one of her friends, a client of mine, said so"

"you sell seashells?"

"yes, i do"

"so you make a profit on something you just pick up out of the sea?"

"excuse me, comrade, but i don't just pick them up out of the sea, i dive under the water to find the most beautiful ones, that's why everybody likes them"

"you dive and pick up tons of shells without paying a cent, and after that you come to sell them in the Big-Man houses? you're a smart guy"

"you could go diving too," Blind Man said

the guard made a threatening gesture but grasped that the old man, in addition to being old, was blind

"you're lucky i can't give a blind elder a punch in the face, or i'd make you dance the *bungula*"

"excuse me, comrade, we do what we do out of hunger, the lady's not in?"

"yes, she's in"

"so?"

"so what?"

"can't you go to call her?"

"i can"

"and you're not going to call?" Blind Man grumbled again

"i can go get her, but if any business comes out of this, i want my cut"

"fine," Seashell Seller agreed, setting down his bag, "if business comes out of it, you get to choose three seashells for your lady"

"agreed"

the guard lowered his weapon, he was about to go inside when Blind Man asked for a glass of water

"no," the guard said, "you can drink the water from the sea where you guys pick the shells," he started to laugh

through the open door, the garden was visible, the grass mown into attractive patterns the seller appreciated for the way they brought together the flowers, roses, cloves, pretty creepers that rose up out of the garden and invaded the porch, cactus, huge porcelain roses and dark green porcelain ferns that reminded him of the sea

"elder, if you could just lay your eyes on that garden... it's a joy to behold"

"i can smell the fragrance, it's got lots of flowers, right?"

the seller's gaze slid over the shining mobiles on the porch, a small bottle rack with whisky, gin, and vermouth, bottles he recognized from the bars where he offered seashells as ashtrays and, inside, voluminous curtains

the guard returned, leaning back against the gate, blocking the view

"the lady's coming, don't forget about our agreement"

"i never forget"

the guard brought a plastic bottle with ice water, opened it with a leisurely gesture, and drank while observing Blind Man's muted reactions.

"you know what i'm doing, elder?" he said when he was finished

"hmm, i know..." Blind Man murmured, "and do you know what you're doing with the other bottles?"

another car arrived at high speed and honked its horn

Blind Man and the seller got out of the way quickly, the gates opened, the car entered on the right-hand side, a body-guard got out in a rush and went to open the back door, where the Minister stepped out

"good morning, everybody," the Minister addressed those at the gate

"good morning, indeed," the guards replied

"don't shut the gate," Pomposa's voice was heard, "is everything all right, dear? i'll be right in, i'm just looking at some things here"

if not for his internalized belief in the persuasive power of the shells, Seashell Seller would have given up on the visit and turned away then and there, the lady approached bursting with gold from her toes to her ears, a long, Indian-style vest of an elegant fabric with suggestive transparencies that his eyes preferred not to contemplate, Blind Man, too, changed his expression on account of the innumerable perfumes that preceded Pomposa, her recently painted nails, her over-shined shoes, hand cream, perfumed neck and deodorized armpits, «a carnival» Blind Man thought.

"this is a carnival of shells," Pomposa joked as the bag opened

"good afternoon, ma'am"

"afternoon! so you're the fellow who's selling the shells my friends are taking to Europe?"

"yes i am, they're shells from right here in Luanda, it depends on what the lady wants"

"i want to look"

"you don't have to pay to look," Blind Man exclaimed, "except that i, even if i had money, couldn't even pay to look"

"your father?"

"no, he's my friend, we sell stuff in the street together"

"you're the first seashell street seller i've met, show me your merchandise"

there was a bit of everything and, knowing what sort of house this was, the seller had already adapted the bag to the occasion, he hadn't brought the simplest, most beautiful shells, nor the flat, almost colourless ashtrays, nor the slender, pendulous earrings that hung from a wire, nor the necklace made of miniature fish-hooks strung together with soft, pink shells

only the bright, the big, that which could be seen and bought for future display

"i think the lady will like these," he started to lay out his goods on the sidewalk

Pomposa made her choices quickly and did not touch the objects, she pointed and the guard set aside ashtrays, long shells for the centre of the table, greenish shells for soap dishes, and a beautiful object which she took to be a candlestick

"so how much is it?"

"you're taking all that?"

"spit it out, i'm in a hurry"

"one hundred fifty dollars for coming to our Minister's house"

"i can see they've given you big ideas, you think this is a bank or something?"

"no, ma'am"

"if you want, i'll give you sixty dollars and a soft drink"

"thanks, ma'am, but let's make it a hundred and a glass of water since i don't like soft drinks very much"

"oh, you're a picky one, you think you're cool?"

"i'm not cool, ma'am, you can bring me the soft drink," Blind Man exclaimed

"a hundred dollars and a bottle of ice water so you don't go around pretending to be hotshots who need to cool off"

she pulled from her wallet a hundred-dollar bill that was surrounded by many others

"this way you won't complain, wise guy" Pomposa concluded

"yes, thank you"

while the guard picked up the things, after opening the bag, nobody moved

Pomposa regarded the movements of the street, mostly from past habit, and waited for the others to withdraw, the other guard returned with a big bottle of ice water with a French label, nobody moved

"don't you have something else to do?"

"we just came in here for a rest, ma'am"

"can't you go rest somewhere else? there's more shade over at the Chinaman's house"

Seashell Seller looked the guard in the eyes, the guard coughed

"are you guys deaf? get out of here," the guard growled

"are you sure?"

"scat!"

they headed out, looking back over their shoulders, waiting for Pomposa to enter the house, but the lady didn't withdraw, intrigued by the slowness of their movements, the Chinese man peaked out from the front-door window, the guard pretended to sling his weapon onto his shoulder and the Chinese man disappeared in a hurry

"we'll just go across the street, they don't want us here any more," Blind Man murmured

they backed away, turned the first corner, then waited a moment, not a sign from the guard

the traffic was heavy on the avenue, Chinese motorcycles threaded between the enormous cars, American, Japanese and Korean jeeps, lots of Toyota HiAces acting as *candongas* to transport the people, for whom this was the only way to move around, plenty of Toyota Starlets, also known as slum-strollers, doing *candonga* service as well, in spite of being illegal and far more risky

"careful when you cross, nowadays nobody respects either traffic or blind men, aren't you coming?"

"just a minute, i'm looking at something," Seller had stopped to read an enormous sign, "this is all over the place"

"what?"

"this sign, it must be a new service"

"what does it say?"

"CIROL"

"cirol? i never heard of it, is it some service, a bank or something from the Party?"

"no...Commission for the Installation of Recoverable Oil in Luanda..."

"never heard of it"

"but Luanda has oil?"

"well, it says oil... recoverable oil... in Luanda, this is Luanda"

"but before that it says 'commission'?"

"yes, commission for the installation"

"well, even i, as a blind man, hear news on the radio, Commission for the Installation is one that goes around installing... and you sit around waiting for it to do the installing"

"and doesn't it install?"

"it installs, except that you don't see the installation, it's a commission for somebody to install himself in a real good spot"

"what do you mean, elder?"

"hey, it's really complicated right now with this hunger, let's find something to eat first, i'll tell you about it later"

"this business is serious, you're the one who can't see the sign" Seashell Seller insisted

"you're the one who can't see what this Commission's about... a group of sometime somebodies who are gonna install themselves! you're still wet behind the ears, boy!"

drawing his shuddering finger across his eyes

Odonato wiped thick, uneven particles of dust, which stung worse for not having round edges, from his eyelids, his discomfort yielding to the ease of improved vision as a tender sadness appeared, causing unease in his eyes and his heart

«tears are what washes away your sadness» he thought

Luanda was boiling with people who sold, who bought to sell, who sold themselves to later go out and buy, and people who sold themselves without being able to buy anything

"i'll be happy when the tears really come back, i'm fed up with false feelings"

his eyes gleamed, they faltered between the hue of white-caps rolling onto the beach and a brightness that imitated August skies pretending it was cold

Odonato's eyes didn't know how to cry the way they used to

he often dreamed that he was descending the staircase of that same building, coming from the terrace, finding his balance, increasing his speed at each flight of steps, smiling and shouting so that the wind would whistle and the birds would shun the imaginary clouds that knew how to conjure up tears, he descended with buoyant feet and the smile of a man who had tasted magic, even rendering a prophecy there, on the first floor of his dream, where, after the stagnant water, his body slipped in response to affected fear and a shout, his hands toyed with grabbing a non-existent banister and his balance failed, waking him up as his knees led the way and he fell, his clothes were soaked, his left knee raised a flag of blood, speeding towards the finish line, and now his throat orchestrated his crying, oh tender, sodden youth! then his eyes were able to cry

all he carried out of the dream was the sweat beneath his arms, the uncertain breathing of someone who had already foreseen that tears were a privilege of those who could cry both on the inside and on the outside

Odonato brushed his hand over his face, rubbed his eyes, brought his fingertips to his mouth and deepened his sadness:

his eyes hadn't been able to produce salt for a very long time.

it was a building, maybe a world
to have a world it's enough to have people and emotions, the emotions, raining down inside people's bodies, spill into dreams, people may be no more than ambling dreams of melted emotions in the blood contained by the skins of our oh-so-human bodies, we can call that world "life."
...
we are the continuation of what it suits us to be, the species advances, kills, progresses, disappoints, remains: humanity is ugly—it wears the marks of its long suffering and has a fetid smell, but it endures
because deep down humanity is good

[from the author's notes]

in the first-floor corridor a family was in the habit of grilling fish in a corner of the hallway then using the rest of the space to three merry lunch parties doused with chilled red wine, leaving a pleasant smell of grilled fish lingering all the way up to the fifth floor

"may i serve you, Comrade Mailman?"

"not yet, thanks very much, maybe when i go downstairs"

the man knew this building well but he hadn't yet remembered to leave one of his official letters concerning his means of transport with the journalist Paulo Paused

the Mailman brought the journalist a small box of considerable weight, this had never happened before, the normal pattern was for Paulo to receive envelopes with magazines, books, or advertising materials from other countries that he often immediately offered to the Mailman for future reading or sale

he rang the bell twice

"it's me, Dom Paulo"

"me who?"

"the Mailman, i always ring twice, haven't you noticed?"

Paulo Paused, sleepy faced, a towel around his waist and his hair wet, invited him in

the Mailman loved to enter that apartment, with its incense fragrances, sometimes even with a blend of them, that was still liable to draw patterns in the morning air like smoky tentacles imitating Oriental dancers

"Dom Paulo, is it just the smell, or do you still have like some international spells?"

"just smells, Dom Mailman, spells are a personal matter"

"what do you mean?"

"a spell depends on the belief of an individual, if you believe that incense casts a spell, then maybe it does"

"just like that? like a kind of invention?"

"yeah, a kind of invention, like life, if you want to see something, it ends up happening"

"oh, but it's not like that, Dom Paulo, i want to see something, i even want a moped, and it still hasn't appeared"

"all in good time"

"speaking of which," he rummaged in his bag, "i wanted to ask you a favour"

"i'm broke, brother"

"it's not that, i'm going to leave you two of these letters on twenty-five-line paper, official requests, i don't have a means of transportation, i don't have any subsidy to take the *candongas*, or even a clapped-out old bus, if you know who to submit them to, please, see if you can do me a favour, the other day i met a minister but i didn't have much luck"

"you should talk to your boss"

"here in Luanda everybody's a boss, and they only want to help afterwards, that's how come i'm going around handing out letters, to see if one of these many bosses can just give me a hand, or rather, a moped"

"okay, you can leave it over there, did you bring me anything else?"

"no, it's a package, i don't even know how it got here, it comes from China, it's really small but it's heavy"

"thanks, you can leave it on the table"

"is it an auto part?"

"yes, it is... my girlfriend's car has engine trouble"

"and parts are cheaper in China?"

"yes"

"i guess they are"

the journalist served him a glass of fresh passion-fruit juice with sugar and ice "thanks very much, hardly anybody here in Luanda's as kind as you are, in the houses i go to they don't even offer me a glass of water anymore, or a little tip, i mean, i know nobody's obliged to, but the gesture's appreciated, a person walks forever in that sun, the distances, the dust, to finally bring somebody information that's important to them, isn't that right, Dom Paulo?"

"yes, it is"

"some people even refuse to give water to a Mailman who's sweating with exhaustion, have you ever heard of such a thing? in the time before they used to say it was a sin to refuse water, a person who was walking down the street would stop in any old yard, clap his hands and ask for water, it was normal, today right away they suspect him of being a thief or a beggar"

"times change," the journalist looked impatient

"in truth, time passed away and didn't take us with it"

"how's that?"

"time passed away and some things were lost—respect, morality, good manners—anyway, i'm on my way, thanks for the juice, it's always so tasty"

"you're welcome, if anything else arrives, let me know"

"sure, no problem, my compliments to the lady of the house"

"thanks"

when Clara came into the living room, after the Mailman had left, her body was half-naked, her slip shrunk to a point that left you wondering whether that piece of fabric could contain such a full waist

"do you think i look fat?" she pointed at her buttocks

"you know i adore a big ass..."

"big is one thing, humungous is another"

"cut it out"

"is there coffee? i thought everything would be ready by now"

"i got delayed, the Mailman came"

"and like always you had to make him a coffee and a bun and a sandwich to keep him going the rest of the day, right?"

"no, not at all, i served a passion-fruit juice to someone who works in the hot sun, without proper working conditions"

Clara saw the two letters on the table, read from a distance

"they're not for you, those letters"

"they're not for me, they're for people i know"

"there's something queer about that Mailman, that's what i say"

"it's not that, he's trying to get some wheels"

"he wants a BMW to deliver letters?"

"no, Clara," Paulo started to lose his patience, "he wants a moped to cover the distances demanded by his profession"

"uh-huh," she went on in an ironic tone, she saw the package, felt its weight, "and what's that?"

"a part for my mother's car"

"it comes from... China?"

"yes, you want to eat? you feel like fried eggs, French toast, regular toast... fruit, coffee?"

"hmnm, nice stuff, i feel like eating and making love, or vice-versa, however you want it, Mr. Newsman..."

Paulo looked at the package, went to put it on top of the cabinet, then tidied up the Mailman's blue letters

"according to the laws of traditional Chinese medicine, it might be good to restore some energy and then move on to that interesting physical activity"

"according to the laws of lust," Clara's voice became sensual, "it's also possible for us to expend our energy right now... for example, on this table, or right here on the sofa, and then restore ourselves with the promised meal..."

Clara pulled off her minuscule black panties, ever so slowly, receiving from Paulo a smile of uncertainty and acceptance, she adored making love like this, with her tight blouse covering the upper half of her body, with no bra, leaving her hot and bothered breasts free to breathe, she herself would thrust her lover's hand inside, as though it were her own, seeking the pleasure of his rough touch on the tips of her hardened nipples, Paulo's breathing accelerated, his hands sweated, he felt himself going mad when Clara stuffed two of her fingers into his mouth

"here on the table..."

"here"

"can i roll over?"

"you should've done it already"

while she moaned, her hand sought out a short flowerpot that was always falling off the edge of the table

she let her body fall full-length across the table and caught the flowerpot, relaxed her stomach, separated her legs some more, raised her ass and they both knew this was the signal, her moans diminished, her voice bristled like that of a suffocating bird, her eyebrows arched and her moist lips twisted with a dull, latent pleasure

she lost the strength in her right arm, the flowerpot flew out of her hand to the floor

absorbed in her heated sensations, she was barely conscious of the strangeness of not having heard the flowerpot shattering into a thousand tiny pieces

the telephone rang

Paulo's body shuddered, he had sweat on his chin, his eyebrows, his fingertips

the telephone wasn't far away but it was as though her body were still reeling him in

"don't answer," she pleaded

and then he answered.

the boss called a meeting that it was not advisable to miss, things weren't going well at work, too many complaints, too much absenteeism, not to mention the different ideological approaches that guided everyone's work, if at times the boss acted like a liberalizer who wanted to set an example at the heart of the national news network, at other times his commitment to members of the upper echelons of the Party was obvious

innumerable questions had been raised on the Luandan political scene in recent weeks, but the fascinating part concerned matters emerging from reliable sources at the core of government but without the confirmation of any official organ, the rumours multiplied without anyone being certain where they originated

accustomed to constant and even radical water shortages, Luanda had never suffered, in this sort of widespread silence, such dramatic, long-running shortages of the precious liquid, it was no longer a question of there being certain days and neighbourhoods where the hours and days of the week when the water came were well known, some of the supply stations for well-water were also beginning to run dry, and the opposition press, even without providing firm data, was already referring to the evidence as a matter to be clarified by the government and scrutinized by the media

"the hitch is that nobody says a word, i'm not getting anything from the official sources and you guys, who are a pack of dipsticks, aren't getting anything from the unofficial sources, it makes us look like a bunch of idiots who only know what we read in the newspapers... is that what you want?"

the first ten minutes of the meeting were dominated by the boss's ritual monologue as he unburdened himself

"as if that weren't enough, a pile of excavations in the city, with billboards of that entity called CIROL, there's already graffiti in the streets saying it means 'Centre for International Rip-Offs of Luanda' and other jokes"

"excuse the interruption, boss... i heard rumours on BBC"

"what rumours?"

"that they started making these excavations because it's clear there's oil in Luanda"

"we always knew that, but i figured there wasn't much of it and they couldn't fuck with the city"

"well, boss," Paulo Paused said, "it looks like somebody now figures they can fuck with it and maybe there is a lot, there are already plenty of holes drilled in the streets, right near my place, i sometimes see people standing next to the holes until dawn with papers and measuring instruments" "all right, enough talk, i want everyone to research this story properly," the boss concluded

Paulo Paused took advantage of being at his desk to make a few phone calls

first he rang his friend, a journalist at National Radio, a tech guy who was often assigned to record important meetings or events, even those reserved for the Party's upper echelons

"hey, Scratch Man, how's life?"

"cool, brother, what's up?"

"hey, hear any rumours?"

"there are always rumours... i don't know what you're talkin' about"

"is this line secure?"

"affirmative"

"first, this business with the water... nobody knows what's going on, the water's not there, and when they say it's going to be there, it's not there, either, and when they say it'll be there later then later they warn that it can't be there..."

"that's almost a poem," Scratch Man laughed at the other end of the line

"a complicated poem... and the boss wants to know all the verses"

"i get it, it's a big deal"

"i already had my doubts... a big deal for big cheeses"

"affirmative, you're lookin' for a turtle, but this is alligator business, like two big alligators"

"then the water's just the tip of the iceberg"

"you're talkin' poetry again, i neither confirm nor deny, you get my drift?" Scratch Man seemed to have somebody within earshot

"that's fine, no problem, can you come by my cubicle this evening?"

"is there sponsorship on offer?"

"affirmative"

"i'll be over, eight or nine o'clock, over and out"

"take care of yourself, man."

when Scratch Man arrived at Paulo Paused's apartment, the table was already set

Clara was in a good mood, which was unusual, particularly when she had to entertain her boyfriend's friends, there were appetizers on the table, Paulo had ordered half a bottle of Chivas Regal from the Jorge Bischoff store since he knew Scratch Man was unable to leave a place without downing to the last drop whatever alcoholic liquids the house might hold

"and the beers?"

"they're cooling"

"how many of them?"

"twenty-some, that should be enough, right?" Clara asked

"enough, nothing's ever enough, but if that's what there is"

Scratch Man was the nickname used by his circle of friends, his real name was Artur Arriscado, a man so blessed with unmistakable good humour that he had never been shaken by even the most destabilizing life circumstances, whether during times of civil war or political tension, or in the fulfillment of his innumerable international missions in the service of National Radio

following independence he had covered a large swathe of Angolan national territory with a team that recorded a vast amount of traditional music, and knew the most remote nooks of the country well, especially those of his native province, Moxico, he was also a man given to tale-spinning and Luandan anecdotes, and the possessor of an extensive history with women

few of his friends and acquaintances, though, knew Artur Arricado's famous military secret, or where he came from

at the end of a certain year in the far-off days of very strict curfews, Artur was moving around thanks to a safe-conduct of dubious authenticity but which had saved him from countless complicated nocturnal situations, when he met up with the police, or soldiers, at a time when circulating casually wasn't authorized, he made use of his document, of his profession as a radio journalist, but above all he was a powerful wielder of bluster, better known as big-city lip

on this fateful night, when the year-end, beneath the intense night-time heat, announced the arrival of the new year, Artur Arriscado found himself at midnight on a small boat, making the crossing from the pier to tranquil Mussulo Island, the lights and sounds of gunshots announced that zero hour had passed beneath the blessing of the motor's engine, the calm waters of the sea, the sad wind and the serene gleam of the stars millions of kilometres away, the boat stopped, the passengers hugged each other, as was the custom at midnight on New Year's Eve, they reached Mussulo three sheets to the wind in wavelets of alcohol they had ingested and flung themselves down right there, on the shore of the first beach they found

Artur Arriscado, better known as Scratch Man, awoke with his shoes wet from the kisses of the rising tide, aside from his discomfort at the light, unsettled voices were arguing far too early on this first day of the year, he opened his eyes, looked with pleasure at the peaceful, illumined blue of the sea, in the distance Luanda appeared not to have awoken yet from the lethargy caused by the previous night's festivities,

he identified his group of friends, who were agitated and terrified of two guards pointing their lustrous AK-47s, the decision was taken in an instant and, while walking with a resolute stride, Artur Arriscado shook sand from his body and his hair, he tidied up his huge beard and, making a strange noise in his throat, came up to the men

"what's going on here?" he said in an arrogant tone, winking at one of his friends and shaking hands with the only woman present

"you comrades realize that you're on private land here? do you even realize where you're setting foot?"

"you fucking monkey," Artur stated, in his serious voice, "you're seeing me here out of uniform, you come with those starter engines, do you know who you're talking to?"

the guard hesitated

the other one immediately backed up a few steps but kept his weapon trained on the group

"lower that piece of shit right now!" Arriscado shouted in the direction of the farther-off one, the one who was closer took advantage of this to withdraw his finger from the trigger, he also lowered his weapon, "don't you know who i am?"

"no, comrade..." replied the younger-looking one

"just because i'm out of uniform! and without my brass, you guys don't even know my house over there?" he spoke without pointing with either his finger or his eyes

the other members of the group took advantage of their fear to mask it as respect for the cranky soldier who had just been disturbed

"cool it, my friend," the woman joined in the spirit of the game

"i'm Colonel Hoffman, you hear me? eh?" Artur Arriscado threatened

"i'm sorry, Comrade Colonel, we weren't informed..."

"scat, right now, and if more people appear from the boat that brought us here yesterday, they're my friends, i don't want any more hassles here, you hear me?"

"yes, colonel," they both saluted

"dismissed!"

"yes, sir"

it was this group of friends, which included Paulo Paused, at that time little more than an adolescent, that knew of the existence of a certain Hoffman, the "colonel from Mussulo"

"we laughed a lot that day, sis," Artur said to Clara, passing her the empty glass so that she could fill it again

"you guys had a lot of guts, imagine if he'd known that there wasn't any Colonel Hoffman"

"how would he know? with the kick in the ass i gave them! no way, you should've seen those kids' faces, all terrified we were gonna be liquidated on the spot"

"the best part was that other dinner two weeks later... with the other colonel" "it's true," Artur Arriscado confirmed, "the guy who was jogging"

"it was an identical situation" Paulo explained "and when some of those young soldiers, well, were a little doubtful about the claims of the colonel here, another colonel passed by jogging, didn't stop and shouted from a distance, 'good morning, colonel!'"

"ha! ha! that's right!" Artur drank his beer in big gulps, "what a life, those were the days..."

they ate and drank to the taste of these and other memories

Artur Arriscado belonged to the generation of great Luandan dancers, he was a friend of Ladislau Silva, also feared at Luanda sprees for step-sequences that included difficult passes, Ladislau being bow-legged and using steps only his arched limbs could perform, Artur was also a contemporary of Edú, in parties, and escapes from parties, which they had sneaked into as uninvited professional gatecrashers,

"bossman Scratch, we can speak freely here"

"and the chick?" Artur was referring to Paulo's girlfriend

"she's cool"

"okay, it looks like there's a big deal, the other day i was at a Party meeting"

"but how can there be a big deal with water? we've been struggling with this since independence"

"the water business is a diversion, my lad, the real deal is the oil on the troubled waters"

"oil?"

"right, and the cirollers"

"who?" Paulo was pretty sure his fifteenth beer had begun to take effect

"cirollers is the code name i gave them, they're the guys from CIROL: Commission for the Installation of Recoverable Oil in Luanda, they're setting up everything underground to get the oil out"

"here in Luanda?"

"where else...? hey, sis, can you see if the next beer's good and cold?"

"remember that study in the '80s? there's no way—that stuff with the tectonic plates"

"but the technology's improved, they've invented metal plates, it looks like the city could stand it"

"i'm gonna need more information, Scratch Man"

"no can do, all of us who were at that meeting were threatened, anything that comes out in the papers is our fault, i never told you a thing, all i've told you is what's already in the rumour mill"

Clara returned with another beer and saucers full of *kitaba*.

"cirollers?"

"right, that's what people started calling them"

Scratch Man only left, in fact, when he had managed to drain the last drops of whisky from the bottle of Chivas, he took his leave, alleging he was in perfect shape to drive home

"take care, bro, careful who you talk to"

"don't worry, it's safe with me"

Cardoso's Store, as it was known, was close to where Odonato lived

Ciente-the-Grand, following The Real Zé's orders, had spent twelve hours without consuming weed or alcohol in order to be minimally ready for his mission, it was simple: two of The Real Zé's other men would make their entrance, neutralizing the guards on the night shift without harming them, when he saw them come out with MPLA caps on their heads, he was supposed to go in, get the safe, use the combination he had memorized in advance, and carry away everything he found there in his backpack, nothing more

it was about two in the morning when the guards were pacified

Ciente-the-Grand went in armed with a flashlight and a knife, made his way to the tiny study on the first floor, on the table lay a cardboard box with some Euros and dollars which he pocketed immediately, behind the bookshelf was the safe, open, with two more boxes inside, Ciente smiled, for in truth he could no longer remember the combination The Real Zé had given him over the phone

a jeep stopped outside and Ciente became terrified, he already had his hand on the door of the safe and he closed it into a fist as he turned around to go to the window to peek out, a short guy with a pendulous belly was getting out of the car

he searched in his memory, this could very well be old Cardoso, the owner of the establishment, panicking, Ciente dropped the knife in the darkness, he wanted to look for it but didn't know what he should do first, he pulled his cellphone out of his pocket and rapidly typed in The Real Zé's number

busy!

by luck the man returned to his car, rummaged frenetically in the glove compartment until he found something, left the car, locked it up, to Ciente it looked as though the man was carrying a pistol in his hand

the connection went through, The Real Zé answered

"how's it goin', everything okay? hello? Ciente? Ciente?"

Ciente had hidden behind a low refrigerator in the corner of the office, Cardoso was moving forward with caution, in a silence that concealed the sound of his steps but not his breathing

old Cardoso, before even entering the office, announced:

"i'm armed, whoever's in there it's better to come out"

Ciente tried to keep quiet, he dropped the phone

"it's better to come out," there was the sound of a bullet clicking into the chamber

"i'm armed too..." Ciente said in a tone lacking conviction

Cardoso realized where the voice was coming from, he managed to glimpse the burglar's body in the shadow, behind the refrigerator

"come out, i can see you, come out slowly"

"if you already saw me, say where i am!"

"come out, you little fuck, or they'll carry you out with a bullet up your ass"

Ciente tried to run and surprise old Cardoso and was rewarded by the effect of his sudden movements, the old man almost fell over when Ciente ran past him, he gave two jumps and made it up the flight of stairs, running clumsily out of the shop, knocking over boxes and shelves on the way

Cardoso recovered quickly, went to the window, and fired two shots

Ciente succeeded in running a few more metres, then he realized his muscles were failing him and his waning strength carried him forward in an attempt to reach the building where his father lived

he covered the final metres with difficulty, on his knees, and finally collapsed on the first floor, stretching out amid the ever-flowing waters

he dragged himself as far as the vacant elevator and in a hidden corner found an old tap, he turned it twice, heard a noise in the pipes, it was a call to whomever knew how to use this warning system

Little Daddy, on the third floor, heard the noise, he got up quickly, went to look for a long dagger that someone had offered him years ago, saying it had been used by Rambo in one of his films, put a red bandanna around his head, picked up a ridiculous little flashlight incapable of illumining even the slightest darkness

he whistled loudly twice

Nga Nelucha, on the fourth floor, woke up Edú

"did you hear that, Edú?"

"hear what?"

"Little Daddy whistled twice"

Edú promptly slid an unusually long wooden broom from beneath the bed, struck a firm blow on the room's ceiling, coughed at the dust that fell onto the bed, waited a moment, and hit twice more, with greater force on the fifth floor Comrade Mute put on his old brown shorts, tightened his belt and grabbed the Makarov pistol that spent the night beneath his second pillow, as he passed through the living room he turned on the record player, cranking up the strident music to high volume, even in the midst of the din, the voice remained in tune

on the sixth floor they all woke up at the same time, Xilisbaba spoke to Odonato

"aren't you going to see what's going on?"

"stay calm... we have to follow procedure, first Little Daddy will reconnoitre, then Edú will take up position in the staircase to make sure no one comes up, then Mute will go down with his weapon, you mustn't do anything, stay calm"

Xilisbaba made her way to the kitchen and returned with the meat cleaver and the stick for churning the cassava meal

"go see what's happening, i'll get everyone into the bathroom"

"okay"

Granma Kunjikise and Amarelinha met in the bathroom

on his way downstairs, Comrade Mute, weapon in hand, met Edú, who was also guarding the stairs with a cassava-stick

"what was it? a thief?"

"i don't think so, i don't know, it was Little Daddy who sounded the alarm"

"how many times did he whistle?"

"twice"

"keep calm, i'm going down"

when the Mute met up with Little Daddy, they carefully descended a dangerous secondary staircase with slippery and missing steps where you had to know exactly where to put your foot

they heard moans, recognized the fallen body

"is that you, Ciente?" Little Daddy said, putting away his Rambo dagger

"they shot me up the ass..."

"at this time of night?" the Mute said

"is there a right time to get shot? just take me to my dad's place"

Comrade Mute was frightened when he saw how much blood had mixed with the waters, it was clear the lad was weak and that it was necessary to get him upstairs as soon as possible

"help me," he grabbed his arms

"there we go," Little Daddy made a huge effort to sustain the weight of the legs without slipping in the middle of the water and blood, "this guy's so skinny, can he really be this heavy?"

"jeez, just keep goin'"

"easy there," Ciente-the-Grand groaned, "my ass hurts"

"that's your problem, couldn't you have got shot somewhere else? i wanna see who's gonna yank the bullet out of there," the Mute muttered

they went upstairs with the already limp body of Odonato's firstborn.

the next day, after speaking with the secretary of Santos Prancha, the Minister's Advisor, Paulo Paused obtained a pre-hearing with a view to investigating, along with more official wellsprings of information, the water question

eventually, thanks to a bit of luck, he would succeed in extracting from Prancha some lesser-known details concerning the other side of the question

Santos Prancha was in the habit of hoisting a glass, even during office hours, and at times this made journalists' lives easier, complicating somewhat the discretion recommended by their occupation

"how are you, Comrade Paulo?"

"very well, thank you, Senhor Santos, and all's well here?"

Prancha slowly shifted in his chair, he made formalities and business matters into pretexts for dragging his feet, lending them an importance they'd never had

he was used to opening the window, smelling the morning air, closing it again, turning up the air conditioning, but his body continued to perspire as though this were its life mission, and then he would pull out a Chivas Regal and serve himself

"Senhor Advisor, the reason..."

"just a moment, Paulito" he grabbed the telephone, "Dona Creusa, bring more ice, please, you know i don't like to see this ice bucket half empty, right? hmm... i don't want to hear about it, send somebody out to buy... what? do you think i have a personal operating budget for the Ministry's ice? perform your duties, Dona Creusa, and don't bother me, perform your duties!" he hung up the phone in dissatisfaction

"everything quiet around here?" Paulo tried to start

"everything's quiet... everything's under control, this Ministry isn't like the others, here everything runs like clockwork, it's just the ice question that irritates me, you heard how that gal—my secretary—asked who pays for the ice? that's a good one!" he made one of his pauses, but Paulo felt no discomfort, "so you're here because you want to see the Minister?"

"if possible... my boss would like to include an interview with him, something big, a front-page story or something like that"

"i see... i see," he stirred his glass of whisky, nursing it

"but the secretary told me it would be better to talk with you first"

"of course... of course... to set things straight, i'm sure you've got certain matters in mind, you're a good journalist... it's possible the Minister might want to grant an opportunity"

"of course, we're ready to cooperate"

"is it going to have a lot of politics in it, this interview your boss wants?"

"look, not really, it would be more about some high-profile matters that are in the air"

"high-profile matters in the air? i'm already worried and getting thirstier..."

"the water mess, water shortages, low supplies, it's all people are talking about, and i actually thought that, to stop the rumours in their tracks, it might be good for the government to take an official position" "i'll see, i'll see... the water mess?"

"the water mess"

Dona Creusa knocked on the door and entered

"Dona Creusa, stop!" the advisor Santos Prancha smashed his glass down, "what's going on?"

"what do you mean, Senhor Advisor?"

"so that's how you enter my office?"

"i knocked on the door, Senhor Advisor"

"but i didn't reply, because i'm in a very important journalistic meeting"

"but didn't you ask...?"

"please withdraw, madam"

"but, Senhor Advisor, the ice..."

"madam, you will withdraw, knock on the door and wait patiently"

"yes, Senhor Advisor," Dona Creusa withdrew

"you were talking about the water mess?"

"yes, everybody talks about it, even the opposition papers have started to speculate"

Dona Creusa knocked on the door again

"come in!" Santos Prancha shouted

Dona Creusa opened the door slowly

"i came to bring the ice, Senhor Advisor, can i come in?"

"i already said you could, are you deaf?"

Dona Creusa headed towards the mini-bar but, as she had her hands full, failed to complete her mission and set down the bag of ice on the small table in the middle of the room

"please, Dona Creusa!"

"yes, Senhor Advisor?"

"are you saying that bag should be on familiar terms with my office? please withdraw and return when you've found a different solution"

"but, Senhor Advisor, these are the bags the ice comes in"

"then take the bucket with you and wet your own table when you change the ice, move it, quickly, perform your duties, in this country time is money and we're working here" "excuse me," Dona Creusa withdrew

"that's why our country sometimes doesn't progress, we're trying to work here and we're constantly interrupted by uneducated employees, oh give me patience!" he sighed, "okay, tell me"

"the water mess"

"yes, the water mess... but what's the mess?"

"Luanda is without water, it happens too often, the supply is completely unreliable"

"seriously? i hadn't noticed anything"

"but the people have noticed it for some time, Senhor Advisor, and as i told you, the opposition is starting to talk"

"to talk?"

"that's my boss's suggestion, that we do a long interview with someone in a position of responsibility to tone down the rumours"

"good," Advisor Santos Prancha smiled, "i don't know much about water," he fanned the glass back and forth in front of the journalist, "i'm just joking... i'll see see what can be done"

"then i should wait for your answer?"

"about what?"

"about the interview, when we'll be able to interview the Minister?"

"oh, yes... i'm going to have to look at his schedule, he's always busy, and even more so now, with the American's arrival"

"the American?"

"yes, that group of... ah, what is it... they even gave them a name... the cirollers"

"i heard about them"

"you heard? what did you hear?"

"no, i mean i read something somewhere"

"what did you read?"

"this Cirol question, there are billboards and everything"

there was another knock on the door

"yes?"

"Senhor Advisor, your brothers are here to speak with you"

"there must be some mistake, i'm an only child"

"no, Senhor Advisor, the brothers This Time and Next Time, whom you called"

"oh, yes, This Time... all right, our journalist friend is just leaving, we'll be in touch, my friend"

"thank you, Senhor Advisor"

"you're welcome, my compliments to your father and mother"

"thank you"

"Dona Creusa, put me through to the Minister..."

when the Minister received Santos Prancha's call, he said they would talk about this later, he was aware of the matter and knew perfectly well that too many rumours were circulating but that the situation was under control

"above all, keep your mouth shut, you talk too much!" the Minister warned

"yes, Senhor Minister"

"good, we'll talk later"

"excuse me, Senhor Minister"

"you can hang up"

"no, sir, you can hang up, Senhor Minister, if you please"

"hang the fuck up, are you making fun of me?"

"my apologies, Senhor Minister, i'll hang up right away, my sincere apologies."

João Slowly wiped the sweat from his forehead, propped up in his hands a notepad where he jotted down the debts and financial commitments of the street-corner moneychangers who sat on the sidewalk outside the building, they weren't run by him, as he himself made a point of emphasizing, "merely-merely advised, in this complicated world of economic globalizations"

in reality, João Slowly was a man who was not very good at mathematics or economics, he merely-merely made use of his wordly powers, and now and then resorted to desultory physical violence to convince the group of female moneychangers to maintain their professional ties with him "*manager!* nowadays everybody has a *manager,* from the soccer player to the shoemaker and even the Comrade President, how can you all want to do business in Maianga without a *manager?* in reality," he paused for effect, "it's you all who need me, not the reverse, as is reported here, comrades, the revolution is an act without end: end of quote!"

he climbed the steps slowly, refreshed his ideas as he passed through the first floor's watery zone, entered his apartment and called his wife, Strong Maria

"they came looking for you today," his wife said

"who came?"

"some tax inspector guys, they said you knew what it was about"

"those sons of bitches again? fucking twins, a guy doesn't even know if they're twins for real..."

"João, it's better just to pay up, they work hand-in-hand with the Ministry, they're the kind of inspectors who've got papers that can close businesses"

"and how are they gonna close my business? close the street? those guys think they're hot shit, but i've got their number"

"quit talkin' like a big shot, you don't understand, those inspectors are always super-well dressed, their names are This Time and Next Time, they're almost family to that comrade assistant"

"you think i'm afraid? i fought in Cuando Cubango Province, i crushed South Africans like ants, you think those two guys are gonna scare me?"

"i guess you know what you're talkin' about, i'm going downstairs"

as she was leaving, the inspectors returned

"can we go inside, Dona Strong?"

"what's it about?" she looked terrified

"can we come in? we came to talk to your comrade husband"

and they came inside, João Slowly went to the kitchen and brought water for everybody

"is this water boiled, Comrade João Slowly?"

"no"

"so?"

"so what?"

"how do you kill the microbes?"

"by praying"

"what?"

"i pray, i beg god to kill them, boiling water ain't progress, i even saw it on TV, our microbes like boiling now, chlorine bleach kills more kids than microbes, too, so i pray"

"are you a believer?" the twins asked at the same time

"still"

"still what?"

"i'm still not one"

"But what do you mean 'still'?"

"the way things are going, i figure i'm still gonna have to become a believer... but what kind of claptrap brought you here today?"

"elder, we know you got a business downstairs with the moneychanger ladies, you take cuts on big notes, exchanges and all that stuff"

"and then?"

"if you don't have permission for a currency exchange, it's an illegal business"

"and then?"

"we can help you legalize your business, comrade"

"i open a currency-exchange office in the street, with the holes drilled here, the flies, people eating my wife's fried food, out in the dust?"

"you don't have to open it, you just need to start to open it"

"what do you mean?"

"we can help, but we'll only help you get started," This Time said

"and we'll help you not finish it," Next Time concluded

"what?"

"yup, you've just got to start and then you have permission for as long as you're waiting for a response, we can help with that, too" "with the response?"

"with the response's non-arrival"

"is that so?"

"yes, it's cheaper than actually getting proper authorization, are you interested?"

"of course, my lads, if it makes everything okay, let's drink a toast"

"sorry, we don't drink water with microbes that have been prayed over"

"that's your problem, stay thirsty then"

João Slowly accompanied the tax inspectors to the nearest street corner, where they went to bother other small business people, hopped into a *candongueiro* and, from a distance, said goodbye to his wife, signalling to her that everything was well on its way

"where are you going?" Strong Maria asked

"i'm going to buy bread, i'll be back soon"

"buying bread," as it was known in the building, could mean a lot of things, because bread itself, the kind that was made at night, with an oven and salt, was available everywhere, going to look for bread was something else, a subject of deep speculation, an occupation of indolent or creative content, a justification as professional as it was human for erratic urban wandering

the *candongueiro* took him to the border of the famous Workers' District, the sky had hauled fat clouds over Luanda that tamed the sunlight's intensity without in the least diminishing the discomfort of its heat

he entered the Workers' District, delighted by the sight of children who played in the clay streets with games from the time before, there were abandoned car wheels, toy cars made out of tin cans, kites, and even broken-down cars serving as shelters for drugged teenagers, above all people with beers in their hands looking at whoever passed by

they were people capable of memorizing gestures and clothing, grimaces and sounds, people who hours or days later, for reasons logic did not reveal, would rearrange the order of events, or their most credible characteristics, in order to transform them into social fictions that were important, even crucial, to the city's normal functioning

"Elder Slowly, please come in," said a gentle voice, "welcome, is it lunch-time already?"

"it's always the right time for love"

"and the right time for a hard-on," the girls laughed, turned up the music on the radio, went to look for good, cold beer

"at least this precious liquid is blessed by god at the distillery, fuck the microbes"

"hey, boy, watch your language," Granma Humps's voice came from the yard

"i'm sorry, mother, you're right, my thirst got the best of me"

tiny rooms, closed off only by flimsy dark curtains, divided up the living space, this was the slack period, and for that reason preferred by some of the more discreet clients

João Slowly sat down in the yard, under the baobab tree, in the company of Granma Humps

he winked at the sisters Ninon and Rosalí and they withdrew inside the house, the ritual was nearly always the same: his arrival announced, the beer kept for him, then the net of conversation he wove with the elder woman prior to getting down to work

João waited in silence for Granma Humps's voice

"before people didn't come here in broad daylight"

"times have changed, little mother, the city's grown a lot, now anytime's the right time, even during the day here in Luanda there's no break"

"it's true, Luanda's changed, i just want to live to see housing projects here in my Workers' District"

"you're going to see them, little mother, you're going to live many more years, the tree grows crooked but it doesn't break, right?"

"d'you guys piss against tree trunks? aren't you ever ashamed?" the old woman snorted and spat "no, don't say that, dear mother," João Slowly smiled, "it's dogs that like to do that at the bottom of the trees"

"that's a lie, with the war the dogs got afraid, now they don't lie down against anything, it's you men who piss all over the place, you don't have any respect"

"you're right..." João Slowly tried to pierce with his gaze the window of the cubicle where the sisters were waiting for him

"listen here, you who are always walking around downtown reading the newspaper"

"yes, mother"

"this talk that i hear here in the neighbourhood, it's like i already heard it on the radio, too, about the 'e-clips' or whatever... what's it called again? they're saying you should buy more glasses, but i still see fine"

"don't worry, dear mother, an eclipse is a thing way up in the sky, everything we see at night, planets with stars and i don't know what else, all in a bright dust, it's just when you look up, it looks way scarier, the sun goes really dark right at lunch time, but you don't have to worry, you just mustn't look at it, but if you want, mother, i can get you those glasses"

"but is this more of god's doing, or is it the Americans' witchcraft?"

Rosalí came outside and tenderly took João Slowly's hand

"with your permission, mother," João set down his beer

"yes, go," Granma Humps consented, picking up the beer, spilling the portion reserved for the dead on the ground, and downing the remaining liquid in a single swig.

"Dona Creusa," shouted the Advisor from inside his office, "don't you hear me, Dona Creusa?" he insisted, unplugging his computer, grabbing leaning stacks of paper and stuffing them into his name-brand purple attaché case

"purple suits me, i must have some French blood," the Advisor was in the habit of saying, being a man of style, dubious style, one might say, but he cultivated a constant concern for the shine of his shoes and the state of his socks

his political rise was swift due to his ties to the Comrade Minister, he exchanged beer for whisky and acquired the habit of scolding his secretary

'i'm sorry, Senhor Advisor"

"you're delaying me then? don't you know that the Minister has commitments that can't be postponed?"

"yes, i know, Senhor Advisor"

"i'm here braying like a billy goat, does that strike you as fair? an Advisor of my stature braying in the corridors of the Ministry?"

"no, it doesn't strike me as fair, Senhor Advisor, i had to leave the office"

"i also have to leave, and it's to go and work, did you remember to warn me of the American's arrival?"

"yes, Senhor Advisor, i left a memorandum on your desk"

"where?"

"it's that piece of paper that you used as a coaster for your whisky glass, Senhor Advisor"

"are you making fun of me? where were you, ma'am? probably off flirting with the Ministry drivers, don't you know that the drivers are all under surveillance? not to mention the virus, eh? the virus," his voice dropped, "the virus... of AIDS..." and he coughed, "where were you, ma'am?"

"i had to go to the *banheiro*, Senhor Advisor"

"well, all right, fine, but you don't have to call it a *banheiro*, that's a Brazilianism from your soap operas... call my driver, we have to go to the airport to pick up the American, is the hotel reservation confirmed?"

"yes, it is, Senhor Advisor, but there's a problem"

"what is it this time? you have to go to the toilet again?"

"no, Senhor Advisor, it's that the driver didn't come"

"what do you mean, didn't come? call him"

"i already called him"

"and...?"

"a funeral! one of his relatives died in Gabela"

"in Gabela... or Kibala?"

"i think it was Gabela"

"that driver guy is going to be dispensed with or maybe even dismissed with unjust cause"

"'unjust,' Senhor Advisor?"

"yes, i'm going to dismiss that little devil: it's unjust because he kills family members every week to get off work, it shows disrespect for tradition, it's one thing to die for real, it's another when we die in the lies of a layabout relative, isn't that right, Dona Creusa?"

"yes, it is, Senhor Advisor"

"then what's the story?"

"concerning what, Senhor Advisor?"

"concerning getting to the airport," the Advisor sat down, served himself another whisky

"do you want ice?"

"no, leave it, this deserves an impromptu sugarcane rum, a real cat-killer, isn't there another driver around?"

"i don't think so, Senhor Advisor"

"well, what i think, Dona Creusa," he served himself for the second time, "is that you, ma'am, are going to have to straighten out this mess, you have five minutes to get me a driver with family members who aren't dead or about to die"

Dona Creusa passed through the Ministry's corridors and courtyards, sweating as she thought of the ways in which her boss might retaliate

with a driver picked up right there on Ministry Square, the Advisor, already late, made his way to the airport

the city was in chaos with new and old construction projects competing for space, and then there were the CIROL excavations, as well as the holes for installing cable television, as well as the holes from the rain and the open potholes that no one ever remembered to pave over and the holes of the kids who lived beneath the city's streets and who now—poor saps—would be expelled to make way for new pipes or even for the installation of the dangerous machinery that would extract petroleum

at the airport, the usual babel of people who were waiting for others to arrive, a zone of opportunities, contacts, of unpostponable business meetings, of easy bilking, the stage for conversations and re-encounters, where ministers mixed with baggage handlers and the highest-ranking public officials, or even intellectuals, cohabited for brief instants with pickpockets or cellphone-card salesmen, moneychangers, transit police who ticketed illegally parked cars, the beggars, the hopeful, those who were sweating in the city's heat and those who suffered from congestion from the powerful air conditioning in their imported jeeps

"excuse me, comrade, but you can't park here"

"what do you mean?" the driver inquired

"i mean this is a traffic-flow area, it's not a place where you can just stop"

"can't you see that this is a ministerial vehicle?"

"so can't you put it in short-term parking?" the policeman suggested

"what's this?" the Advisor finally took notice

"the Comrade Officer says we can't park here"

"tell that officer we're not parked"

"the Senhor Advisor says we're not parked"

"how's that?"

"how's that, Senhor Advisor?"

"the vehicle is not turned off, much less parked"

"it's because the vehicle's turned on"

"but it's not moving" the policeman tried

"Senhor Advisor?"

"what is it?"

"he says that the vehicle is not moving"

"hey, tell that officer to get off my case"

"Comrade Officer"

"what is it?"

"The Senhor Advisor says... to get off his case"

"how's that? are you joking with me, or what?"

"not me, i'm just passing along the message"

"lower your window"

the driver lowered the Senhor Advisor's window

"good afternoon, Your Excellency"

"i'm not yours, nor am i an Excellency"

"then what should i call you, man?"

"in the first place, you shouldn't call me 'man,' but ask, 'what is your title?'"

"and what is it?"

"what's what?"

"your title"

"i'm the Advisor to His Excellency the Minister"

"then, Senhor Advisor to Our Excellency, your car is incorrectly parked"

"Comrade Officer, i already told you through my substitute driver to get off my case, this vehicle belongs to the Ministry and we're here to wait for a passenger"

"but can't the Comrade Advisor to Our Excellency wait in short-term parking?"

"no! i'm here to wait for an important man, an American! have you ever seen an American walk all the way to short-term parking?"

"i haven't seen that yet"

"and you're not going to see it because the vehicle is going to stay here"

"so what do i say if my boss comes to talk to me?"

"say that the Advisor to Our Excellency is here waiting for an American, now let me close the window because the air conditioning is wasting gas"

"Senhor Advisor to Our Excellency, please excuse..."

"what is it?"

"can i just ask you to help me with a cigarette, or even with a hundred kwanzas to quench my thirst?"

"you can," but the Advisor didn't budge, he continued to stare raight ahead with mysteriously calm demeanour "then?"

"then what?"

"the dough?"

"the driver has the dough," the Senhor Advisor closed the window

the driver had already been designated for the mission of identifying the American at the exit to the terminal, and though he insisted that he be provided with a description, even an approximate one, the Advisor continued to smoke in silence inside the vehicle, the driver decided to leave, approaching the mob that surrounded the main passenger exit

"how about it?" the policeman insisted

"how about what? if you didn't get anything out of the boss-man, you expect me, without even a regular salary, to slip you some dough? get some brains in your head"

"i'm going to complain to my boss about you guys," the dejected policeman walked away

people were coming out with suitcases, baggage of unbelievable dimensions, worthy of travelling in the hold of a ship, and others, more restrained, with backpacks

there were people of all colours, with hair and eyes of all shades, the driver was confused as to who might be the American, he asked someone who was fair-skinned but miscalculated, by coincidence he was an Angolan, he asked another, a really tall, very dark-skinned black guy, who even spoke English, but he was Nigerian, and suddenly, with alarm, he spotted a large group of Chinese who were smiling and embracing other Chinese who were waiting for them

and no sign of any American

"my elder, how about one of these spacial glasses?" the boy, a street vendor, tried to empty out an enormous bag of glasses he was carrying on his back

"who told you i had poor sight?"

"these glasses aren't for seeing, my elder, they're for looking"

"are you joking, or what?"

"not at all, elder, these are spacial glasses, one of them en-clips is coming where the sun turns mulatto, and it's gonna be here soon"

"when's that?"

"the Party hasn't announced it yet, they've just been warning about it on the radio, but these here are japie glasses from South Africa, they stand up to the sun of the en-clips and everything"

"how much you askin'?" the disoriented driver tried to ditch the discussion

"five hundred, my elder"

"you kiddin'? five hundred for plastic glasses that look like they belong to a child, all crazy colours, and on top of that for an en-clips that you don't even know when it's happening?"

"but these glasses, elder, at night they see right through the chicks, their miniskirts, their stockings and everything"

"is that so?"

"sure is, they're advantages, my elder, that way, elder, you can size up a lady before making a move on her, you can spot them transvestites"

"not for five hundred... listen, did you see an American here looking really lost, i came to pick the guy up and i don't know him or nothin'"

"American, like one of them guys who speak English?"

"yeah, or he might even speak American"

"i didn't see him, elder, but there was an elder here lookin' half-lost, he sat there inside the airport"

"i'm gonna go look in there"

"and the glasses, my elder?"

"i'm gonna wait for the en-clips"

the American was a young black man who looked like many young Angolans, if it weren't for the English language, for his desperate, sweaty expression, he never would have been identified by his true nationality

"*you Américan saienteest?*"

"*yes, my name's Raago, petroleum engineering... nice to meet you*" *"petroil? yes, here petroil good, gasoil cheapsky, ay, me Kakuarta, Ka-kuar-ta, good playne on TAAG flaite? let's go, boss waitare"*

"ok, let's go"

"watz u name?"

"Raago."

"Rag-ass-o?"

"no, Raago"

"ok, ok"

it did the American good to step inside the ministerial vehicle with its gelid air conditioning, yet the smell of tobacco smoke bothered him

"you not smoke?" the Advisor tried to be sympathetic

"no, thanks," the American smiled, taking advantage of the remark to open the window, *"i really don't smoke"*

"oh, shit!" the Advisor burst out laughing and pretended he was going to put out the cigarette, *"so you come work with us?"*

"yes, it's going to be complicated though"

"no complicated here," the Advsor gesticulated, *"here everee thing is very simples, simples! capiche? good friends, good money!"*

the American let his eyes take in the city, the colours of the women who carried the whole world on their shoulders to feed their infants, their children and their nephews and nieces, their godchildren and their distant relatives who had arrived from far-away wars in search of the expensive, difficult yet safe perch of the Angolan capital

"the women are so beautiful," the American commented

"yes, very biutiful, naice, bonitas... Angola all hot, uorm claimat, uorm chiks... very naice, kizomba dence, you know?"

"kizomba?"

"yes, nashunal dence, kizomba!"

having just arrived, the American believed he'd seen a vision, in the midst of the mass of people crossing the street, selling and drinking water, brushing off dust, mopping their foreheads, the American Raago believed he'd recognized a face

he tried to whistle but no sound emerged, hours of flying had dried his lips "*hey!*" the American opened the automatic window, "*hey you!*"

the *you* had an unconcerned air, his glasses slipping down the bridge of his nose due to the heat and the lost look that always befuddles the expressions of very intelligent people

"Raago?" Davide Airosa, a young Angolan scientist, never forgot names or pages of books

the Advisor ordered the driver to stop the vehicle, they pulled up next to the sidewalk

it had been a few years since they had seen each other, Raago had met Davide Airosa when the latter was doing his Master's in the States, before being called, literally, to make his hallucinatory contribution to the Department of Physics at the University of Oxford

"*long time no see*," Raago seemed startled at finding Davide Airosa here

"*yeah, long time... what's up?*"

"*Tudo bem*," Raago risked trying the little Portuguese he remembered

"nice, how long you staying?"

"i dunno, i here to work"

they both spaced out for a moment, looking at each other as though wondering, after so many years, how many experiences each of them had passed through, how many adventures, how many lessons and challenges

"the vehicle's registration has to be visible," the policeman's voice thinned as he complained the car was illegally parked

"are you joking, or what? you're gonna make me get out of the car in this heat?"

"everybody has to do his job, sir, this vehicle is illegally parked"

"parked? are you all right in the head, or has the sun fried your grey matter?"

"comrade, you must take care not to redouble the infraction, you have already committed it, and now you want to commit it verbally, as well" "you're the one who's going to get committed, did you see this vehicle's licence plate?"

"i saw it"

"do you know my position?"

"i don't have a clue, but now we're under orders to get the vehicle registration, boss, don't take it badly…"

"don't worry, i'm taking it just fine, take the licence number if you want, but you'll be out of a job by the end of the day"

"why, boss?"

"because this is turning into a national obsession, did you guys take some course that made you think all cars are parked? this vehicle is provisionally stopped for reasons of international fraternization"

"what?" the policeman scratched his head, sweated

"this citizen is one of those Americans from America itself"

"what, that guy who looks like he's from Malanje Province?"

"what kind of lack of respect is that? this comrade is one of those scientists who only stops studying when he starts walking with a cane, as it happens, the heat is impossible, Senhor Rag-ass-o, Senhor Raago, we're going to go on our way"

Davide tried to ask for an address, but the American didn't know where he was staying or what contact details to give him and the Senhor Advisor's habit of never being available did not allow them to exchange contact details

"*i can find you,*" Davide Airosa promised, waving goodbye and ingesting the dust raised by the car

"so where do we stand, i don't get it," the policeman commented

"what do you mean?" Davide Airosa asked

"they stop, they commit, they split… and i don't see a thing?"

"all i saw here was dust."

in spite of the heat, the dust, the grit stuck to his body, Davide remained content, meandering in his own mind

and as in New York, where Davide had missed so many classes due to what he called his excessive strolls, so in Luanda it was normal for him to start walking only to have his mind taken over by strange sequences of thoughts which, while they started out making him journey to the past, provided him, as on so many other occasions, with space for the emergence of some brilliant idea, the problem for Davide was precisely that he had been gripped, since early childhood, with ideas more brilliant than concrete, more dreamable than feasible, more beautiful than practical

it was the absence of yellow that caught his attention

the sun had set far enough that the remaining yellow was now a lie that the seawater told the sky and that the sky reflected in tones of pink and purple, announcing to Luanda that it would tell no more by the powerful light of the sun which bathed it every day since night was falling now, and people turned on the fluorescent lights on their porches, not only to provide light for their children's games, but to gradually let the cicadas chime in with their vibrato, awakening the toads, stirring up the fireflies, lulling to sleep the hot stones, making the elders on Luanda Island, both fishermen and their aging wives, tighten their casual clothes around their bodies and light up their cigarettes and bongs, which feed dreams and delight the lungs with a marvellous calm for those who enjoy it

the young scientist, listening to the sound of the cars, no longer felt his glasses sliding down his face, his shoes were full of sand

sand from the beach

he breathed in the smell of meat being readied for the grill, heard the whimpering of dogs shooed away by the women preparing it, the laughter of stone-wielding children who pursued those same dogs in their pendulous, salty gauntness, he was able to hear, in the distance, on the far side of the enormous rocks, children's voices as they delighted in a late dip, savouring the water's lukewarm temperature and readying their bodies, their backs and their cheeks, for the slaps their mothers or elder sisters would give them for arriving home late after their swims in the darkness of the sea,

Blind Man and Seashell Seller were coming back along the beach, both of them tired and satisfied with the results of their day's work, Seashell Seller anxious because his sense of smell told him that the water would be nice and he felt like a swim, and Blind Man's fatigue and hunger making him want to find someone to give him a plate of food followed by a cigarette with or without weed in it

"you guys don't know how smells speak," Blind Man smiled

"you're right, some people don't know, elder, but as for me, i'm a friend of smells"

"but you guys only notice smells now and then, when they're strong... for me smells have all the voices you could imagine, an elder's shout or a child's laugh... i see plenty even with my eyes closed"

"i know, elder, i understand that"

"let it go, son... i'm not talking about things that can be understood"

it is possible that, in his sensorial world of tones and experiences, Blind Man may have noted the far-off presence of Davide Airosa who, smiling to himself, confirming that he had walked too far, shook off his feet, freeing them from the sand and the pebbles that were a discomfort to anyone who was getting ready to start walking again

but see, no, Blind Man did not see

"me, i just fish for shells and on top of that i have to talk a ton just to convince people to buy..."

"are you talking that way because you're sick of the sound of your own voice, or what?"

"or what!" replied Seashell Seller, keeping to himself the smile that he failed to smile.

when Airosa got to Paulo's apartment, he was received warmly

that night Clara was friendly, with her eyes shining—she looked prettier that way, Airosa didn't look at her directly because he was afraid that his gaze would reveal the fantasies he'd cultivated for years, in which his friend's girlfriend played a central role

"Davide, the maddest of our mad scientists," Paulo welcomed him, giving him a hug

"good evening..." Davide Airosa said

there were *quitetas* with lemon sauce, red chili peppers, a bottle of gin, lots of ice and tonic water, Davide's favourite drink

"hey, have you started drinking harder stuff, or do you still have this delusion that you're the Queen of England's nephew?"

"i wouldn't say the nephew... but in some ways our alcoholic tastes are related," Davide sat down, timidly crossing his legs

they opened the windows

the wind brought a pleasant breeze into the apartment, it might be about to rain, for the odours in the air were redolent of murmurs of plants and animals, they felt the turbulent salt air from Luanda Bay and the pressure was different, they were silent for a while, tasting the *quitetas*

"cooked in white wine, or what?"

"house secret," Clara smiled, "all you have to do, sir, is say whether or not they're good"

"i figure they're super-superbly superb, as the unfortunate Odorico Paraguaçu would say"

"enough of your Adolfo Dido sayings," Paulo smiled, as he served him a second round

alcohol and night enveloped the conversation, after dealing with the ordinary, everyday topics, they got to the subject that really worried Paulo

"what's happening with this petroleum business? is it really going ahead?"

"i know only that i know nothing"

"but from the little you do know? i know it's possible that the oil exists, but are they getting ready to exploit it?"

"haven't you seen the cirollers' signs? is there anything that isn't possible here? if the boss has spoken, it's said and done" "and he's spoken?"

"more than spoken, Paulo, wake up, it's all troika'd"

"what do you mean?"

"the same troika as always, Angola, the USA, and Russia"

"and the tugas, poor saps?"

"they're stuck with the leftovers, but now that there are some intermarriages and some identity papers, obtained under pressure, the tuga may eat a little better"

"sons of bitches... and the city? and the consequences?"

"i can send you the detailed report i did on three talks about this, there's no way for the city to withstand it, nor is it possible to get the petroleum out that's under Luanda, it's simply not feasible"

"and how are they going to do it?"

"they're going to try to do it, it would take something very, very sophisticated, high-risk and expensive—replacing the vacuum they're going to create with some other type of material—but it's practically impossible to both extract the petroleum and make this kind of graft at the same time"

"so?"

"so you've got to prepare yourselves," Davide smiled

"who's we?"

"those of you who live in apartment buildings, here in Maianga will be one of the first places to feel the consequences"

"are you serious?" Clara was serving more food

"sure am, i've done some studies on this, the city doesn't have any real foundation, if you take away the top layer the consequences are unpredictable, but at the very least there'll be sinkholes"

"and nobody's worried about this?" Clara looked scandalized

"they may be worried," Paulo speculated

"yes, maybe," Davide finished his gin with a loud slurp, "they may be worried in that Angolan way, you know, we'll see what happens later but first we're gonna fill our pockets, do you know who i saw today, right here in this city that's going to be consumed by fire?"

"who?"

"that American scientist, i think i already talked to you about him once... Raago, he's one of the oil industry's whiz kids, he finds oil where even the cockroaches wouldn't suspect it, he's the one who told the Timorese where the precious liquid was to be found"

"seriously?"

"yes, and in São Tomé, too, and all the new strata in Brazil were detected using his techniques"

"and he's here? in Luanda?"

"i just saw him! and accompanied by His Excellency the Senhor Advisor to the Ministry... okay, let's demolish these curried prawns, which don't have anything to do with the petroleum industry!"

Paulo opened a bottle of wine

"*alea jacta, petroleum est!*" Davide Airosa laughed as he toasted this couple he was happy to call his friends, "this curry is the food of the gods," he exclaimed, "we have to enjoy it now while your building is still standing"

the scientist, lulled into happiness by the wine, made these jokes without noticing the worrying effect they were having on the apartment's owners

jazz was playing on the record player and a pleasing odour of grilled fish settled over the apartment, it being a common practice among Paulo's neighbours, seated late into the night in the third-floor corridor, to grill fish and socialize with their families, even going so far as to invite whoever might be passing by to join them in a delicious eleven p.m. *mufete* and many beers

"i'm sick of saying that we have to move to another building, i can't stand the way people from Luanda grill fish in the halls," Clara complained

"the only reason you folks down in Benguela don't do it is because you don't have buildings with wide hallways," Paulo laughed, leaving Clara even more irate, "or, what's worse, because you haven't thought of it yet... you know that Luandans are always thinking of stuff" "nobody can deny that, except you don't have a clue what you're thinking of, smart asses!"

Clara withdrew in irritation

good whisky kept the men company in the living room, Paulo changed the record and put on Miles Davis's *Kind of Blue*, one of his favourites

"i figure that if a guy's gotta die, it could be to this music... i figure he'd go peacefully, without complaints"

"i think so, too," Davide Airosa smiled

as they listened to the music, the two men took turns nursing their whiskies, the so-called national drink of Angola, and exercising the old habit of letting their words flow out loose and slow, without any clear relationship between them, as happened whenever they got together, Airosa got drunk and melancholy and foolish, his eyes alight, moist

"one of humanity's biggest problems," Davide began, "on the same level as others, obviously... is that people don't want to concede the imagination its rightful place... these days, in our daily lives, we want money, sure, but even when you have money you're not going to buy entertainment, knowledge... and letting the imagination flow doesn't even cost money... you get what i'm saying?"

"more or less"

"to imagine, to imagine... making use of that faculty that separates us from other beings, the stone doesn't imagine—wait— the flower doesn't imagine, it blossoms, the bird migrates, the whale swims, the horse runs, we imagine before we migrate, we can imagine while we swim, and by imagining we can discover countless new ways of running, or even of taming a horse and making him run with us, we had to imagine it all in advance, and that's the beauty of the human condition, it's part of our condition as free beings, prisoners, recluses, the ill, in the final instant of our lives we're imagining... and that's what science and humanity need: imagination"

Paulo poured himself a whisky, he said nothing

Davide pulled a thick notebook with a nut-brown cover from his pocket, he jotted down some phrases and numbers and poured himself another whisky, in the silence, alone with the weight of the night, the notes of the music and the subtle odours of the burned-out charcoal splattered with thick drops of red pepper, lemon, and fish fat that had dripped from the grill.

when Davide had left, Paulo slouched at the window, smoking his last cigarette of the night after putting the dishes in the kitchen and quickly tidying up the living room

the city always seemed different to him at night,

not just because of the play of light that sprang up between zones with few streetlights and those without any at all, but also because the wind temperature seemed to act differently, and hence also the people, their gazes and how they walked, their dress, their routes, the needs they were fulfilling, their way of relating to the cats and lost dogs, their fear of low-flying bats, or even, later—closer to dawn—how the crazies and the drunks were frightened by the roosters announcing the arrival of daylight

Paulo watched the night end for the kids who reeked of gasoline, picking themselves up in their makeshift shanties of cardboard and plastic bags, or in abandoned vehicles now decorated with flair and imagination to build potential dens to shelter them against the frost, the mosquitoes, the wind, and the rain, but above all places that mimicked the tenderness of a home

in a dark corner of the sky, so high up that he would have to strain to grasp the mathematical figure for its distance, a falling star scored Paulo's night sky with light and

inside

he smiled.

Odonato, annoyed, rubbed his eyes

for years he'd nourished the belief that night had been made for sleeping, to allow the body to lie calm and mute, regaining strength, yes, but also giving it, for a few hours, the pleasure of remaining, by way of dreams, in a delicious state of unruffled tranquillity awake and worried, Odonato watched his son's bloodied body being dumped on the kitchen floor

"we found him downstairs next to the pool of water with a bullet up his bum," Little Daddy explained, sweating and asking for a glass of water

"the wound doesn't look serious, Odonato, but he may have lost a lot of blood already," Comrade Mute assessed

the first person to touch Ciente's body was Granma Kunjikise

her eyes were almost closed, whether from drowsiness or simply from the lateness of the hour or the shadowy darkness of the kitchen

"did anybody come after him?" Odonato inquired

"it doesn't look like it, but i'd already heard two shots, i can't guarantee that that one was the shot up the bum"

"that's enough talk about bums, Little Daddy," Comrade Mute criticized, disgruntled, while he tried to find a chair, "can it with that soap opera talk, don't you know how to say ass or fanny?"

"but then i'd be saying ass in the presence of an elderwoman"

· Granma Kunjikise, who was preparing some leaves, only smiled at him, she opened her eyes a little wider, and made a signal for them to roll over Ciente-the-Grand

Xilisbaba didn't say a thing

she glanced at her mother and was already heating the pot of water to boil the leaves for a balm the old woman would need momentarily, she finished it off by boiling the salves in water, this being more of a stopgap measure than a definitive solution

"comrades, neighbours, we're going to disperse! thank you very much for your help," Odonato said

outside the apartment stood João Slowly and Edú, who had a pained expression on his face and long white breeches that resembled a gigantic diaper facing the others' inquiring looks, he felt the necessity of an explanation "on nights when there's a full moon the *mbumbi* swells up more... it's better if i sleep with it exposed to the air... how's it goin', is the kid okay?"

"looks like it," the Mute replied, "it's better if we all move along, tomorrow morning we'll come here an' see if they need help or what"

"was he actually shot?" João Slowly wanted to know

"he actually was," Little Daddy replied excitedly, only to be reprimanded by Comrade Mute's gaze

"where?" João Slowly asked curiously

"can i say, Uncle Mute?" Little Daddy smirked

"in the ass," the Mute said

they all stopped halfway down the stairs and looked at each other

a shot in the posterior region, if we can call it that, was seen in that neighbourhood as a premonition of something ominous, soldier friends and even the elders of the street, hit intentionally or involuntarily in the ass area, had met unhappy ends a few days later, neighbours hit in the head or even in the chest, after surgery or a certain lapse of time, had lived to tell the story, but among the others, those hit in areas that were less easy to describe, not one had survived

"that boy ain't got any sense..." Edú commented

and each of them went to his own bed.

in the building next door and well ahead of schedule

the crowing rooster had decided to try out his voice

he shook his legs, his claws, he picked at parts of his body and walked the fine thread of a barbed wire, which, with the passage of time and thanks to thieves, had lost its barbs, executed a few swift neck movements, as though warming up his singing muscles, blinked his eyes and observed the skies like someone seeking or announcing a scratch of sunlight, opened his beak and would have been on the verge of letting rip his musical cry had it not been for the sudden arrival of a stone that flew swiftly from the window of the apartment where Little Daddy lived a powerful slingshot, made out of tire rubber, had hurled the stone

the rooster couldn't believe the pain he felt, a cold paste drained from his eye, dripped onto his left claw and, lacking a mirror, the rooster was unable to see that his eye was no longer in its proper orifice, what he felt wasn't pain, but rather an icy discomfort spreading through his body

be this as it may, the sun had already risen when the fowl regained the strength and energy to crow, announcing to all in the building the arrival of the curious tax inspectors This Time and Next Time

"good morning," Little Daddy greeted them outside the building as he was hauling water to begin washing the neighbourhood cars

"yes, good morning"

"do you know if Comrade João Slowly is at home?"

"i haven't met anyone yet today, comrades, but anyhow it's really early to be waking people up"

"this is the time when the workday begins, you're working, aren't you?"

"i wake up early to wash cars"

"good for you!" they headed into the building

Little Daddy tried to warn them that at this incipient hour of the day the water gushed more strongly on the first floor and that to cross those waters a fine-tuned dexterity was required, the tax inspectors fell and got soaked

"i tried to warn you, comrades..."

"are you joking, or what? this is a trap, we in our persons are going to bring accusations against this building"

"no, that's just how it is, it's just that in the morning the water's more categorical," Little Daddy hid his laughter

"i'll give you a category"

Edú, on the fourth floor, came to the window

"what's all this ruckus so early in the morning?"

"don't you see, sir, that this building's letting comrade tax inspectors fall over right here in the neighbourhood?"

"the building's 'letting them fall'? are you sure that Portuguese is correctly formulated? a building is immobile, by its nature it doesn't move around"

"are you joking, comrade? we're going to come upstairs to identify you, hey, kid," he said to Little Daddy in a less sympathetic tone, "show us how we can get through the waters"

Edú hurried to warn Odonato, before the tax inspectors were able to reach him, that they were in the building, for it wouldn't be good if they found his son with an exposed wound in his ass

"we've got to distract those men," Odonato said, "what's the deal with them?"

"i figure they just came to give us a hard time, or they want some dough, but i'm broke"

"just distract the men while i think of a way to evacuate Ciente"

Edú went back downstairs to greet the tax inspectors

since he didn't have either food or drink in the house, he sent his partner Nga Nelucha to quickly ask around the building to get the inspectors to settle down at his place for a while

"but who am i gonna ask?" Nga Nelucha whispered, still sleepy

"go ask the neighbours, for fuck's sake, and do it quickly, Odonato doesn't want them to go upstairs"

the inspectors were invited to enter Edú's humble abode and were amazed by the strange arrangement of objects, the table, the furniture, the benches and a series of accessories that helped him to walk, they were misaligned in a way that almost certainly concealed some logic, for their placement suggested something like a track, a route, or even an utterly intentional interior design which, they now understood, provided access to the main paths to the kitchen and bathroom, and also to a kind of seat made out of sisal bags, next to the window, where Edú almost certainly spent a lot of time

the tax inspectors stopped for a moment to look over his gigantic, diaper-shaped breeches "you don't realize, comrades, that the food is on its way, please have a seat"

"can i sit down, too?" Little Daddy asked

"get working, will you, you're already late, car-washers are this nation's first civil servants," he said in a speech-like tone, to the inspectors' shock, "they're among the few people who also work Sundays and holidays, including holiday Sundays that get moved to Mondays... now scat!"

Little Daddy left

"pay no mind, comrades, this is a simple home, and as much as i'm chronically ill and nearly bedridden, though i continue to do a bit of exercise," he gestured towards the room's strange disorder, "because otherwise my health would be in ruins, i'm already somewhat ruined... but have a seat, comrades"

the tax inspectors sat down, their eyes adjusting to the apartment's gloom

"could you open the windows a bit more?"

"of course, but could you help me, sir, as i'm already seated," Edú said, sitting down that instant, "i have motor difficulties"

while This Time opened the windows wider, Next Time sat down next to him, demonstrating a dyed-in-the-wool curiosity

"and that special clothing?"

"i've had this for years," Edú began, then immediately shouted in the direction of the kitchen as though his wife were there, "hey, Nelucha, bring these inspector gentlemen some drinks..." he made himself comfortable in a huge seat and waited for This Time to seat himself also, "it's a long story"

"we've got time"

"a chronic *mbumbi*, of dubious origin, the doctors say"

"of suspect origin?"

"there is no explanation, my friends, no explanation, this *mbumbi*, in addition to being more enormous than the rest of the domestic *mbumbis*, has no reason for its appearance or disappearance" "what do you mean?"

"it's called an autonomous *mbumbi*, it's been identified and catalogued by Swedish and Cuban doctors, not to mention Angolans, Portuguese and Koreans," he started lifting his garments and letting the tax inspectors appreciate the spherical swelling

"yes, sir, it's a fine specimen," tax inspector Next Time commented

"thank you very much"

"please excuse me, Comrade Edú, but you have to find a way of making money from this thing"

"i was just thinking the same thing..."

"thinking is delaying, please don't be offended, but it's time for you to act"

"i can barely walk, let alone act"

"act imaginatively, my friend, imaginatively... do creative things, i'm not sure i'm making myself clear..."

"a few entities have visited me already—the Church, television..."

"you've got to make money from it, take it to an international level, you're not worth less than other people, you understand?"

"i guess so"

"well, i guess not, you've got great potential here," tax inspector Next Time observed, with a nod of his head he intended his brother to see, "you've got to go on CNN... for you Globo and RTP would be a joke... you've got to think big"

"dough? like ask for dough?"

"for dough you should ask the government for a health subsidy," the tax inspector's eyes gleamed, "but in terms of marketing, you've got to aim higher, my friend"

"that South African program where they put cameras in the bathroom? i'd be ashamed"

"even that program could work, but you've got to dream bigger: Oprah!"

"opera?"

"Oprah! the Oprah show, an American program that'll ensure nobody will ever forget your *mbumbi*, Edú..."

after speaking with Strong Maria and João Slowly, Nga Nelucha returned with pots of coffee and milk, sandwiches with butter and a little cheese, and slices of a pre-sliced cake

"comrade inspectors, my partner Nga Nelucha"

"very pleased to meet you, comrade, forgive us for entering your home at this early hour, but our workday begins early"

"i understand, no problem," Nga Nelucha started serving

having eaten, drunk, and conversed, their conversation turned acrimonious when Edú said he wanted to think twice about this idea of publicizing his *mbumbi* worldwide because he'd already had serious hassles for years with the type and number of people who had appeared at his home, including those who, in a similar vein to what was taking shape here, meant to exploit his swollen condition for economic gain

"but you need a cultural agent like artists and people like that!"

"i'm not an artist," Edú complained, "i'm a sick man"

"but it's an artistic illness, let's say..." he paused, "well, we're going to continue our evaluation mission"

"what is your evaluation, if it's not rude to ask?" Nga Nelucha wanted to know

"our evaluation..." tax inspector This Time stammered, looking at Next Time

"our evaluation is to evaluate the conditions of the buildings in Maianga... and namely!"

"namely what?"

"namely the rest, the conditioners"

"which conditioners?"

"the surroundings and the fillng"

"of what?"

"of the building itself! and you, ma'am, are inadvertently interrogating the authorities" "which authorities?" Nga Nelucha laughed her open, brazen laugh, which was more of a diversion than a disobedience, "you guys don't even have papers to prove you're tax inspectors"

"Comrade Titucha...!"

"Nelucha, what are you saying, show some respect," Edú protested

"Comrade Nelucha, we have conditioners of nephewness!"

"what?"

"that's right," the two of them laughed, leaving the apartment, "it goes without saying that we're both nephews of the Senhor Advisor to the Comrade Minister!"

Edú and Nga Nelucha remained silent

the truth was so obvious that it silenced them, the tax inspectors began to stroll through the building, with caution, lest there be another waterfall equal to the one on the first floor, they knocked on locked doors, peered down hallways which they could not fathom, and without wishing to admit this to each other, did not know very well what to do or where to begin

Nga Nelucha went downstairs and asked Little Daddy to warn Odonato as quickly as possible that the tax inspectors were on the loose in the building

Seashell Seller and Blind Man arrived at the building in good time, together they climbed to the fifth floor where the tax inspectors were getting ready to knock on Comrade Mute's door

"don't you buy seashells, comrades?"

"you're selling seashells? seashells from where?"

"seashells from the sea," the Seller replied, "i dive, i find, i wash and i sell, but they're shells that are useful for all sorts of things, and beyond that, they bring people luck"

aware of the issue of Ciente-the-Grand's wound, Comrade Mute allowed everyone into his apartment and, since he liked to talk, put on a jazz record, offered water

his living room resembled a Moroccan merchant's alley, on the floor Seashell Seller had laid out his gleaming shells with their thousands of shapes and smell of the sea, the tax inspectors distractedly allowed themselves to be mesmerized by the shapes and colours, Seashell Seller took advantage of the water, and of being able to escape the sun, to rest his body and his back, and Blind Man relaxed into a corner, accompanying the notes of the half-scratched record playing in the morning heat by tapping the wall lightly with his cane

the setting, then, of a calculated plot

while Morocco was going on in the living room, Ciente-the-Grand's body was transferred from his father's home to Edú and Nga Nelucha's apartment on the fourth floor

interrupting the get-together, Odonato, surpassing the most extreme notions of gauntness, entered the Mute's apartment, making his way towards the tax inspectors

"gentlemen, i'm a resident of the sixth floor and i came looking for you so that you could see the rest of the building, so that you can then leave it right away, since we know our rights"

"do you know who you're talking to, comrade?" tax inspector This Time began

"do you know who we're related to?" Next Time questioned

Comrade Mute had to grip Odonato's sleeve, for an invisible impulse propelled the very gaunt man towards the other two

"show respect, comrades...!" Odonato spoke with such force that no one had the courage to utter another word, "you can be assured that this is a building of honest people"

the tax inspectors glanced at each other, Blind Man coughed and the Seller, very, very slowly, began picking up his shells one by one in order not to ruin the energy that had taken over the room

"by chance, do you know who i am?"

Comrade Mute recoiled, he didn't know of any distinction or occupation of Odonato's worth mentioning, and he wasn't used to seeing his neighbour put on these kinds of airs

"i'm part of this people! the Angolan people, the people... do you know that word? it's a word that contains human beings! now, if you wish, you can come upstairs with me"

"very good, let's go see this sixth floor and the terrace,"
This Time said

the tax inspectors accompanied Odonato up the stairs in silence, they saw his apartment and wanted to nose around more than expected, but in the dark hallway were stopped by the gaze of Granma Kunjikise

"good morning, elderwoman," they greeted her with apprehension

"*good morning*," Granma Kunjikise replied in Umbundu, "*are you poking around in other people's homes?*" her lips sketched something approaching a smile

"no, senhora, we're just on our way out"

when they reached the roof-top terrace, Odonato was far away, in a shaded area, the sun was strong, the tax inspectors regarded the terrace's cardinal points as though appraising them

João Slowly arrived

"take it easy, Odonato, they'll be leaving soon, just put up with them a little longer"

he went over to them in his amiable way, responded to their doubts, enlightened them as to the building's dimensions, spoke of the neighbourhood customs, and of how, in spite of their being in Maianga, in the heart of the city, it was a peaceful building

"and that rooster that's missing an eye?" one tax inspector asked, glancing at the rooster, which balanced with a sad air on the plucked barbed wire of the adjacent building

"i never noticed it"

"it's not a sorcerer?"

"i don't think so," João Slowly said seriously, "these are difficult times for socerer roosters"

"well, my friend," one of the tax inspectors sat down close to João Slowly, "the issue here is that this building is full of irregularities, starting with that swimming pool-thing down on the first floor"

"starting with ecological reasons," said the other tax inspector

"all that water being wasted downstairs"

"but people make use of that water, Senhor Tax Inspector, everybody in the building uses that water to cook, to wash cars, to clean the building..."

"but it's over- and under-utilized!"

"what do you mean?"

"it's over-utilized because too much of it comes out and you people can't control it, it's under-utilized because other members of the community aren't enjoying the benefits"

"you're right," João Slowly agreed

"and this terrace, also"

"what?"

"it must be put to better use, you're a man of ideas..." the tax inspector said, "you must have already thought about that"

"i bet he's already thought about it," the other tax inspector commented

"i might have already thought about it," João Slowly smiled

"an isolated terrace, without any real problems in the neighbourhood... why don't you put in... for example... a homemade movie theatre?"

"a cinema? but what about authorization?"

"but we're the tax inspectors for Maianga... you'd be authorized, and we'd have a public, limited-liability company... that only we knew about"

"what do you mean?"

"it's easy... on one hand, you people from the building, you talk, you get organized and you set up the scheme, on the other hand, us two, providing legal protection and collecting the goodies"

"a cinema?"

"a cinema—low-key, discreet"

"and the paperwork?"

"no paperwork is necessary"

"how's that?"

"only an official cinema requires papers, a disofficial one doesn't need them"

"i understand"

"in that case, it's all settled"

"and the name?"

"the name doesn't matter, what matters is that it has customers"

"and the films?"

"you'll figure it out, afternoon sessions with lots of punch-ups and stuff, some Bruce Lee... and at night something hotter, porno stuff, higher ticket prices and then you can even expand the business, a few closed rooms here in your building..."

pleased, João Slowly shook the tax inspectors' hands and said goodbye, he was a friend of money, especially the easy kind, and he agreed that the terrace was underutilized and would, in fact, be a good spot for cinephilic activity

later, when Odonato criticized him, he played the victim, saying that, trapped by the circumstances, and worried about Ciente-the-Grand's health, he'd been forced to accept the tax inspectors' proposal for the sake of the building.

João Slowly tried again to speak to Odonato about his condition

two days without seeing Odonato was enough time for him to notice the change in something he had no idea how to explain

it was almost lunch time when Xilisbaba appeared on the terrace with a plate with scant food, which she offered to her husband

"no, thank you, love, i'm not hungry"

"i know, but you have to eat"

"i'm not hungry, give it to our ravenous comrade, João Slowly, he eats—and quickly, too," Odonato smiled

"i'd be grateful"

Xilisbaba mentioned that she'd had a phone call with a doctor friend, a friend of a friend, who was willing to come and see Ciente-the-Grand, even though it had been difficult to explain why the boy had been at home since last night with a bullet lodged in his body "i didn't know what to say," Xilisbaba commented

"you don't have to say anything, if he wants to understand, he'll understand, if not, there's nothing to do"

"but he can't stay at home bleeding like that, he's got to go to the hospital"

"it'll work out," Odonato reassured his wife

"are you coming downstairs with me?"

"i'm going to stay here a little longer"

Xilisbaba withdrew, she went to ask Little Daddy and others to carry Ciente-the-Grand back up to the sixth floor to await the doctor's arrival

as the sunlight's position changed, after tidying up some scrap iron that was lying around, picking up and distributing loose pieces of wood, trying to imagine how the space could become an unofficial cinema, in one corner João Slowly found an enormous cracked mirror that resembled a map

it brought back memories of some place he'd seen, he was turning the mirror, and using the rotation to solve the enigma the mirror posed, the sun, strong at that hour, found the position ideal and sprang forth in intense clusterings of light that hurt Odonato's gaze, he crossed his arms before his eyes and stood there, still and leaning backwards, like an emaciated soldier who had just been struck by a hail of bullets

"Odonato... you..." João Slowly stammered, while his hands shook, while the mirror shook, while the light shook, while it was enhanced by a deep yellow in the still-dark tone of Odonato's skin

the bright beam of light faded to mulatto tones as it reached Odonato's body, João Slowly's mouth opened and closed again without leaving time for wonder, in slow motion he laid the mirror flat with a tremor of fear

Odonato uncrossed his arms, lowered them slowly, looking into his friend's eyes

behind him, torn threads of light remained on the wall, as though his body were holding back part of the glow "lay down the mirror, João, before you hurt yourself," Odonato murmured

João Slowly's eyebrows had ridged up so high that Odonato was surprised, his friend tried not to let his hands shake as he kept the mirror trained at an angle that directed the rays of light through Odonato's body so that every second he continued to believe in what he was seeing, in that state of semi-transparency that allowed him, in a single instant, to see and to believe he was not seeing the blood sprinting and dancing through Odonato's veins and muscles

"don't be afraid," Odonato said, "i'm turning transparent."

was i afraid?

to see my city of Luanda in black and yellow tongues of flame, and the houses falling down from sweating in the fire and the voices shouting in fear?

yes, i was afraid, fear was a thing that came from inside me, because the whole city looked like it was about to die;

when did i see him? for the first time?

i was in the street, lost in my thoughts, and i spotted something i'll never forget: in front of me an elder was walking slow and muttering to himself... i glanced at the clouds and tried to return to the vision; the gent had mingled with some of those kids who sell stuff in the streets, i took a quick look for him, spotted him up ahead, ran with steps that tried not to make a sound, and i saw him again and was afraid all over again; and i saw! my near-death fright; the elder was slightly transparent! fear made me stop right there and turn away—but i'd already seen and couldn't forget this miracle of his!

i ran farther, i disconcealed myself behind a tree, the gent glanced around

he suspected i was there but didn't see me, he turned his back in my direction and climbed a little ways up his street, suddenly he disappeared, i went slowly forward and looked at the doorway of the only building he could have entered!

the building where the whole story that i'm going to tell you happens: you see it's not right for me to keep this story just for myself, life is like a sea, you see it and you wade in deeper...

if i saw things, i can speak of them only to set a few more events in the city; if i cried from suffering and beauty, i'll tell you right off that i was happy, if i seem sad today in my voice as i start talking, it's because melancholy, too, comes disguised in sad events which can only be discovered by our eyes...

what i mean is, what i'm saying is, to get it right: life looks bigger than the sea...!

am i shooting my mouth off?

[from Seashell Seller's recording]

the American hadn't slept this badly in years

the air conditioner sounded like it was stuttering all night, but a stuttering that produced nothing cool, expelling lashings of hot air like a blower whose cooling function had packed it in

and that wasn't all

strange thoughts and dreams tormented him to the point of mixing up the sweaty reality of his body odour with the images he thought he was seeing in the darkness

only in the morning, taking a calm look at the light that filled his room, did he confirm it was true

it had been right next to him all night: a flattened insect of a washed-out yellowish appearance, whose long whiskers were in slow but constant motion

it was, beyond a doubt, an albino cockroach

the American wasn't troubled by this, nor was he disgusted by the insect, precisely because he had the feeling that the cockroach had been simply observing him as if it were going to talk,

a strange, serene, enormous, albino cockroach

the American took a long shower and was going to call reception to complain about the malfunctioning air conditioner when it began to function perfectly, the room became cold, very cold, the albino cockroach changed location, climbing onto his nightstand and settling down much too close to his wristwatch when he went downstairs for breakfast, the American had a message from the Advisor to the Minister telling him that they would come and get him later for the first meeting.

the Minister arrived at the Ministry early and immediately called the Advisor, but he hadn't arrived yet

"get him on the phone and tell him to come immediately! in the time before, it was grounds for automatic dismissal if an Advisor arrived later than his Minister... those were different times..." the Minister sighed

he lifted the phone and ordered coffee, strong coffee, the strongest coffee that could be found

the telephone rang, the caller hung up

turning to his cellphone, the Minister spoke with a woman

he smiled, he softened his voice, he delicately scratched his testicles and spread his legs, feeling the heat between them

"that's fine, i'll be there in an hour... but make sure you show up this time because i'm making this trip just for you," the Minister smiled

"Senhor Minister," the secretary entered without knocking, "excuse the interruption," she averted her eyes while the Minister removed his hands from his testicular area, "the Senhor Advisor has arrived"

"tell him to come in"

"yes, Senhor Minister"

the Advisor entered looking worried, possibly they had already told him that the Minister had asked for him

"i'm sorry i'm late, Senhor Minister, it was because of the construction work"

"i drive through construction zones as well, and i got here before you... how is that possible?"

"as it happens, i live a little farther away, Senhor Minister"

"sit down, man, if you live farther away you wake up earlier and spend less time eating breakfast, you eat too much, you're fat, haven't you noticed?

"yes, Senhor Minister"

"well, let's get started, this is going to be a long day, a day of work, Senhor Prancha"

"yes, Senhor Minister"

"is everything ready for the American?"

"yes"

"excellent, i don't want mistakes, either in the meetings or in the reports, that American has to leave here knowing this is a world-class country, am i right?"

"yes, Senhor Minister"

"then get to work! i'm going out for an emergency meeting"

"there's no meeting on your agenda, Senhor Minister"

"don't interrupt me, sir, emergency meetings aren't on agendas, otherwise they wouldn't be emergencies! after that i'll come back here, pick you up and we'll go to the hotel to find the American, at the meeting there are going to be people from the Party, and the engineer responsible for the excavations"

"i understand"

"i'm glad you understand," the Minister got up, put on his jacket, "call my driver and tell him i'm going out."

in the building, the doctor was escorted from the first to the sixth floor, where Ciente-the-Grand rested on the kitchen table with the sweat of his uncontrollable fever and its associated delirium

he was lying half on his side, trying not to press on his bum in the region where the bullet had lodged

Odonato thanked the doctor for his visit and rushed to explain that they didn't have any money to pay him

"don't worry, i'm here to do the family a favour"

with patience, the doctor examined the wrongdoer, touching him where he had to

the white refrigerator framed the painting of Odonato's gaunt, tortured face

rather than worry about the boy, the doctor discreetly observed Odonato

"do you feel all right?"

"yes, thank you, just a little concerned," Odonato replied, thinking that the doctor was questioning his mental condition in the wake of his son's situation

"but, look here, you're very thin and you don't have good colour in your eyes"

"thank you, doctor, right now i'm just worried about my son, what are you planning to do?"

"conditions here won't allow me to extract the bullet, it's stanched at the moment, but there's already an infection, i won't lie to you, the risk is serious," he paused, "we have to act very quickly, because if the infection spreads... your son could die... sir, do you want me to take him to the Military Hospital?" the doctor averted his gaze in the direction of Odonato's hands

Xilisbaba hurried to close the window so that the dark clouds in the kitchen thickened

"don't worry, ma'am, i'm not frightened. i've seen lots of bullets in bodies, but people like this... i have to admit, it's the first time"

Ciente-the-Grand moaned

"the Military Hospital doesn't strike me as a good idea, doctor, how can i explain the bullet?"

"is it you who has to explain it, sir, or your son? we're not talking about a fifteen-year-old boy"

"thanks, but it won't work"

"but, Odonato, maybe," Xilisbaba started

"it won't work"

"the doctor says he could die"

"we could all die," Odonato looked fixedly at the doctor, "every day, with or without bullets in our bodies"

"that's true," the doctor agreed, venturing "and what about you, can i have a look?"

"one thing at a time, doctor"

Little Daddy and João Slowly accompanied the doctor to the building's exit

he was a very observant man, he walked slowly between the floors, observed whether the doors were open or closed, observed the objects left in the halls, the flora cultivated in flowerpots, and that which sprouted through the walls, the delicate, sure-footed way in which the inhabitants crossed the pools of water on the first floor, signalling possible crossing routes to people like him

after passing through the darkness, the doctor smiled on returning to the intense sunlight of the city of Luanda and the sound of the ministerial car's siren, he set off walking in the direction of Maianga Square

"here comes the Minister, we'd better get out of the way before we get in hot water," young Little Daddy said

"come with me," João Slowly said, "let's got up to the terrace, i've got an offer to make you, hey Maria," he shouted, "can you come with us or are you busy?"

"go with you where?" Strong Maria asked her colleague to keep an eye on her washbasins full of things and her lighted grill

"we're going to the terrace to talk about business, this city never sleeps!"

they went upstairs in silence, a strange, minimalist procession

only a few minutes later, having reached the terrace, did the group begin to talk

"right here we'll see the return to the future of the eighth art..." João Slowly said with a strange gleam in his eyes and an incantatory tone ill-suited to the hot sun

"were you out drinking this morning?" Strong Maria sat down on a small box

"that's it, sit down there, yes, right there! now you'll be able to imagine the rest, in front of you a late-afternoon scene, look out at those roof tiles, at this city full of dust, full of people who flutter about, from a distance they can't see us... it's we who can see them..."

Strong Maria sighed and looked at Little Daddy in the hope that he might know what was behind this mysterious speech, but Little Daddy shrugged his shoulders and sat down next to her on the same old box "the return to the cinematic art, except that our cinema is the eighth art... because we're beyond all that, in a conception already based on unparalleled theoretical advancedness, except that..."

this happened at times, late in the afternoon, but especially after drinking, João Slowly went on oral rambles through futile, obscure notions, usually ornamented by a Portuguese which did not approach so-called standard Portuguese, or even, if we may express it this way, standard Angolan Portuguese

"and so the plan sprang up in my head... an open-air cinema, at the top of this building, in the heart of this city, a cinema in which a person brings his stool, his tin can, his seat, like in the time before, and where the hour on the clock dictates the programming, in the afternoon we target the youngsters, at night we can have our soap operas with the support of National Television, and later the sessions for adults"

"pornographic movies? with moaning?"

"films for adults, and our cinema is of an old-fashioned modernity, that's why i called it the eighth art"

"but what are you talkin' about?" Strong Maria stood up impatiently and was on her way out

"we're going to return to the era of silent pictures, where only the crowd's murmurs or comments hang in the air, this is going to be a fucking great business..."

João Slowly's hand lifted slowly, and Little Daddy's and Strong Maria's eyes were obliged to follow it: his finger extended, pointing out the neighbouring building as though it were a far-off road, there, the sad rooster picked at the dry ground, cracked by the daily heat

"let me introduce you to the Rooster Camões Cinema! may our neighbour and future mascot live without the risks of being too close to us"

Little Daddy, narrowing his eyes, gazed incredulously at the rooster: he saw it was missing its right eye, but he didn't get the reference to that other name, "Camões" "so now you're ready," João Slowly's voice changed, now he was talking in a trite tone, less prophetically, "Little Daddy will handle admission and guest seating, and you, Maria, if you wish, can run the food and drink sales, before and after the session, so that we don't get the cinema dirty, i'm going to speak to the neighbourhood and work out how we divide up divide up the profits, aside from my slice, since it was my idea and i'm the manager, on top of that i gave the cinema a name that will make lots of people jealous: Rooster Camões!"

"o-kay," Strong Maria finally agreed, "it sounds like a good idea, when are you gonna start?"

"if everything goes well, tomorrow"

after speaking with the most influential neighbours, João Slowly was completely convinced that the idea was a good one, he mobilized Little Daddy and even Seashell Seller and Blind Man to carry some chairs to the roof

"but didn't Uncle João Slowly say that everybody would bring his own seat?"

"shut up, kid, you don't have any business experience, you don't respect the elders. and the wise old men, are they going to be able to climb these stairs carrying a chair? don't be stupid, this is a cinema with rules from the time before, but also from the future, don't forget, it's the eighth art, the Rooster Camões will be respected and talked about the world over, those chairs are for the group of elders, and so let's get to work because they're already talking a bunch"

Little Daddy helped to carry chairs and Seashell Seller, who had left his bag with Blind Man in a corner up above, was happy because he had finally been introduced to Odonato and Xilisbaba's daughter Amarelinha

over the next two hours Seashell Seller moved his hands slowly, trying to find his rhythm, because he suddenly felt his voice failing him, his callused hands growing weak, when the girl came near and smiled at him

Amarelinha, who normally smiled with a hand in front of her mouth, sensed the Seller looking at her and her yellowed teeth with a simple directness

and she and her sure hands trembled too beneath his gaze

seated in the corner to which he'd been assigned, beneath a small, perforated red umbrella, Blind Man smiled at what he'd been told, that he wouldn't have to pay to get in because at the Rooster Camões Cinema "the unvisualed" had a spot reserved although it wasn't worth sitting them close to the front, blocking other people's view

Blind Man had a reserved corner where, the cinema's manager said, the late afternoon and early evening winds made their refreshing rounds, which would leave Blind Man in a privileged position where he could taste the breeze while listening to the marvellous films that would be exhibited

"but didn't you say this cinema isn't going to have sound? i'll be stuck there as part of the landscape, not seeing anything," Blind Man complained

"i'm more progressive than that, elder, don't worry, the Rooster Camões Cinema is the real cinema of the Eighth Art, i'm not kidding, and the eighth artist, you might say, which will turn this cinema into something monumental, not to say monovocal, is the people, the participatory public!"

"what do you mean?"

"we're not going to have sound, but rather the sounds that people want, it's the people, individually or together, who are invited to create the film's sound from their own mouths... can you imagine that? it's going to be wonderful!"

on her way back to her own business, Strong Maria stopped before crossing the darkness of the first floor

in a humid recess, before she had got used to the darkness, her eyes saw a man's hands, handsome and cared for, running over a young woman's body

the woman, her body soaked from sweat and the open waters, moaned at the man's touch, they kissed ferociously, their tongues seeking each other's throats and ears, their frenzied hands trying to pull off one another's clothes or, failing that, finding routes beneath clothes to stroke or squeeze the woman's hardened nipples or the man's hard sex

Strong Maria looked over her shoulder, fearing that someone else might come down the stairs and though she was far from the place where the water dripped, she felt damp, the sweat hot on her hands and between her breasts, her skin tightened and the spot's coolness made her slide down onto the ground: she saw everything better now

his moans, her moans, and Strong Maria's hand, slipping inside her own clothes and touching her hot sex, made her moan, too, until she quickly closed her mouth to avoid being too loud

Strong Maria's other hand searched for the cool dampness of the wall and daubed moisture onto her throat

Strong Maria let fall a tear, feeling a pleasure that started in her mouth, flowed down through her breasts, ran over her ribs, raised gooseflesh on her buttocks and arrived, by way of her sex, in her tremulous hand at the exact moment when the man shouted in pleasure and the woman pounded the water on the floor in fury as if the noise or the splash of refreshing liquid could either appease or magnify the spasms of her hips in response to the man's still hard sex

pulling together her clothing and her composure, Strong Maria got a shock that stifled her pleasure, not because the man and the girl had suddenly glanced in her direction, or in the vicinity where she'd hidden, but because, in the shadows, she had recognized his face

she was certain, it was the Senhor Minister of the yellow handkerchief.

Paulo Paused woke late, his body swathed in a sticky heat, his girlfriend had gone out long ago

the air conditioning wasn't working, nor the fan, and it took the journalist a few moments to realize that there was no light in the apartment, he decided to take a cold shower, get dressed, and take a drink from the lukewarm water he found in the refrigerator

he realized he was late, he'd finally got an interview with Drybank, the man they called Dom Crystal-Clear for his years involved with aquatic issues, he had worked for many years in the Ministry of Industry, rotating through other positions in the era of now-deceased Scientific Socialism, and was privatizing the places, the factories, and even some of the people who crossed his path

a man with powerful backers, protected by people high up in the Party's Central Committee, he had grown in stature as a figure and a businessman until the Party suddenly grasped that the power dynamic had been turned on its head, and now many people, from the most varied sectors of Angolan society, actually depended on his goodwill and on businesses that Dom Crystal-Clear controlled

among the rumours that had been circulating for some time was that part of the recent crisis in the water supply was a plot by very high-ranking people, in a preemptive attempt to privatize the asset which, in the future, would be the most precious of natural resources on the African continent and in the world

in this sense, and in others, Dom Crystal-Clear was far ahead of his time, for years he had engaged in political and judicial manoeuvring, so that he had already succeeded in privatizing mountains with high-quality wellsprings and abundant headwaters, in buying vast tracts of land selected specifically on the basis of the number of rivers and creeks which bathed them, in this way, little by little, without prompting an outcry, he had accumulated so many pockets of land that it was calculated that a significant slice of the country, rich in water resources, was in his name, or in the names of relatives who lived under his nepotistic rule

a group of well-paid lawyers had spent years preparing the battle that Dom Crystal-Clear was about to win: the privatization of water in Angola, the condition being, and this

supposition was both unknown and simultaneously uncondi-
tional, that the great Leader would have to be his ally

worrying about all of this, Paulo Paused walked towards
Crystal-Clear's business

already irritated, the journalist walked, kicking loose
stones and fruit that had fallen overnight down the sidewalk,
he ruminated in advance on his frustration, after all, in this
long-awaited interview, what questions could he ask? how far
would Dom Crystal-Clear's benevolence extend if he asked
honest, uncomfortable questions?

Dom Crystal-Clear was a much more genteel businessman
than others Paulo knew, he was even an educated man, which
was atypical of many whose luck and strategic social position
had offered either raw wealth for the taking or excellent, available scraps that gave them access, in little time, to astronom-
ical quantities of money

on this checkerboard, Drybank, or Dom Crystal-Clear,
was an excellent player

"weren't you notified?" the secretary blurted

"about what?"

"all of today's interviews were cancelled, Dom Crystal-
Clear is very busy"

"i see, and he didn't say when the interview was resched-
uled for?"

"what interview?"

"the one he was going to give me"

"i just said it was cancelled"

"yes, but there must be an alternate date..."

"ah, but that will be a different interview, you'll have to
wait for us to contact you, sir," the secretary concluded

at that moment, Dom Crystal-Clear, behind the wheel
of his luxurious car, was on his way to a meeting with the
Minister and the American, where questions of concern to
him would also be addressed, as he'd been informed by the
Minister himself who, for some reason, found it interesting
to include him in the first meeting

Crystal-Clear was a man of few words who, in a propitious moment, had decided to associate himself with the then-not-yet-Minister, who at that stage already had a promising political future and close connections to the great Leader,

this association had turned out to be beneficial for them both, as they had complemented each other throughout their respective careers: whatever one of them understood about opening doors, the other knew about financial strategy, and if one of them immersed himself in national political intrigues, the other became a distinguished analyst of the nation's economy

Dom Crystal-Clear had grasped many years earlier that it was the manipulation of social capital that determined the success of all Angolan actors in the post-Scientific Socialism era

«the difference between a guy who's just smart and a guy who's smart and clued-in» Paulo Paused thought, «is that the former has useless obsessions and talks about stuff he doesn't understand and the latter chooses his obsessions and rarely speaks of what he's already grasped... all the rest are just small fry!»

wandering through the streets, lost in his meandering thoughts, Paulo Paused regulated his breathing in a way he hoped would deflect the heat

fortunately he was close to Noah's Barque

he loved this place, which was, in his opinion, one of the most questionable bars in Luanda, in all the interesting senses that the word "questionable" can have in Luandan speech

the bar's owner, an old man of incalculable age with a white beard, a slight hunchback, and hands older than time itself, answered to the name of Noah

"good morning, Senhor Noah," the journalist greeted him, his tone of voice providing advance warning of his acute thirst

"here it's Comrade Noah, i'm from the time before, a good cold beer to kill all the microbes?"

"the very thing," Paulo smiled

the crowd, in permanent attendance, was made up of a set of people who inhabited the borderlands of diluted colours and origins, one of these figures, who for many years had been known simply as the Leftist, arrived early at Noah's Barque, drank his beer very slowly, regardless of its temperature, and carried with him a worn attaché case from which he pulled countless handwritten sheets of paper

"is that book as big as the Bible, or does it run more in the direction of an installation manual for some kind of scientific product?" the other patrons gave him a hard time, chuckling at his shy yet annoyed air

"when the time comes you'll find out..." the Leftist said in a serious tone

the beer at Noah's Barque was among the coldest in the city, and its secret, public and widely known, lay in a huge freezer locker, known as the "ark," that had never been unplugged—so the story went—since November 11, 1975, the wire that nourished it, the voice of the people claimed, was very long and connected to a certain house where the lights never flickered

"that's something lots of people wanted to know... and have, but it's not for everyone! don't forget, my friends," Noah would say, his voice bursting with pride, "it was this ark that supplied the beer to celebrate our national independence day, including the bottles of whisky and champagne that the late Comrade President Agostinho Neto ordered kept here, hours before we got our pure in-*dee*-pen-dence!"

he paused, looking for the right detail, before continuing

"this ain't advertising, even the Cubans, when they reached the Port of Luanda came through here before going on to Kifangondo, this bar has history, my friends..."

the Leftist's eyes shone and his head nodded in approving confirmation

Paulo Paused, his thirst already appeased by an ultra-cold Nocal, asked Noah to turn up the volume, as there was a live interview with the President of Angola himself on the television

"a little silence, if you please," the Leftist said

it was officially confirmed by the figure of the Commander in Chief of the Armed Forces, President of the Republic, Head of Government, President of the Council of Ministers and of the Council of the Republic, and of the MPLA, and patron of the Eduardo dos Santos Foundation, that what Paulo had heard days earlier, from the mouth of his friend Scratch Man, about the commission, now duly constituted, which served under the name of CIROL, was true

but the President clarified that the population should remain patient and ready to help all the workers involved in the project, for the performance of the Commission for the Installation of Recoverable Oil in Luanda would promote the wellbeing of the city and the country, since this activity inaugurated a new phase in the exploitation of *on shore* petroleum and even, he added, *under city* petroleum, according to the standard technical terms, which he went on to explain

the idea was very clear, it was based on intensive, varied excavations around the perimeter of Luanda which had as their epicentre Maianga Square, with the sphere of activity sprawling all the way to the Roque Santeiro Market and, to the south, as far as the so-called Futungo De Belas, former residence of the nation's head of state

"but it's just digging? i already know about the 'pothole problematic,'" one of the regulars said, his beer dying from lack of use, "digging's really quick, what i want to see is who comes afterwards to fill that shit in... my street has a pothole that's older than my son"

"shh! cut the noise, comrade, the Comrade President still hasn't finished"

in his solemn tone, the President continued his explanations, laying out the working methodology, the research that had been done without being revealed to the public because it hadn't yet been clear whether the exploitation of petroleum would be feasible, but now that it was an ongoing reality and the City of Luanda, the country's capital, site of so many revolutions, and host to people arriving from all parts of the country when war blazed in other provinces, would now begin, like the provinces of Zaire or Cabinda, to contribute to increasing the national outpouring of petroleum

the first phase, that of confirming scientific suspicions of the aforementioned possibility, was completed, and the project was now moving forward with the support of the masses but also of the police and the military, to the high-speed excavations that would lead to the imminent exploitation of what was commonly referred to as black gold

more details would be provided to the populace through official communication channels, but the work, the head of state guaranteed, would be carried out in accordance with the most advanced technological and scientific standards, relying on partnerships with countries such as the United States, Russia, France, India, and Brazil

"so this time the tugas don't get to suck the tit?" someone laughed

Paulo Paused sweated as he watched the screens and absorbed the plans for the replacement of countless streets and alleys and their respective underground tubing, for the channelling of water and the installation of enormous pipeline networks designed to transport gas and petroleum

the journalist drank a second beer as the live segment ended and the regulars returned to their places, remaining seated a little longer, perhaps in anticipation of commentaries and reactions

"this means," the Leftist returned to his notes, speaking to no one, "that with this we could finally attain the status of a Third World country"

"what do you mean?" another protested, "we're already in the Third World!"

"don't you wish," the Leftist laughed, "don't we both wish, we must be in the Fifth World, or something like that...!"

with his sweat-drenched body and murky vision, Ciente-the-Grand woke up and stirred with difficulty as a result of the enormous dressing on his ass, his head hurt as well and his feet were swollen

he crept through the kitchen, quenched his thirst, grabbed a fruit, and was on his way out when he ran into Granma Kunjikise in the hall

"*only those who need to flee take flight*"

"shut your big mouth with that shitty language nobody understands, you don't even know how to say 'good morning' in Portuguese!"

"*everyone speaks the language they were taught*"

the young man hurried to get away and Granma Kunjikise put the water bottle back in the refrigerator and arranged the fruit basket according to her preferred colour scheme

Ciente-the-Grand went furtively down the stairs, feeling his strength faltering, stricken by an overpowering fever, but he was hopeful and his heart gladdened as he approached the first floor, where the coolness of the waters made him feel better

"hey, where are you going?" Little Daddy was climbing the stairs with two brimming pails of water

"shut your mouth, you fucking bitch, you think i'm my dad, letting you live in this building in return for them pails of water you go carting around with your stupid little face?" Ciente tripped over his feet, had to grab the banister, he didn't have the strength

"you're sick, Ciente, on top of your rotten ass"

"fuckin' bitch, you're lucky i don't have any strength... who told you that you could talk about my ass like that? just go right on upstairs with your shitty pails, and if you open your mouth," Ciente's voice became terrifying, "two things could happen: either i'll blow you away or, if i croak before that, i'll come back from the next world and find you and drown you in one of them pails, you hear me?"

Little Daddy looked sad

"sorry," he bowed his head, "do you have a message for your family?"

"shut your goddam trap," unsteady on his feet, Ciente-the-Grand stumbled down the stairs, "with you talkin' about my

130

ass at this time of the morning, it makes it sound like i trust you... fucking bitch cunt..."

outside, the sun lashed him with a violent wave of heat, weakening him, his legs gave way, his wound burned, his head turned circles

Strong Maria found it impossible to do anything more than watch it all

a group of six police officers, after kicking the articles she had for sale, and savouring, with guffaws, the food she was beginning to grill

closed in on the collapsed body simply to see what was going on, one of them shouted, "he must be a pot-head, give him a few kicks so he knows you're here," and another, more alert, understood that the bandages strapped to his waist might be concealing something worth investigating

"do you know this individual?" the policeman in charge asked

Strong Maria made a face that could mean anything

"you lost your voice? then you're coming down to the station with us to see if you feel like talking"

Edú, who due to his swollen *mbumbi* spent a lot of time at the window, overheard what was going on

the police carried Ciente into their car

after some protestations and tears on the part of Strong Maria, they decided not to take her away, as she might yield to the temptation to tell their chief all they had done before capturing the individual with the patch on his ass

"it's your duty to notify the family"

"that boy's wounded"

"in the first place this boy isn't exactly a child, in the second place the situation will be studied and we'll act according to conclusive facts..." the policeman concluded, signalling to the driver to pull away.

by the time the toasts were over, the American was almost drunk

he had been convinced, particularly by the Senhor Adviser, that it would be very insensitive, especially from a cultural standpoint, to refuse the good whisky that they were offering him because the meeting had been a success and significant steps had been taken around the Cirolian question

before leaving the room, Raago was warned in Portuguese and English that in no way, shape, or form should he contact the press, either state-owned or private, without the prior consent of the Ministry that had hired him

"shall we have lunch?"

"i wanted to go back to the hotel, i'm tired from last night..." the American tried

"no, we're going to a fabulous place for lunch, *náice pleice, very good,* you're gonna like it, *grillated feesh,* with *feijão,* how do you say *feijão* in English?"

"what?"

"*feijão*—black beans, with palm oil"

"palms?"

"palm! *mufete, mu-fe-te,* you'll see, *let's go*"

Dom Crystal-Clear signed some papers and explained that he had to hurry to an apppointment

"then we'll talk later, to nail down a few details," the Minister said

"certainly"

as he left the Ministry, Crystal-Clear observed that the driver was trying to manouevre the vehicle and, as the sun was too hot, he remained waiting in the shade

suddenly the Mailman approached him

"Comrade Senhor Crystal-Clear, please excuse this interruption, i know you, respected sir, from television"

"listen here, i'm not in the mood for talking, here, take a thousand hard ones and buy yourself a beer," Dom Crystal-Clear was about to pull the money from the inside pocket of his impeccable suit

"sorry, Comrade Super-Crystal, it's not anything like that, i'm not in need of money, thank you very much"

"how's that?"

"i simply came to leave a missive for your consideration"

"what? fuck, that's quite some Portuguese you've written"

the Mailman pulled a long envelope out of his mailbag and passed it to the businessman

"it's a letter, written on paper of twenty-five lines, in the old style"

"what kind of letter?"

"a request for a vehicle"

"but i don't hand out vehicles, my friend"

"but your contribution could be valuable, i don't mean one of those four-wheel vehicles, what i wanted was one of those motorized bikes, it could even be one of those Simsons from the old days, or preferably a Suzuki that could withstand the streets... i'm a Comrade Mailman"

Crystal-Clear's vehicle approached, his driver turned and opened the door, but Crystal-Clear, astonished at the man's enterprise, had already opened the envelope and begun to read the letter

"beautiful handwriting," he praised

"thank you very much"

"what should i do with the letter?"

"if you could get it onto the desk of one of those ministers who pay attention to the mail, i'd be infinitively gracious"

"wouldn't it be easier for me to give you the money for a bicycle?"

"Comrade Crystal-Clear, i thank you for your gesture, if you'd like to give a bicycle to my son, i'll thank you even more, now, for the purposes of my profession, in light of the hills in our city, notably in the Alvalades and the Miramars, i believe that it has to be a motorized vehicle, even if it has only two wheels, but i think that it's the Ministry of Transportation itself, or another one, which must provide my mode of transportation"

"very good, good luck, then, and take the thousand hard ones for your thirst."

when he found out what had happened, Odonato stood still for a long time, unable to move, it wasn't that his body wasn't responding, it was his mind, his so-called spirit, that breath within

"the calamities have begun... i hope god's not asleep..."
Granma Kinjikise murmured

Odonato appeared to be lost in thought, looking out the window in search of a place within time

"i think i suffer from the illness of national malaise," he said to his wife with a thin smile

"what do you mean?" Xilisbaba asked the question without regarding her husband

"my country hurts me... the war, the political misunderstandings, the internal ones and the ones set off by people outside..."

his eyes and body felt a deep yearning for his Sunday walks with the family, close to the sea in the so-called Luanda Island District, even when the surf spray was up and their faces were bathed and gleaming from the cold August waves

Luanda was then, at least when compared with the present, practically an urban desert, where food, clothing, and medicine were in short supply, without water or electric light, often there was no beer or wine, meals were restricted to the famous fried fish with rice and tiny shreds of tomato, canned goods were absent though small amounts of fruit came from the south or the interior, whisky was missing but not dried fish, there were no reliable telephone lines but conversations were blessed by the lazy winds of the sunrise, shoes were worn out but legs rejoiced in inexhaustible nights of *kizomba*, there was the mandatory curfew and for that reason parties filled with people who ensured, with their smiles and animation, that they would continue until after five o'clock in the morning, there were neither CDs nor MP3s but the turntables sweated and electric fans were set on the speakers in order not to compromise the musical conviviality, so many sexual diseases remained unknown like the more recent habits of covering the member with tight-fitting pieces of rubber, but the beaches and the walls and the rocking, clapped-out vehicles were familiar with bodies remade in the celebratory act of love, so many children were born then, so many more died, the parties brought together relatives and neighbours to eat, not to commit nouveau-riche exhibitionism, the sea was richer in fish then

and the people showed each other greater kindness

Odonato began to cry softly, Granma Kunjikise withdrew from the kitchen, leaving him alone with Xilisbaba, who slipped in next to him

this man, his wife knew, was hopelessly in love with another time

"Nato," she said in such a low voice that her husband had to wipe away his tears in order to listen to her, "be brave, comra—... my love!... you're going to find your son"

"yes, i am," he closed the window

"we don't choose those who come into the world through our blood..."

Odonato was on his way out the door when his wife reminded him that he had to take some money because today even information had to be paid for

"you know i don't have money"

"i know, that's why i think you should ask João Slowly or Comrade Mute"

"i figure it's not necessary, there must still be people who know how to talk without money in their hands"

Xilisbaba smiled

and feared for her husband's quaint innocence.

Odonato wiped his hand across his forehead, shielding his eyes from the implacable sun, and grasped that it had been a long time since he had left his home, he felt a contradictory overlapping of sensations, it was hot but he felt cool, he should have been consumed by apprehension at the thought of seeing his son but he was overcome by a peaceful languor that he wanted to sustain

"*time is a place that has come to a halt*," Granma Kunjikise was fond of saying

Odonato didn't know where to begin but he'd always understood that walking as a way of solving things that still didn't have a clear solution

he tried to think of the city as a desert that was open yet surrounded by noise, and many buildings, and the idea made sense to him, unambiguous sense

in the end, what is a place full of humans who worry so little about others? what is a place full of cars containing solitary people trying to run down time and mistreat others in order to get home to greet their own solitariness? what is a place full of rumours and celebrations and burials with so much food, if no one can knock on a stranger's door any more to ask for a glass of water or find a reason to take a break beneath the cool shade of a fig tree

«this city is a desert» he thought as he walked

he pursued the shade that came to meet him, he passed the Mutu Ya Kevela secondary school, he observed the easy smiles of the children in their soiled smocks and their soccer balls bouncing towards the street, he saw the policemen grinning because they had pocketed some cash from the foreigner who had made an illegal turn, and he felt a powerful yearning prick his heart when he arrived at Kinaxixi Square

Odonato's chest was agitated as he felt an undeniable yearning for a Luanda that was there without being there, perhaps time had doubled back on itself to make him suffer, the birds of an older Kinaxixi with mannerisms from the Makulusu District sang, invisible, in his semi-transparent ear

was it he who was speaking to the city or was it the city of Loanda, Luanda, Luuanda, that was flirting with him?

a car horn brought him back to reality, he hurried forward and reached the square, but the horn persisted and the car stopped

"bro, Odonato, how's it goin'?"

he ran forward to see who it was

"how's it goin'? you spaced out or what? standing around lookin' at nothing in this heat?" the man spoke cheerfully from inside a vintage car, "don't you remember? it's me, Superintendent Gadinho"

"oh... Gadinho, great to see you, everything okay?"

"everything's good, and you?"

other vehicles lost no time in honking their horns to cut the dialogue short

"hop in, let's keep talking, you can't really stop here"

they pulled away uphill on Makalusu, following the traffic's slow pace

"how's the family?"

"all well," Odonato began, "i mean, almost all"

"how's that?"

"there's still Ciente with his problems, which then become my problems"

"anything serious?"

"this time it looks like yes, the kid was shot, then he was arrested and i don't even know where he is..."

"geez, what a fucking mess... and those guys in the police are tough now! but how'd he get shot?"

"the problem's not how, it's where"

"how's that?"

"he got shot in the ass"

"holy fuck... in the ass? like right up the ass? in the bum?"

"in the bum, as they say nowadays"

"fuck... but over what?"

"a break-in"

"someone broke into his place? this city's terrible"

"no, he was the one breaking in"

"no way... geez, that makes it more complicated"

"yeah, it does"

"and now?"

"now i don't know, i just need to find him, to get a handle on how serious it is, because he was wounded when they took him away"

"aw fuck, for Christ's sake... hey, we'd better stop some-place and put back some brews, that way we can think about the situation, i'll top up my cell and call a few buddies to try to locate your little bastard"

"brews, at this time of day?"

"it's never the wrong time for beer, Odonato, and anyway, with the heat it always goes down good," Gadinho seemed reinvigorated by the idea.

it was almost nightfall

Seashell Seller insisted to Blind Man that they swing by that building that had cool water in the entrance, it had become an end-of-day ritual, they went in, chatted a bit, cooled their bodies in the lost waters on the first floor of the building where Odonato lived

and Amarelinha

"you want to go there to see the girl..." Blind Man admonished

"but what girl, elder? does only one girl live in that building? you can't even see and you already saw all that?"

"i guess i don't see right... hmm!"

the building welcomed whoever it understood must be welcomed, they took the waters as though they were the last inhabitants on earth

the mysteriously unstaunchable waters spilled, now more, now less strongly, over their naked bodies, Blind Man chanted a pretty melody in Umbundu that reached the ears of Granma Kunjikise above

she smiled alone, remembering images from a time so ancient that she began to doubt in her innermost being that they existed: the time of Elder Mimi dancing, for the first time in her life, on the day her husband was buried, dead in the war, and because of the war, not at someone's hands— because in the end this isn't what's at stake when someone dies—but dead at the hands of fate

"pretty music, that," Seashell Seller ran a hand over his body, with a fleeting gesture, as though he had a real bar of soap

"Umbundu, the pretty language of our south..." Blind Man burst out laughing as loudly as though he wished to shout down the sound of the waters, "i don't even know whether i'm singing as loud as i can or what"

"whatever you're doing, it sounds pretty"

"it's a mourning song... they say an old woman sang it on the day of her husband's death"

"was that here in Luanda?"

"no... that was in Bailundo, a long time ago..."

the afternoon succumbed to the sea's shadow, the motor-bikes growled beneath the urgency of their drivers, young guys who had arranged to go pick up their girlfriends for their daily rendezvous, people came home hungry in the deafening din of car horns and voices on top of other car horns and other voices

Odonato returned to the building, his feet and neck coated with dust, he felt hot and thirsty, and he moved towards the noises he heard on the dark side of the first floor where there had once been an elevator

"you're here? buck naked?"

"apologies, elder, we came here through the heat and this here water is very uncompromising in the way it doesn't stop flowing," Seashell Seller made a move to retrieve his clothes, but failed to do so

"no problem, i'm sweltering, too, i think i'll take a dip, do i have permission to join you guys?"

"it's your home, permission belongs to you and yours," Blind Man concluded

dark glimmerings, sparklings of ember-like colour, an opaque yellow glow and even tiny registers of red played in the reflections on Odonato's gaunt body, Seashell Seller ran his hand across his face a number of times, and his fright was so obvious that Blind Man sensed, from the thumping of his heart, that he was seeing something important

Odonato's body mixed human textures with a heightened clarity of vision, it was now possible to make out, in addition to certain veins, the bones right beneath his skin, his finger-nails looked sharper because translucence lent his body a different geometry, the small bones of his feet were discernible, the edges of his pelvis stood out on the right and left, and uncertain colours danced in his abdomen

he stopped looking, suffused by a deep fear that, at any moment, he might see not Odonato's body, but his soul

"don't be afraid, what's happening here is completely natural"

"if other people saw it, they'd say it was a curse"

"everything that happens to us is a kind of curse"

Blind Man made a brusque flare of his nostrils, as though by sheer sense of smell he had become aware of Odonato's transparence.

Crystal-Clear arrived punctually at the Minister's home in spite of the chaotic traffic and even though his vehicle didn't have a siren

Pomposa had been warned and had prepared everything in her exaggerated style, she had taken a vast number of whisky bottles, chosen according to the colours of their labels, out of the cupboard, as well as bottles of Portuguese and South African wine, French champagne, and the table was divided between appetizers purchased from European specialty shops and light homemade snacks which she'd ordered her cook to prepare earlier, kitaba, sliced ginger, quitetas in a sauce of lemon spice and African red peppers, a shrimp kizaca, everything that anyone could want

"welcome, Senhor Pistol-Clear"

"the name is Crystal-Clear, my lady"

"my apologies, make yourself at home, the Minister's on his way, he apologizes for the delay"

"perhaps i arrived too early"

"no... you arrived at the appointed time, sir, the Minister is still in traffic"

"he has a siren, doesn't he?"

"he does, yes"

"and even so..."

"and even so...! i'll tell you, i can't count on the Minister for anything," Pomposa adjusted her bra as though measuring her own breasts, "not for anything"

"madam, do you always refer to your husband as 'the Minister'?"

"don't call me 'madam'..."

"must i say 'Senhora Minister'?"

"Pomposa, just Pomposa"

"i understand"

"and what will you have to drink?"

"whisky"

"with lots of ice?"

"no ice"

"my grandfather told me real men drank whisky without ice"

"is there such a thing as a man who isn't real?"

"of course, there's faggots"

a cockroach made three circuits of the room before settling on the middle table, a flying cockroach, not at all discreet, with long antennae and an inquisitive gaze, but above all distinguished by its colouration, or, more precisely, its discolouration: it was an albino cockroach, whitened without having been made transparent, flattened without having been lengthened

"oh my god," Pomposa shuddered, immobilized, "could it be one of those witch-doctor cockroaches?"

Crystal-Clear sipped the rest of his whisky, set down his glass nearby, slowly, with his left foot, pried the shoe off his right foot, without taking his eyes off the insect for a second

"it could, in the end, turn out to be a witch-doctor insect... but those beliefs are mainly unfounded," he stirred a little to put the cockroach's attention to the test, "in zoology, Dona Pomposa, that process is known as the moulting of the cuticle, or simply 'to strip it off'"

he reached down, caressed his shoe, and continued looking alternately at the table and at Pomposa's bulging eyes

"the process of the moulting of the cuticle is controlled by
hormones known as ecdysteroids..."

"but a flying... albino cockroach...!"

"calm down..."

the cockroach moved its antennae in the direction of
Crystal-Clear in a gesture that might have been approving,
reproving, or simply demonstrating attentiveness

"this 'stripping off' can be a simple intermediate stage, one
of growth, it's during this process that the insect appears whit-
est, after a few days it'll return to its normal colour, of course,
according to witnesses in our nation, there are cockroaches
that spend their entire lives that colour..."

"i think it's going to fly again"

in a rapid movement, Crystal-Clear's Italian shoe flew over
his whisky glass and struck the table before Pomposa could take
fright, and the woman was gripped by a kind of awe

the Minister came in with an almost humble look

"apologies for being late, it was the traffic"

"in spite of your sirens..." Crystal-Clear looked at him,
"we've already started abusing your whisky"

"well! what of it? ...it's the national drink"

"more for some than others"

"those are the rules of the game"

"those are the rules of our game..."

"is dinner almost ready, Pomposa?"

"here we're always ready"

"it's better if we speak now, i can't stay for dinner," Crystal-
Clear warned

"not at all? what a shame," Pomposa sighed

"go see if dinner's ready"

"but what if our friend's not staying for dinner"

"it's a figure of speech, baby, we're going to talk politics"

Pomposa retreated to the kitchen as though she were using her
natural composure to withdraw her breasts from the dining room

"it's a done deal, my good man, a done deal, and the Leader's already said that he wants this business to move forward"

"seriously? the Leader?"

"yes, i spoke to him after the last cabinet meeting, but there's still one unresolved question""

"tell me," Crystal-Clear was curious

"the petroleum extraction will go ahead, of that there's no doubt, but the Leader is very worried about those scientific fables that are making the rounds"

"those what?"

"Luanda's subsoil, those strata of i-don't-know-what...the Leader wants to hear more opinions, i thought of that crazy kid, the scientist, he's even Angolan"

"you must be joking, Minister... look, we have an American specialist named Ragged Ass who's here to give our research the okay... so we bring this big shot here, he stays with us, he gets a ton of dough, he certifies, then he goes back to his country, and now you're telling me we're going to listen to an Angolan scientist? no way"

"i don't know, Crystal-Clear... the opposition's talking, and the President's worried... it's a question of national security, the capital city..."

"the capital city and all of us... are going to enjoy progress, yes, that's exactly what i want to talk to you about... and you'll want to talk to the President about it one of these days"

"about what? the public tenders? it's a done deal"

"no... it's not done yet, for you and your friends who are bidding to do the hydrocarbon exploration the real security issue has to do to with the drilling and the tubage"

"the tubage?"

"the tubage, the transportation of the petroleum, but also of the water, the sewers and pipes are going to be located, removed, reset... that's the part that can't be left in the hands of any old joker who comes along, and i'm ready for the markets of the future" "the future?" the Minister was drinking more whisky in order to better understand

"the future!"

"how's that?"

"exactly what i'm saying, once the excavations are done, you guys focus on the petroleum, what i want is the water"

"the Leader won't allow that"

"the Leader just doesn't know that he's going to allow it yet!"

"shhh, man, keep your voice down"

"listen to me—because sometimes a guy gets rich only when he listens"

"tell me, Crystal-Clear"

"i don't want the water, water is like whisky, it's a national product"

"what do you want then?"

"i just want to transport the water and get all the pipes and sewers in Luanda privatized cheaply, on my terms"

"ahhh..."

"you see how good it is to listen?" Crystal-Clear served himself another whisky, "listen, Senhor Minister... with so many new pipes to be installed, and so many others to be removed, a labyrinth of petroleum pipelines, gas pipelines and water pipes will be assembled in Luanda's subsoil... we can't take the risk of allowing those pipes to belong to the public sector! don't forget, whoever decides the price of transporting water, decides the price of water..."

Crystal-Clear drank his whisky in a single swallow and sat immobile, impatient, waiting for his logic to echo in the Minister's head

"i got it!... let's drink a toast," proposed the Minister

"with water please!"

when Odonato got home, the daily episode of the Brazilian soap opera had already ended

Amarelinha was in the kitchen with Granma Kunjikise, explaining the nuances of some of the show's dialogues, which the grandmother had failed to follow, and inventing new possibilities for conversations that hadn't yet occurred, it was a post-fiction, running in parallel to the soap opera, a habit which the two had kept up for many years

"are you all right, Nato? your hair's all wet..." Xilisbaba went to meet him in the doorway

"i took a dip on the first floor... has Gadinho phoned?"

"not yet"

"he's going to try to find out where Ciente is"

"you want to eat something?"

"no thanks, i'm fine," he went into the kitchen, poured himself a glass of water, stood appreciating the conversation between the two women, "like two godmothers..." he exclaimed sweetly

"oh, dad... cut it out," Amarelinha seemed to be in a good mood

"did you buy more seashells today? i saw your friend, Seashell Seller, down on the first floor..." Odonato laughed

"i didn't buy today, he offered me some"

"hmm...!" Odonato sighed

"hmm...!" Granma Kunjikise sighed

"come on, enough gossip... i'm going to find a towel so you can dry your head properly," Xilisbaba left the kitchen for the bedroom

"there's no need... i'll head up to the terrace, my hair dries quickly up there, and i can collect my thoughts"

on the terrace Odonato found that the furniture had been arranged in a new configuration, with chairs lined up in rows, abandoned antennae making an interesting decorative installation, a few big boxes, little heaps of garbage that someone had already swept into place, and the people who were there, apparently immersed in some solemn activity

Odonato felt sad, suddenly sad

a smile gripped the corner of his mouth, things changed, that was life, with its rhythms and its rules

the person who let himself linger, in memory and feeling, in the desert landscape known as the past, was bound to suffer for that reason, "his" terrace, "his" decoration, had all been altered—and so it goes, when we sink the roots of our intimate individuality into collective soil

"have a seat, neighbour, we're doing theatrical, cinematographic, and perfomative experimentation..."

Little Daddy, João Slowly, Seashell Seller, Comrade Mute, and even Blind Man were all there with glum expressions on their faces

"sit down, we're going to start an experimental session in human theatre," João Slowly slid his chair sideways, wiped away the dust, looked enthusiastic, "they're gonna be talking about this one on Broadway!"

Comrade Mute agreed to speak first

"people have been calling me Comrade Mute for so long i've almost forgotten my name, to tell the truth, all i look for is to get through to the next day, for pleasure, i turn to music, as for chow, it can be potatoes, onions, fruit like coconuts or some other kind, and even things that take patience"

"very good, Comrade Mute..." João Slowly regarded the stage as though he were visually adjusting some detail, "you see, my neighbour Odonato, this is the theatre of confession... everybody just gets up and talks about something within... it's gotta really come from within, from presentness or pastness, from each person's life... oh, the magic of the theatre!"

Odonato realized that only men were present, a rare event in the city and the building, to be there like that, agreeing to the improvisations devised by João Slowly's mysterious will

a game of talking, of confessing, as the author of that scene said, a game of telling others, even if only for a few minutes, a revealing truth that invades our mouths, a current truth or an old one

just a truth

almost a human celebration and, even more uncommon, was the fact that those who were present had taken up the game in earnest

146

"and something from now, something special?"

"well, to speak that way just a teeny bit longer... to really speak..." Comrade Mute hoped that the words would finally call forth other words from within him to say what had to be said, "it's that... just recently... that Comrade Mailman who visits us with those letters of his... he's bringing around letters that aren't even for me but that he says have to be for me... and he reads them to me... and that's what i came here to say"

Comrade Mute returned to his place and Blind Man caught the odour of his nervous perspiration, a childlike sweat that emerged from between his fingers and mixed with many other odours accumulated in his peeling back what others lacked the patience to peel back

"the elder can go now"

Blind Man waved away help with a casual gesture, between the ripples of sound he had read the space's coordinates and moved forward, he didn't even get close to the edge, as Seashell Seller feared, and didn't lose his way on the path to the speaker"s chair

"me, i'd like to say i just talk about what i see... which is somethin' other people never get because only we know about it, how come i hang around with this young guy? well, young people got old people inside them... from older times that already took place, when you're born that time clicks into place inside you... and you, in your life, just like in the days when you were little, you're never all alone... the reason i hang out with this young guy is because of the way he is, almost like my nephew, or he could be a son, too, and on account of the scent of the seashells that he gathers and sells, i respect his profession of asking the sea and Kianda to give him permission to take away seashells... which are like Kianda's playthings... but to talk that way, to speak like that, it's the same as seeing... it means hearing and feeling things... right here today i saw this cinema with its chairs spread out and i'm enjoying it a lot... even because..."

Blind Man cut himself off with a peep of laughter so tiny that it genuinely seemed like a professional actor's rehearsal, a pretty, soundless smile, like the form or shadow of an absence of sun

"i never even seen them naughty films that they're going to show here with foreign women howling and all... i've heard them when i was far away in another neighbourhood... but to say i saw, no, i never saw them!"

Blind Man returned to his seat, wagging his head from side to side in a contented way, still disbelieving the words he had just uttered, the others' attitudes were of the greatest respect, and, as he returned, Seashell Seller helped him to seat himself

"Little Daddy," João Slowly spoke in a loud voice, "take your place on stage!"

"me, Uncle João...?"

"take your seat, we don't discriminate against youngsters here"

he put down his cleaning rag and didn't know where to put his hands, he avoided standing up, tried to sit down, felt a burning in his eyes that made him seek out the sky, he looked up, prolonged the pause of his leaden silence and, when he finally homed in on the audience, he was another person:

"if i'm supposed to just get up there and talk"—his voice was alien—"then it would just be about the business of the war and my mother... that the war, when it broke over us and terrified me, i was already running,"—sounds danced in the air—"and i didn't even think to return home to see whether my brothers and sisters had the means..."—the voice, which was alien, faltered—"to run, even with hunger and thirst and bleeding feet, that later we walked with a comandante, not even today can i remember how many kilometres, just the days, which were many..."

the tone, which was unfamiliar, grew too close

"and, to tell the truth, at night i still dream about those days, things keep repeating in my sleep, i dream about it at night"—in the air, the sounds ceased their dancing, "and that it's... speaking like this in words... the thing is that i wasn't able to shout... i wasn't able to shout my mother's name... and still today i'm looking for her..."

he picked up the cloth he used for cleaning things again, sat down in the back, catching his breath, returning from the place he hadn't yet succeeded in coming back from

"they just call me Seashell Seller, to speak simply, to speak here, purely to speak, it's not rudeness nor talking out of turn... it's that i'm learning a lot with Elder Blind Man, a person, i mean... you never help yourself all alone, you've gotta have somebody else nearby, sometimes a person doesn't show up just to be helped, it's that it also does the heart good to help another, i'm not talkin' out of my own mouth, i'm sayin' things that Elder Blind Man told me, you see sometimes he don't know that he talks in his sleep... so that's how it is in the city of Luanda, a person can unburden himself by selling seashells, assailing the rich ladies in their big houses who have more money, if people don't have money there's always bartering... and with pretty girls it's just a question of making an offer... but the person... what's really important is to be comfortable, happy... i keep that in mind right before i do anything, i remember i like diving and sell seashells... Kianda protects me..."

Odonato felt he should speak up

he got up slowly, looking at his hands and moving with the deliberate pace of a reticent convict, he'd understood and internalized the rules of the game, and during the short walk he tried to expel from his mind the deep apprehension he felt concerning his son

he settled into the chair and continued to look at his hands, causing the audience to do the same

he lifted both hands, turning them towards the public like someone exhibiting part of his inner being, a light breeze made the oldest antennae dance and awoke the one-eyed rooster in the other building

"shh... go to sleep, ha, it's not the crack of dawn any more, my neighbour, please forgive the intra-eruptions of the Rooster Camões, our cinematographic mascot," and João Slowly fell silent

"first it was my hands, my fingertips... it wasn't that my body was transparent the way it is and looks now... the beginning my fingers felt lighter... and my stomachaches disappeared..."

Odonato turned his hands towards himself and spoke without lifting his gaze from them

"a man, when he talks about himself, talks about things from the beginning... like childhood and games, schools and little girls, the *tugas'* presence and independences... and later, something from the more recent past, the lack of decent jobs, about looking so hard and never finding work... a man stops looking and stays at home to think about life and his family, about feeding his family, to avoid spending, he eats less... a man eats less, as if he were a little bird, to give food to his children... and that's when i got my stomachaches... aches inside me, from seeing that in our cruel times a person who doesn't have money, doesn't have a way to eat or take his child to the hospital... and my fingers started to turn transparent... and my veins, and my hands, my feet, my knees... but the hunger started to go away: that's how i began to accept my transparencies... i stopped feeling hungry and felt lighter and lighter... that's my life..."

and again he looked each of them in the eyes, including Blind Man

"this is the body i have now," he got up to return to his place

a silence could be felt on the terrace

"my friends," João Slowly was unable to hide his emotions, "i don't know how to thank... not for your help in arranging our cinema of the eighth art... it's really for the contribution of human beings, the world needs to know that here, on the terrace of our beloved building, in Luanda, today, at this time, a group of men witnessed by a rooster who maybe doesn't see very well... today this group of men made theatre! theatre in the old style, in the style of the stalwarts!, because... only great men cry alone in the solitary company of other men,"—he crossed his arms on his chest—"end of quote, my friends, good night and be happy!"

without altering the geography of the chairs and the antennae, Odonato lingered for long hours at the edge of the building watching the bustle of cars flowing down the broad or narrow arteries of the city of Luanda

a glow of yearning within him lit up his heart and the man yielded to the temptation to open his shirt and peer down awkwardly at his own chest, but the see-through glow no longer allowed Odonato to observe with his eyes that which was invading his veins

"Nato? what's up?" Xilisbaba found his gesture strange

"what's up where?" Odonato buttoned up his shirt

"chest pains?"

"heart pains"

"seriously?"

"heart pains of feeling, leave it, woman, the doctors have already assured me i suffer from accumulated yearning"

Xilisbaba smiled and, as she had been doing for years, moved her husband away from the edge of the building

"i suffer from a yearning disorder"

"don't make me laugh, Nato"

"it's true, i only understood it completely today, i have yearnings in all directions, not only yearnings for the past, i even have yearnings for things that haven't happened yet"

"you sound like my mother"

"just like her... but do tell, what's been going on?"

"Gadinho phoned"

"and?"

"he's located Ciente in a police station, he left directions, but..."

"tell me"

"he said it's a very tricky police station and that he's already had squabbles with the commanding officer there, he can't help you"

151

"well, at least we know where Ciente is, did he say anything else?"

"he said he got to speak with one of the guards who sleep there"

"so, they want money?"

"no, apparently not"

"what do they want?"

"tomorrow i'll speak with Strong Maria so she can prepare a basket"

"but what do the guards want?"

"steak and French fries! they said that if you bring them more than they can eat they'll give the rest to your son"

"sons of bitches!"

"that's life...! so much the better for us, because steak and French fries is something i think i can lay my hands on, if they'd asked for money it would be a lot worse"

"you're right"

Odonato leaned against Xilisbaba

"are you lighter, too?"

"i am"

"Nato...you've gotta eat, baby," Xilisbaba begged

"i don't have to eat, Baba... i already told you, not eating has done me good, it's got rid of my stomachaches, i feel better, i think better, maybe the rest of you could try it"

"we already talked about that, Nato, all of us except the children"

"i know, i know"

Odonato returned to the edge of the building, looked at the sky, saw the rooster hide, then remained motionless with his body rigid and sweaty, like a statue that had been spit upon

"the truth is even sadder, Baba: we're not transparent because we don't eat... we're transparent because we're poor."

when he opened the box, his hands danced in the light of
the room

they were delicate hands that, for the time being, fingered
pages, rummaged in papers, examined little plastic bags

his fingers became attuned to the intensity of the light, later
they looked for the glass, the glass close to his lips, the breathing-in
of whisky, the return of the glass meeting the table again

the intense silence

it came from far away, farther than the city's borders. a freak
silence, a cloak that invited more silence.

the fingers didn't acknowledge the wait. the last box had
finally arrived. like a puzzle divided into parts. he had decided
a long time ago to assemble the weapon only when he reached the
last part of his secret.

his clean fingers, untrembling, did not betray the impatience
of his gesture or the anxiousness of the wait. twelve boxes. now
there was no escaping fate.

...

a man is made of what he plans and what he comes to feel. of
chains that rivet him to the floor and chain verses that course like
air through his body in echoes of poetry.

truth and urgency

[from the author's notes]

for years now, Paulo Paused, the journalist, had nourished the habit of spending certain mornings alone, reviewing notes in his old diaries, revisiting and taking clippings from old magazines and newspapers from various parts of the world, listening to music, standing for hours on end at the window of his apartment, looking at the city

his girlfriend left early, because she was going to work or because she had her regular meetings with her boring mother or because Paulo was, on these mornings, a different person

buried in the fleeting immersion of his silences, his hands already thirsty for a pair of scissors that would clip the countless pages his eyes had run over days or months earlier

and his girlfriend thought that with the exception of herself and her mother, all Angolans were somehow paranoid about weapons or armaments, they all had a tale to tell that involved a weapon, a pistol, a grenade, or at least a lively tale that involved a shot or a burst of gunfire, some had scars on their bodies, others attributed to various sorts of scars the breathtaking episodes they concocted because they needed them,

to put it another way, a means of experiencing the war and its episodes at a profound level, the battles and their consequences, even if it were just from hearing about them, or listening to them on radio broadcasts, in the time before, in the days when the war, in fact, had been a cruel yet banal part of reality, and, even today, dissociating the war from daily life was almost a sin

from weapon to weapon, from shot to shot, from violent conversation to brutal description, the war remained on the loose—in every corner of Angola, at some moment, even if it were in the first flashes of the clearest morning light, someone would be willing to sacrifice his silence to speak, if only by implication, of a certain war, his own or his neighbour's, that of his family or that of his stepson who came from a province that had suffered more, imbuing marriages, funerals, working hours, dances, the arts and even love, an almost innate ability to speak about that monstrous subject like someone who, smoothly and fearlessly, stroked the shoulder of a raging beast, tormented by a false peace masquerading as mere exhaustion

hence, in his way of acting, reacting, welcoming others, of setting out to tell in great detail the story of the national wound, the Angolan invested a large part of his imagination in memories that in most cases did not belong to him, or in projecting onto the past that which only might have occurred, or making all-too-clear allusions to a future which, fortunately, would not come to pass, and, all things considered, in the end, in dealing with such a societal scar on this scale, the truth is that anyone, without asking others for authorization, could fall back on the magic wand of words to open the gargantuan strongbox where the monster had decided to live

«the war» he said to himself, «is an eternally bleeding memory, and at some point you open your mouth or make a motion, and what comes out is the blood-red trail of things you didn't know you knew»

all Angolans, therefore, had some sort of paranoia about weapons or armaments, they all had a tale to tell or an episode to invent

"i'm going out, love," his girlfriend said, already at the door

the journalist held the scissors in his hand, mountains of magazines were piled on the living-room sofas, the doorbell sounded in a declarative double ring, making him freeze as though he'd been caught in some inappropriate activity

"open the door or i'll break down this piece of shit"

followed by the deep, eccentric laughter of Colonel Hoffman

"isn't it too early for a visit, Senhor Colonel?"

"there's no such thing as early when you live life in a rush, boy! don't you remember what that Brazilian dude used to say? time doesn't stop passing... we have to celebrate while there's time..."

"what are we going to celebrate?" the journalist made his way to the refrigerator

"we're just going to celebrate!... i mean life itself, we don't know which of us will still be here tomorrow, boy... bring them on, the blessed beers and the unsampled whisky... today is to-daily!"

it was one of those days when the city had woken up more chaotic than it really was, uniformed and duly-equipped men had begun to excavate Luanda's arteries and street corners at the crack of dawn, few streets escaped the screaming pulse of the machines, surrounded in some cases—if not in others—by improvised enclosures constructed in such a way that everything seemed to be taking place in the public eye, *It's no secret!*, a newspaper announced, *The latest excavation technology has reached the capital!* announced another, and it was this, the sudden, absurd effectiveness, that had excited Scratch Man, or Colonel Hoffman, so much that he sought out his friend this early in the morning

"for some people the end of the world is coming... for others the beginning of paradise... may there be bank accounts to receive the rivers of money that are going to flow," the colonel got started with two well-chilled beers, his glance suggested to Paulo Paused that he make an omelette in the way Paulo liked, three well-beaten eggs with spicy sausage, lots of onion, dark powdered curry and ginger cut into slender yet visible slices, "a rising tide lifts all boats, hahaha!"

"what about the people who aren't on the inside track?"

"that's how life's always been, boy, ever since they strung up Jesus Christ on the cross: those who can, can, those who can't, wriggle and writhe on the line if you let them"

"so the highroller cirollers are moving full-steam ahead?"

"it's Kinaxixi, it's the Workers' District, it's Alvalade, it's Maianga, nobody's escaped, there's drilling everywhere you look," Hoffman had brought an odiferous *Jornal de Angola*, hot off the press, "you can read it aloud, too, because that way i save my eyes and my voice"

"the headlines?"

"what headlines! that's to put the masses to sleep, the truest news is tiny and discreet, take a look at page seven..."

a brief text, solemn and concise, spoke openly of the role of the Crystal-Clear Waters Company, responsible for the distribution of safe drinking water in certain areas, and also, in a discreet mention near the end of the document, signed by members of the government and of the Party, which ceded to this very non-public company the right, and the duty, to ensure the installation of a new network of pipes "at a recognized international level of quality," for the transportation and supply of potable water in Luanda

implemented by ministerial decree, and approved by the highest-ranking member of the Angolan government, particularly during the period of intense excavations connected to the CIROL project, but with the possibility of being maintained "for a number of years" thereafter, the respective and above-cited authorization, the document reiterated, permitted the transportation and distribution of potable water to the great majority of the population resident in the capital city

"that, for example, sounds to me like an unpublished briefing document"

"unpublished? like hell... i'd already heard about this, and the business's name? did you notice?"

"it's our friend Crystal-Clear!"

"in the flesh"

"now the plot thickens," the journalist sat down to rest his body, breathe deeply, and refuse the offer of a final, small piece of omelette

"it would be discourteous of you to accept the final piece... furthermore, as you're in your own home, and i'm a guest of long standing..."

"that part's certainly true," the journalist's smile was sad, muffled

"don't be like that, comrade," Hoffman smacked him hard on the back, "action... reaction!"

"what reaction?"

"waiting, observing, and then acting"

"it's the excessive calm that distresses me"

"but are there more eggs?"

"in reality, it's apathy... instead of attacking the enemy, everyone looks for a hole in the ground... or an imaginary heaven..."

"cool it with the poetry this early in the morning, bring on our whisky for a few moments of intense reflection and close the newspaper, i already regret showing you that shit"

"all right, cool it, cool it..." Paulo took the plate to the kitchen and put away the newspaper clippings that were spread over the veranda table

the noise of the jackhammers, mixed with various technical idioms spoken in Portuguese, English, and Chinese, reached his window

he peered out

the Mailman was trying to deliver his letters in the entrance of a private clinic, pestering the doctors as they arrived in their jeeps

"hey, man, go do your job," a bad-tempered doctor replied

"that's exactly the problem, Senhor Doctor, that's exactly what i want... to work like a professional, deliver all the letters, all of them, today's and the ones that are behind schedule, but to do that and get to the end of the day content with my profession and my working conditions..."

"let me past, i don't have any money to give you"

"you don't understand, Doctor"

"how?"

"you don't understand, because i haven't even asked you for any money, or am i mistaken?"

"yes, but then..."

"then i'm asking for two different things, since people are used to hearing requests for money, they don't understand my request for attention... please forgive the simple chatter of a poor Mailman"

"i can't help you, man"

"but if you can't help, can't you at least understand, or isn't that possible? i'm going around asking for two very simple things, one is attention, or rather people's understanding, the other is that everyone make a small effort, just this one time, as i do every day of my life: deliver one of my letters, Senhor Doctor! just one!"

"that's it? a letter? but isn't that your job?"

"mine, yes, that's true, i'm a carrier, and on foot, on top of it all, but anybody in this life can suddenly be required to carry or deliver a letter, you understanding me, Senhor Doctor?"

"i guess so"

"and i ask one very simple thing of you, deliver a letter, this letter," he pressed the letter into his hands, "to whomever you can, i need motorized locomotion, Senhor Doctor, each of us has the tools of his profession, you, sir, have this stethoscope, your car, your clinic," the Mailman's seriousness was utterly convincing, "given that it is so, is this asking too much?"

the doctor put the letter in his briefcase

the security guards were already on their way to ask whether the doctor needed help, whether this was a madman disguised as a Mailman or a nagging drunk, but then they recognized the Mailman and, smiling, stood back

"life is made up of understandings, comrades, to each his labour, i'm going to deliver more letters"

as he was so close, he decided to go to the building

he fulfilled the ritual of his smiles, greeted Strong Maria, who had already processed more than forty-some Motorola sandwiches, as her oblong bread slices with sausage inside were known, recalling in their design Angola's first cellphones

"a Motorola, Comrade Mailman?"

160

"i had breakfast this morning, Dona Strong Maria, but thanks anyway"

"you're welcome..."

"i'm on my way upstairs"

"then do me a favour, Comrade Mailman"

"yes?"

"tell Comrade Mute that he can start to peel it all off, at lunchtime we're going to have a special session"

"so what's a 'session'?"

"ah, you don't know? i'm going to invite you, if you're nearby, to go up to our terrace right away, my husband is organizing a completely new kind of cinema"

"so he's doing it after all?"

"yes"

"thank you"

the Mailman was about to slowly climb the stairs

he stopped

there, among the strange waters, a dance of a forgotten flavour sprang up from inside his body

"i tell them this building is bewitched..."

his feet stirred like notes on an epileptic piano, his knees trembled, muscle spasms gripped his neck, and the sudden swelling in his pants gave clear evidence of an exercise unsuitable for the hour

the Mailman stood still, in the sudden coolness that washed over his intoxicated but abstemious soul, closed his eyes, and listened to the building's orchestra of soft sounds

voices of people waking up, feet that dragged across the upper floors, stray phrases in Umbundu that descended slowly through the vertical corridor once used by the elevator, sounds of water splattering onto the floor, the sharp sound of a rooster pecking the floor of the neighbouring building, the abrasive but smooth sloshing of the Maianga leaves, the noise of Little Daddy's pails on the third floor, Nga Nelucha's voice as she scolded her husband Edú that he couldn't always use his gigantic *mbumbi* as an excuse for not taking a bath the Mailman opened his eyes and began to climb to the fifth floor where a polished vinyl record relayed Ruy Mingas's suffering voice as he intoned a song that the Mailman hadn't heard for years

mother of mine, you taught me to wait, as you waited patiently in the most difficult hours

Little Daddy saw the hypnotized Mailman pass by without greeting him and also felt the call of the music, but it was too early to go up top and also too late, because he was behind in his car washes and water-pail deliveries

but in me life killed that mystical hoping, i don't wait... i'm the one whose arrival they're awaiting...

on the fourth floor, Nga Nelucha left home dressed as though for a beauty contest, and even though he didn't want to look, the Mailman couldn't help but notice her purple shoes, her tight skirt, her breasts sticking out like verandas over the top of a bra too small for her, the strong fragrance of her perfume and the way her body took advantage of the stairs' uneven terrain to simulate little dancing oscillations that contrasted with her powerful legs

we the naked children... the kids without a school, playing with a cloth ball...

when he reached the fifth floor, Comrade Mute was smiling patiently, almost inside his head, guardian of the secrets of his vinyl music, a perpetual soundtrack—even when silenced—of life rambling in celebration through that mysterious, broken, poor building

on the midday sands, we, the cheap labour...

the sharpened knife swung back and forth in rapid cutting movements, the peelings fell at his feet as though laughing, the open door danced in the occasional gusts, the gramophone needle read the disk as the oracle's voice reads life

we're your children, from the poor neighbourhoods, hungry and thirsty

ashamed of calling you mother

afraid to cross the streets, afraid of men

it's us, hope in search of life...

with a sluggish step, the Mailman finally approached Comrade Mute, who separated the knife from the damp potato, leaving his thick fingers to tap across the morning's silence, when the music stopped

"excuse me, elder, but this music is too much," the Mailman wiped tears from his face, embarrassed

"leave our worries behind, son, i cry a lot, too... it's just that we're more used to crying alone... you used to know this music, right?"

"i knew it, but i hadn't come across it for a long time"

"hmm... the thing about music is that it follows us," Comrade Mute returned to his rhythmic peeling of innumerable potatoes, insinuating with a discreet series of signs that the Mailman should come inside, serve himself water, and turn over the record to the B-side.

up top, teasing out new furniture arrangements, João Slowly rehearsed his controlled nervousness in the service of the event scheduled for around lunchtime on that splendorous day: the inaugural special session of the mysterious performances of the Rooster Camões Cinema, at the peak of the building among the holes drilled in the streets of the Maianga neighbourhood, at the heart of his beloved city

"if this sunlight weren't so strong, we'd have a beautiful session here!"

João Slowly had already spread the word, scorning the strong light of day with rushed efforts to overcome his lack of professional preparation

it would be obvious to other open-air cinema professionals that the lunch hour wasn't the ideal time to inaugurate a project of this nature, but João Slowly frequently rode roughshod over his own plans, the truth is that he was equally good at the art of social improvisation, he had summoned his wife to make snacks and stock up on drinks, he had invited neighbours and people of influence in the Luandan art of indolent amusement, including some friends from distant neighbourhoods, and even some professional journalists, securing in this way the media coverage that the event deserved, even the journalist Paulo Paused had received an invitation transmitted via his third-floor neighbour, who regularly grilled fish in the building's corridor, and, as he was in a solitary conversation with Colonel Hoffman, this person, perhaps due to quantity of whisky he'd drunk, would end up attending the event too

the crowd was led to the spacious terrace by Little Daddy, who was able to lend only a few water-hauling services that morning, given the number of new commitments he had in this regard, carrying chairs, cleaning grills for the snacks that Strong Maria would cook on skewers with lemon and red peppers for the more resilient customers, and with mustard or olive oil for those condemned to certain heartburn

as always happens in Luanda, many of those present joined spontaneous entourages without knowing the reason for the social gathering, but rather because they learned there would be food and drink in a ventilated spot at lunch-hour, in a singular makeshift venue, the terrace of a famous Luandan building bursting with tales of a first floor with mysteriously cool waters which, as those who had passed through them confirmed, produced a special, revivifying glow that turned out, they now knew, to be very difficult to explain to anyone who had never been there

the men who usually frequented Noah's Barque were summoned, including potbellied Noah, who, in order not to feel out of place, arrived in the company of the friend known as the Leftist, who came with his old attaché case and its respective notes, groups of curious young people were also allowed to attend, the singer Paulo Flores was passing through Maianga and was welcomed with an ovation, the building's residents also attended, Edú brought his tiny stool and, assisted by Little Daddy, seated himself in a strategic corner where he could alternately observe the smiling gathering,

João Slowly's verbal and gesticular activities, and even the shifting, now vertically, now diagonally, of the rooster's head from the building next door, as though the bird were trying to participate, though he had not been invited, by listening to the voices and music that surrounded him

close to the bench with the food, which emerged at a steady clip, beers of all sizes and brands stood in ice-packed styrofoam coolers, Strong Maria smiled happily at the pace of sales, continually requesting that Little Daddy replenish the stock, Odonato's daughter Amarelinha set up a small bench at the entrance where she sold bead necklaces and wristbands decorated with tiny pieces of wood, or shells she'd bought from Seashell Seller who, at that instant, daunted by the size of the crowd, arrived in the company of his elder friend, Blind Man

"Amarelinha... you're here?" Seashell Seller didn't know which words to speak to the girl

"yeah... lots of people, i came here to sell, i don't know if it's going to be like this every day"

"is your father in the building? or is he not coming?"

"my dad left, he's looking for Ciente, there's no real news"

"hmm, oh well, and your granma's well?"

"yes, thank you"

João Slowly asked the crowd for a minute's attention, somebody shouted, "i doubt it'll be just a minute," they laughed, they drank more, but gradually they allowed silence to fall

João Slowly's strategic pause caught the crowd's attention, the smell of beer-breath mixed with the sweet smoke from the enormous grills, the noise of bottles being set down at the edges of the terrace, the shuffle of Blind Man's feet, which was heard close to Edú, the not-very-discreet sound of Edú's hand vehemently scratching his gigantic pet testicle, in addition to the nearly uniform aroma of collective body odour

João Slowly knew how to use these elements to call the crowd to order he waited, drawing out the pause and, when it became unsettling, extended his arm in search of what some thought was the future, but was actually in the direction of the one-eyed rooster, Blind Man found out, without seeing the things others saw, that over there was a being who in his way saw things before they could actually be seen

"at times business... leisure... and our social obligations are very close to us," João Slowly coughed deliberately, "the city's fresh air, our country's marvellous climate, and here in our city, particularly, this proximity to the sea and to the country's modernity, and the simple vision of a rooster"

the crowd finally saw the rooster, and the rooster, smitten with the weight of so many gazes, lowered his head, stole away to a more remote corner, and the crowd laughed

"yes, let's say a fearless performer of a rooster, with an aesthetic worthy of a major figure of the literatures of a certain Portuguese language... almost an actor, but on the other side of the wall... a rooster is what inspired and gave me this idea, ladies and gentlemen"

they clapped, they whistled, Colonel Hoffman ordered another beer, the tax inspectors This Time and Next Time crept into the vicinity, as did a young woman with fair hair and dark eyes

João Slowly did not allow himself to be disturbed

"it's in this cultural... gastronomic context," he pointed to his side, where Strong Maria acknowledged his words with a smile, "that we inaugurate a new locale in our own inimitable way here in Luanda, let's say a cultural locale... with us today are members of our artistic community... journalistic community... socialistic community... peoples from our neighbourhood, from other neighbourhoods, and i believe even individuals from the international sphere, except maybe the UNs and NGOs," he smiled in the direction of the young foreign woman who hadn't understood that this was a reference to her, "nevertheless, it's important to mention two points... this cultural space is going to receive the very illustrious name of Rooster Camões," the crowd sighed in unison, "out of the highest respect for our little mascot who will remain over there in the far-off neighbourhood... because we know that in these times... in some emergency of appetite, we know that certain elements of our society," João Slowly regarded Little Daddy, who tried to feign innocence, "are prone to roostering, er, roasting tendencies with regard to any living animal wandering around the neighbourhood..."

"cut to the chase, man, the beer's getting warm!" somebody shouted

João Slowly didn't like this, but as the crowd burst out laughing, he judged it better to go along with them

"our hurried and ethylic friend is right... we shall move on to the finallys"

"long live Odorico!" the same man shouted, causing a general uproar of laughter that shook the building

"i would ask the comrade to have the decency," João Slowly said, irritated now, "to abstain from speaking, and to sign up in advance should he wish to do so... let's show respect, this is a solemn session, furthermore we have elders present here," he pointed to Blind Man, "and even people who've been on television due to utterly extraordinary physiological conditions," he pointed at Edú, "or even goodwill ambassadors and representatives of one of the greatest voices on the national musical scene," he pointed at Paulo Flores, and the crowd broke into another loud ovation

the young woman journalist smiled and took photographs of those present, failing to realize at least two things that Angolans don't like very much, one—which has nothing to do with the present situation—is for a woman to come to a party and not dance with anyone, and the other, this one certainly more relevant to the case, is for someone to suddenly start taking photographs without identifying herself or explaining the reason for these shots

"so culture, that immensely vast field that always has a place in Luandans' daily lives... and even, according to some reports, in the daily lives of people from Malanje... culture requires neither a schedule nor complicated explanations: i declare this cultural space open and inaugurated, a place where, as we'll see later, we're going to listen and sit and drink... it will accommodate the widest possible range of forms in the areas of performance, both on film and on stage, as much the ultra-modern theatre of improvised confession as other cultural forms that i won't divulge here for reasons of our leadership's strategic planning, end of quote, i have spoken!" João Slowly lifted his bottle of now-warm beer and the crowd clapped its hands hard, mixing its applause with comments and laughter

"bravo," Hoffman said in his loud voice

"long live Odorico!" the drunk shouted again

the tax inspectors This Time and Next Time accepted, without paying, the beer that Strong Maria offered them, strolled through the party, looked at the distant rooster, exchanged a few words with Edú and moved deliberately towards the young female journalist

"young lady, are you supplied with the necessary authorization?"

"sorry?"

"young lady, are you accompanied by the appropriate documentation?"

"sorry, what do you mean?"

"we're in Angola, my young lady, here the cohorts of the mass media require a variety of documents"

"i don't understand"

"but you're going to understand," This Time smiled

"yes, you're going to understand," Next Time confirmed

"and the other journalists, do they need these documents, too?"

"domestics are inherent"

"what?!"

"domestics are inherent, my lady, documentation for news reports, particularly of photographic content, costs money, i hope you're prepared for that, my lady" "i don't know if i understand"

"fortunately we're tax inspectors of multiple functions, perhaps we will be able to impart to you some information, maybe even the appropriate authorization"

"you gentlemen provide these documents?" the girl, in a serious mood, tried to solve this problem so she could keep taking her photographs, "i work for the BBC and i'm accredited"

"but are you accredited for this event?"

"for this event in particular, no... but in general..."

"in general is one thing," This Time said slowly

"in particular, even in the hypothetical case..." Next Time said, "is a different story"

"who are you gentlemen?"

"we're This Time and Next Time, the tax inspectors"

"inspectors? from which ministry?"

"from various ministries"

"various? but which ones?"

"various, meaning those that issue this type of authorization"

"i don't know if i understand"

"that i can see, that you are having difficulties understanding, the more difficult it is for you to understand, the more difficult it will be for you to do your work"

"but is special authorization needed to cover events?"

"yes, because there is a difference between attending and covering," This Time announced

"yes, there is a difference," Next Time confirmed

"but normally..."

"my lady, this is not a normal situation, this is a cultural opening of parallel proportions..."

"what?" the journalist was beginning to think the tax inspectors were drunk

"look at it this way, the issue is that you, my lady, need an authorization, but only we know that you need it... isn't that it?"

"i suppose so"

"and only you, my lady, know that you don't have it, so why make it complicated?"

"it's you gentlemen who are complicating things"

"no, it's you, my lady, who's not facilitating matters, if you don't get down to it and facilitate, complications appear later"

"and how do i 'get down to it and facilitate'?"

"for example, with half a big-head"

"what?"

"half a big-head," Next Time explained, "is a bill, normally green, of fifty American dollars, so that we don't charge you in Euros, which we're doing in this case only because we're dealing with a Madame Journalist"

"and if i were a man?"

"a man?" Next Time looked towards This Time so his brother could size up the situation

"a man would be one hundred Euros or more"

"and why's that?" the journalist was irritated

"because Angolans are kinder to ladies"

"and if it were an Angolan who likes men?"

"who likes men? but what's that?" This Time was nervous

"for men, if it were a tax inspector who likes men... you know? in that case maybe he'd charge a half big-head to a male BBC journalist... and he could charge one hundred Euros to a female journalist..."

"i'm not aware of any such case," Next Time, also, looked confused

"i was told that the tax inspectors here in Luanda... are usually kinder to male journalists... i don't know if this is the case with you, as a matter of fact i was going to write about exactly that question... i saw so many men here at this party... including you gentlemen, who arrived together"

"we're brothers on our father's side"

"but nobody at the BBC knows that..."

"well, then, we're going to settle this without any trouble..." This Time coughed, "this time, my lady, you may proceed with your work with this verbal warning" "i thank you for your indulgence, Senhor Tax Inspector"

"very good," This Time said

"yes, very good," Next Time said

"then go forth and be glad, as they say in church"

"thank you, Senhor Tax Inspector"

the crowd was dispersing, there were no free drinks left, from the moment the speech had ended, everything had to be purchased, which displeased some members of the crowd, especially those known as "gatecrashers," a social stratum composed of people who, blissfully and almost in a spirit of social reform, devote themselves from an early age to showing up at weddings, funerals, baptisms, social or sectarian meetings, anniversaries or associative assemblies, with the intention of eating and drinking without paying a thing, being particularly aware and proud of not having been directly or indirectly invited

Nga Nelucha, Edú's wife, came to look for him on the terrace, not only because her husband had already exposed himself to the sun and the vagaries of social, and even journalistic contact for too many hours, but also because his sister, a famous Luandan cultural agent, was downstairs ready to figure out a strategy for the commercial exploitation of Edú's singular anatomical issue, he was lifted to his feet, with Little Daddy's help, nor did he forget the tiny stool that had accompanied him for so many years

after answering some questions from media representatives, during which João Slowly avoided concrete revelations about the type of activities that would happen in that space, leaving almost all possibilities open, reiterating with greater or lesser eloquence what he had just said in his improvised speech, the event's principal organizer saw the tax inspectors This Time and Next Time approaching him

"you gentlemen are here?"

"we weren't formally invited, unfortunately, but news travels quickly in Luanda"

"it's just as well"

"so you haven't yet settled that question of the exchange problems..."

"problems?" João Slowly queried, "i don't have any exchange problem, Senhor Tax Inspector, you must be getting confused, as you're drinking on the job," he pointed to the bottle in This Time's hand

the tax inspector gave him a serious, irritated look, and swallowed the rest of the beer in a single gulp, taking responsibility for the bottle and the rest of the liquid

"you think you can joke with us, Senhor João Totally Slowly?"

"i don't think anything, Senhor Tax Inspector"

"you want me to order the arrest of your wife and her friends, who are sitting outside downstairs pretending to sell fish and meat and peanuts cooked in sugar from the time before, and have dollars hidden under the food?"

"but you have to understand... i'm not actually involved in parallel exchange procedures..."

"and this cultural centre or whatever it is? what's the deal?"

"it started today, as you can see"

"and without commercial licences, i imagine"

"you imagine very well," João Slowly confirmed

"well, now, that's the complicated part," This Time commented

"that's the complicated part," Next Time agreed

"in that case, and the way things are going... from the look of the inaugural session... with so many people from our country and even from abroad," they looked again at the young female journalist who winked at them, "it would be best for you to take measures"

"what measures?"

"preventive measures, that way you're not going to have a surprise visit from some branch of the tax services"

"what's your proposal?"

"we'd like to hear your proposal"

"how's that?"

"neither we nor anyone else here understood... what is this going to be in the end?"

"it's going to be a new cinema... in a modern sense, we're still not sure"

"stop talking like you're from Sucupira and roll out the plan"

"it can be anything... we're going to have some sessions for adults at night... we might have afternoon matinees, with dancing or movies, we're still not sure which"

"plus your wife's gastronomic profits, grilled foods and such-like..."

"yes, eventually"

"but we also tax the eventually"

"i understand"

"so let's leave it at that... we're going to be stopping by to see how your business is doing and you're going to stop what you're doing to pass us the dough so that we won't officially be seeing how your business is doing..."

"understood"

"and we don't have to pay for our tickets at the adult-film sessions"

"fine"

"just one question"

"what, Senhor Tax Inspector?"

"what's with that journalist with the BBC accent?"

"i don't know her"

"then i'll give you a piece of friendly advice... be careful with her"

"why?"

"everything she says is completely off the wall, and on top of that we have the risk that the BBC'll go and write things for the rest of the world about us Angolans..."

"like what?"

"be careful, that's all i'm saying"

"fine, i'll take care of it, but is she with the opposition, or what?"

"you know, my friend... opposition is a matter of whom you're in favour of, i don't know if you understand me..."

the journalist had taken advantage of the event to get to know other people from the building and, not missing an opportunity, had conversations with both Seashell Seller and Blind Man, introduced herself to the silent Comrade Mute, and was now on her way downstairs with them to get to know the apartments and the people, fascinated by the building's peculiar and diversified human scope, and struggling to understand who, among so many strange names and occupations, actually lived in the building

"and the water? hasn't anybody solved the water problem?"

"but what's the problem?"

"the water downstairs, where it looks like a waterfall and everybody has to take such care to go upstairs"

"no, no, it's not necessary to take such care, it's necessary to know," Edú replied, serious, "if you don't know, you mustn't go upstairs, but if you don't know, that's also a warning for us: what's this person doing here?"

"meaning me?"

"no, not you, people in general, you understand?"

"so the water isn't a problem?"

"but is water some sort of problem in your country? water's for everybody, it arrives here at the building and it's distributed through the building, what's the *maka*, young lady?"

"*maka?*"

"*maka* means problem"

"i understand"

"*maka grossa* is a more complicated problem"

"*maka grossa?*"

"yes, *maka grossa*, and then there's *maka mesmo*"

"*maka mesmo?*"

"which happens just to you, which affects you in your life or your heart"

"you can have a *maka* in your heart as well?"

"you mean *you* can't? so young and you don't know about that?"

the journalist laughed and nodded, now it was Nga Nelucha who wasn't much enjoying the situation "oh, Edú, a minute ago you were so tired, you had to go and rest your *mbumbi* at home, and now you're giving classes in Kimbundu?"

"it's not like that, baby"

"well, i'm sure seeing a *maka*... a blonde *maka* is a different type of *maka*"

Nga Nelucha's sister, a mulatta with pronounced, slightly droopy lips, arrived in the hallway just as they were about to enter their apartment

"my favourite brother-in-law!" she greeted him cheerfully

"my sister-in-law with the prettiest lips in Angola!" Edú hugged her as best he could, allowing for the fact that the swelling in his crotch always became an embarrassment in situations like this, "let me introduce you to this worldly girl who says that she doesn't have *makas* in her heart"

Fató did not move, she gave the foreign woman a penetrating look, causing the journalist a level of discomfort that Nga Nelucha hadn't succeeded in giving her

"let's go inside and talk business, i don't have all day," she hurried into her sister's apartment, "my apologies, young lady"

"bye-bye," Edú murmured, excusing himself with a look at the astonished young woman

"thanks for everything," her words bounced off the closed door

Little Daddy was nearby and, eager to help, he offered again to keep showing her the building, the young man answered her questions cheerfully, relating the building's little secrets, such as how to enter without being noticed, how to leave without passing through the ground floor, and the whopping tales that got bigger and better with time

"some people say this building has its own free will... that things happen," the journalist spoke in a muted voice, observing the strange, calm way in which the waters flowed incessantly from the walls of the first-floor hallways

"it's up to each person to wait and see... lots of things happen right here, when i pass by, unusual thoughts enter my head"

175

"are you from here, from Luanda?"

"no, i'm from the south, i left because of the war"

"what was the war like?"

"the war's something you don't talk about, lady... were you yourself ever in a war?"

"only in photographs, my grandfather was in a war for many years"

"photographs? how's that? you can see war in a photograph?"

"no... no you can't..." the journalist lowered her eyes, "and who's the elder-woman who lives here in the building?"

"she's a lady who's also from the south"

"do you speak to each other in your language?"

"i disremembered my language, maybe on the day i find my mother"

"where's your mother?"

"i don't know, i'm looking for her, in fact today i'm going on television, on the program that finds people"

"and do they really find them?"

"first you have to believe..."

Little Daddy smiled

his sodden body hoisted another pail of water.

in the chambers, behind Dona Creusa, who was given permission to attend, sat Advisor Santos Prancha and the Minister

the tax inspectors This Time and Next Time entered just as they were about to drink a toast, without knowing the reason for the celebration, they were pleased with the snacks and the quantity of champagne on offer

"long live Crystal-Clear Waters!" Dom Crystal-Clear said

"long live the precious liquid," the Minister winked, "and the preciousness of liquids in general!"

"cheers!" the tax inspectors said together

Dona Creusa remained more distant and withdrawn, hoping to be offered a glass, something that nobody would have done had it not been for Crystal-Clear's politeness

"don't you drink, senhora?"

"it depends," the Advisor interjected

"what do you mean it depends? it only depends on her thirst and her wishes, so," speaking to her alone, "will you have some champagne?"

"thank you, Senhor Crystal-Clear"

"i'm glad, drinking is good luck"

"and it quenches thirst!" the Minister concluded

through the half-open door, the telephone rang in the secretary's office, Dona Creusa went to answer

"who? yes... just a minute," she went back into the chambers, "excuse me, Senhor Minister, the American is at reception"

"what American?" the Minister had completely forgotten

"the one with the ass... what's his name, Dona Creusa?"

"Rambo... Rango..."

"Raago," Crystal Clear corrected

"yes, him"

"so?" the Minister turned to Crystal-Clear

"so he should come up and join us, there's still champagne left"

"tell Rambo to join us, Dona Creusa!" the Minister seemed to be sincerely delighted

the American entered carrying preliminary reports from the initial field visits

his mood of disquiet and the handwritten notes he put forward were worrying, confirming suspicions, the excavations—already underway—hadn't been surveyed properly, the risks run by the drilling and the tremors it set off, did not meet, not even remotely, acceptable levels of international security

the danger extended, therefore, to the city's buildings and inhabitants, which even included government edifices, the Assembly of the Republic, the Port of Luanda and the residence of the Comrade President of the Republic himself

Crystal-Clear grasped that the American was mentioning these cases to underline the alert he was issuing "let's proceed with calm, Senhor Raago! i believe there is a correct way to do these things, this was studied, it was planned"

"yes, but it wasn't planned very well"

they hadn't taken into consideration the recently discovered, and now correctly measured, natural gases, nor the location, which is to say, the exact depth at which the petroleum was found, the nervous American citizen explained, an initially controlled yet threatening scenario was now unravelling into a dangerous combination of apparently unavoidable risks

the tax inspectors served themselves more champagne, Santos Prancha, nervous, opened another bottle of whisky, the Minister answered his noisy cellphone

"gentlemen," Crystal-Clear almost shouted, "we're going to put this house in order!"

the tax inspectors stopped drinking, Dona Creusa withdrew, closing the door, Santos Prancha sipped very slowly from his warm whisky, the Minister immediately turned off his phone

"Senhor Raago, i'm going to say something important in Portuguese, but if you don't understand, sir, tell me so that i can translate"

"okay," Raago said, apprehensive

"there are no unavoidable risks in this country..." Crystal-Clear spoke so slowly he appeared to be articulating a biblical revelation, "did you understand my sentence?"

"okay, i got it"

"construction has already begun, thousands of tunnels and holes are being dug at this precise moment, the pipes have been purchased, the equipment hired, the machinery of modernity is already in action..."

"i understand"

"and the Comrade President himself signed all the dispatches relating to petrolem exploration in Luanda, all of these people, including those here in this room, are part of what's called CIROL, you're one of them, you're a 'ciroller,' as people say"

"i understand"

"therefore, there are no unavoidable events, there are solutions, there is the future! are we in agreement?"

"yes, yes"

Crystal-Clear sat down, pensive, and looked out the window

right there, very close by, noisy excavations were also taking place, and then he smiled, like someone listening to a well-rehearsed orchestra

"now you can ask for your ice, Senhor Advisor," Crystal-Clear said

They called Dona Creusa on the phone and completed the ritual of bringing the ice, the tax inspectors drank more champagne, Raago was invited to put away his notes and revise his final report

"now let's move on to something just as interesting, Senhor Raago, how about all this talk of an eclipse?"

"what about it?"

"Angola really is one of the best places to witness the phenomenon?"

"yes, it really is"

"this country is incredible," the Minister said, filling his chest with air and his mouth with champagne, "another toast!"

"to the world's best eclipse!" Santos Prancha brought his sweating body erect.

out in the street there were enormous announcements about the eclipse, they were already calling it, "The Most Angolan of All Eclipses," the newspapers and radios talked of nothing else, not in terms of scientific explanation, or anything that might enlighten the most superstitious sectors of the population, but above all as a munificent event that could deliver financial and political gains, the Party itself was responsible for some of these placards, which concentrated on a vast gamut of activities it had organized around the distant phenomenon, dates and details, times and places, remained to be confirmed, but Kwanza Sul Province, for example, which after all lay so close to Luanda, was actually one of the best places in the world to witness "the event," as it was called, among other curious titles that appeared in the headlines during those days

Luanda Brings its Sun Festival to the City of Sumbe, wrote one editorial

The Sun Unvisits Angola for a few hours, wrote another

Angola Greets the Sun, a neighbourhood billboard read

diners with good vantage points offered package deals for lovers, or for single people—"don't let the sun extinguish your relationship"—that included special drinks with appropriate names—"blessed eclipse," "half-light martini," "sonic boom gin," or even, in the case of traditional drinks, "sunless moonshine"

«this is going to be a party...» Odonato thought while he walked down Luanda's potholed, raucous streets beneath a burning, pre-eclipse sun

gigantic placards had been hung from the Party's offices, the T-shirts and sunglasses the Party had ordered from China were already available, and right next to the big screen, which remained lit even in daylight, could be read, *The Eclipse is Fleeting but our Party Always Shines!*

Odonato wore a light-coloured, long-sleeved shirt because recently, due to the effects of his growing transparency, the heat of the sun bothered him more than it used to, nor did he want to call attention to himself in the streets, he hid his hands in his pockets and avoided making eye contact

in spite of this, various people stopped for a few seconds to look at him, without having any particular reason for doing so, enticed by a firm premonition or an irresistible attraction, after all, the man possessed the least normal body in the world from the point of view of someone who saw him without knowing him, his veins were sharply visible, his bones were starting to stand out in their strange shapes and conjunctions, his skin tone was beginning to lose its vitality as it dissipated into a colour that, though difficult to describe, clearly departed from the normal human or even animal standards habitually used to describe skin colour

this man carried, hanging from his arm, a plastic bag prepared by Strong Maria, with several tender steaks well-done
in red pepper and onion sauce, two fried eggs that danced as
they bounced against his leg, a substantial quantity of French
fries, and raw onions sliced into large rings

this was the detailed special order placed by the the policemen whom Odonato was going to meet, according to what he
had learned, these policemen had custody of his elder child,
who for years had been called Ciente-the-Grand, a thief well
known for his glaring lack of talent and for being constantly
pursued in his profession by unusual bad luck

"i'm here to see Agent Belo"

"Agent Belo?" a policeman just inside the station door
queried, "is this personal, or is it corporate?"

"i think it's personal"

the policeman looked at Odonato with distrust

"and that gastronomic fragrance?"

"it's an order"

"for Agent Belo?"

"in person"

"then it's a personal matter"

"where can i find him?"

"you see sometimes, comrade," the policeman relaxed,
"even a personal matter can be dealt with by many people,
everything can be talked through"

"that's true, but i was instructed to find Agent Belo, it's
about a detainee"

"we've got lots of detainees here, but they move through
here fast"

"what do you mean?"

"the detainees are sent here to await judgment, but since judgment can take a long time, we send them on to another county"

"what county?"

"it depends on the detainee, the crime... and the rest"

"what rest?"

"what i was telling you about, comrade, it depends on the

rest of the conversation, all matters can be dealt with, i heard that even the eclipse is being dealt with by the government"

"but the eclipse is a natural phenomenon"

"yes, but in any event"

"so where can i find Agent Belo?"

"well, in fact, as i stated at the outset, he's not here, but he shouldn't be long"

"ah, so you know where he went?"

"more or less"

"but you said you didn't know"

"no, i just said that everything can be talked through, fortunately we're already talking because your order smells delicious... there are times, comrade, when you might be able to find someone who's better able to help you with the matter that brought you here than Agent Belo"

"you said he shouldn't be long"

"that's what i said, but i can't swear to accuracy on another agent's business, the truth is he's not in the station, but i am"

"i came to look for my son, they told me he was imprisoned in this station"

"do you have his name, or a reference?"

"he's known as Ciente-the-Grand"

"the grain?"

"the grand"

"lots of bad guys have been brought in here in the last few days"

"he's wounded"

"just a flesh wound, or wounded bad?"

"wounded bad"

"that's kinda strange... we don't usually get the wounded ones"

"and at what time does Agent Belo arrive?"

"Pops," the policeman acted as though he were telling him a secret, "i'm going to tell you where he is, but i don't want his old man walking around with that heavy bag of food"

"how's that?"

"the bag stays here and the old man goes to find the agent at the place i'm going to tell you about"

"then what do i give to Agent Belo?"

"you give him the news"

"what news?"

"that the Deputy Superintendent kept the bag"

"you're the Deputy Superintendent?"

"no, i'm not, Pops, that's why you're gonna say it was the Deputy Superintendent, that way nobody hassles me"

"fine," Odonato agreed, passing him the fragrant bag, "if i come back soon, will you still be here?"

"it depends on the schedule, it's unpredictable"

"what do you mean?"

"i'm supposed to attend a lecture, right here in the neighbourhood, they're going to talk about the 'cirollers,' the whole excavation *maka* and all that stuff, you see, i live in the sheds behind a house"

"so?"

"they're saying that with the excavations, when they find petroleum, the property's owner will also receive a share, but since i rent the sheds, i want to know what happens to me, because of this my rent's already gone up, you live in a back-yard too, Pops?"

"no, i live in an apartment building"

"wow... in an apartment building the division is even more complicated, if i were you, Pops, i'd move to a house, or even some sheds, it's an 'investment,' as a friend of mine says"

"so where's this house?"

"let me explain, Pops, because it's in an alley, for anything you need to know, just ask for Granma Humps, everybody knows her"

"thanks"

"you're welcome, Pops, just excuse me," the policeman was thinking as he opened the bag, "there isn't any mustard or ketchup here, is there?"

"no... it wasn't included in the order"

after twists and turns and questions, to which people replied here with boredom there with a strange enthusiasm, Odonato succeeded in finding Granma Humps's house

the door of the yard, made from wood that had long ago ceased to stand upright, was ajar, and through the crack escaped an odour of burnt charcoal, and of embers that had been visited often by mackerel shads

Granma Humps, seated in the colossal shade of her modest yard, made the sign of the cross and said something in an incomprehensible Kimbundu, focused on the man's face without regarding his hands, which Odonato opened as though he were making a corporeal confession,

the man came to a stop after his first steps into the yard, and awaited the old woman's verdict, a skinny dog—very skinny—fled into the house and the parrot started to talk until the elder-woman ordered it to be quiet

and only then did she smile

"those beasts, too..." she made a terse gesture, grabbed another stool and offered Odonato a spot, "you'd think they'd never seen anyone who was the least bit different"

Odonato walked slowly and, perhaps for the first time, became aware of the limitations his new appearance imposed on a social setting

he sat down without speaking a word, out of respect, since it fell to the old woman to speak first

"did you come to look for a girl?"

"no, i came to look for a man"

"a skinny cop?"

"that's him"

"he's in the room, just let him finish, then i'll call him, will you have a drink?"

"thank you," he accepted out of courtesy

"hey, boy," she shouted towards the kitchen, "a beer, good and cold"

"there isn't any, Granma"

"go get one from next door, you insolent twerp," then she turned towards Odonato, looking him in the eyes again, as though seeking his inner being, "the drink's on its way, we'll stay here in the shade"

"yes, mother, that's fine"

"i'm Granma Humps"

"i'm Odonato, thanks"

the elder-woman lit her cigarette

the skinny dog returned to the yard, skulked in the corners, sniffed the trunk of a stunted banana tree and, obedient and lazy, came to sit down at Granma Humps's feet, it yawned and set its eyes on the parrot, which was whistling an extended melody

"but this dog... so skinny and all..." Odonato seemed puzzled, "doesn't he eat?"

"him?" Granma Humps stroked his head and hindquarters, "this dog eats a ton... we just don't give him anything!"

they half-laughed, Odonato realized that, without meaning to, he had asked the classic question that had been part of the collective repertoire of Luanda anecdotes for years

the parrot repeated its melody

"i heard that tune earlier today"

"he's always singing that song, who's it by?"

"Ruy Mingas"

"ah..." Granma Humps passed him the beer the kid had fetched, "listen here, you insolent twerp, beer with the cap on? is the gentleman supposed to open it with his teeth?"

"sorry, Granma"

"just go and open the bottle on the gate"

a metal orifice, halfway up the gate, served as a bottle opener

"thanks," Odonato smiled at the child

"sorry"

"it's okay"

"kids these days..." Granma Humps stroked the dog but continued looking at Odonato he was going to say something, any old thing, his chest expanded to prepare the words, but his body desisted before he could make the necessary vocal movements, the curtain opened, fluttering, Agent Belo came out tightening the belt of his trousers, repositioning his pistol and nightstick at his waist

"this gentleman is waiting for you"

"yes, good afternoon," Belo shook Odonato's hand

"hey, boy, bring another stool"

"yes, Granma"

"yeah, and a beer, good and cold," the policeman ordered

"but we don't have be—"

"that story again? are you kidding me? go get it from next door"

the boy got ready to leave

"hey, kid, first you bring the stool, are you going to leave the officer standing?"

"sorry, Granma"

the beer arrived, Belo drank most of the bottle's contents in a single swallow, he became more serious

"so, tell me, comrade, i hear you want to talk with me"

"my name's Odonato, i'm the father of Ciente-the-Grand, i got a phone call and i wanted to know how we can resolve the situation"

"well... your son's situation, it's complicated. you know we don't have the power to help very much, right?"

"i understand"

"but we can always help in some way, at least to make sure the other offenders treat your boy right, it's a small comfort, you know, jail's not an easy place"

"that's true"

"but our lives aren't easy either... beat cops who make the neighbourhood rounds, or even transit cops, who shake down the *candongueiros*, get extra salary, you know... now us guys, assigned to the station, all we can do is wait for the end of the month when we get our tiny little salary..."

"that's true"

"so that's how it is," Agent Belo finished

"so where do we stand?"

"as it stands, family visits haven't been authorized yet, and if you, sir, went to bother the Deputy Superintendent, that makes it worse, the best thing you can do is wait calmly, and we can go in and get you a visit, but maybe only a week from now"

"and now—what can we do now?"

"now, sir, you can bring food, i'll hand it over, there's still time today, did you bring the special order?"

"i brought it... i mean i brought it but i left at the station"

"at the station? who with?"

"unfortunately, with the Deputy Superintendent"

"oh fuck... we're off to a bad start," Belo finished his beer, "sorry, Gramps, i'm talking out of turn now... so if we could just settle on tomorrow"

"that's fine, i'll come by tomorrow, the same order?"

"the same, did it have fried egg?"

"it did"

"and onion?"

"that, too"

"so it's g-o-o-d"

"what time should i come?"

"the same as always"

"but are you always here at this time, or are you at the station?"

"i'm collateral"

"what do you mean?"

"if i'm not here, i'll be there, you just bring the merchandise and i'll hand it over"

"but you'll really hand it over?"

"oh, so you think i'm not going to hand it over? i'll take a sample, the rest is for your son"

"can you tell me if he's well? he doesn't need medicine?"

"medicine?"

"yes, he's wounded"

"well, i can ask tomorrow, geez, what time is it?"

"it's well after—" Granma Humps said

"then i've got to get going, Senhor Ornato..."

"it's Odonato"

"yes, Odonato, see you tomorrow, it's business hours for me, if i don't move they're going to say the police don't do any work"

"until tomorrow"

"excuse me, mother," Belo shook Granma Humps's hand

"have a good day and be careful not to trip on your way out"

"i already know my way out," Belo, laughing, left

but Granma Humps, a lady steeped in ancient wisdom, wasn't referring to the gate

"did you see that, Senhor Odonato?"

"see what, mother?"

"i don't want to meddle in other people's suffering, but you know that men lie a lot, right?"

"thank you, Dona Humps"

the sun had softened a bit and in reality Odonato felt tempted to let his body lie where it was, in that cool, appetizing shade, but it didn't make sense, nothing now held him to this place

"are you going already?" a coy voice said from the window

Ninon took advantage of the afternoon, and the sunlight, to put a huge smile on her face

"don't you want to lie down for a bit? to rest? or maybe to tire yourself out?" the young girl laughed

"no, thanks"

"then come back another day"

"all right," Odonato got up, cast a last look at the dog, whistled a farewell at the parrot, and did not hide his hands when Granma Humps looked at them, confirming what she had suspected from the beginning

"thank you, senhora"

he left through the gate, holding in his nostrils the dull odour of the grill where the fish had burned.

at nightfall Luanda was suffused by a pleasant coolness and the sound of car horns and jackhammers was replaced by a lulling lethargy, and by the sound of radios, which turned the metropolis into an almost pleasant place in which to idle away the time

the *candongueiros* undertook their bewildering work, transporting the population from its more or less official workplaces to its more or less comfortable, more or less dignified homes, for on the subject of dignity much may be said or conjectured

that which in some countries is a hearth, made up of a certain combination of objects and possibilities, in another might not be so at all, since, in human terms, on the most varied continents, it's force of habit that dictates which circumstances each citizen regards as acceptable, collectively unbearable, or democratically fair and just

"as somebody else used to say," the Leftist proposed a toast, "to Caesar that which is Caesar's and to the rest whatever they can grab!"

drinks flowed steadily at Noah's Barque, sometimes in silence, sometimes in words half-spoken, listening to the news, or the rumours brought in from the street, here time seemed to have come to rest in some broad net that beckoned the people and things of this world into idleness

"you have to be careful with this thing called progress," the Leftist was saying, pointing at a nearby sidewalk, where an enormous placard with the acronym CIROL stood next to other advertising

"don't tell me you know something other people here don't," Noah opened the ark, checked that everything was in its proper place, cast a quick glance at the lighted lamp, closed up again and served another round of good, cold beer

"i know what everybody knows: haste makes waste"

"haste?"

"you have to read between the lines, my friends... everybody's lost it, they're convinced they're going to find oil in their own backyard... but i'm not going around with my eyes shut, i may be going around drinking, but i'm not going around asleep..."

"how's that?"

"you only reading the big stories? the banner headlines? you have to read everything that's in the papers, from the most official to the most officious... did anybody here read the name of a certain Raago, the American? did anybody hear or see the first interviews he gave?"

"the specialist guy?" somebody said

"but what kind of name's that?"

"the specialist, yeah... the great scientist, i've read about him before, it's not the first time i've heard about that guy"

"spill it, man"

"there's a controversy, my friends... in his first interviews he spoke about exercising care, about risks, potential consequences, now you never hear him... the system must have already set its course, now they just talk about the advantages, they've already opened a new water distribution system... where have you ever heard of such a thing!... privatizing water..."

"but isn't it just the distribution system, keeping track of the pipes and so on?"

"wake up, guys... what distribution?! so now the state needs somebody from the private sector to distribute water? and we just sit here in silence, is that it? the state admits, 'i can't distribute quality drinking water, but this gentleman, whose name is actually Crystal-Clear, yeah, sure, he can do it! from now on, water will be well distributed, well purified! long live water privatization!' but where have we seen that before?"

"you don't have to act like that either, man"

"keep sleeping, then..." the Leftist said with an ironic and sad and disappointed and serious air, "keep sleeping while they stick their finger up your ass with their unclipped nails... keep sleeping while they anaesthetize you with doses of supposed modernity! and pretty cars, and an internet that doesn't even work, and a new Marginal with buildings put up on land dredged without asking Kianda's blessing, and drill the city's body without listening to others who already drilled their own cities' bodies, about how it didn't work out... listen here, sleepyheads, it didn't work out there and here, because we're stupid, blind, and conniving, that's to say, because we are globally corrupt, here, too, the city is going to be drilled, water is going to be privatized, oil is going to be sucked up from under our houses, under our noses, from beneath our dignity... while the politicians pretend to be politicians... while the people sleep... while the people sleep..."

a harsh silence, the sound of thoughts finally being processed, was broken only by the sound of four or five men doing what seemed to be all they could do at that moment, chugging noisily from their beers, staring into the distance without looking each other in the eyes, scratching their heads and their chests, letting the walls of the place speak in muted voices, raised over men's the muted voices

"don't fuck with me..."

the Leftist concluded, seating himself at his table, pulling his endless supply of papers out of his attaché case, and beginning to write without stopping.

far off, in that limited far off that Luanda allows, close to the sea

walking along the Marginal, allowing the salt from the whitecaps to seep into his skin, Odonato wandered as he hadn't done for a long time, absorbing the voices and the noises, the honking of car horns and the shouted insults, the finely tuned horizontal beauty of the National Bank of Angola, the smells of Baleizão Square now with no ice cream for sale, the strangely chaotic vision of the ruined buildings beneath the hilltop foundations of the São Miguel Fortress, the bay's extensive, elongated breadth, like the smile of some Luandan adolescent, the peaceful murmur of the coconut palms that had withstood time and construction on the Marginal's sidewalks, taking in the spectacle of billboards announcing the latest and most expensive cellphones and jeeps

he smiled in the manner of those accustomed to smiling to themselves a few years ago he could count his friends with cars, allowing for the fact those cars might be owned by the State, or even borrowed, back in the time when you could ask for a ride in the street or a glass of cold water at the gate of an unfamiliar backyard, in the time when carnivals were danced by weaving bodies in front of crowds of smiling people

the people always find an excuse for a celebration, their joyfulness remains their own, it cannot be predicted or bought, at most it's induced, and even then doesn't happen as expected

Odonato smiled

watching the sea and the bay now infested with human intrusions that shrank it, the areas reclaimed by dredging revising the original contours of its body shaped only by the sea, the currents and the gales, or by time, that greatest of machines which, in the final instance, is the force freest to suggest that we change or cease our human activities

«it's time»

the semitransparent man thought, heading home, not wishing to delay and concern his wife, already much given to the arts of supposition and chronic worry.

"it's time," the production assistant said

and Little Daddy, more nervous than he'd expected, was taken to an enormous room with intense white lighting, where three television cameras pointed at him as though it were judgment day

"and what do i say now?" he asked

"you have one minute to explain that you're looking for your mother, the important thing is to say where you fled from, the last time you saw your family, the province and the neighbourhood you come from, and also say where you are... if you're lucky..."

the word "luck" stuck in his head, it had taken him a number of years to understand the mysteries of this term, he'd slept in the street, he'd taken drugs, he'd stolen food and clothing, and in some way life had seen fit to arrange his time and his activities, he approached the building, he didn't really remember how, he began to wash cars and earn people's trust until he was given permission to spend the night there, first at the back of the building, in the company of countless cockroaches and mosquitoes, later inside its doors, a spot where it was unclear whether he was on the ground floor or on a landing on the notorious first floor with its mysterious waters, until, by virtue of a consensus reached among the residents, during the business of a condominium meeting, he was granted the very much abandoned third floor, if he accepted it and wouldn't take offence, it was completely emptied out and dark, well-ventilated by missing doors and windows, and he accepted it with emotion and gratitude, and on that first night, thrilled finally to have a roof over his head, he was unable to sleep, he spent the night feeling the strangeness of the silence created by the night and the absence of cockroaches, confirming that the permanent coolness kept the mosquitoes away and that even on the hottest nights the site remained ventilated, a powerful upheaval shook his chest and his eyes, he cried quietly in a corner, and he remained still for a long time until day broke, accepting the salt of his tears on his hands and the tremulous spasms of his stomach making his whole body quiver, and only later, beneath the first rays of pre-dawn sunlight, did he think of that word that they now applied to him—luck—not with a thorough consciousness of its meaning, but making do with whatever the word's echo might be, and his body grew still, and his tears stopped and he tried to believe that yes, Luanda and some of its people had granted him a big, lucky break, which started right there, on the third floor of that building, during a night of nervous invocations and self-admonishing memories,

"hey, buddy, you ready to record?" the Brazilian assistant understood the boy's suffering, brought him a glass of water and gave his shoulder a gentle touch, "it's like getting a vaccination, you know? just a little prick... and before you know it, it's over... are we gonna record?"

in the studio next door

they brought a special, comfortable chair, and Edú said he was ready to record

before he'd had a long conversation with Fató about the key points to raise and the questions to which he should not, under any circumstances, reply in order not to compromise himself relating to either the past or the future

the lights irritated his eyes

for Edú the experience was more like a music hall, a world that exercised a certain attraction and fascination over him, he had even inquired whether the lights would be sufficiently strong to illuminate the bulk of his seated body, as well as the *mbumbi* swelling in his crotch

"no worries, guy, everything's cool, you're gonna do great," another Brazilian assistant understood his anxiety, brought him a glass of water and gave his shoulder a gentle touch, "it's like getting a vaccination, you know? just a little prick... and before you know it, it's over... ready to record?"

with aching feet, the Mailman made a detour before going home, he'd spent the whole afternoon imagining the moment when the end of his shift would find him with his feet immersed in the cool waters of the building in Maianga

"excuse me..."

he had to say, for feet other than his were already present, in a spontaneous human gathering there, and packed in more tightly than it might at first seem, those who for various reasons, among them fatigue, had been taken with the same idea

"if you please," Strong Maria smiled, not having seen him for a few days

from her countless bags she offered some snacks, she apologized there were no drinks left, but invited him to sit down because the water was lovely, a line sometimes heard on the building's first floor, less in reference to the water's taste or temperature than to its inexplicable powers of relaxation "i've got to say, it is really categorical water," the Mailman said from up above, on the fifth floor, a piano-and-saxophone melody descended like a gift from the gods at the day's end, a soft, faltering, soothing sonorousness

"there's always good international music here," Blind Man commented, already seated

"not always, elder, just the other day he played Elias Dia Kumuezo, and Waldemar Bastos, the great Ruy Mingas, and Uncle Paulo Flores"

"it's true, he plays everything," Amarelinha murmured, bent forward over her own body, a little scared of having accepted Seashell Seller's invitation to be there, seated at his feet, without knowing what to say, and fearful of the behaviour of her own body which, as a result of the lack of space, was leaning as never before into Seashell Seller's firm, warm arms

"are you comfortably seated, Amarelinha?"

"yes, i am, thank you"

"and your father, he's well?"

"he's well..." Amarelinha burst into tears

"don't cry like that"

"i'm sorry"

"what is it?"

"i don't know, i always feel like i want to cry, lots of stuff is happening at home, my father's very worried that he can't find out where Ciente-the-Grand is"

"you don't have any information?"

"almost none, just today Dad went out to see if he was in that police station there"

"everything works out in the end," Blind Man murmured, trying to soothe the conversation's mournful rhythms

"thank you, elder"

"take this shell, it's special," Seashell Seller opened his bag and pulled out an enormous pink shell so vibrant that it looked as though it were about to glow

"thank you"

Clara said when Paulo Paused passed her the package
"what is it?"

"open it and see, a present, it's been such a long time since i gave you a present," she sat down next to him, "or received one—"

"oh, cut it out, i give you a lot more presents than you give me"

"open it"

it was a small, carefully polished seashell in a format so unadorned that threaded on a necklace it would look like a deluxe piece

"it's beautiful, Paulo, thank you... really beautiful"

"you deserve it, my love"

"where did you buy it?"

"professional secret, i can't tell you"

"just tell me, in which store?"

"curiosity killed the cat, Clara"

"please, i want to buy something similar and i don't even know where the store is"

"it wasn't a store"

"it wasn't?"

"no, it was from a guy, Seashell Seller, he came by here the other day, i liked it so much i bought it"

"what? that guy who's always hanging around with a stinky old man?"

"you see? your world depends on interpretations... i don't suppose you've ever stopped to chat with them?"

"not me, you're the one who's friends with those kinds of people"

"what do you mean by 'those kinds of people'?"

"the ones you like to talk to, weirdos, you collect weirdos, weird words, weird places, like that old-timers' bar where you like to go to eavesdrop on their conversations"

"you should talk more with 'those kinds of people' instead of spending your life gossiping with your mother"

"if you went out more often with me and my mother you might actually know what we talk about, but no, of course...

you prefer to talk to blind weirdos who sell seashells..." Clara closed the package, leaving it on the table

she went to the bedroom and returned quickly, with irritated, determined gestures, and tossed a mass of newspapers and magazines on the sofa

"and let's see if you can put away this crap that's all over the bed"

they were the magazines his clippings came from—the clippings Clara avoided asking about, and about which Paulo Paused shunned giving extensive explanations

"isn't shopping your hobby? mine's collecting magazines..."

the journalist's girlfriend locked herself in the bathroom

while he smoked at the window listening to her movements, he knew her gestures by heart, he knew where she was and what she was doing from the slightest sound issuing from the cubbyhole bathroom, imagined her body's movements, the shades of the towels, the amount of toilet paper that his partner was unrolling from the roll, he almost mentally measured the water she used to take a shower or to brush her teeth, the languid or more nervous way in which she put on her clothes or her pyjamas, and the precise location where her feet trod the floor's light-brown ceramic tile

"Paulo..." she said in a voice so soft that it could scarcely bear the weight of the most explicit feminine worry, "if you could please not forget to take your pills"

"no problem."

Edú walked with difficulty, climbing the first flight of stairs and smiling openly at finding the sea of people on the first floor

Nga Nelucha, his young wife, who had taken in her sister's wary advice to keep quiet about audiovisual happenings in her husband's career, was avoiding areas of conviviality, particularly the crowds of neighbours and acquaintances standing in the flowing waters of the local bathing spot, who were bound to ask about their all-afternoon adventure on National Television "how did it go on TV?" asked João Slowly, who had just come down from his terrace

his smile and stare suggested the question was really directed at Little Daddy, who had got a ride with them

"everything was just great," Little Daddy replied, "it's all really big, really pretty just from the lights!? it looks like a soccer stadium"

they all laughed out of a shared sense of joy and wellbeing and the secret, so simple after all, lay in those feet resting in the marvellous water that was neither hot nor cold, neither still nor really flowing, that stroked their toes, tickled their heels and gave their calves a rested feeling that induced a temporary drowsiness

"are you falling asleep, elder?" Seashell Seller nudged Blind Man

"hey, who are you to wake me up by giving me a shove like that, how come you don't show any respect?"

making room for the new arrivals

Amarelinha laughed at the fake quarrel, and, after laughing together, they all made themselves comfortable, finding it curious that only Nga Nelucha did not take off the red, highheeled shoes she was wearing, even though the others advised her that doing so would be appropriate given the place and the occasion

"we're not all the same, neighbours, we're going to respect our differences," Nga Nelucha grumbled, revealing an unusual bout of bad temper

"hey, look who's here, it's my neighbour...!" João Slowly exclaimed, having just set his feet in the collective almost-swimming-pool, "excuse me for not getting up to greet you, come and join us"

"may i?" Odonato inquired, his face visibly tired, or sad

"by all means, there's always room for one more"

only after taking off his shoes and letting his eyes adjust to the gloom did Odonato recognize, with shock, the body, face, and hands of Amarelinha who, on the other side of the water, gave him a timid wave "are you all right, my dear?"

"how was your day, Dad?"

"i'll tell you later," Odonato said, taking a deep breath, and plunging his feet into the water, "is your mother at home?"

"yes, she is there"

the words themselves killed the conversation without killing time, as though the place and the waters demanded silence and contemplation

but the silence was broken by someone who was unable to refuse to speak if the elders present asked him a question

"how about you, Little Daddy, how did your first time on television go?"

"even if it's not worth the trouble, it's too... just really beautiful"

"did you record your message?"

"i recorded it, yeah, a cool Brazilian guy gives you tips, but i talked about my province and just said i was looking for my mother"

"you did good, it's great that you got a spot, it's tough to get on there," João Slowly made implicit reference to the friends he had called to get the young man into the recording session for the much-solicited family reunification show

"you left them your contact details?"

"what do you mean?"

"how's she going to get in touch with you?"

"i left the name of the neighbourhood and the building"

"not even a telephone number, boy? you could have left mine"

"but i didn't even speak with you, godfather"

"well, forget about it, they have people's contact details, we'll hope that everything works out"

"yes"

and as though the silence wished to descend again

"we don't always get what we want, that's what life will teach you one day... at times we don't get even the simplest things" the Mailman said, making some people aware of his peaceful presence "a simple moped... so many letters, so many ministries, and it seems like they're ignoring me on purpose, how much would it cost? i'm sure it's just a question of a signature, a simple order... other people who don't even need transportation drive around in big cars, i'm just asking for a moped, i even tell them explicitly in my letters that it can be a Chinese moped, although i'd prefer a Japanese one, they last longer..."

it was night in the city of Luanda

with its placid tides, in spreading horizontal beauty, as it says in poems written by dreamers who prefer this way of describing the sea and its aquatic configurations

a strange heat permeated Odonato's body, Amarelinha assumed she shouldn't stay any longer and withdrew, the Mailman bid farewell, resigned to his moped-less condition, Edú, unable to reach the itch caused by his famous swelling, suggested to Nga Nelucha that she scratch it with her own hand, Blind Man sniffed three times as a secret signal to Seashell Seller that it was time to leave, the rooster from the neighbouring building recovered its ability to crow and must have realized that its remaining eye didn't guide it very well either, it bumped into pails and abandoned buckets on its terrace and, as a result, felt what might be called rooster sadness

on arriving at the humid sanctuary, Xilisbaba saw her husband strip off his oversized shirt, exhibiting a nudity that offended all known notions of human density

"this is my body, this is the sight of my pain," he murmured

"let's go upstairs, dear," Xilisbaba comforted him.

i entered that building

a coolness dampened my skin, i know that area well and i had never felt such coolness, i saw some cracked steps and i thought it was better not to tread them, i jumped, i climbed further, the seashells in my bag got noisier, yet my heart told me to keep climbing, i continued,

an elder-like child passed me going downstairs with a huge watering can, he was a drawer of water, without a doubt; on the second floor i still hadn't seen anyone else; on the third floor i saw no one, fourth floor, a neighbour woman peered at me without seeing me; fifth floor, a huge stockpot was on the floor, i had to walk around it to get by and on the sixth floor i knew i was there, i did as i always do in places i want to scope out, i spoke up,

"look at the pretty seashells, who wants seashells...?"

i carried on, it wasn't necessary to knock because the door was open and Dona Xilisbaba—i was seeing her for the first time—came to shout down the hall

"hey, Nelucha, i left the pot on the fifth floor"

only then did she look over and see me, she looked me in the eyes

"Auntie, i'm here to sell seashells, i only sell pretty seashells"

she went in and lingered, at first the door almost closed, then i heard the words of

an argument, the voices stopped shouting and i had to peep in, i trembled, it was him

the gent was backlit by the window and i was afraid again, the light went straight through him like a bullet, you could see the inside of his body, just like that, if you know what i mean, it's not so as though the gentleman's body was missing much, it was more like he was not of that body

"that's him," the gent said to the woman

she pushed him into the darkness of the kitchen, they disappeared, then i peered in even more carefully

the living-room floor looked emptied, there was little furniture, a big chair full of holes, a black-and-white television, a candle in front of the television *and i saw the prettiest eyes in the world emerge out of another darkness, the timid eyes of someone who cries often, i wondered at that gaze as at the gaze of the whelks i can't be bothered to harvest*

she approached slowly to gaze more closely at the seashells i had hung from my belt, all of my materials, my oh-so-beautiful seashells, dried algae, the bones and scales of big fish, stones and trash from the sea

she approavched and the conversation in the kitchen stopped, back there the gentleman and the lady didn't make a sound

"do you have more seashells in that bag?"

i looked at the gentleman again, you could see in his eyes that he was her father, he moved his eyes up and down, the girl moved her eyes also

"i'm selling seashells from the sea, i only sell pretty ones"

i hauled the bag off my back and halted in the middle of the floor, we all stopped

the transparent gent looked at me, i tried to look at him, the gent looked at his daughter, the daughter looked and felt the sea in my shells

they say that to hear the sea it's enough to place the seashell next to your ear and wait for the sound, i don't know that i ever experienced this as i've never been alone with any sound, i prefer to go right to the edge of the sea to find sunken seashells

"i want other seashells as well, even if they're not pretty…"

and she suddenly went away into the darkness

my mission was now to find i-don't-know-what-all kind of shells for that dishevelled girl

but i was okay with the mission, i was able to return under the plausible pretext of being a supplier and that's my life, too: other people tell me which roads to take so that i can go and come back, as i liked to say

"i'm selling seashells from the sea, i only sell pretty ones"

[from Seashell Seller's recording]

days before the beginning of the short circuit and the gigantic blaze

Odonato's body was a shadow that had fled from what it had been throughout his life, as not even his tightest clothing fit his body, and he now walked in a series of clumsy movements

every day—he was already tired of it—he re-learned how to walk, taking into account the meagre ballast now provided by his body, altering the most basic notions of gravity, teaching his knees how to communicate with his shrivelled muscles and even teaching his lips to obey the motor commands that give rise to words, that final, pronounceable redoubt of the ideas and wishes that we utter

"*you see, life has many sides,*" Granma Kunjikise would say

"speaking your own language, mother? that's good, that way you won't forget it"

"*hum,*" the old woman laughed, "*we don't forget the language of our heart. i speak Umbundu to see whether the dead are still listening to me...*"

"i'm going out, mother, tell Xilisbaba that i went back to the police station to take Ciente food"

"*go with open eyes, where you think there's a tree, there's only a shadow... it's your paternal eyes that don't want to see the truth...*"

with eyes wide open, Odonato walked through the torn-up city, barely recognizing nearby street corners and alleys due to the amount of scaffolding and enclosures, cranes and machinery, men and accents heedful of the rhythms of his light, free-roaming body, the transparent man steadied himself beneath the weight of the bag of food he was carrying, some very powerful, very fragrant cut of steak with plenty of French fries, in the hope that something would be left over for his son

and he even had time to stop in at Noah's Barque to ask, as a favour to a friend, for a little plastic bag of mustard to please the police officers

"it's even got mustard? yes, sir," Agent Belo smiled, licking his well-fed lips, "now that's what i call a picnic even a dead man will remember..."

"do you think i can see my son today? it's been almost a week"

"hide the goods for fuck's sake, if the Deputy Superintendent sees that, he'll take it all for himself!"

"but how do we do this?"

"meet me out there at the corner and we'll settle everything, order something to drink and you can rely on me"

"i don't drink"

"don't worry, i'll drink yours."

Agent Belo entered the tiny street-corner bar but didn't see Odonato

he looked again, waited for the indoor gloom to forgive the intense outdoor brightness and imagined he had seen a form seated in a corner, frowned and stepped closer to confirm that this was the same man he had spoken to earlier

"but you..."

"don't worry, that's how i am"

"have you talked to a doctor?"

"sure, but tell me, when can i see my son? i'm worried about his wound"

"naw," the policeman said, pulling out the food, asking for a plate and cutlery, "with these steaks you've got nothing to worry about"

"but you're eating the steaks!" Odonato said, speaking seriously "i'm only eating half the steak, someone else will eat the other half"

"when will i be able to see my kid?"

"he's a kid?"

"you didn't see him?"

"yeah, but i mean... how old a kid?"

"how old, man?" Odonato's voice sounded tearful, a dark, paternal presentiment, "when can i see him?"

"well... i'm not sure... i can neither promise nor dispromise, i've already tried to bring in the Deputy Superintendent, but he doesn't accept French fries unless they're green"

"green?"

"greenbacks, bucks, hundred-dollar bills"

"that part's going to be more complicated"

"well, everything's more complicated here in Luanda," Agent Belo chewed with satisfaction, "just look at you, comrade."

Little Daddy, in the burning heat, took his frequent work breaks on the first floor, lying down in the area where the waters fell hardest to reinvigorate the muscles of his body and the rhythms of his mind

he had mastered the secrets of those waters to the extent that they allowed themselves to be understood, just as the mysterious Noah's Barque never experienced a power outage even when the whole city had been plunged into more or less permanent blackness, the first floor never succumbed to the most dire general water shortages and this secret, though it might be of great value to more business-oriented minds, was kept by the building's inhabitants, almost as a matter of pride

"if the world runs out of water, i know where there'll still be a drop to drink," João Slowly joked, "when you're finished, come and see me, i need to speak to you, Little Daddy"

"yes, Uncle João, i'll be right there"

the terrace was now impeccably clean, Little Daddy officially received a miniscule salary from João Slowly for the morning cleaning and tidying up he did up there "we have to give this movie house a sense of dignity," João Slowly had explained, "our Rooster Camões over there won't let us act inappropriately, cleanliness is the dignity of the poor, as my grandmother used to say"

"tell me then, Uncle João. what's wrong? isn't everything clean?"

"it's excellent, boy, you're a serious, hard-working guy, you know that sloth is the worst enemy of your profession, you know that, right?"

"what?"

"that sloth is the mother of all vices?"

"the mother?"

"yes, the start"

"i get it," the lad went on his way to clean everything again

"cool it, boy, calm down, we're talking here, have a seat," João Slowly pulled a bottle of whisky, so well cooled it was sweating, out of a styrofoam cooler, "we're going to commemorate"

"we're going to what?"

"commemorate, celebrate your job here in the cinema and your TV appearance"

"thanks, but i don't even like whisky"

"so what? just shut your mouth, you don't refuse whisky, especially when it's free, i'm not charging you a cent... drink it down like a man"

"thanks, Uncle João"

"take a drink, then, so you can't say i treat my advisors badly"

from his pocket he pulled a Nokia, battered by time and the countless hands it had passed through, no one could say for certain whether its peculiar colour was an ash-grey that had once been silver

"is that for me, uncle?"

"so you can be contactable, available... you see this thing? now you go buy a cellphone card from Auntie Strong Maria and bingo, we're in the age of global communication, we ain't in Huambo any more!" João Slowly laughed "but people say that in Huambo the network coverage is better"

"okay, sure, but this is a real Luandan cellphone, with all the latest gadgets! you get the picture?"

"yeah, uncle, i get it, thank you very much, doesn't it need credit?"

"shut your goddamn mouth, what we need around here is for you to learn to drink whisky, who ever saw an Angolan your size not drinking a good cold whisky at this time of day...!"

"thanks, uncle"

"you're welcome, listen, tonight you're going to have to stay late, we're going to have a special session"

"an adult film?"

"that's right, but it's not just adult... tonight you're going to see pornographic internationalism"

"what's that, uncle?"

"it's called *An African Man's Hard Revenge*, it was recommended to me by some friends, i already saw part of it and it's promising... come and see it, you'll like it, it's like a blue movie!"

"is that like a blue moon?"

"blue movie, like a movie from Sweden, you people from Huambo...! well kid, we'll talk soon, tidy up here because tonight we're going to have an extra-big crowd"

"yes, uncle," delighted, Little Daddy looked at his new phone

"go downstairs and give this whisky to Comrade Mute, it's got too much water in it"

"sure, uncle."

at the agreed-upon time, the English journalist found Odonato halfway up the staircase and helped him up the remaining floors to the sixth

finding Granma Kunjikise in the hall outside his apartment, seated with Amarelinha at her feet, the two of them amused themselves threading necklaces with seashells and beads sold or given to them by Seashell Seller the smile on Granma Kunjikise's face was the soothing sight that, without knowing it, Odonato was looking for

"good afternoon, mother"

the old woman smiled at her son-in-law and the journalist

Granma Kunjikise took a liking to her, even without knowing her, from the movements of her hands, she seemed like someone who had an impulse to learn rather than make deductions based on scant knowledge, as was the usual practice among other journalists, whatever their nationality

"Baba," Odonato hugged his wife, "can we offer this girl something? she wants to record a conversation with me"

"yes, we do, will you have a tea?"

"yes, thank you very much"

they sat down in the living room, remaining still, as if both enjoyed watching the time pass

"do you send the things you record to the BBC?"

"i'm not going to record anything, i just want to chat, and take some notes, if that's not a problem"

"but they're for the BBC?"

the young woman smiled in a way that was both discreet and open

"no, i don't send anything to the BBC any more, they don't want it"

"oh no?"

"no, nobody wants my stories any more, it seems they're too good-news"

"but if they're good-news... that's good news!"

"no, nobody wants good news about Angola, or about Africa, not too good, you see? a small good-news item from time to time is one thing, but always reporting interesting things is something else"

"i see," Odonato appeared slightly startled, "so what are we going to talk about? i don't know any more than you about the excavations, maybe less... as for the eclipse, i just know what i see on the billboards and in the newspapers..."

"we're going to talk about life, about the building, about whatever you like"

Odonato rolled up his sleeves and the journalist had to suppress a start, his arms were even more transparent than his face; the movements of his bones were visible, perfectly visible, as was the flow of his blood from one extremity of his body to another, the tendons obeying the movements of the nerves, or perhaps the reverse,

she gradually managed to meet Odonato's gaze again

"you know, aside from becoming transparent, i'm getting lighter and lighter"

"how do you deal with all of this?"

"how would you deal with it?"

"i've never been transparent, i wouldn't know what to say"

"i wouldn't know what to say either"

"how did it begin?"

"are you recording?" Odonato asked

"no, i'm not"

"i think it's better if you record, we may not have another chance... it started with hunger, i was hungry and i didn't have anything to eat"

"here in Luanda, in this building? there's always a helping hand"

"but i was sick of eating out of helping hands, i wanted to eat from the hand of my government, but not the way our rulers eat, i wanted to eat from the fruit of my labours, from my profession"

"you were fired?"

"i was being fired"

"what do you mean?"

"i was being prevented from doing my work, i was being forced to leave"

"physically?"

"not physically, no... anyway, i ended up without money and, in Luanda, if you don't have a gift for money-making schemes..."

"i understand"

"i was eating less and less so that my children would be able to eat what little i didn't"

"how did this happen? you should have become weak, ill"

"but i didn't!"

"what happened?"

"life freed me"

Xilisbaba, her eyes moist with tears, glanced into the kitchen, shaken by her husband's detailed confession

"life freed me little by little from the burden of hunger and pain"

"may i ask how this came about?"

"i had aches at the beginning, hunger, stomach cramps, but for some reason my instinct told me not to eat any more, it was a kind of relinquishment, but i can't explain it very well because it wasn't thought through, i just kept going... i just kept going, and at a certain point i stopped feeling hunger, i even stopped feeling my stomach, it got so that i had a drink of water and i felt great, better all the time, until the day"

"until the day...?"

"until the day when my hands started to become transparent"

"weren't you afraid?"

"you want the truth?"

"i want your truth"

"i wasn't afraid, it seemed appropriate"

"appropriate? the outcome?"

"the appearance"

"aren't you afraid of dying?"

"i think i've already got past that fear"

"you said you felt the appearance was fair?"

"because it's a symbol, transparency is a symbol, and i love this city to a point where i'd do anything for it, it was my turn, i couldn't refuse"

"what do you mean?"

"i don't know how to explain it very well, and that's what i keep thinking about, when i go and sit by myself on the terrace and feel the wind and stare out at the city, a man can be a people, his image can be that of the people..."

"the people are transparent?"

"the people are beautiful, merry, arrogant, fantastical, crazy, drunken... Luanda is a city of people who fantasize about anything they can imagine"

"it's not the people who are transparent..." the journalist tried

"no, it's not all of the people, there are some who are transparent, i figure the city is speaking through my body..."

"that's the truth of your life," the young journalist murmured

"it's important to let the truth appear, even at the cost of disappearing, are you recording?"

the building shook, its motion slow, but everyone was able to feel its trembling

Xilisbaba sought out her husband in the living room, Granma Kunjikise and Amarelinha appeared also

it was a small, brief earthquake, which left dents only in everyone's certainties and in their faces

"either this passes or it splits right open," Odonato murmured

"*they dig up the tree's roots and they think that the shadow will stay in the same place...*"

Granma Kunjikise murmured in the direction of the journalist's recorder.

the people who had just landed at Quatro de Fevereiro International Airport, while still in the line-up for Immigration, concluded that some sort of earthquake had occurred

"don't worry," an Angolan joked, speaking to the foreigners in the line-up, "this is just part of the welcome celebrations"

the other locals joined in his laughter

"celebrations for the Angolan eclipse have already begun, our government's really efficient!"

and they continued, smiling, while searching for suit-cases full of items purchased in Brazil, South Africa, or the Europes

brightly coloured T-shirts for summer, warm suits in spite of the Angolan heat, expensive dresses for wives, high-heeled shoes for lovers, soccer balls for nephews, dynamite necklaces for daughters, goddaughters, and nieces, fancy running shoes to give to friends or even sell under the counter, thousands of lacy feminine panties to sell to black-market clothing guys, silk pyjamas, ties, dress shoes for weddings or funerals, bands for girlfriends' frizzy hair, caps with the monograms of American basketball teams, hi-tech gadgets, MP3s or MP4s, next-generation cellphones with services not yet offered by local networks, miniature televisions and DVD players for the cars, bluish LED lamps for automobiles' interiors or exte-riors, apparatuses to annoy neighbours at more than a hun-dred metres' distance

plus

digital photo frames compatible with all kinds of chargers, GPSes that could speak and receive spoken orders, sensors to prevent cars backing into others, dry fruit, Serrano cheese, Minas Gerais cheese, condoms of different colours and tastes, expensive brand-name silver or gold watches, more shoes, more ties, more warm suits, name-brand sunglasses, televi-sion remotes, security alarms, articles for the kitchen or gar-den, inflatable swimming pools, televisions with screens of uncountable inches, external hard drives, books on manage-ment, business, or international law, Blue-ray DVDs, wireless phones, kitchen frying pans, tiny electric shavers, earphones with mute buttons, waterproof cameras, children's car seats, many expensive perfumes

"you don't mess with an Angolan when it comes to shop-ping," they said, emerging from the airport's filthy bathroom, "even if your suitcase gets delayed, that's life, you bought it, now you put up with it! we've got people here travelling with twelve suitcases, are you kidding or what?"

214

many foreigners belonged to the so-called international scientific community and had come to Angola, precisely now, to study the eclipse from one of several privileged viewing points

as per the flyers and publicity right there in the baggage area

"Angola has never seen an eclipse like this," a foreigner explained, taking notes, photographing, commenting to another that he found this national appropriation of a universal phenomenon very interesting, but in reality, looking at it clearly, there was no denying that it was also local

Don't get eclipsed, use appropriate sunglasses, was legible on a billboard underwritten by the Party, in minuscule letters, but with an enormous partisan symbol that glowed in the half-light

Made here, watched here, said an ad from the satellite-dish company and all the television stations

An eclipse seen live is worth two watched on TV, said the flyer from the Kwanza Sul government, whose capital, Sumbe, as we know, was the most propitious spot from which to enjoy the full spectacle, and was the likely destination of the majority of the scientists present

"we've been here for two hours and no suitcases, is that what it's like here?" asked a Brazilian scientist, paunchy and drenched in sweat

"you just got to put up with it, Pops, just put up with it," an equally sweaty but upbeat Angolan replied, "do you get one of the best eclipses in the world in your country?"

"that's by chance..."

"we do here! this is Angola, brother, put up with it a bit and everything'll work out"

"tell me something, brother, is there jungle here? am i going to be able to see the Angolan jungle?"

the Angolans around the Brazilian killed themselves with loud laughing, confusing him for a few seconds

"there's jungle here, don't worry," an Angolan replied

"just step out of the airport and you'll see it... the urban jungle," another said, the gathering burst out into a laughter that intensified the heat "because they told me there's jungle here, i'd like to see wild animals... hey, there's my suitcase, what luck, well, guys, i'm on my way," the Brazilian concluded, wiping his forehead after pulling his suitcase off the belt

"have a good eclipse," the Angolan said

"you, too"

the enormous group of scientists, divided by nationality, went to face exacting agents who checked the numbers of their luggage tags and made the appropriate inspection

"there's nothing in there," one of the Brazilians said, "just observation materials, research..."

"but everything has to be examined, you get it, mah honey?"

"i have to pay money?"

"maybe... let's take a good look at those suitcases, open up, please"

the agents, equipped with impeccable white gloves, searched the scientists' baggage, some were searched more than others, last-minute airport taxes were invented and by luck nobody had to hand over dollars because the reception committee included people from Angolan travel agencies well versed in the process of verbal resolution with airport workers

"these are scientists, what's going on, just let them through, they've been authorized by the government and everything"

"can't they just leave us a favour? a favour is a voluntary thing, brother, nobody's asking for anything," one of the white-gloved agents growled, closing a suitcase that had been examined

"tell me something, young man," the Brazilian insisted, "are we going to pass through some jungle on the road to Sumbe?"

"jungle? how's that? you gentlemen are going to Sumbe and Sumbe is a city, it's the capital of Kwanza Sul Province"

"but does it have jungle? like jungle with wild animals?"

outside, baptized by waves of heat and body odour while they waited for the tour bus that would take them to their hotel, they were approached by countless youngsters who tried to sell them soft drinks, water, telephone cards, stolen cellphones, or more specialized products

"what's that?"

"pure en-clips sunglasses, elder, you've gotta buy them now so you're not taken by surprise, the eclipse is almost here"

"and i came here precisely to observe the eclipse, i'm a scientist, do you understand?" the Brazilian smiled at the young vendor

"then the gentleman must know that he can't just stare at the sun, the sun doesn't like it"

"that's right, i know, let me see what those glasses are like"

"these are the real deal official sunglasses, boss, they're even authorized by the government, i ain't sellin' any ol' product, y'know, it's fifteen dollars, boss, but Euros are okay, too"

"and the real? can i pay with the real?"

"no, boss, for the moment i'm not working with Brazilian currency"

"so you know the real is the Brazilian currency?"

"yeah, i know, boss, but you can pay in dollars or tell me the hotel where you gentlemen are staying and i'll come round later with products for your whole retinue"

"how did you know the Brazilian currency is the real?"

"we know all the currencies here, boss, even Chinese money"

"and is the city of Sumbe far away?"

"it's pretty close, boss, in a *candongueiro* you can do it in less than four hours, but are you going to take the real-deal shades?"

"the shades?"

"the goggles, the anti-en-clips sunglasses, the ones i'm selling... look, boss, they've got a stamp and everything"

"who knows... i'm not prepared now, but we can talk later, look, here comes my bus"

"just a few dollars, boss, even if it's only ten, i'm gonna give you a good price, boss, Brazilians are like our brothers, like Mr. Lula..."

"are you from here in Luanda?"

"no, boss, i'm from Uíge"

"Mweejee?"

"Uíge, the city of Uíge"

"is there jungle there? have you been in the jungle?"

"jungle?"

"yeah, jungle, with wild animals"

the travel agent told the young man to move along, even gave him a disrespectful shove, and made the scientists enter the poorly parked tour bus

"did you have to shove me like that? you guys get violent when you're escorting foreigners, it's as if you think of even Brazilians as foreigners..."

"shut your goddamn mouth and go get a job," the agent said, grumpy about the heat and about his work

"aren't i workin' at my job now? buy some goddamn en-clips glasses so you don't go blind"

"who told you i'm going to look at the eclipse?"

"and who told you that you don't have to wear them even if you're not looking? there are people who are going to start wearing them the night before"

"hey, leave me alone, i've got my own stuff to worry about"

the tour bus, with hazard lights on, pulled away with its door still open, but was intercepted by two police officers who, to the agent's despair, lay in wait for it up ahead

"good afternoon, comrades, who is responsible for this vehicle?"

"i am," the agent replied

"please step out with the bus's complete identification, we're going to have to see everyone's papers"

"but they just left the airport, they waited three hours for their luggage, Mr. Officer, this is a group of scientists who came to bear witness to our eclipse"

"here outside the airport we're in a national situation, this is what you might call a daily occurrence"

"but they've already been identified, Mr. Officer"

"so give me all the passports together for a simple verification"

the Brazilian got out of the tour bus to smoke and approached the policemen

"everything in order, Mr. Officer?" he smiled at the men

"everything's in order with me, and you?"

"fine, i'm beating the heat, just fine... we're on our way to Sumbe, y'know?"

"yeah, i know, i was born near there"

"ah, so you know the area?"

"yeah, i know it"

"do you know if there's jungle there?"

"jungle?"

"yes, jungle, i'd like to see wild animals of the African jungle"

"it's better to talk about that with your guide once you get there," the policeman disguised his laughter, glancing in complicity at the other officer, "you just arrived from Brazil?"

"yeah, just now, i mean, three hours ago, eh? the baggage carousel was a shambles"

"yes, sir, and you're here for the arrival of the eclipse?"

"yeah, we came to observe, to study..."

"very good, and did you bring monetary values?"

"how's that?"

"values in dollars or Euros?"

"no, no, we didn't bring anything, they said it was all included"

"but it's always good to carry some *cumbú*"

"*cumbú?*"

"*cumbú* is money, what you guys call *grana*"

"oh, yeah, *grana*, right"

"right," the policeman said calmly, "but sooner or later you're gonna need *grana*... *cumbú!*"

"right," the Brazilian pretended, with his cigarette in his mouth

"do you have a cigarette, Mr. Scientist?"

"yes i do," he pulled the pack out of his pocket

"can we keep the pack? we're going to be here all afternoon, you see..."

"fine, you can keep it, can we get moving?"

"yes, you can, sure, have a good trip, the National Police wish you gentlemen scientists an excellent stay and concomitantly a correspondingly good eclipse!"

"your Portuguese is wonderful!" the Brazilian appeared to be genuinely startled

"thank you, have a good day," the policeman saluted and went to divide up the pack of cigarettes with his colleague

"the police here are nice guys except that they like to smoke other people's cigarettes," the scientist commented

"they're like me," the agent remarked, "i smoke but i don't assume"

"you don't inhale? you got some kind of health problem?"

"no, i smoke but i don't like to assume the losses from actually buying cigarettes"

the Brazilian laughed, he liked the joke, he hung his head out the window and began to look at the city, several billboards mentioned the eclipse, the city, at a number of points, had been painted or rearranged for the occasion, but as soon as they left the airport area endless scaffolding appeared, walled-off buildings and streets, recently dug-up red earth, cracked concrete, blocks of tarmac torn out of the streets and everywhere plaques that named CIROL

"cie-roll? what's cie-roll?"

"it's the Commission for the Installation of Recoverable Oil in Luanda"

"a commission? for oil? what's that about?"

"excavations, we're headed for the future"

"which future?"

"they found oil here, underneath the city of Luanda"

"and you can drill?"

"of course we can, it's our land"

"yes, but in terms of the safety of people and buildings, can you drill just like that?"

"we have really advanced techniques, people came from other countries and everything, the government's overseeing it all"

"you believe in this government?"

"i can't compare, i've never known any other government," the agent said

"are they still prospecting?"

"they're getting started, the excavations are for the installation of tubes and machinery, any moment now oil's gonna start gushing out, and they say that if they find oil in somebody's backyard that person gets a commission"

"so what i heard in Brazil about people having oil wells in their backyards is true?"

"no, those are just Brazilians' stories"

"Brazilians' or Angolans'?"

"well, they're stories spread by Angolans who go to Brazil to tell those stories, and they're Brazilians' stories when people like you, sir, believe in them"

"don't call me 'sir,' we're practically friends... what's your name?"

"Bernas"

"Burn Ass?"

"Bernas"

"oh, Bernas, pleased to meet you, i'm Serginho, what a funny name, is that your tribal name?"

"no," the young man laughed, "it comes from Bernardo, i'm Bernardo, but in my family they call me Bernas"

"i see"

after two hours in heavy, noisy traffic, they reached the hotel, unloaded their suitcases, and said goodbye to the driver and the guide

"well, Bernas, if you find out something about our route, if we're going to pass through or we're able to visit some jungle you let me know, eh?"

"okay, sure, have a good stay and a good eclipse"

"a good eclipse to you, too."

as the cockroach got closer

and in response to some of its movements, the television in Raago's room stopped working or broadcast static that caused the occasional appearance of images from a pornographic movie with two blonde women and a black stallion endowed with an enormous sexual organ, of the type that in Luanda is known as a *kinjango*

or which, in certain family circles, answers to the spiritual name of *salardote*

the American smiled, watching the albino cockroach whose antennae stirred in an even more fidgety way when subject to direct observation

"i wonder how many stories you could tell me... if only you could speak," the American murmured, lying on the floor looking at the steamy little cockroach

he was surprised by the sound of the ringing telephone but avoided abrupt movements because he knew that the cockroach was easily frightened, and the friendship he had achieved through time and patience demanded that he move slowly

he answered the phone and was glad to hear the voice of his friend and fellow scientist Davide Airosa, who would come around later to pick him up for a big dinner at Paulo Paused's place

"should i bring something, a bottle of wine, perhaps?"

"no, no, you don't have to, don't worry, if there's one thing there's no shortage of there, it's booze," the other said.

"a bottle of Portuguese wine, preferably from Alentejo," João Slowly ordered, smiling

"here it comes," Noah replied, heading for the ark, "good and cold, or natural and warm?"

"good and cold, so my throat doesn't lose the habit, Senhor Noah"

"here it is"

"we'll open it to celebrate"

"so?"

"so didn't i tell you i was coming here right away so we could settle this business?"

"oh, yeah, the stuff about the yard," Noah remembered, opening the bottle of wine, preparing the glasses

222

"bring more glasses, i'm paying for a round of red wine for everybody"

at his table, the Leftist smiled and thanked him with a nod, at another table two others imitated the gesture and hurried to finish their warm beers to free their glasses of prior commitments, the wine was served and the toast proposed

"to our Angolan eclipse!"

"to the eclipse!"

"so how do things stand, Senhor Noah?"

"in theory the Chinese are moving out today, they didn't want to move out, i rented it for one year, it expired more than a month ago and they didn't move out, when you told me you were interested, i went to talk to the men"

"and they didn't move out?"

"you can't even imagine the trouble this caused me, they threatened me with Kung Fu tricks, the Bruce Lee fuckers..."

"and you didn't show off your skill in mixing karate with Angolan *bassula*?"

"not me, i'm too old for that, i left them in peace and came back the next day"

"you came back with the police in tow?"

"no, i came back towing an AK-47"

"oh, nice, those chinks wanted to fool around with Noah the commando"

"certain matters can only be resolved with an AK-47"

"did the boys rub them out?"

"i got there, i fired two shots in the air and i asked where that Bruce Lee guy was, but the guy i asked panicked and took off on his hind legs"

"sure, you're right, after all, we were trained by the Cubans"

"that's right!"

"so what about today?"

"we're going back there, if you want we can go right now, they must be clearing everything out, i gave them the end of the afternoon as a deadline" "but should we go there right now, just like that, to catch them off guard?" João Slowly was not exactly the most courageous of Luandans

"of course we'll catch them off guard," Noah opened the ark and out of an opaque plastic bag he pulled his gleaming AK-47

"are you certain, Senhor Noah, that it's not better to go well prepared? with these Chinese people you never know..."

"what could be more prepared than this? all that's missing is the psychological factor "

"what do you mean?"

"we take our buddies along, have a quick rough-and-tumble in the yard, then return from our mission for another glass, are you on board, comrades?"

"i'm on board after i finish my drink," the Leftist affirmed

"us, too," the others said, gesturing with their hands to indicate they wanted their glasses filled up again

"well..." João Slowly murmured, finishing his glass, "i declare initiated, by unanimous vote, Operation Enter-the-Dragon's-Lair!"

"then bring another bottle of wine!" one of the regulars urged

fired up, the group strengthened its martial enthusiasm and, ready to rumble, with their bodies reeling and their faces twisted with venom, entered the backyard that Noah had rented out to seven Chinese one year before, demanding in Portuguese mixed with Kimbundu where the boss, a certain Bruce, was, for it was time for them to withdraw from their sanctuary, it had already been allocated to other people, who were on their way

"Bruce not here," said a weeping woman, a very short Chinese with a child in her lap

"okay, let's keep it cool," Noah lowered his weapon and suggested that the others hold their alcoholic breath, "has he left for real?"

"everything gone already, person come get pillows and beds"

"very good, very good," Noah said, without knowing what else to say "then let's proceed with the countdown," João slowly said

from within the outbuilding came beds, pillows, baskets, fruit and vegetables, oil lamps, candles, a tiny generator and gas cans, kitchen utensils, suitcases, and enormous bags of clothes and other objects, all carried out the back door to a truck also driven by more-or-less smiling Chinese

"wait up... have i been drinking too much? how many Chinese have already left that place?" Noah appeared confused

the rest of the group made gestures with their fingers and their eyes, it was puzzling, they entered and left, went to the car, their clothes and faces were too similar and there were children thrown into the mix so that at the end, when they had finished removing everything and a woman came to hand in the key, Noah climbed up onto the back of the trolley, his weapon slung over his arm, and a strange silence fell among the Chinese

Noah climbed down with a defeated expression, joined his friends to stare at the departing vehicle, then finally offered his verdict

"these Chinese are fucking unbelievable!"

"how's that, bro?"

"well, when i rented out the place there were seven of them, just now i counted eleven, including two babes in arms and two pre-adolescents"

"scientifically speaking, that's complicated..." the Leftist commented, pointing towards the bar and suggesting that they return right away

"scientifically? don't fool around with the Chinese"

on their return they opened two more bottles, Noah wrapped up his AK-47 again in a long plastic bag then tightened it with two small tethers and locked the imposing weapon away

"there are things that surpass the scientific dimension, Senhor Leftist, you can be sure"

"i'm sure, but in one year, Noah..."

"haven't you ever heard those stories? you, who are almost a writer, haven't you heard?"

"i've heard incredible stories about the Chinese," somebody commented

"so they learn Kimbundu in three months on some intensive course, who are you kidding?"

"yes, it's one thing to learn to spout a few words of Kimbundu, it's another to gestate a child"

"gestate? now you whip out those hundred-dollar verbs? isn't it true that right here in the Rocha Pinto district a Chinese woman was admitted twice to the same clinic in the space of a little more than a year?"

"a little more than a year, Senhor Noah? let's not exaggerate..."

"it's true, the case was in the papers, it seems that here in Angola Chinese women are mixing ginger with their own spices, and the length of their pregnancies has been reduced to six months"

"six months?!" the Leftist was doubtful

"well, six and a half, sure, bah! twice that... gives you thirteen months, they're pumpin' out kids like they're still back in China... didn't you just see it with your own eyes? there used to be seven of them, but eleven moved out"

"those Chinese..." commented another of the temperamental fellows

"those Chinese have secret techniques to defy the laws of maternity... well," Noah opened another bottle, "a toast to my new tenant"

"a toast," João Slowly filled and lifted the glass

"are you sticking to your plan?"

"i'm sticking to it, but it's better to keep it half-secret"

"what's half-secret?"

"well, in technical terms it's what you call being incorporated, me, you, and my faithful"

"so you're still going to open a church?"

"i thought about calling it Sacred Barque, but i already know that you won't like that, sir" "either it's an incorporated company or it's not... don't do that, the tax inspectors already give me enough headaches over my bar, now one more thing, no, it's not possible"

"yes, i understand, i was doing some research, and i received a message from heaven," João Slowly said in a sarcastic voice

"oh yeah?"

"yup, i was preparing biblical citations to defend my church, and a certain animal really caught my attention"

"which one?" Noah, and everyone else, looked curious

"the sheep! i think i might be close to a certain revelation, Senhor Noah, and i've dreamed a lot about sheep"

"in fact, it's an interesting animal"

"the faithful will be informed shortly, and they'll want to become acquainted with the Church of the Sacred Little Lamb"

"amen," the Leftist joked

"therein lies one of the great differences in my parish, Senhor Leftist, and here i cite Matthew 25:31, 'when the Son of Man comes in his glory, and all the angels with him, he will sit on his glorious throne; all the nations will be gathered before him, and he will separate the people one from another as a shepherd separates the sheep from the goats; he will put the sheep on his right and the goats on his left'"

"well, then, i prefer the goats," the Leftist affirmed, "and i cite Genesis 27:16, 'she also covered his hands and the smooth part of his neck with the goatskins!'"

"then i'll send you back to Matthew, 25:41, 'then he will say to those on his left, "depart from me, you who are cursed, into the eternal fire prepared for the devil and his angels"'"

"then i'll send you back to the whore who gave you birth! fucking bullshit-artist, because the left will always be better and your Matthew, up there in heaven, could have his directions mixed up," the Leftist roared

"cool it, comrade, João Slowly is our friend, and those Bible quotations are in preparation for his church..."

"and can't i choose other quotations? the people on the left-hand side are evil and are going to hell, is that it?"

"calm down… i just wanted to quote part of my biblical research to show you some of my preparation… it was to tell you that our word of celebration will be different, it won't be 'amen'"

"what will it be?" Noah tried to divert the conversation

"am-baaah!" he made the serious sound of a sheep responding to a religious call, "in homage to that much-sacrificed animal… i propose a toast to the Church of the Sacred Little Lamb!"

"am-baaah!" replied a chorus of those present

Noah served more wine, João Slowly bid farewell to everyone while the Leftist was grumbling again

"that's it, go on your way to your little sheep church, otherwise let's stick to Genesis 29:7, '"look," he said, "the sun is still high; it is not time for the flocks to be gathered, water the sheep and take them back to pasture"'…give the sheep something to drink, Senhor Noah!"

the session was scheduled for seven o'clock, with a forty-five-minute allowance for Luandans' chronic lateness, João Slowly smiled when he arrived on the terrace better known as the Rooster Camões Cinema and found it tidied up, clean, and with a smell resembling perfume, with flowers in the corners, the flames of the grills beginning to let off reddish sparks, Strong Maria in a pretty, modest dress, Little Daddy finishing tidying-up and arranging the chairs, at the back, near the second entrance was an alcove of more comfortable chairs that served as the VIP area, the borrowed projector was already in place and on the neighbouring terrace even the rooster's comb looked less fallen, his gaze more youthful and revived

"i'm thinking, Maria"

"tell me, baby"

"if we shouldn't go over to that other terrace and give our rooster something to eat"

"then the neighbours will ask why, and you'll have to explain everything" "you're right, it's not worth it, just toss any old thing from this distance and what makes it, makes it, he'll understand"

"fine"

"the guests could arrive at any minute"

"we're all set, i'm just getting the coal ready"

"it's gonna be quite a night here"

"you've got the film, right?"

"it's safely stored... hey, Little Daddy," João Slowly called

"uncle?"

"when you're done, go downstairs and help Edú get up here and bring his little bench so he doesn't take up a seat"

"right, uncle"

when the film started the theatre was packed with people seated in the chairs and others standing up in the corners or even next to the entrance, getting in Little Daddy's way as he acted as a general-purpose waiter, going down to look for beer or whisky in order to supply Strong Maria's enormous styrofoam coolers, serving plastic plates of grilled snacks, with or without napkins, hauling pails of ice purchased at the last minute, and even responding to special orders from the VIP area

all went as planned, the younger members of the audience began to speak out loud lines from the film's scenes, superimposing their words on certain dialogues, making up others, in a chaotic fashion, then leaving the floor free to give way to anyone who hadn't expressed themselves, which included, without bias or joy, the lines and groans of the blonde women who, endowed with a pornographic and nordic voluptuousness, took care of the African plumber for more than forty-five minutes

João Slowly opened his eyes in ecstasy, caught his wife's eye from where she stood in front of the grill, watched, hypnotized, the crowd's reactions of laughter or open pleasure, and, considering it in retrospect, was pleased to be proved right in his prediction that the future would imitate the silent cinema of the past using the absence of sound, stimulating the crowd with this intentional lack of synchronicity, João Slowly became the orchestrator of a self-generating and self-sustaining theatre, the crowd took charge of bringing to life the ideas he had announced earlier in the fields of "theatrical, cinematographic and performative experimentation," or, in short, the imagined echoes of his eighth art

"a beautiful thing... beautiful"

João Slowly shed a tear

and observed the vertical movements of the Camões Rooster's neck.

"where's the bottle? did you hide it or what?"

Colonel Hoffman asked

"in the usual spot,"

Paulo Paused replied, worried about hosting the American, who seemed uncomfortable with the mess in the apartment

the television was broadcasting a Brazilian soap opera in which everyone was arguing, the radio was tuned to the news, and even this late in the day the Cirolian jackhammers were putting in poorly paid overtime hours

as arranged, though an hour and a half late, Davide Airosa had come by the hotel to pick up the American, who seemed upset and a little scared by Dom Crystal-Clear's verbal threats and the Minister's silent compliance, backed up by the Senhor Advisor's consent and Dona Creusa's laughing eyebrows, he described all of this in a mixture of the Portuguese and American languages, with a wealth of detail, to the point where Davide Airosa felt compelled to appease the young American

"cool it, they're just shooting off their mouths, while you're there, just keep quiet"

"yes, i'm already quiet"

"so that's the story, you did your work, you gave your opinion, the rest is up to them"

"i'm afraid everything's going to go wrong"

"everything's been going wrong for a long time, Raago, don't worry, later on people will find a way to patch it up, that's how Angolans deal with stuff, if we did everything right the first time there would be countless disadvantages, first it would look like work was quick and easy, then we wouldn't have a pretext for looking brilliant by fixing things, you get it?"

"more or less"

"more or less is good enough, don't worry about it, when you leave you'll write your articles, draw your own conclusions"

"even leaving is going to be a problem, or am i mistaken?"

"what do you mean?"

"the other day Dom Crystal-Clear gave me a lift back to the hotel"

"and?"

"he told me i could be arrested"

"arrested? but why?"

"just that, arrested, in jail"

"no, they can't grab an American citizen, far less at this stage, don't worry, it was just a bluff"

"no, he said i'm married"

"you're married?"

"but i didn't know about it"

"i don't understand"

"he says i'm married to an Angolan citizen now, and for that reason i can be jailed as an Angolan citizen"

"but did you get married to an Angolan?"

"he married me"

"are you kidding?"

"he said that when the Ministry had my passport they could've made up other documents, but i don't even know my Angolan wife, who knows, maybe she's pretty," Raago laughed

"and you haven't even paid the dowry, it's gonna be expensive"

Clara had prepared huge, delicious aperitifs, she turned off the television in order not to bother the American, she came and went from the kitchen many times until everything looked pretty and the table was well laden, in addition to the food that her mother's maid had prepared, a special main course of a super-large seafood curry with a special sauce, followed by a wicked meat pie with a topping made of blood sausage and fried eggs

"the blood sausage came from South Africa," she said

"this sister of mine is my salvation," Colonel Hoffman commented, his mouth full

"i can't eat another bite," Paulo said

"i'm full, too," the American confessed

"really great," Davide Airosa concluded

"watch out, i might take that amiss," their hostess replied

"look at these fakers," Colonel Hoffman said, in his booming, serious voice, "so many people with nothing to eat right now and these idiots claim they're stuffed, honestly," he struck the desk with his fist, "get down to it and eat! my apologies, sister, if i didn't yell at them, these youngsters would never learn, they goddamn well should have fought in Cuando Cubango to see what it's like to have a hunger that never goes away"

"sir," Raago said in halting Portuguese, "were you a colonel in the charmed forces?"

the guests laughed softly at the American's mistake

"sorry, Raago, it's not charmed forces, they're armed"

"oh, sorry, sometimes changing a letter gets you into trouble... i meant armed forces, they were known as FAPLA, weren't they?"

"yes," Colonel Hoffman replied, serious, "that's more or less it," and he returned to his food to avoid further explanations

"there was a huge battle in Cuando Cubango, i saw a good documentary on that, about the Cuban presence in Angola, a really good film"

"yes, yes, *los compañeros*..." Hoffman relaxed again, smiling, remembering his Cuban colleagues, soldiers, but they had worked with him at National Radio during the campaign to record traditional music undertaken in the war years, "you know, Rambo..."

"it's Raago, his name's Raago," Paulo corrected

"Okay, listen, Raago... the Cubans, *los cubanos*... they were really funny people, except everything in Cuba was better than it was here, it led to a lot of stories..."

"what do you mean?"

"everything was better there—*las playas, las chicas, la comida*... everything... but they also had this obsession that they knew Angola better than we did because they were soldiers, it was true, they'd been to lots of places that we didn't even have access to"

"i understand"

"i remember well, once, in a combat zone," he paused in his theatrical Luandan manner, the professional pause of any Luandan when he starts to tell a more-or-less true tale, trying to figure out whether anyone present is going to refute him, "once in Moxico, i was with a Cuban, and i began to tell stories about some of the places where i'd been"

"yes"

"and i'm telling this guy that i've already recorded music in Lambala, and the bastard says in Spanish, 'sure, Lambala, i was there with my unit,' and i'm thinking all right, it's possible, then i remembered a time when i was in Chiume and the guy goes, 'hey, Chiume, sure, right next to Cuando Cubango, that's where i fought the South Africans,' and i already get this guy's drift, i start to talk about my childhood in Lumeje and the bastard reacts right away, 'hey, *compañero*, Lumeje, sure, that's where we were last week,' and now i'm getting pissed off with all this shit, so in a soft voice i say, '*Sundu ya manhenu*,' and the bastard turns to me bald-faced and says, 'hey, *Sundu ya manhenu*, sure, we ate there yesterday!'"

Paulo and Clara burst out laughing, unlike the American, who smiled in sympathy with his fork dangling in the air, not getting the joke, while he watched Colonel Hoffman's exaggerated theatricality as he nearly choked with laughter at his own joke, until they explained to him in English that *Sundu ya man-henu* meant "your mother's cunt" in Kimbundu

"oh, man, those Cubans were too much! Jesus, every little story..."

after they had eaten and drunk to their hearts' content, the colonel encouraged his band of internationalists to put in an appearance at a stodgy wedding to which he had not been invited

"we'll do it like in the times before, every *pato* brings three more with him"

"we bring three ducks? *pato* means 'duck'?" the American asked

"*pato* means a non-invited person," Paulo Paused explained

"okay"

"trust me, you've go to go in looking important, that's how it is here in Luanda, if you want to get into a place you have to look arrogant"

since the party was nearby they headed off on foot, avoiding the holes in the sidewalks, circumventing the most dangerous areas, and finally arriving at their destination followed the deafening noise of heavy, throbbing *kizomba* music

in the entrance, as usual, were the bouncers, formally dressed in dark suits and heavily waxed shoes

Hoffman made a rapid visual inspection, took a quick scouting excursion down the sides of the house, "in case of some emergency," as he explained, and, gripping the American's arm, offered a final hint

"keep your mouth shut and don't speak Portuguese, if you've gotta say something, do it in the language of Shakespeare"

"okay," the American laughed

"how's it going, young man, everything combat-ready?" the colonel said loudly to the security guard

"yes, everything's fine"

"we came for the wedding, we were invited, we just brought this American as a gatecrasher so he could get to know how we party here in Angola, get it?" with a sweep of his arm, he conducted Paulo Paused and Davide Airosa into the room

"so you guys...?"

"hey, 'you guys"!? what kind of talk is that? didn't you see this gentleman in yesterday's newspapers? he's a special guest of our Comrade President and came here to explain all those oil excavations"

"i didn't see it, boss"

"'boss' no! we're not on the same wavelength, hmm! i'm Colonel Hoffman, but you can be at ease, were you guys in the army?" he took advantage of this question to give the security guard a powerful slap on the arm

"no, boss, we weren't called up"

"then be careful, you can get called up at any time, can't you?"

"yes, boss, but this party here..."

"enough of this chit-chat, now we bosses are gonna try out a few old-style kizomba steps, if there's any confusion here at the door, i'm Colonel Hoffman, you guys can call me"

"okay, boss, thanks"

they made a grand entrance into the party, Hoffman smiled and bragged about his verbal manoeuvring, made his way straight to the bar, brought drinks for everybody, proposed a toast, and let his gaze wander over the party, appreciating the big-boobed dames, the withdrawn elders with their whisky glasses in their hands, some smoking, others not, the swaggering bodies of the young women who smiled with their mouths and their eyes

and then he saw that, on an improvised stage in a corner, a band was playing live and it was Paulo Flores himself who was there, also with a glass in his hand, clearly at ease as he sang for the dancing crowd

Colonel Hoffman, truly moved, made a signal with his hand, waved in greeting, and Paulo Flores replied with a slight bow and his open smile, this kept the situation under control, the party's hosts couldn't help but note Colonel Hoffman's familiarity with Paulo, and Hoffman rushed to hug his friends so that everyone else would understand that they were with him, the American tapped his foot in a hesitant and suspect rhythm, Paulo Paused went over to greet a few politicians and media people, after which the group reunited for another round of drinks, Davide Airosa found leftovers from a gargantuan plate of *cachupa* on the table and brought over a fresh plate, Hoffman thanked him and ate in a hurry in order to go and dance with a young woman who seemed to be smiling at him

Paulo Flores, over the sound of the guitar and drums, after giving a brief introduction, began singing *Meu Segredo*

"this goes out to my boss-elder who's here tonight, Artur Arriscado, or Scratch Man, better known in Moxico and the surrounding environs as Colonel Hoffman...!"

the group of friends whistled and clapped, the young woman looked impressed and joined her hands around the Colonel's neck

"so, young lady, are you ready to dance with a Luandan from Moxico?" Hoffman joked

"this young lady is ready for anything," she said into the Colonel's ear

her feminine body came closer to him, he made two twists to the left and pulled the girl behind him in a swift manoeuvre to gauge her dancing abilities

"very nice, let's go"

"you ain't seen nothin' yet, colonel"

"call me Artur, what's your name?"

"Manucha"

"pleased to meet you, Manucha..."

"the pleasure's all mine, Artur"

the colonel was having a great time and wasn't about to quit now, he took a few breaks between dances to top up his whisky glass with lots of ice

"what is this, are you joking, or what?" he complained to the young barman, "you're giving me this watery scotch, cooked up in the Roque Santeiro market, with a fake J&B label?"

"no, elder, i apologize"

"don't apologize, just pass me the goddamn Black Label you've got hidden there, you think i didn't see it? i'm from here, too, you little jimmy-fuck"

"yes, elder"

"elder no, we never studied together or sweated together on the same football field, it's 'colonel, sir,' to you, didn't you hear Paulo Flores welcome me at the microphone?"

"here's your whisky, colonel, sir"

"hey, are you kidding or what? two rocks of ice? you think i'm a kitten who's afraid of the water?"

"sorry, colonel, sir"

Paulo Paused and Davide Airosa were explaining to the American how Luandans behaved at parties, how masculine conventions were expressed insofar as drink, food, women, and elders were concerned, who was there and was married, who was already flirting, those who had retreated to dark corners, those who had the confidence to drag someone into a back room or underneath a tree, who had come here to eat, who had come mainly to dance and, in a jocular manner, they bet on whether anyone, other than themselves, might be a gatecrasher at this party

that was when, pumped up by his seventh whisky and wrapped up in Manucha's arms, Colonel Hoffman felt his dancing being interrupted when the music suddenly cut out, everyone's initial reaction was to look in the direction of the light to see whether it was a lack of electricity, but no

"comrades, please excuse this break in your dancing," said a man in a dubious state of sobriety, "but too many gatecrashers have arrived at this party, we're gonna set everything straight"

murmurs, complaints, and barks of laughter were heard, Davide Airosa became nervous and was unable to disguise it, Hoffman made a quick coded signal that Paulo Paused failed to catch, the colonel apologized to the girl and came over to talk to them

"we're going to assume preventive positions, but nobody should abandon the place" "what?" Paulo couldn't hear very well because the man at the microphone was continuing his speech

"we were already given permission by the dude himself, Paulo Flores, we've just got to put up with this sermon then the gatecrashers will beat a retreat and we can stay here taking it easy, don't let me down," Hoffman pulled the chair upright and was already off to look for another whisky, "look at the ice here, dude..."

a few people were voluntarily retreating from the party, the security guards let them leave without any trouble, it looked as though everything was going to return to normal, had the man at the microphone not become inspired

"excuse me please, but that's not good enough, there are still too many gatecrashers, here's what we're gonna do..." he strung out his alcoholic pause, "the bride's guests on the right of the yard, ple-e-e-ss-e... this won't take a minute"

in lowered voices, the crowd commented on the oddity of the situation

"the groom's guests on the left-hand side, let's get moving..."

but few people obeyed his orders

"this is getting really weird," Davide Airosa commented

"keep your cool, you're all young, i know all about this trick, it's been around for a long time, you'll see," Colonel Hoffman laughed with the anticipatory pleasure of an elder and an accomplished professional in the art of gatecrashing Luandan parties

"Now, all of those who are on the right... and all of those who are on the left..." the man made an effort to keep his eyes open and his voice strong, "get out of this party, you pricks! this isn't a shitty wedding, it's my daughter's christening!"

the crowd broke into an easy chortling, the gatecrashers, both on the right and on the left, were escorted to the exit, the party started again and picked up a good pace, with people clapping their hands

on leaving the microphone, the man was embraced and greeted by Hoffman, who looked very satisfied with the cultural manoeuvring that allowed him to show the American a bit of local reality

"hey, Rambo, you guys over there in the Americas don't have those tricks, eh?"

"a very good trick, really..."

"yeah, right, if we were in Texas you guys would call the FBI to investigate the gatecrashers," Hoffman laughed, "here it just takes silver-tongued off-the-cuff words to send the whole gatecrashing gang out the door... and we're here sitting pretty, no doubt about that? hmm?"

"it's true"

"learn it and you can take it back to your country"

hours of dancing ensued, countless bottles and cans of beer were consumed, the bottles of J&B whisky were downed by the younger people and the Black Label reserved for the elders present, the women danced in a joyful circle to Brazlian rhythms

it must have been close to two o'clock in the morning when the elders showed off their prowess in the circle, shaking up their aching backs and their stiff knees, taking advantage of the dance to toss off their boozing and delight their wives with an impromptu clinch to the sounds of samba music

there were people of all ages, including the elderly and small children holding hands, the people in the circle sang in tune with their bodies into the first light of dawn, Colonel Hoffman himself, more at ease than ever before, barked out commands, "ladies to one side, gents to the other... ready..." the bodies followed the rhythm of their stout asses and lips wide open in smiles of celebration

"*fogope!*" Hoffman shouted

in a harsh voice and with an attentive eye on young Manucha, who was ever more impressed by the huge colonel's performance, young people, adults, and the elderly bumped their pelvises together, wheeled their bodies into each other, insisting on bodily gyrations "*fogope!*" Hoffman repeated

laughing and opening his arms for the embrace that the young woman asked him to give her, he let his hands run over Manucha's naked back, the force of gravity carrying them down to her ass, testing how far the girl would let him go, she smiled, pretending not to understand, and at that moment Hoffman sensed the security guard approaching him

"is there a problem, bud? can't you see the colonel is putting the moves on a lady?"

"there's a problem with a thief outside, my elder, we've neutralized him, now we're coming to call you, elder"

"good work, just let me finish this dance, i'll be right there"

the young security guard, with an expression too serious for the mood that surrounded him, saluted and returned to the front door, from where the now undisguisable sounds of a skirmish filtered into the room, the host made mention of the possibility of interrupting the party, but Hoffman whispered into his ear and promised to settle the situation

"as long as you guarantee the Black Label won't run out, this party still has a long time to go"

he took his leave of Manucha, danced across the room gyrating his waist, straightened his shirt, and went out the door with a triumphal air

"what's goin' on? who came to interrupt my niece's christening?"

"this is the guy we caught trying to rip off the elders' cars"

the young man's face was already somewhat swollen, his shirt torn, his expression demoralized from being punched and slapped by the party's security guards, and Hoffman, still under the influence of the whisky in his blood, failed to recognize that this was The Real Zé, one of the most notorious and audacious thieves in the city of Luanda

"hey kid... so you came here to bust up somebody else's party?"

"no, elder, that's not it, i was like just passin' by, i was gonna clean them jalopies" "clean them? clean what? clean them out? or wash them?"

"yes, elder, i was gonna to wash them, i was just dismantling the mirrors so i could wash them real good"

"at this time of night? you came here to jinx yourself, kid"

"don't say that, elder, they already beat the shit out of me"

"well, first you should know there's no 'elder' here, i'm an army officer of nocturnal rank"

"ah, elder, don't say that"

"shut your goddamn mouth, fucker, you come here to interrupt my party, and you're still giving me lip? washing cars at this time of night? yeah, right...!" Hoffman looked pensive, he had to get back to the party but he also had to uphold his fame and standing as a colonel, "here's what we're gonna do," he said to the security guards, "if he can make a lemon-face, he's free to go"

"how's that, colonel?" the security guard asked, confused

"lemon-face, if he can make a real lemon-face, you release the guy, if not, punch him some more, make a lemon-face, you!" Hoffman ordered in a harsh voice, looking at The Real Zé as though this were in fact possible

"elder, i don't know..."

"make a lemon-face, fucker," Hoffman gave him the first smack

"like this?" The Real Zé attempted an ugly, ridiculous grimace

"no, that's not it, you can give it to him"

the security guards began to hit him hard, imitating Colonel Hoffman's strange, unknown phrase, "make the lemon-face if you want us to let you go"

"like this?" he made another grimace

"no, that's no good, that's not a lemon-face," the security guards regarded him with care as though giving the grimace a meticulous evaluation

the colonel entered the party, danced two more songs, got the phone number of the young woman with the exposed back, and advised his gang to beat a retreat because this party might end badly they said farewell, understood at last which child was being christened, Hoffman went to embrace Paulo Flores, thanking him for his gesture at the microphone, he gave the host of the party a big hug and was introduced to the family, to the little girl's mother, her grandmother, and even her great-grandmother, who was present and wide awake, accompanied by her large glass of whisky, he welcomed the in-laws and the nephews and nieces, the wife's brothers and sisters, the host's cousins, then it was the godparents' turn, then the godfather's older brother and the cousin who had come from Portugal, in addition to the neighbour who was an immigrant from the Cape Verde Islands and their respective daughters, finally he bid farewell to the husbands of the Cape Verdean's daughters, as he did to the man's sisters, and he was accompanied to the door by the host of the party himself who, along the way, made sure the colonel met his cousin as well as his brother, his brother's wife, and their four children

"it was a pleasure, Senhor Colonel"

"i'm always here to help, my friend"

"so what about the crook?"

"severe punishment for him, beyond the lemon!"

"what do you mean?" the security guard asked, tired already from having punched The Real Zé so many times

"everybody who leaves the party has to punch this kid, he has to learn that stealing is really ugly," Hoffman gave the thief a crushing blow to the face, "now the rest of you, my gang"

Davide Airosa positioned himself at the end of the line, he really didn't want to hit anyone, he didn't think it was right, or necessary, Paulo Paused said the same thing as he tried to calm the American, who had a horrified expression on his face

"look, the host, my buddy, might get blamed, you just don't do that, especially not you, an American, a last-minute guest, as we might call you"

Hoffman insisted, he shoved them towards the thief, and they had to give him a more or less hard punch, the thief took the beating in silence, now and then wiping sweat or tears off his face

"listen here," he said to the security guards, "everybody at the party has to punch the thief, by order of Colonel Hoffman, including the birthday girl!"

"hey, elder, you said it was a christening," the thief whispered

"fairy son of a bitch, are you still making fun of us...? give it to him good..."

they walked through the dark streets of Luanda

Davide Airosa smiled timidly, wrapped in an alcoholic haze, the American could no longer disguise his astonishment at the way in which Angolans solved the issues that had arisen during the party

"here you are back home, senhor, *gud naite, suite dreems!*" Hoffman bid farewell to Raago at the door of the hotel

"thanks very much, it was a very... well, you know... a very interesting experience"

"we'll talk tomorrow," Davide Airosa said goodbye, adding in English, "sorry about all of this"

"sleep well," Paulo Paused said

the three of them walked back to Maianga, to Paulo's apartment, and Hoffman would have invited himself in had the journalist not explained that if they entered in their current happy state it would be too much for his partner, and that this could bring him serious conjugal problems

"conjugal problems are shit, haven't you learned that?"

"what?"

"if the chick gives you a hard time, make a lemon-face and everything's cool"

they hugged, laughed, and spent more than forty-five minutes prolonging the night by saying goodbye, including reliving the party they had just left

Artur Arriscado, or Scratch Man, after accompanying Davide Airosa to the door of his home, went for a walk, as he used to do years ago, giving his body the opportunity to shake off the alcohol's unwanted effects, feasting his eyes on the heated spectacle of the Luandan sun rise

"a *muzonguê* soup... with good hot red peppers, please"

the colonel placed his order, beneath a sun that was already yellow, at a bar that had just opened its doors.

"but who gives the orders here?"
"the higher-ups"
"higher... like god?"
"no, really higher! here in Angola there are people who give more orders than god"

[from the voice of the people]

it's well known that bad news travels fast

and there were no clock-hands or ways to measure it, yet before the news was official the whole country already knew it, a wave of sadness and melancholy gripped the elders' faces above all, the younger people weren't indifferent but it didn't disrupt their day, though they knew to adopt a more restrained tone

soon after, there was an official declaration, first on National Radio and later on television, the condolences and preparations for the ceremonies ensued, the city muffled the sound of its collective musicality and the *candongueiros* slowed the rhythm of their movements, even people dancing the *batucada* tried to be more discreet

in the outlying neighbourhoods there was civil and political mobilization so that the event would not go unnoticed, the professional mourners oiled their dry heels and prepared potions to soothe their throats, girls' hair was coifed in the latest style, medicine men were ordered to begin farewell ceremonies so that the other world might receive the deceased woman in peace

flags were lowered to half-mast and the President decreed a two-day halt for reflection with the right to fire off guns in the air in all eighteen Angolan provinces precisely at 6 p.m. on each of the days

the priests increased production of wafers for the eucharist, the altars were dusted and the saints took pleasure in being polished by the hands of nuns and children in the service of the church, the interiors of the cathedrals were swept and the churchyards were tidied

in the more remote corners of the country, where military orders travel faster than civilian news, some people reckoned that armed conflict was flaring up again, an idea refuted by the gunfire's isolation and its excessive punctuality

people drank with that furious inner turmoil that death incites, a blend of anxiety and revolt, nostalgia and indignation, the country boozed up gradually to the sound of soft music and incessant chants of resignation

"death spares no one,"

Granma Humps commented

"and it's like the rain: when it falls, everyone gets wet"

the girls of the Workers' District stopped providing their services during those days, drawing the flimsy curtains of each cubicle, they changed the naphthalene in their trunks, scrubbed the floor with vehemence, leaving the intriguing odour of Creolin disinfectant floating over the poor neighbourhoods

all the churches spoke in the dense voices of their bells, inside the churches lengthy masses were recited in Latin, Umbundu, Kimbundu, Kikongo, Chokwe

surrounded by his gigantic battalion of bodyguards, the President appeared at the ceremony for a few instants, leaving in his wake a vast trail of flowers that had arrived, hours earlier, from the best florists of Namibia and South Africa

the family, it was later learned, received an abundant sum of money and the promise of lifelong pensions for immediate family members, particularly the young who remained motherless, many of whom were also fatherless

the material published in the official newspapers spoke of a pact of silence, nobody else would make a statement on the subject, neither of free will nor when provoked, as during those days, beyond the drinks poured, the parties thrown, the hushed celebrations and secluded farewells, there remained, for those who do not forget what they read, the title, the enormous black headline of the *Jornal de Angola*

"Senhora Ideology is officially deceased."

at Noah's Barque nobody spoke of anything else, the old man was clipping headlines from the newspapers to stick on the wall, staring at them and rereading them aloud, visibly sad and depressed by the sudden news

"were you acquainted with the lady?" the Leftist asked

"very well indeed, ever since i was a child. she wasn't even that old"

"but did you know her biblically?" someone who was drunker said, fooling around

"show some respect, comrade, her body's not even cold and you're already starting with the jokes? careful you don't get a red card and be expelled from the bar before half-time"

"my apologies, elder"

"she was a lady who deserved respect, i'm acquainted with the family... the times are really changing, i don't know what's going to happen to us..." Noah looked from a distance at the obituary clippings gathered on the wall near his ark

"we're going from Ba'ath to worse, as they say in the Middle East"

"that's the truth," the Leftist agreed, ordering another beer, "that's why you have to write, leave a legacy," he returned to his written notes, "young people have to know about the past and have other points of reference, today everything's just soap operas, satellite dishes, and discotheques, but we've got to leave behind a statement of our displeasure!"

there was scarce mourning for the death of Senhora Ideology for the workers of CIROL, as the excavations continued at a good pace as though, on a last-minute mission, Angola's politicians had decided to bore incessantly into the city until they saw the jet of the first geyser of Luandan oil.

leaning his weight on Little Daddy's shoulder, Odonato decided once again to go to the police station to meet Agent Belo, carrying with him the enormous tupperware container with the delicious steaks, the greasy fried potatoes, the swollen raw onion, and the little bags of mustard that Little Daddy had discovered in the Chinese store

"Agent Belo, please"

"he went to a burial service, can i help you?"

"i don't know... really, i don't know"

"but tell me, sir, if there's something we can do, i'm the right person, don't you know who i am?"

"at first glance? i'm sorry, but no"

"i'm the Deputy Superintendent here at the station, and there are rumours that i may be promoted any day now, so you should take advantage of my being available while you can"

"i came for news of my son"

"his name?"

"he's known by the name of Ciente-the-Grand, he arrived here wounded..."

"oh, so you're here for news of the body?"

"what do you mean, the body?" Odonato's voice was as transparent as his own body

"your son was consigned to the fourteenth district cemetery three days ago, i thought you knew... i thought you'd come here to make an affadavit"

a sudden dizziness knocked Odonato over and he fell against the Deputy Superintendent, catching himself with one hand while seeking with the other Little Daddy's powerful shoulder, the sun perturbed him, breaking inwards through his line of vision, the city spun in his head, but he didn't faint, he succeeded in breathing deeply, telling himself that he'd already sensed this days ago

images of his son burst into his mind and, after drinking several glasses of water, he pretended to feel better and thanked the Deputy Superintendent for the information

"how many days can the body remain over in the fourteenth district?"

"well, that's a warehouse, you know, sir... if nobody claims the body, it goes into a common grave, i think you'd better hurry up, sir"

"thank you"

Little Daddy being unable to persuade Odonato to go home to his apartment for help, they went directly to the fourteenth district they caught a *candongueiro*, then another one, they walked beneath the abrasive sun, people watching with astonishment and terror the man hurrying along, exhibiting his translucent appearance

when they reached the gate of the fourteenth district cemetery, the earth barely made a sound as Odonato's feet trod upon it, not even the leaves sank beneath his weight

"you have to keep an eye out, Little Daddy"

"no problem"

"i seem to be getting lighter as well, if you hear the wind, it's up to you to hold onto me"

"yes, uncle"

"so how do we do this, with this door all locked up?"

"we do like in the time before, uncle, we clap our hands and see if someone comes"

they whistled, they clapped their hands, they shouted, but received only a hard, empty sound as a reply

they heard the sounds of birds that divided their attention between the search for crumbs and materials to construct their nests, a gaunt dog paced inside the enclosure and looked at them through the grating, as though getting the attention of the two observers, who were solitary and unaware of the power just one of their gestures might have had in solving its sudden affliction

"we're going to go in over the wall, like in the time before"

"what do you mean?"

"we're going to go around the corner and find a place to climb up, where there's a wall there's a man to climb it, as the poet used to say"

"pardon?"

"nothing... there're two of us, we'll manage it"

searching with their eyes and their hands, they found a stretch of the outside wall that had cracks and exposed bricks where their feet found purchase and they were able to climb up, first Odonato helped Little Daddy who, seated on a low parapet, hauled up the distraught father behind him, ushering him into the large yard "what now?" Little Daddy regarded the vast stretch of tombstones at rest, with their fluttering birds and morbid, fleeting, necessary decorations of dried flowers

"now we're going to go get my son's body"

"we're going to find him?" they both set off, Odonato, who appeared to possess an instinct for blood-ties stronger than any logic, deciding their route

"we have to find him, look over there," a tiny hut, like a badly finished shanty of unpainted brick, expelled a minuscule thread of smoke pungent with the smell of grilled meat

they approached, clapped their hands again, but nobody appeared, there were two little seats, dirty plates, and embers collapsing into the ashes of faltering fires to announce that a meal had ended

"let's go," Odonato continued, resolute

there's a soundless singing in cemeteries, where fresh flowers lean against each other, the brightness of their colours exhaling a life force

"there"

Odonato had glimpsed a clearing without tombstones, a helter-skelter zone of red earth and a fetid stench where a pile of bodies lay, Little Daddy went into convulsions and began to vomit

"let's get on with this," Odonato said, very serious, intimating that Little Daddy should control himself, "you haven't even eaten today and you want to vomit?"

they made a quick tour of the corpses, Odonato walked uneasily from one side to the other, his eyes nearly closed, moving more by virtue of his paternal instinct than by way of visual confirmation, they heard a far-off shout

"hey, what yous doin' over there?" the gravedigger approached them with an ancient shovel in his hand

Odonato's body shook in time with his shaky breathing

"i came to look for my son, for fuck's sake, they've been telling me for i-don't-know-how-long that he's in jail and it turns out he's here"

252

"and you entered a closed cemetery without authorization from the authorities?"

"i'm the authority over my son," Odonato spoke in a strange voice, half-blocked by the tremors of emotional exhaustion, "i came to look for my son to care for him, i'm going to take him," he went through the bodies, pulling on arms, twisting heads around

"it doesn't work like that, comrade"

"leave me in fucking peace," Odonato shoved the grave-digger, who tripped on the leg of a corpse and fell over, "does this country work? eh? does this country work somehow, Senhor Gravedigger of open-air cemeteries and documents from the authorities?"

Odonato wasn't looking at anyone, not even at the bodies that surrounded him, his own body was a blind entity, sobbing and transparent, less in search of a body than of an urgent necessity

the gravedigger got up, picked up the rusty shovel, and tried to crack his ribs, Little Daddy moved in quickly but didn't get there in time, the outraged father, cowering in the shade, watched the gravedigger's movements, before the blade could hit him, he neutralized the gravedigger with military swiftness, Odonato crouched down, whirled around, stretched out his leg and, in a movement worthy of a capoeira dancer, pulled the rug out from under the gravedigger's feet

"there he is, Little Daddy, there's my son's body"

on the far outer edge of the sea of stinking corpses, humming with flies, his son lay on the roots of a huge fig tree

the gravedigger tried to get up but couldn't reach the shovel, his back hurt and a thread of blood was seeping from a cut on his neck

"you're tryin' to get me riled up," he managed to say in reaction

but Little Daddy, moving in swiftly, kicked the side of his stomach hard, following up with a shot at the gravedigger's long-suffering back, making a lengthy, high-pitched sound like one he'd had heard in a Bruce Lee movie

Odonato was already prone, fondling his son's face, brushing away a film of reddish mud that had formed over his cheekbones, he burst into tears, the neutralized gravedigger was moaning on the ground, in the sky the swift swooping of a tumult of birds announced the men's misery in that repulsive setting

"we're going to carry the body," Odonato said, "help me carry my son's body"

"but, Uncle Odonato, i'm sorry, but where are we going to carry him to?"

"home"

hampered by the body's astonishing weight, the two men, the young man and the transparent man, worked their own bodies into a sweat as they stumbled along the path, finally reaching the cemetery's entrance, Little Daddy had taken the gravedigger's keys and opened the rusted padlock when he was overcome by the strangeness of the situation, there at the main gate of the fourteenth district cemetery, with a corpse in a dubious state of conservation and a man lacking normal skin density, whose body was outlined by the drably coloured contours of his loose clothing, damaged by the struggle

"what do we do now?"

"where there's a will there's a way," in the tone of his voice, Odonato's utterance contained, for the first time, a sign of hope

a mini-taxi skidded into the cemetery's park and drove towards them at high speed

"The Real Zé?" Little Daddy was astonished

"so it's true after all," troubled, The Real Zé looked at his friend's body

"is this car yours?"

"this isn't the time to ask questions," Odonato said, "The Real Zé, we're gonna take Ciente's body home," he pleaded

"okay, let's do it"

in the precise instant the word "home" was uttered, Ciente-the-Grand's body, already very heavy, fell hard on the ground, slipping from Odonato's and Little Daddy's filthy hands, the three men looked at one another like people peering into the depths of a mystery, each with the mild foreboding and hollow suspicion that the body might have shaken loose of its own free will, they waited a few seconds, leaving the body inert on the ground, waiting to make sure nothing else happened

death is unendurable and, in most cases, enduring, men have known this for millennia, yet they fear feeding any hope of a return

The Real Zé joined them with slow movements, crouched down and grabbed the corpse again, inviting the others to do the same

frightened, they heard a noise coming from the gate

"take it easy, i'm just coming to help you carry the body," the gravedigger said

he joined the others, and with great difficulty they raised the corpse, depositing it in the vehicle's cramped trunk

"could you just give me back the key to the padlock?"

"here it is," Odonato said, gaping at the man

"but you... you have no body colour..." the gravedigger trembled

"my apologies for the way i came to get my son's body, but i've got to prepare for the funeral"

the gravedigger, still sore, closed the padlock on the front gate with his shaking hands, retreated to his smoky shanty, and the vehicle carrying the extremely heavy corpse, with the trunk open, took off along the potholed Luanda streets towards the building that was once Ciente-the-Grand's home

"can a corpse really weigh that much?" The Real Zé asked

"i think i know the reason"

"what is it, then, Uncle Odonato?" Little Daddy was in the back seat, nauseated by the corpse's proximity and stench

"once he told me, 'even when i'm dead i won't return to your house,' that's the only possible explanation"

"that must be it," The Real Zé confirmed with a serious air

lethargic, with the exception of the Cirolian workers, the city looked as though it had been evacuated, the silence inside the houses interrupted only by radios or sad satellite dishes, the children seemed constrained from playing in a natural way, the dogs' eyes filled with a more pointed melancholy out of respect for the premature demise of Senhora Ideology

five more men offered their help when they arrived at the building, but with eight of them now trying to haul the corpse out of the car, they succeeded only with great effort

passing along the first floor, the deceased became even heavier, "what's that stench?" Comrade Mute asked, having come downstairs to help, on the third floor they stopped and had to set down the body, Strong Maria unleashed a weeping that accompanied each step with a fresh moaning chant, out of respect no one told her to be quiet, but the sound got on their nerves, it disturbed the silence they were trying to preserve to lend solemnity to the stinking upwards procession

upstairs Granma Kunjikise and Xilisbaba were preparing the living room to receive the body of the deceased

Amarelinha sobbed in silence on the broken-down living-room sofa, Seashell Seller's bag had been left on the first floor, next to the elevator with the ever-moving waters where Blind Man was refreshing himself while waiting for his friend's visit to finish

on arriving at the apartment's entrance on the sixth floor, Edú and the women had to help because the weight had become truly unbearable, Granma Kunjikise moved objects out of the way and rolled up the carpet to let the dead man pass

"*a burden in life and a burden in death*," the old woman murmured

the dead man was set down hard on the huge table that had been displaced to the kitchen, the floor creaked on receiving the weight, a crack opened up below the lower corner of the window, passed under the table, traced a line parallel to the area of the toilet, and headed towards the living room like a cobra fleeing the light of the kitchen

"careful," someone shouted

everyone saw the table slowly split, Xilisbaba lifted her hands to her mouth and broke into silent tears as Odonato hugged her, Edú left the apartment because for the last few years he'd been afraid of tales about evil spells, Granma Kunjikise raised her hands into the air as though the sky were drawing closer and watched the table crack in two, the body fell onto the shards of wood, the crack in the floor opened up little by little and everyone understood that the inevitable was on the verge of happening

the floor swallowed up Ciente-the-Grand as though gravity had turned solid and barked an order to descend

everyone saw the corpse disappear from the sixth floor, opening up a hole the exact size and shape of a corpse lying flat on its back, they peered down and saw the floor of the fifth floor yield with a piercing sound

the fourth floor collapsed more swiftly and violently, following the corpse like a dead weight, if you pardon the expression, smashing everything it found in its path, ceiling or floor, kitchen or living room, partition or the first-floor wet zone, until it plunged, with a thunderous crash, into the open space of the building's main entrance

"so it was true," Odonato peered sadly from his sixth-floor kitchen, "he didn't want to come home... we've got to find a place to bury him today"

they broke into two groups, one to try to immediately repair the damage to the building, the other to find a prompt resting place for the body, if only to neutralize the equally prompt rumours whose spread would attract the police or bring someone from the morgue

João Slowly quickly suggested that they carry the body to the Church of the Sacred Little Lamb which, aside from being a normal place to lay out the deceased, was a peaceful place where family and friends could proceed with the wake

Odonato agreed, sad and too transparent to think of anything else, and they made provisions to start repairing the sequence of holes

"but the last... the last hole should remain in memory of my son," Odonato pleaded

another group tried to get a "contribution" for the dead man's flowers, clothes, and shoes, but, above all, someone said with unexpectedness frankness, it was necessary to organize the gastronomic part of the *komba*, which would obviously include kilos and kilos of good food, countless litres of wine, beer and whisky, and in sufficient supply to last unbroken for at least three consecutive days.

just before they took him outside, the dead man was dressed in donated clothing that was a little large for him but worthy of his final condition, Strong Maria and Xilisbaba washed the body and cut his hair and nails with water carried by Little Daddy

on a small borrowed wagon, the body, already a little lighter, was finally taken to the back of Noah's Barque, where a yard decorated with dry flowers awaited the deceased, João Slowly made a point of monitoring the situation in person, and though he was not in complete charge of the management of the Church of the Sacred Little Lamb, he interrupted the service that was taking place there and begged the recently contracted Brazilian pastor to prepare the ceremony

"but just like that? not even god realizes yet that he's passed"

"don't start causing problems, man, this is a question of life or death"

"just of death, you mean"

"you still tryin' to be cute? the door's right there if you want to be fired!" João Slowly threatened

"fired already? you said this was a training period, that the first month was like an internship, hey, we've got good results, lots of the faithful have already understood our philosophy and know the whole 'am-baaah Maria'"

"good work, keep it up, you'll be my only pastor, who knows, maybe someday you'll get to be a bishop"

"you think i might make it?"

"go for it, today's your big chance, i want this service to be remembered forever, the victim's father will be here, the family, and i can ensure some politicians are here, go prepare the service, man, i want this mass to have a speech that's almost apocalyptic...!"

"good grief, man, we don't make speeches in church, we only preach to the faithful," the Brazilian said seriously

"preach, pastor, preach, but i want this ready by late afternoon, the deceased is the son of my buddy Odonato"

"very good"

"one more thing"

"tell me"

"you don't know him..." João Slowly said

"who, the dead man?"

"no, the father"

"what about him?"

"don't be shocked when he arrives, don't start making faces, try to act normal and, whatever happens, go ahead with the mass and let everything take place normally"

"Brother João Slowly, our lord Jesus said, 'do not judge so that you will not be judged, for in the way you judge, you will be judged; and by your standard of measure, it will be measured to you, whether it be physical or moral in nature, am-baaah!'"

"am-baaah!"

his hands still trembling, standing close to the hole in his kitchen, Edú sipped the verbena-leaf tea that Nga Nelucha had prepared to calm him down

once the tea was served, his wife arranged a series of objects into a perimeter around the recently created cliff in her kitchen

seated on his tiny stool, Edú heard the telephone ring but felt no desire to get up, he sucked up his tea with withered lips and a face where only his staring eyes revealed his horror at the departed's final downward movement

"oh my dear, drink, the tea will soothe you"

"but haven't you heard?"

"what?"

"that men shouldn't abuse verbena-leaf tea"

"and why not?"

"verbena-leaf tea and avocados both calm men down too much"

"but you need to calm down right away, you're agitated, my dear, look how tense you are"

"calming down is one thing, but for men verbena-leaf tea is downright dangerous"

"enough of that"

"you say that because you're a woman, verbena-leaf tea calms the parts down below," he pointed in the direction of his swollen crotch

"don't make me laugh now, you don't need to worry about that"

"you never know"

the telephone rang persistently, Nga Nelucha wiped her hands and went to pick it up

"it's Angolan Public Television, they want to talk to you, it could be news about our tour, there must some interest, maybe from an embassy"

"all right, let me answer"

with great effort, he moved over, carrying his tiny stool, and sat down on it again, buttoned up his shirt, and made a point of patting down his hair before replying

"yes, hello..."

but it had nothing to do with him or the popularity of his gigantic testicular swelling, a public relations clerk from the show *Courageous Nation* was looking for a boy named Little Daddy

"he's not here, but listen, can i give him a message or something?"

from the expression on Edú's face, Nga Nelucha sensed that it was good news, he was breathing more deeply, gasping, sweating, he looked happy and sad at the same time, his tongue licked his lips

"i don't have anything to write with, can you call back in the evening? yes, today in the evening, he should be here then, is that all right? yes, thanks..."

he hung up the phone and sat still in woeful silence, which might as easily have been prompted by good as by bad news, Nga Nelucha sat next to him on the sofa, and caressed the kitchen cloth as though it were a beloved marionette, not wanting to intrude on her husband's silence, the wind gusted against the window, opening it a little farther, letting in the soft, respectful sound of Comrade Mute's record player, in the next building Camões the rooster broke into sporadic murmurs of coughing

"what was it, Edú?"

"they found Little Daddy's mother, all the way up in Huambo..." he covered his mouth as if hiding an uncomfortable truth, "they found Little Daddy's mother!"

gripped by contradictory emotions, Strong Maria, on learning the news, smiled and hurried to tell the others, she was entrusted with finding Little Daddy and giving him the good news, they had said, also, that the interested party should contact the television program's public relations department right away in order to finalize the details, as the mother had already been contacted and arrangements to transport her to Luanda for her televised re-encounter were already at an advanced stage

in Huambo, it can be assumed, at that same hour, the lady had been informed and had already shared with her friends and neighbours not just the whereabouts of her son who had disappeared during the war years, but also the news that she was going to Luanda on a plane specially chartered by the Ministry of Social Reinsertion, with the right to one companion, male or female, as might be the lady's wish

the best clothes would already be laid out that afternoon, the lady would even have visited a talented young woman to have her hair combed into pretty braids, finally, after years of avoiding thinking about this subject, somebody from Huambo television had come to inform her, as suddenly as it was possible to pass on news, that her son was alive

"god is great," she must have said, in tears

"and the Party, as well, my lady, don't forget, all of this forms part of the Party's efforts and action plan"

Strong Maria, after looking everywhere, concluded that Little Daddy wasn't in the building, he must have been sent out by João Slowly on a mission to find flowers or doilies for the religious altar where the ceremony would take place later

"and João?" Strong Maria asked

"Uncle João went out, too, he said he had to go all the way to the airport," said one of the girls who was playing next to the building's front door.

when he arrived at the airport, late

João Slowly had no difficulty in recognizing the women who were so anxiously waiting, two genuine blondes, as he confirmed immediately, kissing them loudly, looking them over to celebrate with concealed satisfaction the fact that even their eyebrows and the fine down on their upper lips were absolutely blonde, yellow, to put it that way

"how are you doing? is everything okay? *tudo bem?*" he asked

"yes, very nice, *too-doo* okay," one blonde replied in English

"*too-doo* very good, we are officially scientistas!" the other blonde said in English

inspired by the pornographic film they had shown, but motivated above all by the collective masculine reaction of the crowd, João Slowly, who considered himself a multifaceted entrepreneur, with various undeclared business interests under way, including the Rooster Camões Cinema and the recently created Church of the Sacred Little Lamb, had decided on impulse to import two blonde prostitutes directly from Sweden, he had activated former contacts from the former Yugoslavia to Bulgaria in an effort to find two women with open minds and, preferably, equally open bodies, ready, they had said by email, to develop their careers in a country that everyone said was growing at an absolutely exceptional rate, in whatever field one might be working, even more so in the experimental field of multiracial contacts "very welcome *bem-vindas*, very nice ha-air," João Slowly was beaming, "you arrived on a good day, on the eve of an international event"

"we know, that's why we're scientistas..."

"Angola is about to introduce the world to an eclipse of unprecedented quality, never before seen, you understand?, never before seen"

"me think eclipse international in world," one of the smiling Swedes said in Portuguese

"yes, but we're coordinating the event, NASA can't compete with us, you get it? we're heading into outer space... have you ever slept in a church?"

"a church?"

"a church... of god, *deus*, also *ngana zambi*"

"amen," the prostitute joked, making the sign of the cross over her voluminous breasts

"yes, good, but in my church it's 'am-baaah'"

"am-baaah?"

"yes, like sound sheep make: Church of the Sacred Little Lamb!"

João Slowly tried to reach Little Daddy by cellphone to confirm the boy had completed his assigned chore, but a strange signal seemed to indicate the telephone was outside its network area, or even disconnected

in his rented *candongueiro* he continued straight to the church, for Odonato wanted the ceremony to take place as soon as possible, Superintendent Gadinho, along with friends, had already provided for the opening of a sepulchre in a far-away cemetery and even for the death-certificate papers to be supplied in order that there be no repetition of the mourning scene nor any increase in the "tip" due to its being a "last-minute" request

everything seemed to be set when, after Amarelinha and Granma Kunjikise had got ready to go, Odonato called Xilisbaba into the room in a tone of voice that verged on pleading

"Nato? Nato?" Xilisbaba repeated, not seeing her husband in the small space of his room "i'm here, Baba, up here"

shoeless, his socks already on, and with the old-fashioned brown suit in place, the tie well knotted and even the hat set on his head, Odonato floated near to the ceiling

"Nato!" Xilisbaba sighed, fearing for her heart, not even in these recent days had any other fear touched her so deeply

"i'm here, Xilisbaba, i haven't been able to get my shoes on"

Odonato, almost totally transparent, his hands practically invisible, bobbed close to the ceiling with a cloud-like docility, he spun slowly above her body, pressing his hands against the ceiling, and steadied himself on the wire from which the light was suspended, avoiding touching the hot bulb

"i'm too light"

"so what do we do?"

"take out my shoelaces, tie them together, and pass me the end"

Xilisbaba, controlling her tears, managed to calm down, she pulled the laces out of his shoes, tied them, slid off her own shoes, climbed up onto the bed, and passed Odonato the end of the reasonably long string, Odonato struggled to navigate against his weightlessness, but quickly tied the string around his ankle with a firm movement

"all right, we're ready to go."

Granma Kunjikise left the sixth-floor apartment, followed by Amarelinha, who wore an equally old-fashioned flowered dress worn threadbare by countless washings, and, finally, Xilisbaba, moving with a particular care, gripping the laces and her suspended husband, who struggled to maintain a tranquil expression in spite of his weightless condition

"let's go, they must be waiting for us at the church"

on leaving the building, the entourage was joined by Comrade Mute, dressed in a conservative black suit with well-shined shoes, Nga Nelucha and her husband Edú, who walked with effort, having refused to leave his tiny wooden stool at home, and Strong Maria, who carried huge flowers in her arms, they were joined by Blind Man and Seashell Seller with his ubiquitous bag, the noise and smell of the beautiful seashells pitting the noise of whitecaps, which sounded like a weeping song, against his muted strides

"aren't you coming with us, sir?"

Strong Maria asked the Mailman, who approached them

"to where?"

"they found the body at last, we're going to bury Senhor Odonato's son"

"then i'll go, yes"

the church was "composed," as they say in Luanda, with last-minute flowers and some snacks served discreetly at the entrance, the body reposed in the hurriedly purchased open casket of inappropriate dimensions, the pastor was nervous but tried to disguise it,

the family arrived and was received with tears and wailing, Odonato was pulled by his wife and tied to a metal-edged flower bed still without flowers and remained there for long minutes, suspended, ethereal, and transparent,

"is everything to your liking, sister?" João Slowly asked Xilisbaba while seeking to maximize the curious stares in the direction of the two blonde bombshells who accompanied him

"everything's fine, thanks"

"and you, brother, are you parked?" he laughed at Odonato

"as best i can be," Odonato replied

"as god wills," the pastor murmured

the blondes were given a place at the end of the row of plastic chairs, they forced themselves to put on a more serious and dignified expression for the purposes of the event, they thought that Odonato's condition was due to some Angolan ruse, they had doubts about the nature of the ceremony but quickly realized, from the sincerity of the suffering, that this death was not part of a circus trick, they tried the Angolan snacks with gratitude and smiled even more on receiving glasses full of whisky with lots of ice in their delicate hands "that prick Little Daddy hasn't shown up," João Slowly said

"it's true," Strong Maria confided, "i haven't told you yet, they called from National Television, they found his mother"

"the guy's gonna be real happy, wonderful… this country's wonderful!" he raised his glass to the two Swedes

"and who are these two? this is how they come dressed for a funeral?"

"they just arrived, Maria, i went to pick them up at the airport"

"but who are they?"

"they're two Swedes who've come straight from the Europes to maximize business"

"what business? the church? they're the 'sacred little lambs'?"

"they came here to maximize revenue in the world's oldest business, imagine the success, you can see how everybody's looking at them…"

"and how they've got their boobies nearly hanging out, go see if you can get them shawls, they need to show more respect, even if this is just the Church of the Sacred Little Lamb"

"i'm already looking into that…" he glanced at the main door and saw the tax inspectors come in, "look who's here, that's all i need"

the tax inspectors entered dressed in formal black and with appropriately funereal expressions on their faces, they went first to Xilisbaba and her floating husband to express their most elevated condolences and then cast an appraising gaze over the church's amenities, they spoke briefly with the Brazilian pastor and only then headed towards João Slowly

"nice set-up you've got here, new floor, pretty plastic chairs"

"thank you, were you acquainted with the deceased?"

"to a certain degree," This Time said

"yes, to a certain degree," Next Time agreed

"then, to a certain degree, are you staying for the ceremony?"

"yes, and afterwards we want to talk to you about business"

"i understand"

"and the two blonde babes, are they new acquisitions, or friends of the family?"

"new propositions, let's put it that way"

"and in what area are they propositioning? the cinematographic?"

"maybe, maybe, you never know... it all depends on how much we talk"

"oh, you mean we can already start to talk about how much"

"one can always talk about 'how much,' my friends, we're in Luanda!"

"that's true," the tax inspectors smiled at the blondes, who responded each time with open laughter and light nudges to rearrange their voluminous brassieres

"we can talk later, the ceremony's about to begin"

"fine, and what are we listening to?"

"classical music, the parlance of angels, appropriate for a ceremony of this gravity," João Slowly explained

"yes, sir, people are going to be talking about this church"

"let's hope"

"stereo sound, plenty of speakers, very nice, god is in the details of Dolby Surround, very nice"

"it's a direct connection to the system of my friend Noah, the one with the bar, but in the future we'll have our own set-up"

Strong Maria handed out napkins to all the guests, except for the Swedes, and once they had wiped their hands and mouths, they fraternized, whisky glasses in hand, while the pastor began the ceremony

"my brothers... Angolans and other nationalities," the pastor winked at one of the blondes, "we're here to celebrate..."

João Slowly gave a deliberate cough, looking at the pastor

"it's Ciente-the-Grand," Odonato corrected, secured now to the armrest of one of the chairs, he drifted above the level of the pastor's eyes

"yes, our brother Ciente-the-Grand, now departed to the gates of the garden of our lord god... here and now we invoke his name, i mean both their names, that of our lord on high, and the name of our beloved brother, whose family is gathered here, and also his friends, both Angolans and those of other nationalities," the pastor winked at the other blonde, "lending this simple homage a spirit that rises to the heavens"

the pastor met Odonato's eyes, regretted his phrasing, coughed

"let us be aware that the house of our lord god, and that of his son, Senhor Jesus, is present everywhere, in the physical and psychological space of this world, in all places, including in our hearts," he made a deliberate pause

"am-baaah," João Slowly said in a loud voice, inviting all those present to repeat after him, and after the pastor

"am-baaah!" repeated the multitude

"thus, in this religious homage, availing ourselves of the hospitality of our recently inaugurated Church of the Sacred Little Lamb, we are gathered here in the company of the body and the spirit... not of a saint... but of a good man, good at least during his infancy on the streets of Luanda," he hesitated, "and later... his career evolved through certain moral and even physical errors, as he chose a path little approved of by our lord god or by his son, Jesus, fruit of the artificial insemination... i mean the immaculate insemination, of his mother, the Virgin Mary, may god protect her and keep her free of sin"

"am-baaah," João Slowly said, very loudly, regarding the pastor with a threatening air

"but god chooses the roads and detour, god places the stones where we will trip over them, god knows the suffering of our stumblings and the swellings of our bodies," the pastor looked in the direction of the Swedes, who were re-arranging their brassieres with sensual smoothness, "it is god who gropes... i mean grows, in our bodies and our suffering, god who speaks through our sinful mouths, now and in the hour of our death"

"am-baaah," everyone said

"our beloved Ciente-the-Grand is now seated next to our lord god, speaking with him... facing him, giving him an account of his days and his actions... who knows? who here can say what they may be discussing at this moment? Ciente-the-Grand grew up and was born in Luanda, here he was a child, here he became a young man, with his own very particular activities, and, as people say here in Luanda, who knows what rumours Ciente may be passing along to god at this very moment?"

the multitude almost broke into open laughter on hearing such religious speculation, of a supposedly cultural nature, but João Slowly, making use of a strange hand signal, urged the pastor to continue the ceremony without fewer digressions, of whatever nature they might be

"the power and will of our lord is great, as is that of his immaculate son, Jesus... therefore, let us pray, brothers, let us pray for our brother who ascended to the heavens at the hour and in the instant that god called him to his side... let us pray... in the name of the father, the son, and the holy ghost..."

"am-baaah," everyone said

"in the name of our blessed Little Lamb, who is in god's presence, at his feet..."

"am-baaah"

"brothers... let us pronounce in silence our prayers of the ushering of our brother Ciente into the house of our lord god... let us pray that his moral wounds be cured, and that god take note with excessive clarity of our brother's wounds... i'm not speaking, of course, of the wounds in the region of his rump, but of his moral wounds... which are the deepest, and which god pardons and has already pardoned in others, and of himself... just as we shall one day pardon those who trespass against us," he fixed his gaze on the Swedes' chests, "who trespass against us with their visions... with their bodies... with their fiery eyes... let us pray in silence, brothers... am-baaah!"

"am-baaah," murmured the faithful and the rest over the whispers that fluttered around their prayers the sad rhythm of a Beethoven sonata stretched out, spurred on here and there by the swift hands of the pianist interpreting it

Noah was at the door, he hadn't come to this sort of place for years, and he strained to prevent himself from laughing at the Brazilian pastor's homily, the people closed their eyes, with the exception of Odonato who, like a distracted child, spun, his body suspended, his arms opening as though embracing the air, making the string tethering him to the chair's armrest the axis of his slow rotation, his body winding around, spinning to the left and remaining very still, awaiting the inverse motion that the string would initiate, regarding his son's face with tenderness and sadness, and appreciating, by virtue of the full view afforded him by his tightrope routine, the faces and gestures of the others present, until his movements ceased and he looked at his wife as she, feeling herself being watched, opened her eyes

"close the casket, Baba, this tale's gone on long enough"

everything that looked planned in advance was due, according the version of the true believers, to divine will or, as the Brazilian pastor would say, "to god who knows all and plans all"

when Xilisbaba closed the casket the pastor extinguished the candles on the improvised altar and initiated a ceremony for the distribution of flowers, one for each individual present, in a movement that began next to the altar and extended, by way of the flowers' passage, to the chairs at the back, where the blondes sat peacefully, and, when the crowd got to its feet in respectful silence, the sonata was abruptly interrupted and the voice of the National Radio announcer was heard saying

"we interrupt this broadcast to transmit, through the whole national territory of the Republic of Angola, a message from His Excellency, the Engineer, the President of the Republic of Angola..."

people looked at each other, then at the pastor, who for his part turned towards João Slowly who, as surprised as everyone else, tured his gaze upward in the direction of Odonato "let's listen in, it could be something important..."

those who were outside squeezed into the church in order to better hear the message that National Radio would transmit any minute now, a few moments of silence followed, hit songs were being cued up, two slaps to the microphone preceded the Comrade President's cough, and then his voice was heard and continued in a serious tone,

"dear citizens of the Republic of Angola, representatives of other countries accredited in our nation, religious and civic bodies: in the name of the national government of Angola and as the outcome of an extraordinary session of the political bureau of the Party, i am fulfilling my duty to inform you of a decision that will have implications in the social, political, and cultural life of each of us, after analyzing the most recent national events, taking into account the relevance of their moral implications and political significance, since the days of our independence, taking into account also the deep consternation of the entire population of the Republic of Angola, much mature reflection has been given to the events and phenomena scheduled to take place on the nation's soil, perpetrating in our lives events of incommensurable magnitude, even so, the Party in power understands that, in Angola, this is not the most propitious moment for the fulsome celebrations that are so quickly approaching," the President coughed lightly, "it being so, and given the recent passing of Comrade Ideology, one of the moral and civic pillars of our nation, the Party in power has decided to cancel any and all collective celebrations, declaring a period of three days of national mourning, in this context, and imbued with the power that is vested in me, i am taking advantage of this communiqué to affirm that Angola announces to the nation and the world the cancellation, i repeat, the absolute cancellation, of the eclipse scheduled for the coming days, efforts will be undertaken to minimize any economic damage that this decision may cause, but from this moment forward the Party declares utterly cancelled the much-awaited total eclipse."

"that's all we needed"

"holy fuck, if i'd known i wouldn't've come here"

the foreigners moaned

it was frustrating to witness, in this way, the alteration of the course of events and collective expectations, not by acts of nature but rather by human will, even when that alteration was depicted as the fruit of a wise decision taken by a group of people, in the present case, a political collective

"do you think they're serious?"

said the voices expressing the general shock and disbelief out loud, since, at least within narrow circles, freedom of speech had not yet fallen victim to control

the young BBC journalist reported live using her cellphone, pressed up against a speaker broadcasting the sound of National Radio, which was followed by her diligent but abridged translation, which initially provoked laughter and derisive comments in the world's main news services, but shortly afterwards the news was confirmed scientifically by NASA and other equivalent agencies, something in the planet's movements had been changed

and it was true that the eclipse, cancelled by the Angolan nation, was no longer going to occur, as per the announcement made by Our Excellency, the Engineer, and Comrade President

"the Party's going to have to rethink the situation," Dom Crystal-Clear commented

"well, changing an eclipse's agenda is a complicated business, even for the Party..." said the Advisor Santos Prancha

"they'll have to come up with something"

"yes, the population's already been stockpiling beer and food..."

"good god, there must be some scheme behind all this that we're not seeing"

"you really think so?"

"of course, man, the Party doesn't lift a finger without some purpose"

"is that what people are saying?"

"ha! they don't lift a finger without *scoring* a point"

National Radio, underlining the feeling of loss, followed the President's remarks with a well-rehearsed rendition of the National Anthem, during which those attending Ciente-the-Grand's funeral, the ladies and their dresses, the men with well-waxed shoes and glasses of whisky in their hands, the smiling Brazilian pastor, those not invited to the burial and Odonato, safe in his wife's firm grasp, floating in a sudden gust of wind, left the Church of the Sacred Little Lamb to the measured tones of the National Anthem, which gave the funeral an absolutely unforgettable and highly appropriate feel

"onward?" João Slowly asked

"of course," Odonato replied, "oh how lovely, João, National Radio playing the anthem at my son's funeral!"

with the exception of the Swedes, everyone returned to the apartment building

carrying in their hands the leftover food to be consumed over the next three days, their stomachs filled with alcohol, their eyes shining, now with tears, now simply because they were moistened by the beers and wine and whiskies they had consumed

the funeral cortege made a silent, symbolic pause on arriving at the apartment building's entrance, Odonato asked to be lowered to the level of the other people and so, glancing up from the floor down below, he set himself to pondering the strange hole his son had made right down to the ground floor of the building

Granma Kunjikise murmured something inaudible in Umbundu and glanced at her tired feet, Amarelinha rubbed her arms, brushing away a sudden shiver

on the first floor, around the waters, the temperature was so superhumanly pleasing that it became difficult to resist the spot

Edú set down his tiny stool and eased the weight off his back by leaning against the wall, Nga Nelucha stood next to him, stroking his head, her husband closed his eyes, pretending to succumb to a premature sleepiness and wearing a childlike smile on his lips, Granma Kunjikise folded one of her cloths and sat down on the floor, the string that tethered Odonato to the world of those who walked the earth was tied to a railing, Xilisbaba seated herself next to him, at an angle, crossed her legs and drew a deep breath, Amarelinha excused herself and went upstairs, Comrade Mute did the same and asked the family of the deceased whether the sound of "appropriate light music" would offend them because it was his custom to fall asleep to a few bars of jazz, João Slowly, already seated, tugged his wife's hand and Strong Maria leaned towards him, Blind Man was led to a corner and also wore on his face the indecipherable smile of those who cannot see the world through the daylight, Seashell Seller left without anyone noticing, headed upstairs and it was then that, softly, the old woman's voice was heard, at first light and sweet, an imperceptible murmuring of many voices beneath the stroking of an intense light, then at a slow cadence with a soft slapping of her hands in the water that covered the floor keeping them company, their heads kept time with the free-flowing rhythm that Granma Kunjikise imprinted on her venerable song, several imaginary instruments fitted within her one-woman chorus, and the water appeared to run out of the walls in counterpoint to her vocal rhythm, and they all seemed to be hypnotized when they were interrupted by the freakish sounds that the rooster Camões gave off at that late hour, the interruption being followed by the less-acoustic music that Comrade Mute had chosen to play

"hey, Little Daddy, go upstairs and tell him Granma's singing is better than that jazz"

"who you talkin' to?" Strong Maria asked

"ah, it's a habit, that boy took off on me today, he's not even answering the phone" "i'll go up there," Nga Nelucha offered to help, "but i'm not coming back down, my legs hurt"

"and you're so young," Edú laughed, lazily scratching his gigantic *mbumbi*.

"young people work a lot, didn't you know that?"

"young people were made to dance," Edú sighed

a few moments later, up above, Comrade Mute's turntable stopped its droning and Odonato's sad voice was heard between the drip-dripping beats of the water

"sing, mother, your voice is so beautiful"

Granma Kunjikise, her eyes closed, sang in the sad rhythm of a sordine murmur, in the brief pauses she slapped her hands in the water, swayed her head from side to side, and trembled with her eyes closed

"*i'm going to sing a sad song...*"

up above, on the terrace, below the abandoned seats of the Rooster Camões Cinema, Amarelinha's bare feet soothed the floor and the night, the moon waited to find its voice in other choruses, her peaceful gaze concentrated on the rooster, which calmed down and began to regard the body of the young woman and that of the young man behind her

"don't be afraid," Seashell Seller murmured, embracing her very gradually, "i'm the sea approaching a shell..."

"i'm not afraid," Amarelinha smiled, "i'm looking at the moon"

"and i'm looking at you"

"you can't see me"

"i see you every night when i think about you, miss"

"you think about me every night?" Amarelinha turned around to look at him, resting her face and mouth close to his

"almost every night," he tried to kiss her

"if you want to give me a kiss you have to ask my father or my grandmother"

"i'll ask later," Seashell Seller gave her clumsy kiss

she laughed her open laugh, then composed her face and straightened her dress, gripping the Seashell Seller's strong, lean arms, tugging his bag off his shoulder, embracing him with all her strength, and kissing him again

"you've got to go slowly, kisses have to be slow"

"okay"

Seashell Seller's body shook and, feeling naked, he groped with his hands in the air, seeking a gesture that might calm him, with his foot he assured himself that the bag was nearby, he heard the sound of shells inside the bag as he touched it and they sank down to stretch out on the floor, the white moonlight ambled over their bodies, few stars were visible in the sky

"i like the stars," she said

"i like your shells and your hands," she said

the wind passed over the first floor, Granma Kunjikise opened her eyes now and then, rested her gaze on each of those present, sang, intoned sounds that imitated those of instruments and insects, allowed the echoes to assist her whenever more than one voice was required, and spoke very slowly to spill out her truths in Umbundu

"*it's an elderwoman's song... her husband went away to war... he went away to war many times, there were many wars... now she weeps for her husband's death... there are many people around her...*"

Odonato's body dangled, slowly lost its axis, spun back on itself trying not just to listen but to see the old woman's mouth as it went on singing and speaking, drawing the rhythm of the tale she told into the rhythm of her voice, speaking and singing at the same time

"*only she can sing or speak... this old woman has a name, her name is She-Who-Doesn't-Dance... who doesn't know how to dance... she cries, slowly gets up, tells her tale... about how many times she prepared her husband's weapons for war, how many times he promised to return... and of that time he left early in the morning, very early, he didn't say anything... he went away without saying anything... the old woman cries, sings, and begins to dance... the children are shocked... "the old woman's dancing!"*"

*they say in chorus... "the old woman who doesn't know how to
dance is dancing" ...only the children and the old woman can
speak...the old woman starts to dance little by little, a rhythm for
her body alone... she cries... my husband went to war to die... my
husband went to war to die... my husband didn't say goodbye... i
didn't clean my husband's weapons... she cries and dances for the
first time in her life... the old woman dances slowly and cries...
she looks at the children... my husband went to war to die and
today i'm dancing... i'm dancing because my husband died in the
war...and the children shout in chorus... "the old woman who
doesn't know how to dance is dancing" ...she's dancing out of sadness... at her husband's death... "the old woman's dancing..." sing
the children... the old woman dances slowly and, alone, she enters
her reed hut... only the children stay close to the fire to sing... "the
old woman danced!" "the old woman danced!""*

Xilisbaba grabbed hold of the string, pulled her husband
behind her, and went up the stairs in silence

later, Granma Kunjikise will reach her bed, remove the
traditional cloths from her body and, after many years, will
sleep naked, Granma Kunjikise will sleep naked, Granma
Kunjikise will sleep naked with the wind brushing over her
body, smiling, she is naked because she senses that her granddaughter is naked on the terrace with wind brushing over her
body, Amarelinha will arrive much later, will enter the apartment with a smile hidden behind her hands, she's going to go
to bed next to the old woman, she's going to sleep naked, her
heart secretly aflutter, she's going to gently cuddle her still-
hard breasts, she's going to caress her stomach

Seashell Seller is going to descend the stairs slowly, he's
going to find Blind Man sitting in a corner with his lips open
in laughter, Blind Man, silent and awake, is going to allow
himself to be led to the faraway beach without asking a question, observing the respect that elders know how to show for
younger people, he's going to smile in silence, within himself,
with the inner smile of those who are certain of a secret,

Edú is going to go home and wake up his wife, Nga Nelucha is going to pretend that she's still sleeping and that she wants to sleep, she's naked, she's sweating, and the wind that makes the window rattle and reminds her of her own presence tastes good to her, Edú is going to take off his clothes and come to bed naked, he's going to let his hands awaken the young woman's body, he's going to kiss her breasts and whisper ancient words in her ear, Nga Nelucha is going to take his sex in her firm, moist hand, she's going to say in a serious voice, "you want to start these games today, on the day of a burial," she's going to let her voice flow out in languid provocation, "love doesn't offend death," Edú is going to reply, pulling himself into an acrobatic pose to hold his swelling obliquely away from her and slowly penetrate his wife, "i can't fall asleep like that..." she's going to say, his hand is going to caress her back along her spinal column, his fingers are going to touch her mouth, her tongue is going to vibrate and her buttocks will make fresh movements, "let me sleep... let me sleep," she's going to say at each of his minimalist, pleasure-inducing retreats and advances intended to provoke more pleasure, "sleep... sleep, woman," he's going to murmur in her ear, more slowly and erotically with each repetition, in contrast with the rapid undulating movements she's making, "ay!" he's going to shout when she deliberately strikes his swollen *mbumbi*, "oh, sorry," she'll say ironically, hitting it again, "let me sleep," her voice is going to say, panting, waiting, and extending her delayed orgasm, "sleep... sleep," he'll say, leaving their bodies to speak in the drowsy heat, naked, happy, waiting for soothing dreams or no dreams at all,

Strong Maria will be in her apartment tidying up the kitchen, it's never her preference to leave this chore for the wee hours, she's going to smile when she hears the sound of moaning coming from the lower floors, she will put away leftovers that she'll ask Little Daddy to take to the rooster tomorrow, she'll listen to the sound of João Slowly entering the apartment, sitting down in the living room, taking off his shoes, the radio will be turned on for the last news broadcast of the day, the international community is troubled, not to say outraged, by the Angolan government's decision to cancel the eclipse as though this phenomenon were its exclusive property, João Slowly, smiling, will remember again that he has to call Little Daddy

and he's going to call, and Strong Maria will be in the kitchen hearing her partner's incredulous voice

"hello, Little Daddy? finally"

"it's not Little Daddy! what Little Daddy are you talking about?"

"i'm sorry, the lines must have got crossed, these phones are crap"

Strong Maria will feel a shiver run up her spine

another woman, much older, in the country's south, in the city of Huambo, seated in her yard looking at the bright white light, will also feel a shiver run up her spine, a common tear will appear in both women's eyes, the white will unsettle them for a few seconds, they'll feel a strange tremor in their lower lips and both will think it's nothing in particular, Strong Maria will feel another, more palpable shiver listening to her husband's voice again, as he calls the same number

"hello, Little Daddy?"

"i already told you there's no Little Daddy here"

"but who am i talking to?"

"it's the thief!"

"what?"

"it's the thief talkin' here, you get it?"

"but what thief?"

"the thief, man! i stole this cellphone, you're talkin' to the thief, you got a fuckin' problem with that?"

"enough kidding around, just pass the damn phone to Little Daddy"

"oh, was that his name? hey, listen, i already told you, this is the thief talkin', you want to negotiate or what?"

"i'm talking to the thief, for real?" João Slowly became irritated

"yeah, you could say that, how much are you going to give me for the phone?"

"i'm gonna give you one hell of a beating, that's what i'm gonna do"

"not so fast, dude, i already drilled the guy, now it's just you who can get a return on this Nokia"

"listen to me, you fucking son of a bitch, you know who you're talking to?"

"what son of a bitch is that? are you going to pay or not? fuck, you're making me waste the phone's battery, on top of that i don't even have a charger here! hey, i'm gonna get off the line…"

Strong Maria dropped the dishcloth on the floor, sat down close to her husband, moved closer, grabbed his hand, her hand was cold, João Slowly's was warm, it was trembling, his breathing was shuddering with anxious rage, he hesitated before dialling the number again, he looked at his wife as though about to ask a crucial question, but Strong Maria did as wives do, she sat quiet and motionless

a mere mirror turning her husband's question back on him

"hello?"

"yes, all right, tell me, how much is it going to be?"

"we'll talk about the price later…" he paused, deflected his gaze out the window, perhaps looking for the moon, "but what happened? where's Little Daddy?"

"i already told you, i robbed the guy, he went crazy and refused to give me the phone, i drilled the guy with a shot in the back"

"where did this happen? are you kidding or what?"

"i'm not kidding, fuck, what do you think happened? i went ahead and swiped it, the guy wasn't moving"

"where did he fall?"

"someplace in Vila Alice or something"

"listen to me, you fucking son of a bitch, fucking prick, your mother's cunt…"

"whoah, who do you think you're talkin' to?"

"shut your fucking mouth," João Slowly shouted with swollen eyes, "i just want to know where the kid is?"

"what do i know? i already told you, he was on the ground, i'm not an ambulance"

"where's the kid, you fucker? where's the kid gone, you fucking son of a bitch? where's the kid?"

the thief hung up, João Slowly, shaken by tears, fell to the floor, crying compulsively and repeating, "where's the kid...where's the kid..." countless times, with his wife plastered to his body, enveloping him with as many arms as she could, trying to adopt the rhythm of his breathing, both of them gasping, both of them crying, "where's the kid, Maria...where's that kid gone?," in order, little by little, to draw him into a calmer rhythm, silent tears, so she could stop squeezing him so hard, so that she, too, could begin her tardy tears

"what happened?" Xilisbaba, frightened, had entered the apartment

the couple paused for the time it took them to share a glance and their pain and say in a single, muffled voice

"they killed the kid"

"who?" Xilisbaba was trembling

"Little Daddy"

João Slowly hugged Xilisbaba and his wife as though he had no more strength in his body or his voice

"they killed the kid... they killed the kid, Xilisbaba!"

when he found out what had happened, Odonato was overtaken by a sadness so deep that Xilisbaba was afraid

she was afraid his condition would worsen and she didn't know how to anticipate which direction this worsening would take, she prepared a verbena-leaf tea but her husband remained absolutely silent, only his sad eyes spoke, he drank the tea, taking nearly an hour to finish it

"take me up to the terrace, Baba, i need to be alone"

"to the terrace?"

"yes, i'm going to spend the night up there so i can look out at the city... to think about life... can you take me?"

it was so early in the morning—so early in the morning inside her—that Xilisbaba had difficulty discerning what she felt, among the various emotional truths her body had absorbed during the day, she grabbed the string, climbed the stairs, reached the terrace with her husband, the Rooster Camões woke up and came to look out at them with curiosity, but since no one paid it any attention, or even looked in its direction, the rooster avoided making noise and returned to its corner

"leave me here, please"

"here, where? i can't just leave you like that"

"tie me to those antennas, i'll stay here at the edge, looking out over the city"

Xilisbaba lashed him to an antenna, tied two or three knots, fearful from having agreed to this request

and if her husband untied himself? and if a strong wind visited him during the night? and if the knots on the antenna or his ankles weren't strong enough and her husband came undone and soared through the skies of Luanda?

"are you all right? i'm afraid to leave you like that, Nato"

"i'm fine"

"are you tied up tight?"

"yes, i am, Baba: nostalgia ties me to this city"

Xilisbaba went home to her kitchen, and found Granma Kunjikise completely naked in the kitchen

"Mother! you gave me a shock"

"*i came to boil water*"

the old woman, dragging her feet and her wrinkled skin, returned to her bed, kissed Amarelinha on the forehead, and covered herself with one of her cloths

in the moonlit darkness, Xilisbaba prepared her tea, looked in the kitchen drawer for the leftover end of a candle that she liked to light when she meditated or prayed, lit the candle and felt more at ease because across the street from the building, on a broad wall, she was able to see her winged husband's oscillating shadow dancing slowly, spinning from one side to another in accord with the rhymes whispered by the night-time breeze

to prompt her thinking, one hand dropped bits of wax into her other hand, later switching hands, she imitated her own gestures in a trance

the brief pain of the wax hardening
in her solitude

a woman with a burning candle in her hand needed to be somewhere else, or not to be herself, or to be in another life

a woman with a candle in her hand who had long ago accepted her body, her destiny, now and then turned to glance at the door, then ascertained that a few drops had escaped from her hand and hardened on the table

the window was opened gradually by an unlikely breeze and she smiled as though she were going along with it

if the woman hadn't smiled, would the window have closed again?

the same breeze nearly extinguished the flame, signals such as these brought the woman back to her reality, seated in the kitchen, the woman travelled so far in her thoughts that it was difficult to remember where she had been

a woman needs to remain still in order to go so far
and she goes

she comes back from there with a tear that doesn't reach her mouth, she intercepts the tear before the taste of salt can dye her tongue, for that would be to know a tear twice

coming from so far away, it's enough to have tasted the tear once

and she thinks

«the candle has to stay in the kitchen so that others, who are in darkness, may make use of its light.»

then he knew
a delicate chill in his ribs
and saw the map of his own blood spread on the ground —
feeling that this was how he would die, longing for his mother

[from Little Daddy's sensations]

thousands of balloons, black, yellow and red, were distributed through all the neighbourhoods, and the colours mixed with the children's smiles as well as with the sound of the Party's cars announcing that night's celebrations

people reacted with an outpouring of relief in response to the sadness and upheaval they had lived through recently, radio and television ran interviews with people who declared with conviction that they smelled or saw residues of a dark compound that signalled the presence of black gold right in their backyards

"the government has to come to my place right away, the road to the future goes through my backyard, i'm sure of it," a middle-aged man shouted, as he rambled down the street, gripping his seventh early-morning bottle of beer

"there's more oil than oil tankers," a young poet bawled, "i've devoted my work to the era we're presently living through in our city, i'm only a few pages shy of reaching the fateful conclusion of this masterpiece," he concluded, exalted, hugging a young woman who was as drunk as he was, "therefore... here's a high alert to the nation's poetry publishers and general publishers of other genres... i'm taking my place in Angolan literature, right from my neighbourhood, which will be the biggest oil producer of them all... my work is based on real facts, the oil will be real..."

people reacted with hollow fury

it's often like that in Luanda, there's a generalized feeling that fantasy and celebration are the obligation and moral duty of each Luandan, the citizen is genetically programmed to join the party, paying little regard to either prior explanations or future consequences, but only to its intense homage to human sloth in that time known as the present

few were aware, during the early hours of the day, and in spite of the news in the main organs of the press, that the party that would take place that night was as a result, precisely, of the first oil geyser discovered the previous morning, in a neighbourhood whose identity had not been divulged

and that the event, announced in the morning by the distribution of balloons, brightly coloured T-shirts, flags and crates of beer, would enable the observer to behold, during the late afternoon and all night long, a monumental concert that would feature huge light shows, the most modern speaker systems on the planet, a gamut of A-list national musicians assembled at the last minute and paid big bucks in real dollars, a show of semi-naked beauty queens motivated by the thought of making their lives comfortable in a couple of hours and even a megalomaniac pyrotechnical performance taking place simultaneously in several neighbourhoods of the city that would culminate, precisely, with a wicked explosion over the meandering Luanda Bay

"you're our first little geyser, the materialization of the Angolan dream," the Minister said, opening the bottle of French champagne ordered for the occasion

"you're a man who thinks ahead, Minister," Dom Crystal-Clear laughed

"i knew the great day would arrive... Dona Creusa, bring us the appropriate glasses for this liquid"

"yes, Senhor Minister"

"are you having champagne, Advisor, or something else?"

"i'm having something else, Senhor Minister, don't be offended, but our national drink is the best remedy to ward off bodily ailments," the Advisor said, opening his bottle of thirty-year-old whisky, "this whisky... to tell the truth, it makes me choke up" "choke up?" Dom Crystal-Clear asked

"choke up completely, Senhor Crystal-Clear, take a good look at this beauty," and he grabbed the box, pulling from inside it a bottle and various printed contents, "have you ever seen a whisky that came with a dictionary? whoah, the stuff those whites come up with!"

the buddies laughed, the champagne glasses arrived, the bottle was opened

"to our little national geyser, the most difficult of all petroleums"

"to the most difficult!" the Minister toasted

the Advisor's two tax inspectors, This Time and Next Time, were invited to the celebration, as was the serene Dona Creusa, beneath the disapproving eye of the Advisor, who was not in the habit of sharing drinks or toasts with his subordinates

"let's make an exception in honour of this event," the Advisor murmured, then said in a low voice, "Dona Creusa, this ice is a disaster, i've been waiting five minutes for the whisky to cool down"

"don't you want to try the champagne, Senhor Advisor? it's really cold"

"don't meddle in political issues of a liquid nature, Senhora Civil Servant, just because you got a lift with Dom Crystal-Clear now you think you can weigh in on the temperatures of the leaders' whisky?"

"i'm sorry, Senhor Advisor, it was just a suggestion"

"then i suggest a whole lot more planning to get an icier ice cube, this one's an embarrassment to the Senhor Minister's office"

"yes, Senhor Advisor"

the tax inspectors accepted and redoubled their appreciation of good champagne, not understanding in the least what this celebration was about, but according to Luandan logic a series of toasts involving a French drink in the company of a Minister did not need to be questioned "and that chore i assigned you, was it successfully completed?" the Advisor felt good speaking out loud about work in the Minister's presence

"yes, Senhor Advisor, it was duly completed"

"what is the practical outcome?"

"up to now, we've assembled fifteen new dates"

"only fifteen?"

"we only went to the major embassies, Senhor Advisor, we still haven't visited the consulates and other diplomatic delegations"

"look, get it done, the cabinet ministers' meeting is only a week away"

"yes, Senhor Advisor"

"what mission was this?" Dom Crystal-Clear asked in a serious voice

"pragmatic data for a new proposal to cabinet based on my personal advice to the Senhor Minister"

"about what?"

"the national adoption of 'solidarity holidays'"

"what?"

"Angola must adopt a position of greater solidarity with influential countries as well as with the so-called emerging countries"

"what do holidays have to do with it?"

"i asked the comrade tax inspectors to make a list of other nations' most important holidays, and we're going to try to get the cabinet to approve a plan of adopting the pertinent dates"

"to be holidays here?"

"exactly, Senhor Crystal-Clear, exactly! here in Angola we work too much"

"i understand," Dom Crystal-Clear discontinued

"for that reason, we're going to have new holidays to consider, or even to see if we introduce new dates to support three-day weekends, without losing the weekend perspective"

"the weekend perspective?"

"yes, maintaining the official position of delaying until Monday any holiday that falls on a Sunday and also, within the scope of the country's national reconstruction, a new philosophy for three-day weekends"

"three-day weekends?" the Minister, also, was unaware of the stringency of the Advisor's planning

"mandatory three-day weekends, that is, a holiday that falls on a Thursday is a three-day weekend! a weekend that goes on until Monday, if it's a really, really important holiday, let's say, for example, a friendly power's independence day, let's imagine Mozambique, if it falls on a Wednesday, we declare an extended three-day weekend, by automatic decree, the Thursday and Friday working days are cancelled, and you only go back to work on Monday, or even, with a certain amount of respectful tolerance, on Monday afternoon, that's to say very nearly on Tuesday morning!" the Advisor served himself another whisky, "but fifteen holidays strikes me as not being enough, because, after all, the year has three hundred sixty-five days, not counting leap years"

"can i try this whisky, Senhor Advisor?" This Time asked

"are you crazy or something?" the Advisor grew serious, crinkling his eyebrows in a manoeuvre that was nearly physically impossible, "you think you're old enough to drink whisky that comes with a dictionary? are you of age? you young guys really like to push it"

"i'm sorry, Senhor Advisor"

"even if you'd come up with more holidays... you guys have got to be smart about this, it's not just following the lead of powerful countries like the United States, it's also looking at the others, for example, Burma or Cambodia, the Kosovos, the Chechnyas, those places that have massacres and complicated histories, those are the ones that deliver good holidays, you get it?"

"yes, Senhor Advisor"

"you've got to take into account religious holidays, historical data, the deaths of historical leaders, the Gandhis, the

African leaders, even if they're from past centuries, are you listening to me?"

"yes, Senhor Advisor"

"read up on it, boys, do some research, even if it's on the internet... when did the great Shaka Zulu die? isn't there any information out there? was it more than a month ago? if there aren't any facts, Angola could even make a contribution as the first country to celebrate, with a holiday, of course, this trivia of Humanity, you get the picture, boys?"

"yes, Senhor Advisor"

"be clever about it... we've got the Irelands, with bombing *makas*, the Spains, with separatist *makas*, the Palestines, look, Palestine alone is a holiday gold mine... the Indians massacred by the Spaniards... the Americans' Indians, as well, the others... ay, what are they called...? those Mayans, all those people should be considered, the First World War, the Second World War, the Cold War, journeys to the moon, the first journey, the second journey, and the frustrated attempts? why doesn't anybody talk about those? the question isn't just who got there... it's who didn't get there? how did they die? those are the kinds of facts we want"

"yes, Senhor Advisor, we'll deal with that"

"then get going! you should've already left... use your heads, boys, your heads, don't forget the Middle East or the Far East, either, or even the distant past, the Romes and the Greeces... Europe is full of massacres, it's necessary to remind those guys that they were barbarians! go take care of that... and that's without talking about papal issues..."

"are you guys going to the speech today, late this afternoon?" Dom Crystal-Clear interrupted, containing his laughter

"today?" the Advisor served himself another whisky and looked irritated at its lack of ice

"yes, the President is going to speak, he's going to make a speech"

"on the radio?"

"live"

"that's why there was so much security on the streets today..."

"that's why, he's going to speak, i'm guessing about the latest events, he also has to give an explanation to the international community, it seems they were furious about the cancellation of the eclipse"

"the international community are a bunch of drama queens," the Minister said.

when he opened the box, the man's hands danced beneath the light of the many oil lamps set up in the room, he first read the instructions meticulously, in spite of having read them already on the computer

his were delicate hands, fingering pages, shuffling sheets, checking the little plastic bags contained in the opened boxes, the fingers' movements tuned the light's intensity, then sought the glass

the glass close to the lips, the breath of dry whisky, the glass returned to the table

there was a deep silence, something that had come from far away, farther away than the city's borders, an unusual silence—a warm cloak, so that following the right interior frequency, people could seek and find secrets residing at that dense silence's core

the silence

the hands opening the box

his fingers did not betray the days of waiting, the last box had finally arrived to complete the puzzle

he had decided shortly before to put together the weapon only when the last part of his secret arrived, he'd made a thorough investigation, he'd awaited delivery of the parts at unlikely addresses and under false names

the scent of newness, the dull glow beneath the weak light of the oil lamps, the scent of the oil close to the cacti in his apartment, the books, the carpets, the endless dust, his clean fingers, whose shaking didn't betray the impatience of his gestures or the anxiety of his waiting

twelve boxes, twelve months, now his destiny was unavoidable

each order was a letter, written to fate, or to himself, announcing fragments of a deadline, or a task to be completed

the hours, the research, the dreams, the fears, the certainties: a man is made of what he plans

«a man is made of truth and urgency» he thought

"Paulo!" Clara shouted in a tearful voice from outside the door, "open the door, Paulo, please, i know you're in there"

but the journalist was moving in another dimension, he didn't let the sounds from the street disturb him, he had closed the windows in the early afternoon, lighted the lamps after filling them with oil, he had left only a small aperture the width of his weapon's barrel and his line of sight, all afternoon he had monitored the increased security on the streets, observed the operation of setting up the stage where the President would speak to the nation, and had taken care to leave an identical scratch of light in another window in case the vehicles took a different route

"Paulo, open the door, i just want to talk to you... i just want to talk to you, Paulo... speak to me, what are you doing locked in there?"

he lifted a piece of velvet to his mouth, touched his tongue and recognized the odour of whisky, then lifted the cloth to the long pipe, washed the oblong piece of metal an infinite number of times, the scents of whisky and the burnt lamp oil hanging in the air, and with the dry part of the velvet cloth the journalist washed the front glass of the telescopic sight and laid the cloth on the kitchen table

next to the window, he wiped his sweaty right hand on his bluejeans, glanced at his bare feet, shook his fingers, cracking his knuckles, and took a deep breath, the sirens of the Presidential retinue were audible in the distance, he got his weapon ready, his chin touched the cold metal and the wooden stock, he became calm but continued breathing deeply, the woman's weepy voice outside the door was bothering him, thousands of flags were waving in the square where the people awaited the arrival of the Comrade President, a few balloons, yellow, black, and scarlet, were released from uplifted hands and flew upwards to the heavens

"the door's barred?" Hoffman asked, panting, after climbing five floors

"he's in there, Arriscado, i know he's in there," Clara wept

"i came as fast as i could, what's going on? did you call his cell?"

"he's not answering, he won't open the door, he won't talk to me... he was all weird this morning, with that spaced-out look"

"and what's that smell?"

"i don't know, it could be oil lamps"

"but the electricity's on in the building," Hoffman moved the woman away from the door and struck it with force, "Paulo, Paulo, you there?"

the sirens grew louder, the motorcycle outriders travelling ahead of the Presidential vehicle arrived, the crowd was in an uproar of alcoholic euphoria, the bodyguards rushed to set up the security corridor, vehicles with smoked-glass windshields approached and from one of them emerged the figure of His Excellency and Engineer Comrade President, who waved to the population and smiled, from the opposite door his spouse stepped out, waved to the population, smiled

the President took his first steps towards of the rostrum decorated with ribbons, flags, and flowers, moving, after having greeted a few of the leaders, to where a confused mass of microphones had been set up for his arrival

the crowd was shouting, the sound reaching the building as a blending of voices, chants, and human roars

"Paulo, for fuck's sake, open the door," Scratch Man, angry, was kicking at it

the journalist, his body draped over the weapon and his weight spread across the table, observed other leaders through the rifle's sight, moved from face to face, distracting himself with thoughts of the very real possibility of striking each of them, laid his finger very lightly on the trigger, felt the sweat pour down his face to his arm, he didn't move, he didn't get excited, he didn't worry about the shouts or the kicks at the door of his apartment, the President smiled as he reached the microphones, camera flashes rained down on him and the music grew softer as the President waved to the population with a gesture that announced the beginning of his speech

"get out of the way, i'm gonna break down the door," Hoffman said

a large bundle of balloons was released on either side of the stage and the population responded with a fresh ovation, the President smiled, the Ministers smiled, Dom Crystal-Clear smiled, observed the brightly coloured balloons rising into the heavens, and the crowd, there to listen to the nation's leader, naturally returned to its silence

"dear citizens, as was announced earlier by the national organs of the press," the President began, "early yesterday morning Luanda finally witnessed the first oil geyser to be discovered beneath the soil of this city"

the multitude roared, clapping their hands

the tip of the weapon's barrel wavered slightly, tapping against the window, the journalist reset his position with both hands, laid his finger on the trigger, leaving the decision as to when to fire at the mercy of this gesture

"all comrades of the Commission for the Installation of Recoverable Oil in Luanda, also known among you as the 'cirollers,' are to be congratulated... the government is to be congratulated for the work undertaken so far, our city is to be congratulated... long live the oil already discovered in Luan— "

a sudden darkness, preceded by a low, intensely muffled sound—the sensation of receiving a shot in the forehead

beneath out-of-control shouts and the chaotic surge of human motion, feet trampled other feet and nearby bodies, the shot set off a generalized confusion but the soldiers were well trained and the evacuation was prompt, the first lady was carried away to a vehicle parked behind the rostrum, the President's head was immediately covered by the hands and bodies of countless body guards

and he was carried to a separate vehicle

without another shot being heard.

Hoffman wrecked his shoulder but the door yielded on his third attempt

the colonel came to an immediate halt in the living room, he abruptly extended his arm to prevent Clara from moving forward, hugged the journalist's girlfriend and she fell against her friend's chest, a ribbon of thick blood from Paulo's forehead seeped from the kitchen, passed the side of the weapon, his outflung arm on the floor, reached the wall and turned slowly in the direction of the colonel, who did not have time to withdraw his foot

"let's get out of here," Hoffman said

"no!" Clara shouted, "i want to see Paulo"

"let's get out of here, Clara!"

they rushed down two flights of stairs and were intercepted by the President's security which, heavily armed, had invaded the building and detained along the way the inhabitants who liked to grill fish on the staircases as well as a doctor who said that he was answering an emergency call from a woman called Clara

"doctor... Paulo... Paulo's up there in the kitchen"

"shut your mouth," one of the guards, dragged her brutally downstairs

"what happened?" the doctor asked

"we don't know for sure," Scratch Man said

they were taken away by a special security unit, National Radio immediately began playing music without having broadcast the six o'clock news

in London, the BBC reported that there had been an assassination attempt on the President of Angola, confirming simultaneously that the head of state was alive and that everything was in a state of great disorder, as a matter of fact, the young woman journalist commented live from the site of the interrupted rally, the lone shot had emerged from very close to her location and had been taken by a sniper from the Presidential guard, though the true course of events remained unclear

"Clara," the doctor whispered, "had he taken his pills?"

"i don't think so..." Clara was crying, her wrists hurting from the handcuffs and her eyes burning with tears, "i don't think so..."

"what pills?" Hoffman asked

Clara looked at the city streets, the potholes, the flags, the balloons gripped in the hands of children who were fleeing from the rapid passage of cars from the President's security detail, thinking, perhaps, that there, comfortably seated, was the Comrade President

"did you guys see Paulo?" the doctor whispered

"i saw him, he was lying in the kitchen"

"lying? he'd fainted?"

"no... dead, he was shot in the head... he was in the kitchen with a gun"

"oh my god, what a mess"

"it must have been a mistake," Scratch Man looked up so that the doctor wouldn't see his tears, "it was a Diana"

"a what?"

"a pellet gun... to kill birds"

the doctor, too, looked away, he tried to loosen the handcuffs that were chafing his skin, he took a deep breath

looking, secretly astonished, at the brightness of the balloons that filled the sky, he murmured

"why did someone invent weapons to kill birds?"

«the name» is what the Mailman thought about, the name

about the names he'd had already and that he'd gathered in his life, the names parents choose for the most serious or most absurd reasons, the family name, «the one that's imposed on us by an uncle or a cousin and then the name of the street that's sometimes paired with that other, more familiar, one that's going to be your family nickname, and then the names that life gives to us»

he brought his tired body to a halt to gaze with amazement at the enormous mountain of garbage that separated him from his home, this had been his route for years, his parents had always led him home this way, in the darkness or beneath the light of so many moons, the Mailman entered his *musseque*, passing various houses, he veered down alleys of rough earth dampened by mucky water, and, before reaching home, crossed the enormous mountain of garbage that divided what were in reality two different *musseques*, a rivulet of dark water drew curves on the ground that looked, however much he might want to deny it, like an enormous map of Angola, the Mailman confirmed the treacherous river's sinuous curves, he extended his stride and crossed it, discovering on the dump's outskirts a pathway of compacted garbage that led him, one hundred or more metres farther along, to the door of his miserable house, but

the Mailman brought his tired body to a halt and used his eyes to confirm that his pathway had disappeared, everything was occupied by towering extensions of the mountains of refuse accumulated over years, he turned, looked around, was unable to find a way through, tried to climb over the top, slipped without hurting himself, grabbed his mailbag and tried again on the other side, but the impossibility of access became more and more unremitting, he smiled, imagining that he had misjudged the path, he glanced towards the trees that he used to orient himself and saw that he was on the path to his house

he drew a deep breath, identifying each odour, let himself be borne away by a strange sadness, an ache that was at the same time a penetrating nostalgia for home and a fear of never returning there, he could take the long way, it would be a huge detour, but it wasn't so much the impossibility of locating his hearth and home, it was more an offence that the city and the garbage had made against his person, preventing him from taking the pathway he had always used, the same dirt lane, filthy and strange, yet a trail that was also a little bit his, and thus, saddened, silent within, he sat down on a twisted tree trunk, set down his mailbag next to his feet, and began to read the only official letter that had been addressed to him

«mail for the Mailman» he thought

he opened it slowly, looked again at the edges of the dump without locating a pathway through, remained still, as though the same entity that had dumped the garbage had come to take charge of opening a passage for him

the letter, written in a pompous officialistic idiom, with a lengthy introduction on the reception of the letters he had left with various people in some of the country's major ministries, someone had taken the trouble to put them all together, to consider them as stemming from a single correspondent, the Mailman, the man who wrote, by hand, on twenty-five-line paper, letters of a serious, official tone, requesting that he be granted a moped to improve the fulfillment of his duties

the letter explained that, the pertinent entities having analyzed his strange request, they had decided to deny the concession of the vehicle, in recognition of the reality confronted by other national mailmen who, for their part, even in provinces far more afflicted by slopes and inclines, continued the normal exercise of their duties without ever, until now, having wasted time and paper on requests that could be considered as absurd if not, depending on who might receive and interpret them, offensive

the Mailman, incredulous, read more similar justifications and also thought of the time wasted by whoever had put together all of the letters that were found in the envelope, and who had gone to the trouble of replying with such tenacity and care in a denial composed in severe, demanding Portuguese, written on a computer, with each page stamped by some dolt who hadn't even taken the time to call him in for an interview where he could have explained himself,

he let the letter fall to the ground in the mud trampled by his feet, which were now still, and with both hands on his chin began to gaze at the dump as he had never looked at it before, slowly, his eyes roaming over the waste installation in its unbelievable dimensions, its height and breadth, the variety of its colours, the filthy balance of its odours, the forms he was able to imagine, here almost seeing a sleeping dinosaur, there a cross-legged giant, over here a crooked flower or a felled tree, almost human figures, or figures of beings who were more or less alive, in this awe-inspiring accumulation of what people tossed out, either because they didn't want it or because it had no use or simply because it smelled bad,

this jumble of useless, putrefying things physically prevented the Mailman from reaching home

and wrapped up in the calmest rhythms of his sweaty breath, he decided to sit still, dozing off, waiting for a concrete action on the part of that entity known as time.

"for how long?" João Slowly asked

"don't include that clause, leave it like that, you can always go back on what's not written down"

"that's going to increase the price"

"money's not the problem, just say how much and it'll be there," tax inspector This Time said

"will you guys be able to place this money overseas?"

"where?" tax inspector Next Time asked

"maybe in Portugal"

"maybe, depending on the amount"

"then it's a deal, are you going to keep the enterprise's name?"

"yeah, it's a good name, it's produced good results, people are already used to the Church of the Sacred Little Lamb"

"and what do i say to the pastor?"

"don't say anything, just announce a change of management, the church will have new owners, but for the moment his duties will be the same, going forward we'll have to make certain modifications in the services"

"new services?"

"yes, funeral services, commending souls to god, absolving sins five minutes before death, that sort of thing, here in Luanda everything revolves around money, if not nobody will take the business seriously"

"you're right"

"we're also going to include commercial packages for *kombas*, funerals move too quickly these days, we have to return to our traditions, old-fashioned *kombas*, with drinks, food, and professional mourners like in the old days"

"i can see you guys have a knack for that"

"thank you, João, will you be available if we need to consult someone?"

"you know everything has a price"

"sure, sure"

they settled the deal, the brothers had brought part of the money with them, the dollars were counted out and again deposited in a huge bag, they agreed that the tax inspectors would be able to go ahead and set up the new office in the room next door to the sacristy the next day

"now leave me here with my lady friends, i have to say farewell, i'm going to miss this church"

"do you need help?" This Time winked at João Slowly, running his tongue over his lips in excitement as he looked at the Swedes

"no, thanks, i can handle it myself"

João accompanied the tax inspectors to the exit, stepped back inside the church, and bolted the door

the Swedes wandered slowly around the edges of the church, they changed the arrangement of the chairs, opening in their midst a huge bright space, João Slowly took dozens of candles off the shelves, which the Swedes lighted until they formed a circle of fire that cast dancing shadows on the walls "i always wanted to make love in a church"

the Swedes began to take off their clothes

João Slowly did the same, he imitated their feminine gestures and they soon understood the game, taking off their blouses, he undid his buttons, leaving his shirt open, they took off their high-heeled shoes, he took off his shoes, in an almost parallel gesture the Swedes approached each other and undid one another's bras, followed soon after by their panties, and João Slowly smiled, he dropped his pants and ran his hand over his hard sex, the Swedes, who were almost on the opposite side of the circle of flame, touched their own breasts and then each other's breasts, squeezing the nipples hard without ceasing to look at him, he didn't approach, the women kissed, slowly, in a lascivious way that allowed the entrepreneur to see their tongues and their daring fingers alternating paths between their moist lips, their breasts and their sexes with clipped, blonde hair

"Ave Maria, this is heaven..." João Slowly murmured

he closed his eyes and lost himself in the Swedes' rhythmic energy, the candles began to go out, the spreading odour of wax inside of the church mixed with the odours of sex and sweat

the tax inspectors were peeping in at the scene from a crack in the window

at the other door, the Brazilian pastor tightened his fingers around his sex, moving his body with intense rhythm he followed the action within the house of his lord Jesus

"long live Sweden and all of Scandinavia!"

in his tiny cubicle, the man kept looking at the candle's scarlet, self-sculpting stub

the Leftist didn't realize it, he didn't imagine anything similar, but, in fact, the mirror-image of that candle existed elsewhere: it was shaped exactly like the body of an ancient tree in an abandoned yard on Maianga Square, and soon this candle would disintegrate, though perhaps not the tree the man didn't think about this, he lit the candle and caressed the only pen he ever used for his writing, the pages looked yellower beneath the fleeting glow of the tree-like candle, the man's thoughts slid over the poetry of the image but quickly returned to the axis of his thought, the important manuscript that he had set himself the task of writing

at his side a glass of water, a skimpy glass filled with water of dubious quality, the heat of the night, bats' far-away cries and then an intense silence

he tried to turn on the enormous radio in the living room, but the radio refused, the candle light trembled, and the man looked at the flame

«don't go out now, my light... you're the light i rely on to create, don't go out now»

and he sat down

to wait, as always, for the words to come from within, to enter his bloodstream and make him write

the scarlet candle cast dancing shadows on the hands and face of the man bent over his yellowed pages

calmly, with his hand shaking, the man peacefully finished what it had taken all of those years to compose

then he walked to Noah's Barque where

Noah killed a cockroach and wondered at the fact that this was the third one he'd found that night

the critters seemed more befuddled than normal and he assumed this was caused by some product the Brazilian pastor had spread around the church

"sons of bitches, you haven't got a chance with me, you can come into my ark, but i'm not going to leave you alone," the old codger grumbled

he fulfilled his ritual of sweeping the whole bar three times, and after cleaning the floor with water mixed with cresol, he stood in the doorway, smoking his short, rank cigarette, waiting for whoever might yet show up

"good evening, Senhor Leftist"

"good evening, Noah"

"are you loaded down with notes, as usual?"

"the usual... bring out a red wine to give the night a shock"

"sure, i'll bring it out"

Noah made his way to the ark, pulled out two tall glasses for special occasions, filled them to the brim, sipped from his, gave an exclamation, approved with a brief nod of his head

"are we toasting any particular occasion?" the Leftist asked

"we're going to toast an unoccasion"

"have you become a poet, Senhor Noah?"

"we're all poets, the question is whether we allow it to happen"

"i couldn't agree more... but which unoccasion are we going to toast?"

"whichever one occurs to us... whatever undoes the sadness of these days, wafts us far away... sometimes, you know, it happens that i feel the same sorts of thing that Senhor Odonato is always talking about"

"what things?"

"city-related things... the emotions and sadnesses we feel inside when something happens in this city"

"i understand"

"all the worlds get mixed up, pardon my poetic speech, but we're all water from the same river"

"minus those beyond the third bank, as the master Guimarães would say"

"minus those beyond each individual's bank," the elder Noah raised his glass, made the toast before heading off to piss, holding his bladder at bay with his left hand

"go ahead, man, pissing is a fundamental right"

Noah turned on the bathroom light, stumbled on another cockroach, failed to capture it prior to its speedy, zigzagging escape

"son of a bitch, i'll get you next time, i'll give you a cresol bath and burn your shitty little shell," he began to relieve himself, "do they think they own the place, or what?"

the Leftist swiftly pulled his disorganized notes out of his attaché case, gave them a farewell glance, crammed them into an opaque bag and opened the ark, finding right away a spot deep down and at the edges where he could hide his papers

«one of the safest places in Luanda» he thought

on top of the papers he deposited a bag containing three scorpion fish and some little boxes that he knew would be of limited use

"the wine bottle is on the counter, man"

"oh, sorry, i hadn't seen it."

the young BBC journalist almost tripped on the false step and would have hit her head on an outjutting section of the wall had Davide Airosa not caught her

"oh, i didn't see it," the journalist said, relieved

"we can't always see what we're looking for," Davide said

"i can see that this is going to be a serious interview"

"i took advantage of your fall to give you a quote, but it wasn't just a joke"

"and whose words are those?"

"i don't remember"

"they wouldn't be yours?"

"no, they're not, that happens to me sometimes, i don't remember where my words come from, i'm sorry, i should have kept my mouth shut"

"you always say that to me"

"i do?"

"yes, every time we meet you end up saying those same words, or something similar"

"we haven't met that many times," Davide Airosa sat down, inviting her to do the same

"one more reason why this is important," the journalist made herself comfortable and pulled a recorder from her bag

"are you already taping?"

"i'm always taping... in my memory i'm always taping, Davide"

"that's risky"

"or lucky, think about it, some day i can tell someone the important things i've seen and lived through in this city"

"don't worry, that's all that Luandans do"

"what is?"

"each Luandan is a creator of his own tale, just be careful you don't pick up the habit"

"that sounds lovely, inventing, making up another version of your own life"

"it can entail the risk of forgetting the original version"

"yes, there's that"

"or something worse"

"are you sad, Davide?"

"a little bit... i got a difficult piece of news, the death of a journalist, a great friend of mine"

"he was your friend?"

"you know about it? about Paulo?"

"i practically saw it happen"

"what happened, anyway? what was it like?"

"i think it was a reflection, a reflection in your friend's window"

"he was at the window?"

"he was at the window with a weapon, Davide..."

"he wasn't doing well," Davide rubbed his face, hid his tears, searched in his breathing for the calm that was missing in his chest

"don't let it get to you"

the building's waters seemed to be speaking, they spouted at fresh, rhythmic intervals, their echoes scurried down the stairs or the elevator shafts, which carried them away to hidden zones of the building or the street, the wind swooped down into that enclosed spot, enabled by the waters and their strange flow, the whistling of the wind mingled with voices from the time before that spoke to those who knew how to listen to them

the journalist caressed her face

in one ear she was listening to the watery orchestra raise its tone, imitating or stirring up the wind, in the other she felt

Davide's troubled breathing, the pulse of his pain in the air he inhaled, she let her hand slide down his neck, she felt his veins tremble, and she liked it, the journalist liked the feeling that she could make their closeness contain a man's pain, his loss, his soothing weeping, she liked to feel the sudden, boiling will to kiss the awkward scientist rising from her feet and passing through her knees and her sex

Davide did not open his eyes

he saw, with his eyes closed, within an imposed darkness, isolated images of laughter and toasts made with Paulo Paused, then voices from childhood

the journalist's tongue, tender and moist, grazed the side of his sweaty neck, the images sped up, he tried to slow the beat of his heart

she liked to appreciate the man's slightest reaction to the touch of her tongue, encircling his ear, penetrating it, then returning to the lobe, and then, suddenly, touching his closed eyes, attacking him in this sensitive spot which, rather than exciting him, moved him

"i always think..." Davide Airosa said in a very low voice, "that lovemaking begins before bodies touch"

"mmm-hmm," her eyes closed, she allowed her tongue to make its gradual progress

"lovemaking is when bodies know they're going to touch"

the scientist's hand slid firmly up the journalist's back to her neck, lifted her blouse, confirming, as he broke into a smile, that she was not wearing a bra, his other hand ran down the front of her body until the tip of his finger touched the earring in her navel, he caressed the aroused nipple of her left breast, he touched her throat

they kissed with open, clumsy mouths, inaugurating a fire in their stomachs that took this as its cue to grow and spread.

the fire

began with a short circuit in the heart of Maianga Square, where thousands of kilos of explosives had already been set, so that later, as programmed, they would have the promised fireworks show that the Party had paid for and promoted

"did you hear that?"

"i didn't hear anything," a woman said

"it sounded like an explosion"

shooting sparks ignited the fire, the tunnels that had been dug out, the now-installed pipes, the dangerous soup of volatile gases, all formed a perfect labyrinth for the fire's will and direction

in a few minutes the oxygen was bearing the flame and the heat was finding avenues through which it could expand

the explosions happened one after another, the sounds blending into the memories of the peoples of Luanda

"oh, my god, another war has started," shouted an elderwoman whose path had crossed all of the city's wars

"calm down, mother... calm down," a woman's voice shouted in terror, "it's not always a war!"

on the little boy's face

rough-edged drops glimmered, nearly dried by the heat of the approaching flame, they glimmered in the spittle that drooled from his trembling mouth, or, since his black face had become a series of yellow tracks, in subdued threads of snot that flowed from his nose

exhaustion made his weeping calm and free flowing

lost in his home from the fire's earliest moments, he first sought visual references that the smoke had erased, he tried to advance by touch and burned his fingertips, and walked, pressing on with the courage of a gigantic little boy who refused to surrender to death, he walked, looking for his brothers and sisters, or a recognizable voice, looking for life, or a spot where there might be an exit, he walked as though the streets where the fire had taken least hold offered an escape from the labyrinth

he moistened his body and hair and mouth with the first water he came across and, amid strange noises, the boy, tired out from crying, began to discover a kind of silence, a respite in the unmusical sounds born from the crackle of falling trees and houses

all of the liquids in his face—from spittle to snot, from tears to terror, evaporated in a sudden sensation in which the incredible monster of solitude whimpered and fell to pieces—the little boy saw a gasping fish hopping, sniffing, if that was what it was doing, tiny droplets of water that might contain its possible salvation,

on the other side, as though it were two different life-saving creatures, a white bird, singed and lame, arranged the setting that, suddenly, like a force for renewal in the world, made the little boy, trapped in the middle of the fire, begin to smile

without hesitation, the child—bringing with him his smile, his burning fingers, his aching fingernails, shouldering the burning hunger in his stomach—carried on one side of his

chest, for security, the remains of a palpable fear, on the other,
half snuffed out, a keening need to see his mother and assailed
with an unexpected wisdom, he grabbed the shuddering fish
and gave it to the bird as food—as though this gesture would
resolve the world's problems.

[from the author's notes]

the city writhed at each twist of fire

the oil fumes fed the flames and created volcanoes that exhaled tongues of fire, the night first insisted on the darkness of an absence of lights, but then took on a yellow shade too searing to support human life, the beings who knew how to fly soon fled

all the city's foundations shuddered, the oldest buildings began to collapse, others leaned over as though about to crumble, gas cans and gas pumps lit up the Luanda night, poisoning the city with smoke and foul vapours

"oh my god!" shouted the American, Raago, locked in his room, feeling himself hemmed in by the smoke and by the scorching heat radiating from the hotel's hallways but also from the burning trees that surrounded the building

he got down on the floor, crawled to the bathroom, soaked a towel in a washbasin close to floor-level, succeeded in regaining control of his exhausted breathing, and, on the flat *azulejo* tiles on the floor he saw the cockroach, strangely peaceful, beckoning to him with its dexterous antennae, the American tried to imagine that this would be his last sight and remained motionless while he mixed improvised prayers with glances at the albino insect, whose appearance had become shinier

the cockroach walked for a few seconds and stopped moving, it looked behind itself, turned its body, Raago thought he must be hallucinating, but, seeing the fire sizzling inside the windows, he decided that, vision for vision, he preferred to follow the cockroach in its skewed trajectory, he wrapped another towel around his back and, wriggling like a bigger insect, set off to follow the cockroach

on the veranda, a door opened into a larger room, the cockroach ran forward and he followed close behind, they passed through the door, everything was ashy smoke and suffocation, they went through another door and reached a tiny corridor that ended in some narrow stairs

the last thing he was able to see was the albino cockroach sneaking away under the crack at the bottom of a door that was bolted shut, he got up, and, with all his strength, broke the lock, more smoke came in from outside, this time accompanied by a strong smell of burning rubber, and, when he was about to stumble over, giving up on saving his own body, he saw a water tank and succeeded in pulling away the wooden lid and diving into it, he felt terrible, he drank a little of the water and remained still, immersing himself each time he was assailed by a particularly explosive burst of flame, breathing however he was able, beginning to appreciate the silence he experienced whenever he submerged his head completely in the water

and he thought, finally, he thought about the albino cockroach, but he didn't see it.

on the first floor, hurrying along in the collective procession and the disorderly shoving of bodies, the whole group arrived

Edú carried his tiny stool in his hand and set it down immediately in order to sit close to his wife, Nga Nelucha, who was crying compulsively and holding her hands over her ears to avoid hearing the explosions that followed one after another, Comrade Mute was carrying a bag full of LPs, some with covers, others without, and allowed his body to fall into the water

Amarelinha arrived with Granma Kunjikise, who was barefoot and wrapped in various coloured cloths but unable to speak, not even in Umbundu

"what's going on?" Comrade Mute shouted

"my mother's upstairs"

between the torrents of smoke that poured out of the elevator shaft, Davide Airoso only had time to quickly pull on his trousers and head upstairs barefoot, already suffering an asthma attack, making his way more by the touch of his outstretched hands than by sight

when he reached the sixth floor, he bumped into Xilisbaba's stumbling body trying to climb the stairs that led to the terrace

"where are the stairs? but where are the stairs?" she bellowed like a madwoman

"come with me, madam"

"no... my husband"

she tried to resist, but Davide grabbed her firmly

"come with me, madam"

as if the smoke were actually very thick, the woman lost her strength and almost fainted in the scientist's arms

"don't faint now, madam, if you do we're both going to die here, please, i don't want to die yet"

"neither do i," Xilisbaba's voice was already lifeless

"then wake up a little"

they descended without touching anything, they listened to objects collapsing or falling to the floor inside the apartments, windows shattered, vases exploded, and on reaching the second floor they both thought they had glimpsed the peaceful image of a terrifying ghost, a body lay in repose in the centre of the corridor, as though it were consigning itself to the fire of its own free will and wished to be carried far away by the oncoming disintegration

"do you see what i see?" Davide asked

"is it a person?"

the sound of weeping howled out like an appeal, Xilisbaba recognized the murmuring as that of Strong Maria, the three of them descended in utter blindness, guided by the life-saving sound that the waters, now grown stronger, sent out to whoever was looking for them they sat down near the others, now quiet and huddled in what they took to be the centre of the corridor, where the flux of the waters was strongest and windows of oxygen appeared to be opening up

Xilisbaba, her body pooled with water, was breathing with difficulty and coughed slowly despite her efforts to stifle it

in her hand she gripped a small piece of sisal, similar to the piece her husband had tied around his left ankle, her sweat and the frenetic movement of her fingers untied the chord into fine, soaked threads which covered her feet, the others looked at her, guiding themselves by sound and by the sight of her wavy hair

outside, human voices were shouting

the women's hands reached towards each other in a delicate, almost secret gesture, more to share fears than temperatures, Strong Maria felt she must appeal to higher forces to placate her sister's tears, her gaze sought out Xilisbaba's face, she divined the tracks of her tears, foresaw her sadness in the defiant set of her nostrils, tried to take her pulse, but the pumping of Xilisbaba's heart, as she thought of her husband marooned at the top of the building, was nothing more than a silent murmuring in her veins

"Maria... i want to see my husband one last time... to talk to him about the things people keep quiet their whole lives"

Maria's hand exerted a comforting pressure and Xilisbaba let herself slide down with her back to the wall, lying nearly flat in her friend's lap

her clothes, her shoes, her hair and her soul, all were sodden from the water that protected them from the fire

"take it easy, sis... fire's like wind, it shouts a lot but it has a tiny little voice."

the only calm bark of laughter came from the Mailman

seated in the same position for hours, he remained still, confident that the fire would not reach his body, he remained still imitating the serenity of a baobab tree that had no idea how to flee, he observed the fire's progression from the edges of the dump, he saw adults and children disappear into the gigantic flames, he heard the far-away explosions, he swivelled his head slightly to see, in the distance, the airport emitting a series of gasoline-nourished flashes, he scoured the sky for the sight of a gleaming star, then restored his attention to the fire that was entering the huge garbage dump right in front of him, he laughed like a madman awaiting the moment of vengeance and, still peaceful, he danced

he created for himself a seated dance, he stamped his feet in time with music he believed he could hear, he laughed in hot guffaws and made circular movements with his hands that, above all, were incitations to the invading flames to consume the garbage dump so that hours later, his hair and clothing scorched, still laughing

he might reach the door of his house, its doorbell broken, and see the glowing embers of everything in his home that had burned, breathing deeply from the atmosphere of tragedy, to affirm in a loud voice

"finally i can say that i made it home."

worried at first, then consciously calmer

Odonato saw the rooster's agitation, its body enclosed by the fire that had finally invaded its terrace, he saw it's feet and its hesitant hops

even maddened and enclosed by heat, the Rooster Camões felt no yearning to jump, various times he went to the edges that were least hot and regarded the city from the vantage point of his final dwelling, he ran frenetically and looked at Odonato, who was calmer now, bobbing, his foot tethered to the highest antenna, the man pulled away from the rooster's gaze and looked around

in every direction the horizon was a sea of yellow flames and twisted smoke, sounds dwindled only to return to feed fresh explosions, the devouring flame died down in burned-out corners only to reignite immediately in oblong, vertical, spitting flames stirred up by the wind from his left pocket Odonato pulled out a tiny scrap of paper and, beneath the cool gaze of a tender farewell, rapidly scrawled a few lines, then leaned over in front of himself and began to gnaw with his upper and lower teeth at the length of cord tying him to the building

the rooster saw Odonato progress rowards the skies, unbound, free, fanning his body from side to side in response to the wind, overflying the building, where the rooster sat, shocked into silence, then climbing suddenly, crumpled into lopsided ball, the wrinkled note that the rooster, for lack of anything better to do, heightened by a certain appetite, pecked at, opened and, seeing that the sodden material was mushy and could be devoured, finally ingested it

letter by letter, word by word.

seizing Blind Man by the wrist, forcing himself to run without letting him go, Seashell Seller shouted

"aren't you going to say anything, elder?"

lying out of fear of telling the truth, feeling the fire's heat too close to his skin, the old man preferred to remain silent in order not to have to speak of his fear

yet he yielded to the request of the man who still hadn't abandoned him

"it's not my turn to speak, just between you and me, which of us is the elder here, isn't it me?"

"so it is"

"then i just have to endure..."

they wandered around, following their instincts, they ran, they stopped, they awaited gaps in the flames to locate fleeting corridors, wherever there was a puddle they slurped water over their bodies, and, during a long pause, Blind Man grasped that the boy was breathing with the rhythm of someone attentively awaiting something

"what's up?" Blind Man asked, "are you looking at the fire?"

"no, at the sky..."

"what about it?"

"the sky is full of balloons, elder"

Blind Man suddenly rubbed his hands together and Seashell Seller parried the gesture as though he didn't understand the reason for this agitation, he remained with his neck stretched from craning up at the sky through the rivers of smoke, Blind Man's hands finally reached his mouth, Blind Man intended to read the shape of his smile

"yellow, red, black balloons"

Seashell Seller looked but did not see, in the midst of the thousands of balloons, a body rising, outdistancing the dangerous tips of the flames

there were still occasional explosions and some of the balloons burst from the intensity of the heat, they continued wandering at random, Seashell Seller's hand firm and sweating on Blind Man's wrist

"let's run, the fire's really big here"

"leave me behind, old people have to die," Blind Man said in a tearful voice and mentioned that he was going to stop running

"old people! but do the blind also have to die today?" Seashell Seller joked, "come with me, elder, we're close to that bar"

they ran, they felt the fire scorching their backs and feet, Seashell Seller's bag fell to the floor and for a few moments the young man left the elder behind to go back, metres back, to pick up the bag with his most precious collection of seashells, they ran together and entered the door of Noah's Barque

the night was a like braid coming undone and losing its blackness, the hide of a nocturnal beast with mud dripping from its body, there was already a timid gleam of stars in the sky, the languor of certain whitecaps, and the seashells overheating and clattering open, human bodies undergoing involuntary cremation and the sleepwalking city wept, unaffected by the moon's consolation

Blind Man, his lips a sad smile, laid his hand on Seashell Seller's leg

317

"just tell me..."

the city sweated beneath a scarlet glow, getting ready to experience, in the unsteady bodies and skins, a deep dark night such as fire alone can teach

"what's your question, elder?"

"the colour of that fire," Blind Man seemed to be imploring him

Seashell Seller felt it would show a lack of respect not to reply

"if i knew how to explain the colour of the fire, elder, i'd be a poet"

but, his voice hypnotized, Seashell Seller followed the inclinations of the heat, the surly circles of that flaring jungle driven on by the wind in unending provocation

"don't let me die without knowing the colour of that light" Blind Man said over the huge flames' powerful roaring

"elder, i'm waiting for a child's voice inside me"

Seashell Seller got up, opened the ark, which was still working, and found so many objects piled inside that it was difficult for him to decide what to grab, he seized two bottles of water from a corner, passed one to Blind Man

"water?" the old man tasted it, spitting a second later, "go see if this ark doesn't have a goddam beer, good and cold, or even some whisky"

Seashell Seller dipped his hands into the ark again without letting the lunging flames out of his sight, the bloodied city was shackled and about to keel over and die

"just tell me the colour of that fire"

he repeated in a very low voice

so that Seashell Seller, caressing Blind Man's hand, was able to tell him

"it's a lazy red, elder... that's what it is: a lazy red."

Odonato's letter was drawn from the following verses:

> [...]
> nothing remains from that time
> the peace of placid days
> and long nights
> poisoned arrows
> dwell in the hearts of the living
> the time of remembering is finished
> tomorrow i'll weep
> the things i should have wept today

Ana Paula Tavares

GLOSSARY

alea jacta, petroleum est—Latin: "there's no going back, petroleum it is." The first clause is attributed to Julius Caesar while crossing the Rubicon River.

azulejo—Glazed blue ceramic Portuguese tile.

Bastos, Waldemar—Angolan singer (b. 1954). His music mixes African, Brazilian, and Portuguese influences.

bassula—Ancient Angolan martial art, or a blow from this martial art designed to knock down an opponent.

batucada—The sound of a festival, including that made by both music and people.

Burity, Carlos—Popular Angolan singer (b. 1952), known for his traditionally inflected *semba*.

cachupa—Traditional dish from the Cape Verde Islands, made of ground corn or refried black beans stuffed with meat or fish, cassava, banana, and baked vegetables.

Camões, Luís Vaz de—(1524–1580). Classical Portuguese poet.

Chokwe—Bantu language spoken in eastern Angola.

candonga, candongueiro—Minivan running on a regular route to provide cheap urban transport, or the driver or owner of such a van.

Cuando Cubango—Province in Southern Angola. It contains the hamlet of Cuito Cuanavale where, between September 1987 and March 1988, MPLA and Cuban troops on one side and South African and UNITA troops on the other fought the largest battle in Africa since the Second World War. The South African Defence Force's failure to capture Cuito Cuanavale is seen as an historic turning point whose consequences included international recognition of independent Angola's borders, the independence of Namibia, Cuba's withdrawal from Africa, and the fall of the apartheid regime in South Africa.

Dido, Adolfo—Narrator of Ondjaki's novel *Quantas madrugadas tem a noite* "How Many Dawns Has the Night" (2004), not yet available in English. His name is an obscene pun.

Dos Santos, José Eduardo—President of Angola from 1979 to 2017.

FAPLA—People's Armed Forces for the Liberation of Angola. The name given to the army of Angola's MPLA government from 1975 to 1991.

Flores, Paulo—One of Angola's best-known contemporary singers (b. 1972). His songs address the difficulties of life in Angola.

fogope—An instruction to grab your partner when dancing.

Globo—Full name "Rede Globo" (Globo Network). Private television network, based in Rio de Janeiro, Brazil, and widely viewed in Portuguese-speaking countries.

japie—Derogatory term for a (usually white) South African.

Kassav'—French West Indian band formed in Paris in 1979; musically influential in Africa.

Kianda—Goddess of the sea in the mythology of the Kimbundu people who originally inhabited the area around Luanda.

Kifangondo—Decisive battle, fought on November 10, 1975, which secured Angolan independence. MPLA forces, with Cuban support, severely defeated Holden Roberto's Western-backed FNLA (Angolan National Liberation Front), which was aided by South African, Zairean, and Portuguese troops.

Kikongo—Bantu language spoken in the Republic of Congo and in northern Angola.

Kimbundu—Bantu language traditionally spoken in the area around Luanda. Though many urban young people of Kimbundu heritage speak only Portuguese, Kimbundu words are prominent in Luandan slang.

kitaba—A paste made from roasted peanuts.

kizaca—A dish, which often includes seafood, made from soaked, cooked, and seasoned cassava leaves.

kizomba—A popular Angolan dance.

komba—Traditional religious ritual, performed seven days after an individual's death, in which the deceased's favourite drinks and foods are consumed.

Kumuezo, Elias Dia—Angolan semba singer (b. 1936). Singing in both Portuguese and Kimbundu, he was dubbed the "King of Angolan Music" in the 1960s.

kwanza—National currency of Angola.

maka—Problem, dilemma.

Marginal—Scenic waterfront boulevard that separates downtown Luanda from Luanda Bay.

Mingas, Ruy—Popular Angolan singer (b. 1939), who was also a distinguished athlete and government official.

MPLA—People's Movement for the Liberation of Angola. Angola's ruling party since independence in 1975.

muzonguê—A fish soup prepared with palm oil.

mufete—A dish typical of Luanda Island, consisting of grilled fish, brown beans cooked in palm oil, sweet potatoes, manioc, plantains, manioc flour, and a sauce made of onions, vinegar, red pepper, and salt.

musseque—A poor neighbourhood, generally far from the city centre, distinguished by informally constructed housing and dirt roads.

Neto, Agostinho—First President of Angola, from independence in 1975 until his death in 1979.

Nga—Popular abbreviation for "senhora."

ngana zambi—Abbreviated Kimbundu form of "god the father."

Nocal—Popular Angolan beer.

November 11, 1975—Angolan independence day.

Paraguaçu, Odorico—Comic character on Brazilian television. He is the mayor of a remote town called Sucupira.

Rosa, João Guimarães—(1908–1967). Brazilian writer of fiction. His best-known short story is "The Third Bank of the River."

quitetas—A type of edible shellfish.

RTP—Rádio e Televisão de Portugal. Public Portuguese television station, widely viewed in Lusophone Africa.

Sucupira—See "Odorico Paraguaçu" above.

tuga—Derogatory term for someone from Portugal.

Umbundu—The most widely spoken Bantu language in Angola; traditionally, the language spoken by the Ovimbundu people of the central highlands.

UNITA—National Union for the Total Independence of Angola. Anti-MPLA movement led by Jonas Savimbi until his death in combat in 2002; from the mid-1970s until the early 1990s, UNITA was supported by the United States and South Africa.

ACKNOWLEDGEMENTS

thanks to manuel rui who one day passed along the true tale of a child who had invented that colour: "lazy red";

i thank the patience, revisions, and words of:

r. figueredo, l. apa, z. coelho, i. garcez, a. murano, e. coelho, j. campino;

these pages were written and experienced with the music of wim mertens, paulo flores, cat power, joaquin sabina, keith jarrett, ruy mingas, antony and the johnsons, thomas feiner & anywhen, lavoura arcaica soundtrack, sigur rós, lhasa, bon iver, beethoven, mozart, among others.

michel laban diá kimuezo: from Luuanda we embrace you.

Luanda, Lubango, Lisbon   /2001/2009/2012/   Laranjeiras, Luanda

ABOUT THE TRANSLATOR

Stephen Henighan's previous translations include Ondjaki's *Good Morning Comrades* and *Granma Nineteen and the Soviet's Secret*. He is the author of five novels, including *The Path of the Jaguar* (2016) and *Mr. Singh Among the Fugitives* (2017), as well as four short story collections, most recently *Blue River and Red Earth* (2018). Henighan has been a finalist for the Governor General's Literary Award and the Canada Prize in the Humanities.